Dame Catherine Cookson was born in 1906. She was the daughter of a poverty-stricken woman, Kate, whom she believed to be her older sister, and was raised in Tyne Dock by her grandmother and step-grandfather.

From an early age Catherine was determined to become a writer. She wrote her first short story when she was eleven, sending it off to the *South Shields Gazette*.

She left school at thirteen and worked in domestic service and in a workhouse before moving to Hastings. Here she bought herself a house, taking in lodgers to supplement her income. At thirty-four she married Tom Cookson, a local grammar-school master.

During the next few years Catherine suffered several miscarriages and fell into a depression. She returned to writing to recover and joined the local writers' group for encouragement. Her first book, *Kate Hannigan* (1950), was partly autobiographical.

Although she was originally acclaimed as a regional writer, Catherine's readership soon began to spread around the world and her many bestselling novels were to establish her as one of Britain's most popular novelists.

For many years Catherine and Tom lived near Newcastle-upon-Tyne. Catherine died shortly before her ninety-second birthday in June 1998 having completed 104 works, nine of which were published posthumously.

www.rbooks.co.uk

By the time of her death Catherine Cookson had received an OBE, the Freedom of the Borough of South Tyneside, an honorary degree from the University of Newcastle and the Royal Society of Literature's award for Best Regional Novel of the Year.

The Variety Club of Great Britain had named her Writer of the Year, she had been voted Personality of The North-East, appointed an Honorary Fellow of St Hilda's College, Oxford and created a Dame of the British Empire.

Catherine's novels have today been translated into more than twenty languages and more than 50 million copies of her books have been sold in Corgi alone. Eighteen of her novels have been televised starring such famous names as Sean Bean, Catherine Zeta Jones and Jane Horrocks.

Catherine Cookson was the most borrowed author in UK public libraries for twenty years. She only lost this title in 2004 — a sure testament to the ongoing popularity of her stirring, timeless novels.

THE BLIND MILLER

Catherine Cookson

CORGI BOOKS

TRANSWORLD PUBLISHERS
61–63 Uxbridge Road, London W5 5SA
A Random House Group Company
www.rbooks.co.uk

THE BLIND MILLER
A CORGI BOOK: 9780552156769

First published in Great Britain in 1963 by Macdonald & Co.
(Publishers) Ltd
Corgi edition published 1971
Corgi edition reissued 2008

Addresses for Random House Group Ltd companies outside the
UK can be found at: www.randomhouse.co.uk
The Random House Group Ltd Reg. No. 954009

The Random House Group Limited supports The Forest
Stewardship Council (FSC), the leading international forest
certification organisation. All our titles that are printed on
Greenpeace approved FSC certified paper carry the FSC logo. Our
paper procurement policy can be found at
www.rbooks.co.uk/environment

Typeset in 11/13 Palatino by
Phoenix Typesetting, Auldgirth, Dumfriesshire

Printed in the UK by
CPI Cox & Wyman, Reading, RG1 8EX.

2 4 6 8 10 9 7 5 3 1

TO THERESA AND COLIN

'Though the mills of God grind slowly, yet
    they grind exceeding small;
Though with patience He stands waiting,
    with exactness grinds He all.'

HENRY WADSWORTH LONGFELLOW

PART ONE

'I should have known.'

'Why should you?'

'Me mother should have told me.'

'How did she know that they were going to give you fruit with your tea? And, anyway, you said you used the fork all right.'

'I felt clumsy. It was awful . . . awful.'

'What's up with you, our Sarah, worrying about using a fork to fruit? Lord, if I was in your shoes I'd be thinking about what they thought about me . . . along that line.'

'Well, I am . . . that's what I'm doing. What'll she think about me using a fork as if it was a pick shovel?'

'Look, forget about the fork and tell us what it was like, the house and everything.'

'Oh, it was lovely, lovely. You've no idea, Phyllis.'

The two sisters sat on the edge of the bed, their thighs brought together by the sagging mattress. They looked at each other, one bursting to unload her experiences over the hump of humiliation brought about by a new venture in table manners at a Sunday high-tea, the other waiting to be warmed in the glory that had befallen her elder sister.

'There was a beautiful linen cloth on the table; everything was to match, china and all that, and tea-knives besides the knives and forks. I knew what they were for all right.' She pulled a face; then her features flowed into a quick smile that illuminated her surroundings like a light through a dirty window. 'And they've got a proper dining-room, they don't eat in the kitchen.'

'That's because it's a corner house, it's double like.'

Sarah nodded quickly. 'And there's a carpet in the front room, and there's a whole suite; and a piano, and a cabinet – glass-fronted you know, with best china in it. Oh, Phyllis, it was lovely.'

'Did you get upstairs?'

'Yes, she took me up to take me things off.'

'All of them?' Phyllis pushed Sarah in the shoulder and they swayed from each other before the bed brought them close together again.

'Don't be nasty, our Phyllis.' Sarah's eyes were blinking; her face was straining not to laugh now. 'That's what they do. An' you know something . . . they've got a flush lav.'

'No!'

'Yes, truly.'

'Coo! Did it wet your things?'

'Don't be silly.'

'I'm not; I sat on one once and pulled the chain, Ooh, lor! I was wringing.'

'You are a fool you know, our Phyllis; you don't pull it till you get up.'

'I know now. But go on. Did they leave you in the front room to do your courtin'?'

Now it was Sarah's arm that shot out, and so quick was the thrust that it knocked Phyllis from the edge of the bed on to the floor. Within a minute they were back into position again, holding each other as they rocked silently together.

When they were sitting upright once more, their faces wet with their controlled convulsions, Phyllis said, 'I wouldn't have been surprised if they did, you know. Coo! He's not slow on the uptake, is he? You've only been going with him for three weeks and he asks you home. There's May Connor, she's been going with Harry Willis for six months and never darkened his mother's door, and they're supposed to be goin' strong.'

'That's different . . . I don't suppose Harry's particular for May to see inside the house.'

Phyllis wriggled her buttocks on the bed, which brought her feet from the floor, and she lifted them upwards and looked at them as she said, 'They're talkin' about you next door. Old Ma Ratcliffe had her head over the wall the minute you went round the bottom corner. She said to me mother: "Sarah's looking bonnie the day".' Phyllis nudged Sarah with her elbow and stuck her tongue well out.

'That was a sure lead-up to the old snake sticking her fangs in. Will I tell you what she said?'

The eyes of the two girls were now slanted towards each other. 'I'll likely have heard it all afore,' said Sarah.

'You haven't, not this bit . . . we're all one family now.' Phyllis drew her upper lip to a point, showing her large white teeth, and, thrusting her chin out, brought her face into a good imitation of that of their neighbour as she said, ' "Well, Annie, you know nothing can ever come of that, we being at the bottom end." We, you note . . . we're all one big family now . . . no looking down her nose the day. "Stink-pots like the Hetheringtons couldn't be expected to walk this way with wedding rings." That's what she said.'

'Who's talkin' of wedding rings?' Sarah's voice sounded hoarse and threatening.

'Well, I'm only tellin' you what she said. And she didn't forget to rub it in an' all about them being chapel. And then she fired her last gun afore saying she had to get the tea ready. "You'll be having the priest sitting on the doorstep from now on," she said.'

'Damn her!' Sarah got to her feet and walked the two steps to the window, and Phyllis, looking at her straight back, said, 'Eeh! our Sarah, fancy you sayin' that; I thought you had said you'd promised Our Lady never to use a swear word in your life.'

Sarah did not turn her head but stared through

14

the lace curtain to the row of chimneys opposite. Her whole being was flooded with an anger that was not just the outcome of the moment, but stemmed from years of puzzled thinking, of probing and groping blindly to know the reason why. She had been protesting constantly for ten years now from a particular day when she had seen, as if in a revelation, the whole of her life being spent in the lower end of the Fifteen Streets. She'd had a bad cold and her mother had given her nearly half a bottle of cough mixture. It had knocked her silly, and she'd seen funny things, most of which she had forgotten. But she hadn't forgotten the mud picture, as she now thought of it. In the picture she not only saw her mother and Phyllis and her new step-father, wallowing, choking, in a sea of mud, mud like that which filled the huge timber pond at Jarrow Slacks, a mile down the road, but all the people of the Fifteen Streets, all of them, were choking in the mud; there wasn't one of them who wasn't up to the neck in it. And she knew that they all knew there was no hope of getting out. Yet they still struggled. Some upheld others, but some, like Mrs Ratcliffe next door, put their hands on the heads of those nearest them and pushed them under.

'I hate that woman.' She was glaring down at Phyllis now. 'She's never so happy as when she's goin' for us. But I'll show her. I'll get out of here, you'll see.' She bounced her head at her sister, and

Phyllis nodded back, saying under her breath, 'An' the day you go I'll be on your heels.'

Again they were seated close, and Sarah's voice, stripped now of all anger, asked softly, 'But what about me mother?'

Phyllis, sitting straight on the iron frame, eased her hip to one side before she said, 'She wants us to go, an' as soon as possible. There'll be no peace until we get out.'

'She told you that?'

'No, no, of course she didn't, but she could manage him if we were out of the way.' Phyllis sighed now, and tossing her head back and her long fair hair from her shoulders, she supported herself with her hands, gripping the iron frame of the mesh base as she looked up to the ceiling, and said dreamingly, 'I wish I had a bust like yours.'

This remark brought from Sarah a quick downward jerk of the head. The movement showed impatience and an effort to crush down laughter. She got up from the bed, and with her back against the narrow window-sill she looked down on Phyllis, and once again tried to understand this mercurial sister, who could change not only a conversation but her manner so quickly as to leave you bewildered. She said, 'You can have it, and welcome.'

'That's what they go for, a bust.'

'Don't be nasty, our Phyllis, I've told you.' In embarrassment Sarah gathered the frayed end of the lace curtain in her hand and laid it in a bunch on the sill.

'I'm not. I tell you I've watched you going past the bottom corner. An' I've seen the men. Some of them look at your legs sometimes, an' others at your face, but their eyes nearly always finish up on your bust.'

'Our Phyllis!' Sarah was now kneeling on the bed with one knee; pinning her sister down by the shoulders with her hands as she hissed, 'Stop it! Stop such talk! And you only seventeen. You're as bad as the women up the street standing round their doors.'

The bed began to shake and once more they were enfolded together, their arms tight round each other, rocking from side to side, the springs making a zing-zing sound as they moved, until Sarah choked, 'Stop it! You'll have me mother up.'

'I can't help me bust.' They were lying quiet now, their faces wet with their laughing.

'Don't try, you've got something there.'

Again their arms were round each other; again the springs were zing-zinging.

'Do you know you'll have to go to Confession?'

'What for?'

'Well, talking about such things.'

'Oh, our Sarah! You know you are a bairn in some ways. Do you mean to tell me you'd tell Father Bailey about your bust?'

Sarah pulled herself off the bed; a battle was

now going on inside her. This too was an old battle. She wanted to laugh loudly at Phyllis's suggestion, but she knew that it was no laughing matter, for if she had been guilty of bringing up the conversation about her bust she would definitely have had to confess to bad thoughts.

As she stood up there came from below the sound of a door banging, and the sound brought Phyllis from the bed too.

'Better get in.' They were whispering.

Quickly they began to undress, standing where they were in the two-foot space between the wall and the iron bed. As they bent down to pick up their clothes their buttocks bumped and this brought a suppressed giggle from Phyllis, but Sarah, swiftly hanging her things on a hook behind the door, motioned her to silence. Then almost simultaneously they knelt down side by side and, crossing themselves, said their prayers.

Sarah, holding the spring taut with gripped pressure from her hands, waited for Phyllis to crawl cautiously to the far side of the bed, and not until her sister was settled did she take her hands away. Then, sitting on the edge of the bed, she slowly allowed her large frame to sink towards her sister; and when they were close once again Phyllis whispered, 'He'll be disappointed that we're in; he'll have to find something else to yell about.'

Sarah nodded, then whispered, 'Goodnight.'

'Goodnight,' said Phyllis.

They both turned slowly on to their backs and lay looking up at the flaking ceiling, fading now in the light of a summer evening.

It was ten o'clock on this Sunday evening. It was warm and nice outside; couples would be strolling up in the country still, yet here they were packed off to bed as if they were still bairns. Well, Sarah supposed Phyllis wasn't much more being just seventeen. But she herself was nineteen, nearly twenty. It couldn't go on; it mustn't go on. She thrust her long legs down the bed, and when her toes caught against the iron rail she bit tight on her lower lip and screwed up her eyes and in the bright sparked-off pain patterns in the depth of blackness in front of her lids she saw pictured in vivid detail the tea-table in the Hetheringtons' house. And once again she was overwhelmed with shame about the fork business, until the shame was suddenly flicked away and her eyes sprung wide with the thought, It'll come to nothing, them being chapel.

All along she had known it would come to nothing – what hope was there for a Catholic and a chapelite? It was a greater barrier than a social one. The Hetheringtons might live in the Fifteen Streets, but the gap between her family and them was as wide as between a prop man in the docks and one of the managers living in his big house down Westoe end in Shields. The fact that the four

Hetherington men all went to work in collars and ties and that three of the men living in one house were actually in work, whereas her own father – as her mother had insisted she call him – hadn't done a batt for the past seven years, and would have fought shy of it now if he had the chance of it, even this barrier, the difference which meant living with bugs behind the wallpaper or without them, could, with a miracle, have been surmounted, but not even time or death could alter the religious difference. And yet here she was, yarping on to herself about making a mess of using a fruit fork. That's what she did, she told herself heatedly: she never faced up to things, always started worrying about some little thing that didn't matter a damn, trying to cover up the bigger issues, like trying to cover the sky with a blade of grass. If you held the grass or anything else close enough to your eyes you could blot out what was behind it. At least for a time, then your arm got tired, so to speak. She had to face up to things in the end, but it was always in the night that they caught up with her, which was why she was so tired in the morning.

Well, she had known who he was from the word go, hadn't she? When he had stood outside the shop waiting for her she had known he was from the posh house at the end of Camelia Street. Everybody knew the big house at the end of Camelia Street because it wasn't divided into two.

It had seven rooms and a brass knocker on the door, and the curtains were always beautifully white.

He had said to her 'Hello', and she had answered 'Hello', while sweat had suddenly burst into her oxters and the palms of her hands.

'I hope you don't mind.' He had stopped, as embarrassed as she was, and then she had answered. 'No, no, not at all', in the swanky tone she tried to adopt at times. She had got it from the people who came into the sweet shop – some talked swanky. But they didn't get many like that, although it was a good-class shop.

He said, 'Can I walk home with you?'

The shop was in Ocean Road in Shields and she always took the tram from the Market Place to Tyne Dock and there changed to the Jarrow tram. In the mornings she usually walked part of the distance to save the fare, but at night, her feet were nearly always swollen with so much standing, and her heavy build didn't make them any better, so she was glad to sit down in the tram. But this first night they walked all the way from Ocean Road to Tyne Dock, then up through the arches, past Simonside Bank, which led up into the country, past the respectable New Buildings flanking the Jarrow Slacks, past the dark jumble of houses built on a rise and called Bogey Hill, and on to the Fifteen Streets. It was a long walk and she really only came to herself as they neared his street,

Camelia Street, and she stopped as if she had been pulled to a halt with a rope and said, primly, 'Thank you, but I can see me own way now.' It was such a silly thing to say and she blushed with the stupidity of it, but he smiled and said, 'Can I see you tomorrow night?'

To this she merely nodded shyly.

'The same time?' he said.

'Yes.' She was on the point of moving away when again she was halted, by the fascinating sight of a man raising his hat to her, a trilby hat.

She had tried to walk straight because she knew he was still standing watching her, but her legs were tired, and they felt wonky, just as if she was slightly tipsy.

There were men grouped at the bottom of all the streets past Dudley Street – Dudley Street was the sixth street from the top end. The men looked at her, they always did, but none of them spoke until she came to the corner of their own street. There were about a dozen men here; some were on their hunkers, some leaning against the wall, all with their coats and caps and mufflers on, although the night was stifling. The older ones hailed her, while the younger ones just spoke with their eyes.

'Brought any bullets with you the night, Sarah?'

She smiled, and with a feeling of gaiety answered them, saying, 'There was only a box of chocolates over, and I knew you wouldn't like them so I gave them away to the bairns.'

'Oh, aye!'

'Well, Aa never liked chocolates,' said another; 'acid drops is more in me line.'

'Sherbet dips for me.'

'I like suckers, oh! I'm very fond of a sucker.' She was well past them when this remark was made; it came from a man who lived three doors down from her, a nasty man. She heard one of the older men saying, 'That's enough, shut tha' gob.'

The man who had spoken in the pitmatic was Mr Ferris and lived opposite to them. He had often slipped her a ha'penny when she was a bairn. They had no children of their own. She liked Mr Ferris . . .

So that had been the beginning, only three weeks ago, and every night at half-past eight he had been waiting for her when the shop closed and he had walked her home. He had wanted to take her to the pictures, but she had refused. When at the end of the second week he had again asked her to go to the pictures and she again refused he had seemed puzzled. How could she tell him it was because she felt shabby and hadn't any Sunday things. It was different being met coming from work, you weren't expected to be dressed up then. Then last Saturday night he had asked her if she would come to tea on the Sunday, and she had stayed up late washing and ironing her skirt and blouse.

The odd thing about all this was her father had

never mentioned the matter. If he had known that she was seeing a lad of any kind the place would have been raised; he simply went mad if he saw her talking to a lad. He had belted her when she was sixteen because he had seen her coming up the road three nights running with the same lad. None of the lads around the Buildings made up to her – perhaps because she kept herself aloof, but she also knew that they were slightly afraid of Pat Bradley. This had puzzled her in her early years because her stepfather was an undersized, insignificant-looking man, but lately she had come to understand people's fear of him, for there was an innate vicious strength about him that had nothing to do with his stature.

Of one thing she was sure: if he had known about her meeting with David Hetherington she would have heard about it. There were a number of people who had seen her with David, Mrs Ratcliffe next door for one, yet none of them had split on her. She felt a warm feeling towards the whole population of the Fifteen Streets. But the warm feeling fled with the thought. Perhaps the longer he's in the dark the bigger the bust-up there'll be, and that's what they're waiting for. Her father was known as a know-all, and likely a lot of the men were laughing up their sleeves at the way she was hoodwinking him. They would think of it as hoodwinking although she had done nothing on the sly.

Her mother had said last night, 'There'll be murder when he finds out; I would drop it if I were you.' And to this she had answered, 'I will after tomorrow night. He's asked me to tea, I'll tell him then.' Her mother's answer had been, 'My God! And them chapel!'

She turned on her side now and began to pray: 'Holy Mary, Mother of God, pray for us sinners now and at the hour of our death, amen. What am I going to do? Make him turn . . . don't let him be bigoted, Holy Mother. Oh, Queen of Heaven, the ocean star, guide of the wanderer here below.' Her praying trailed away and slowly she turned her face into the straw pillow and pressed her nose until it was pushed to one side and her mouth bit on the rough ticking. Was she mad altogether? She had only known him three weeks and here she was thinking he would ask her to marry him. Yet why had he asked her home? Why was he meeting her every day if there wasn't something in his mind? You didn't ask a girl home unless it meant something. Yet he knew where she came from, he knew she came from the bottom end – in fact the bottom, bottom end, for they lived in the last street, the last habitable street. Beyond, the houses were so dilapidated, so overrun with bugs, that they were only inhabited now and again by flitters, and there was talk of them being pulled down any time. Yes, he knew where she lived, and his mother must know too. She had been afraid of meeting his mother; she hadn't been afraid of meeting his father, or his brother, or his uncle. She wasn't afraid of men as she was of women; not really, except perhaps her father. But his mother had turned out to be . . . well, all right in a way. Cautious; oh yes, very cautious. Scrutinising, looking her over from the side, and quizzing in her talk. How long had she worked at Bentons?'

Since she was fourteen, she had said; it was her first job.

How long had her father been out of work? What was he when he was in work?

He had been a platelayer, but that was before the War, and then he had been in the Army, but could only get odd jobs since he came out. Work was very scarce. She had said this as if they didn't know, and found the eyes of the three men on her – the father, the uncle, and David. The other son wasn't there. He was married and lived in the next street.

Where did her sister work?

She worked in a cafe in Shields.

She was glad they didn't ask where the cafe was.

David sat opposite her through the tea, and every time she became slightly overawed or embarrassed she would look at him. His eyes were always waiting for her. She thought he had the kindest eyes she had ever seen in a man. They were clear grey. They were his best feature, although he had a nice mouth too. All his features were nice, yet they didn't make him good looking. She supposed that was because of his skin. It was rough, with red veins high on the cheeks, like a man who had worked in the blast furnaces all his life. His face was more suited to what she classed a working man than a man who worked in the dock offices. But his voice was not that of a working man. He had a lovely voice; soft, warm, kindly. She liked his voice and his eyes; she liked him altogether.

His father must have looked pretty much the same at David's age, but now his hair, instead of being brown, was wispy grey and he had a twitch in one eye. But he, too, was nice. Then there was the uncle. She had laughed when she was introduced to the uncle. David hadn't called him uncle but Dan. 'This is Dan,' he said. 'He's really my uncle, but he's only six years older than me so why should I call him uncle? And he's a rogue, so you look out for him.'

She had been at home with Dan right away, more than with any of them, even David. Dan wasn't as tall as David, who was close on six feet, but he was broader, much broader, with a big square face. You could call Dan good looking. And from the start she had seen that Dan was what was known as a joker. He could keep the conversation going and make you laugh. And yet there was something about Dan that she couldn't fathom; it was linked up in some way with his sister's attitude towards him, the sister being David's mother. She had noticed right away that Mrs Hetherington's manner towards her brother was different altogether from the manner she used to either her husband or her son. Either she ignored him, or when she was forced to speak, as when she thanked him for passing something across the table to her, she did not look at him and her voice took on a prim sound as if she was displeased, like a teacher's attitude towards an erring pupil. Sarah hadn't realised this fully until now, when she was going over the whole scene in her mind.

But there was one thing she was sure of: all the Hetheringtons were wonderful; and if only David would ask her she would die of happiness.

And so with another prayer to Our Lady to get him to turn, she dropped into fitful, dream-threaded sleep.

2

The last customer was a boy about seven years old. He couldn't decide whether he wanted jube-jubes, everlasting strips, or walnut-tray toffee. Sarah said as gently as she could, 'We're closing, hinny; come on, make up your mind.'

The child thought a little longer, then, looking

up, he asked, 'Can I have a ha'porth of each of two of them?'

Sarah sighed, 'Which two?'

Again there was some consideration and Sarah raised her eyes from the top of the boy's head to the glass door and to the figure walking slowly past.

As the boy's mouth opened on his decision a voice from the back of the shop called quietly, 'It's time, Sarah.'

'Yes, Mrs Benton.'

She flung the sweets into a bag, then pushed them at the boy, who had the temerity to say, with no small indignation, 'Why, you've put them in the same bag? The jube-jubes'll stick to the taffy.'

'Go on,' she hissed at him now.

Having pushed him out of the door, she stooped quickly and shot the bolt in while keeping her eyes averted from the street beyond.

She was getting into her coat as she said, 'I'm all locked up, Mrs Benton. I'll away then.'

The elderly woman smiled quietly. 'Yes, get yourself away ... I wouldn't like to have to pay for his shoe leather.'

The colour flooded up into Sarah's face. She hadn't imagined that Mrs Benton had noticed David.

'Is he a nice boy?'

'Yes, very nice, Mrs Benton.'

'Be a good girl.'

Sarah said nothing to this, only her eyes widened a little as she turned away with her head bent. She felt she should laugh, but she couldn't, for she was slightly annoyed. The admonition hadn't been spoken in a jocular way, as one of their neighbours might have said it, but more broadly, more casually. 'Divn't dee what I wouldn't dee unless ya want the priest after ya.' No, Mrs Benton's words had sounded like a warning and they made her feel hot. And so, when she came out of the side passage and he was standing there facing the alleyway, his first words were, 'You look warm.'

She stood in front of him, smiling widely now. 'I am . . . I've just finished a big deal . . . a shipping order.'

'Yes?' His smile too was wide as he waited.

'That bairn you saw coming out. He couldn't make up his mind how to spend a penny. He wanted jube-jubes, everlasting strips, and walnut toffee. He just couldn't make up his mind.'

'What eventually did he plunge for?'

'A ha'porth of walnut taffy and a ha'porth of jube-jubes, then he went for me because I put them in the same bag.'

Their heads back but their eyes holding, and still laughing, they turned away and walked as one, not touching, yet their bodies joined through the rhythmic swing of their limbs. But at the corner of Fowler Street, where it branched off

Ocean Road, he stopped and said, 'We'll get the tram here.'

She turned her head quickly towards him. They had done the journey on foot every night since they had first met. It was the only time they had together. She watched his eyes flick down towards her ankles as he said, 'You've done enough standing for one day.'

She had the desire to crouch down, covering her feet with her clothes, as she had done when a child, when they had played mothers and fathers in the back-yard and she had always wanted to be the baby which had occasioned her doubling herself in two. But now she looked down at her ankles and she hated them. They were the only part of her body that she hated; in her opinion they spoilt her. For she could not help but be aware that her body earned her the northern compliment of being 'a strapping lass'. In the morning her ankles were as thin as her wrists, but they always swelled if she stood on her feet for any length of time. With her build she supposed she should have tried for a sitting-down job. As it was, there wasn't even a stool behind the shop counter.

'They get like that with standing.' She didn't want him to think that they were always swollen.

'I know; Dan's swell too.'

Dan, she had been surprised to learn, worked in a grocer's shop in Jarrow. She imagined that he would have worked in the dock offices, seeing that

David and his father did. She didn't know where the other son worked; she supposed it was in the dock offices too.

She said, 'But I don't mind walking, they don't pain.'

'Nevertheless we're taking the tram.' His voice sounded firm, nicely firm. 'Here it is; come on.' He took her arm and hurried her across the road.

As they were going up the gangway of the tram he spoke to a workman sitting in the back, saying, 'Hello there, Fred.'

'Hello there, Mr Hetherington.'

The distinction in the form of address pleased Sarah. She felt proud, as if she was bathing in the glorified reflection of a title; the workman had called him Mr Hetherington.

David's hand was on her arm now, pulling her gently back, and he ushered her into the seat in front of the man; then, twisting round, he asked him, 'Did you get it, Fred?'

'No-o.' The word was drawn out, it was a long deep thick syllable. 'There was about thirty waiting for it. It's no good, man; even a bit of influence isn't any good any more.'

'I'm sorry.'

'Oh, don't you worry, Mr Hetherington, man. It was good of you to put me on to it.'

David turned to give the conductor the fares, then he looked at Sarah and said under his breath, 'It's frightful, this business, trying to get a job.'

Sarah didn't catch all he said because of the rumble of the tram-car, but she gauged he was speaking sympathetically about the man. Then he turned again and, looking over his shoulder, said, 'Try Fullers, Fred, first thing in the morning. There might be something doing, you never know. You'll find our John somewhere in the yard.' His voice dropped. 'If you can get a word with him on the quiet, tell him I sent you.'

'Oh, thanks, Mr Hetherington. Thanks, I'll do that. I'll be up afore the lark. Man, this life gets you down.'

'Good luck, Fred.'

'Aye, good luck, that's what we want. And good luck to you, sir.' His eyes nicked to Sarah's profile and back to David, and the jerk of his head was an open compliment. He rose to his feet, jabbed at the bell pull, as the conductor was upstairs, and brought the tram to a stop.

David did not look at her as he now said, 'It gets me down, to see them standing about, rotting away. I remember him as a big man when I first started in the dock office. Now he seems to have shrunk to half his size. It has effect on all of them in the end: it shrivels up something inside of them, I suppose.'

Sarah glanced sharply at him, her face quite grave. She had heard all he had said and somehow she didn't like it; she didn't like to think of him associating with workmen, talking to them as man

33

to man. He was from a different world, from the top end. He worked in an office. She wanted to keep him, at least in her mind, secluded, away from all contact with labourers, riveters, plate-men, propmen, trimmers, pitmen, and the like.

And then he said, 'My brother's a foreman joiner, it's a small firm, but he'll set him on if it's at all possible.'

His brother a joiner? This news came in the form of a blow, even with the title foreman before it. She hadn't imagined one of the Hetheringtons working in the docks, actually working among the rough-and-tumble. Oh, she wasn't an upstart, she wasn't, and she didn't want to be an upstart, she didn't. Her mind reiterated the phrase as if she was answering in agitated defence some voice that was spitting scorn at her, and her environment-encumbered mind, being unable to put forward any argument to uphold her snobbishness, ended helplessly. Oh, I just want to get away from it all.

She was looking at her hands encased in thin cotton grey gloves – an outward sign of gentility. And from her hands her gaze dropped to David's feet. He was wearing nice brown shoes, very highly polished. He had worn black ones last night, but then he had been wearing a dark suit. Fancy having different shoes to go with different suits. She had seen him in two different suits besides grey flannels and a tweed coat.

'Have you dropped something?'

'No.' She jerked her head up to him. 'I . . . I was only looking at your shoes.' She hadn't meant to say any such thing.

'Oh . . . the polish?' He brought his lips tightly together and his eyes twinkled as he bounced his head before saying, 'My mother. She polishes all our shoes. You would think she had been trained in the army.'

She answered his smile, but weakly. It was as her mother was so fond of saying . . . you got everything in batches. And it was true in every aspect of life. He had talked to the workman as if he was on the same level as the man. Then he had told her his brother was a fitter, and now he had pricked the illusion of the exclusiveness of his family, by telling her his mother cleaned all their shoes. Why, even her father, as bad and as lazy as he was, cleaned his own shoes.

The tram was rumbling its way down Stanhope Road now, and as it passed the Catholic Church, the church that she had attended from when she first went to school, she bowed her head deeply in obeisance to the Sacred Heart that was ever present on the altar. It was an involuntary, almost an unconscious movement.

That the action had not been lost on David was given to her just after they alighted at the bottom of the dock bank and had crossed the road, beginning the walk through the arches towards East Jarrow.

'Are you a regular attendant at church?' he asked, smiling quietly.

'A regular attendant?' She repeated his phrase as if muttering a foreign language, and then said hastily, 'Yes, yes, I go every Sunday. We have to.'

They walked on in silence for a few minutes before he said, 'I used to go every Sunday too. To chapel, that was.' He smiled, rather apologetically, following this statement.

'Don't you go now?'

'No ... no. I've never been since I was eighteen.'

There came a lightness to her mind. This could make things easier, oh, so much easier. 'Why?' she asked.

He moved his head slowly. 'I just couldn't stand it any more. The narrowness, the idea that God belonged to the Baptists and he would shoot you down sort of business if you didn't think along the particular lines they laid down appeared mad to me. Of course I didn't see it all in a flash, I had a long time of troubled thinking to go through. But now I think people are quite bats, almost insane, to believe that if there is a God he's there just for them and their particular way of thinking, while the rest of the community – and not only the community but the world – is damned if they don't come in with them.'

Her mind for a moment was devastated. If he thought that about the Baptists what did he think about the Catholics, for the Catholic religion was

36

the only one true religion, and every Catholic knew this and maintained it. They might stay off mass, they might get drunk, the men might knock their wives about, but when they went to Confession and their sins were absolved, they knew that they were receiving a privilege given to no one except a Catholic . . . The devastation moved its dull sickening weight to allow for a ray of brightness. Didn't his attitude make things easier? The very fact that he was no longer a chapelite made the battle half won. But even as she thought this she said, 'But you believe in God?'

'I just don't know.' He shook his head. 'Sometimes I know positively that I don't, at others . . . well, I just don't know. I could cry for the greatness, the simplicity, the naïveness, in Jesus. I could wring his hand for his detestation of the holier than thous. I could walk beside him as he smiles on the publicans and whores. But I can't see eye to eye with him when he tells me that the slow, slow force that urged a seed into a tree, then compressed it into fuel for firing for man it had not yet conceived – is my Father. But does it matter all that much? Does it matter much?' He was walking close to her now, his face, long and serious, turned towards her, and she did not look at him as she answered quite untruthfully, 'No, no.'

Again they were walking in silence, and now they were on a quiet stretch of the road bordered by high stone walls that ran between Simonside

Bank and the Saw Mill, and it was at a spot where no one was in sight that he suddenly took hold of her arm and brought them both to a stop. His hand still holding her, his eyes roamed round her face, and in a way that she termed quaint he said, 'Hello, Sarah.' She had the desire to giggle; it was funny the way he said it, as if they had just met, and her lids began to blink as his eyes slowly picked out her features. It was as if he were detaching them from her face and examining them. When his eyes came to rest on hers again he said, 'What about it, Sarah?'

She didn't know how to answer. She wetted her lips, which were trembling, and, like the fool she told herself she was, she remained dumb, and he went on speaking. 'I've never spoken your name before. We've come up this road twenty-five times. I've kept count – and I've never called you by your name. And tonight is the first time I've touched you, when I helped you on to the bus. You know something, Sarah . . . you're very beautiful.'

'O . . . oh!' It was an inarticulate sound, like a groan.

His eyes flicked from her now up and down the road and then he said softly. 'May I kiss you?'

Still she could make no answering sound, but her whole body spoke for her and the next moment they were close and his lips were on hers, gently, softly, as if afraid of what they were about. It was over in an instant, and then silently again they were walking up the road, their arms rubbing every now and again. Her body felt light, there was no longer any heavy tight pressure around her ankles, she seemed to be afloat. They passed the open space of the Jarrow Slacks. The tide was high and there were children playing on the timbers. They passed the tram sheds. They passed Bogey Hill. And not until they walked up the bank that led to the plateau of the Fifteen Streets did he break the enchanted silence.

'Will you come to Newcastle with me tomorrow night, Sarah, to a show?'

'Ooh!' It was another groan, but a different kind of groan. Go to Newcastle and do a show. That would be living indeed; hitting the high spots. Oh, if only she could say yes. She had her pay in her pocket, eighteen and six; it was good money and she could have been dressed up to the eyes if she had been able to keep at least the eight and six, but no, she had to tip up fourteen shillings each and every week. Then there was two shillings out of the remainder for her clothes club. That left half a crown and she wouldn't have had that if she hadn't stuck out for her bus fare each day. If only she could have managed a five-pound club she would have been able to rig herself out. Well, she would get a club. Her chest moved upwards on the decision. She would get a five-pound club and get herself a new coat and shoes . . . But that wouldn't fix tomorrow. Her chest moved downwards again, and she answered, 'I'm sorry, I can't tomorrow.'

'Why? You said last week it was your early night off this Saturday . . . Sarah.' Again they were standing facing each other, 'There isn't somebody else?'

'Somebody else!' Her voice was high, right up in her head, and she laughed as she repeated, 'Somebody else?' Then, putting her head on one side, she dared joke. 'And where do you think he's been every night for the last three weeks?'

They laughed together, his head back in his characteristic style. And when he was looking at her again he asked, 'Then why won't you come?'

Now her eyes were steady and travelling over his face. It was a good face she was looking into, a kindly, honest face, and as she stared at it, it came to her that this man had no side. The knowledge was warming. She felt wise, even superior, being able to appraise his character. She knew it was because of his lack of side that he was to the workmen one of themselves. That was why he could talk about his mother cleaning their shoes and his brother being a fitter. He had no side. Her revealed knowledge of him supplied her with the courage to touch the front of her coat, lifting it outwards, and say, 'I haven't any clothes.'

'What!' His eyebrows moved up in genuine surprise. Then his long face seemed to crumple into agitated concern and the end of his nose twitched with a rabbit-like movement before he went on, 'Oh, my dear. Why, fancy you worrying about that! I've never even noticed what you've got on.' His features spread outwards again into an amused smile. 'Nobody will ever notice what you're wearing, Sarah. You carry your clothes like . . . well, like someone who doesn't have to have clothes to make her out. You know what I mean,' he finished swiftly.

Her lids were lowered. 'It's nice of you to put it like that, but a girl needs clothes. It does something to you to have nice clothes . . . new clothes.'

'I tell you people will never look at what you're . . . Oh, come on.' He swung her away now, holding on to her, laughing. 'You're coming to Newcastle tomorrow night and the dames in their rabbit skins won't be able to hold a candle to you.'

Her chin was on her chest, her large body was shaking with a gurgle of intense happy laughter. Then abruptly it stopped. She was looking ahead, speaking quietly. 'You know what?'

'No.'

'I think you're the nicest man in the world.'

'Oh, Sarah!' She was about to be pulled to a stop yet once again when she said hurriedly, 'Eeh, no! Look, we're nearing the streets. There's people about.'

She was blushing all over; she hadn't intended to say anything like that, about him being nice. It was a bit forward at this stage, she supposed, like

41

pushing herself, throwing herself on to his neck. But he wouldn't take it like that, he wasn't that kind, and she had meant it – he was the nicest man in the world. And he was a man. He looked a man, not a lad, or a chap; he was a man. She wondered how old he was, he had never said. He appeared about twenty-five or twenty-six. She seemed to have no control over her tongue tonight, for she heard herself asking quite boldly, 'How old are you?'

'What do you think?' There was laughter in his voice again.

She cast her eyes slantwise towards him as if taking a measure of his age, and then she said, 'Twenty-six.'

'Twenty-six?' His eyebrows went up. 'Three years out.'

'You're not twenty-nine?'

'No. Are you disappointed? I'm twenty-three.'

No, she wasn't disappointed, but he looked older. She was startled now as he said, 'And you're nineteen.'

'How do you know?'

'Oh, I know when you left school.'

'You do?'

He leant near her and whispered menacingly, 'I've had my eye on you for years, Sarah Bradley.'

Again she was flooded with a happy gurgling feeling, an unusual carefree feeling. Fancy now, he'd had his eye on her for years . . . But if that was so, why hadn't he come forward sooner? Perhaps because she had never looked at him. Now and again she had passed him on the road but had always averted her gaze, knowing he was from the top end.

As they were passing Camelia Street two women came round the corner, and he said to them, 'Good evening, Mrs Talbot. Good evening, Mrs Francis.'

'Good evening, David,' one of them said, while both of them nodded, with their eyes tight on Sarah.

A coolness touched her warm body. What were they thinking? Oh, she knew what they were thinking: that he was mad. Well – she bridled inside – he wasn't the only one that was mad, she was mad in her own way too.

She stopped at their usual place of parting.

'Why don't you let me walk down with you?'

She looked straight into his eyes. 'Do I need to have to tell you?' It was a relief to be honest. Since she had told him about her clothes she felt she could tell him anything.

'Don't be silly.'

'I'm not being silly, but you know what it's like down there.'

'Well, I'll have to come sometime.'

The coolness was pressed from her body, she was warm again. She dropped her eyes from his.

'I'll call for you tomorrow . . . that's fixed.'

Her head was up. 'No, no. Please, oh please.' She was pleading now. 'Don't come to the door, I'll meet you here.'

He was about to say something when a group of boys who had come tearing down the roadway now raced round them on the pavement, and one of them, as he swung away from a pursuer, grabbed at Sarah's skirt. As she almost over-balanced David's hand went out to steady her, and he cried at the boy, 'Here! Here! Let up on that, will you?'

The boy scrambled back into the road again, but the one who had been doing the chasing stopped in the gutter and peered up at Sarah, and without a preliminary lead-up remarked, 'There's hell going on in your back-yard, Sarah. Yer da's taken the belt to Phyllis. She's been screaming blue murder and he's locked yer ma in the netty.'

Sarah's lips moved without any intention of uttering words. For a moment they were like the lips of a very old woman chewing the cud of unformulated thought; only Sarah's thoughts were not unformulated. In a matter of seconds the faint sweetness of life that she had tasted was smudged out with the picture conjured up by the boy's words. She could not bear to look at David but turned away and with a swing of her body sped from him and raced up the road. Then he was by her side running with her, and she was forced to stop. Gasping, she almost barked at him, 'No, no! Don't come, please. I don't want you to. Don't you see?'

He remained still, saying nothing, and once again she was running past the street corners. There were no men standing at the bottom of her own corner tonight, nor were they in the front street. The street was strangely bare, except for Mrs Young, the neighbour on the right-hand side. She was coming out of her house as Sarah hammered on the front door, and she said quietly, 'I doubt you'll not get in that way, hinny; he's been at it for the last half-hour. You know, something should be done with him. I would go to the Cruelty Inspector, I would an' all, if it wasn't for your ma. He's belted that poor lass within an inch of her life. Sam Ferris just got over the wall in time. He's mad, you know, vicious and mad when the fit takes him. I wouldn't care if he did it in drink, but for a man who's tee-total and acts the way he does there's somethin' radically wrong with him.'

'But what'd she done, Mrs Young?'

'Aw lass, it's none of my business, you'll know soon enough. But I'd go round the back if I was you.'

Running again, Sarah entered the back lane. There were groups gathered together all along its length, the men mostly by themselves, the women likewise. Outside of their back door were four men standing and a woman. The woman turned and said, 'Oh, it's you, Sarah.' And one man,

45

taking hold of her arm, said, 'I wouldn't go in for a while if I was you, lass; let him cool down. Your mother's with him now.'

'He's not all to blame,' another man was addressing her, his head bouncing as if on wires. 'You've got to do something when it comes to that, you know.'

'What are you talking about, Mr Riley? Comes to what? What's happened? . . . Leave go of me.' She turned to the man who was holding her arm, and when he released her the other man said, 'Arabs, to put it in a nutshell.'

'Arabs?' Sarah was aware that she was showing all her teeth, that her lips had moved back from her gums as if the word itself smelt.

'Aye, that's what I said, lass. Young Phyllis's been with an Arab. Now your da's no angel, we all know that, but I would have done the same in his case.'

'No bloody fear you wouldn't; he's a maniac!'

As the woman spoke, Sarah pushed past the group and went through the open back door and up the yard. There was no sound coming from the kitchen, the whole place appeared quiet. She opened the door and stepped into the little square scullery and noted that the tin dish, which usually stood on the cracket behind the door and in which they did the washing up and used for everything that required the use of water, was lying against the wall end up, and that the floor surrounding it was covered with soapy suds. She opened the kitchen door and stepped quietly into the room. Her father was sitting at the corner of the table. His thin sour face looked yellow, and the red marks that always streaked the whites of his eyes seemed to have spread completely over them. They looked a bloodshot blur except for two dark jets pointed at her from his narrowed lids. His short wiry body and equally short legs were held taut; he looked as if he were jointless.

She glanced quickly from him towards her mother, who was standing with her hands gripping the mantelpiece, her head hanging forward, gazing down into the low fire in the bottom of the deep grate between the black-leaded oven and the pan hob. Her mother was a big woman, almost twice the size of her father. She had been bonnie too at one time, with a fine figure and a laughing face, but Sarah hadn't seen her really laugh for years. A thought that she had asked herself countless times she asked again now. Why did she do it . . . marry him? A man ten years younger than herself. Perhaps, as she had told herself before, it was just because he was ten years younger and she had been flattered.

Her words came out on a stammer as she asked, 'W-what's the matter?' She couldn't believe what they had said in the back lane, that Phyllis had been with an Arab. Her father would jump at

47

anything that would give him the excuse to use his belt.

'So you've come in, have you?'

Ignoring his words, she said again, addressing herself pointedly to her mother, 'What's the matter?'

Pat Bradley was on his feet, glaring at her now from his bloodshot eyes. 'You're goin' to make on you know nowt about it, that's what you're going to do, aren't you? There's a pair of you. Oh, aye, there's a pair of you. What she doesn't know you'll put her up to. Not that she needs much coachin'.'

Her mother turned from the fireplace, speaking for the first time, her voice heavy with a dead kind of weariness. She said, 'Go on upstairs, Sarah, and see to Phyllis.'

'She'll go when I give the word.'

'Leave her alone.' Annie Bradley turned on her husband, towering over him, threatening now. 'You've done enough for one night, I've told you. You've gone too far this time. I told you what would happen if you lifted your hand to one of them again, didn't I?' She turned from the staring eyes of the man and said again to Sarah, 'Go on up to Phyllis.'

Sarah turned away slowly. She wanted to go up to Phyllis and yet she didn't want to go, at least not yet. She wanted to face up to this man too, to tell him what would happen if he dared raise his hand to her. She knew that she had been waiting for a

48

long time for this opportunity and praying for the courage to use it, but she obeyed her mother. Moving between the square wooden table and the leather couch, she opened the staircase door and, groping for the rope balustrade, she pulled herself up the almost precipitous staircase. One step across the four-foot square of landing and she was in the bedroom, standing by the bed looking down at Phyllis.

Her sister was lying on her side. Her jumper lay in shreds across her back; there were two rents in her skirt from waistband to hem, and the seat of her bloomers were all black as if she had been dragged around the yard. Sarah brought her face closer to the torn blouse. There was no sign of blood, but, lifting the shreds of material apart, she saw a criss-cross of rising dark-blue weals.

'Oh, Phyllis!' She put her hands gently on her sister's shoulder, but Phyllis did not move or speak, and Sarah said, urgently now, 'Phyllis, sit up. Phyllis, do you hear me? Come on . . . Phyllis.'

Phyllis moved slowly; then with an effort, as if her body was tied to the bed, she turned on to her hip. Her eyes were closed; her face, except for a dark weal that started at the top of her ear and came down across her cheek to the corner of her mouth, was a sickly white. But Sarah was not looking at her face, she was looking at her breasts, the small undeveloped breasts that Phyllis was forever trying to enlarge. They were bare and

49

criss-crossed with lines, similar to the one on her face.

'Oh, my God!' Sarah sat down on the edge of the bed and gently enfolded the slight body within her arms, rocking her like a mother with a child. And again she said, 'Oh, my God!' She stayed like this for some time, gently rocking and making sounds that expressed pain; and then she said, 'I've got some Pond's cream; I'll rub it on, Eh?'

Phyllis still did not speak, but when Sarah released her she moved her legs and sat on the edge of the bed. She looked as if all life had been whipped out of her, not a protest left. But this impression was shattered as Sarah went to apply, with gentle fingers, the first dab of cream on to the weal on her sister's cheek, for Phyllis's hand came up and gripped her wrist and in a whisper, cracked and hoarse but laden with a fierce strength, she said, 'One day I'm going to kill him, Sarah.'

Sarah did not reprimand her for the statement, but, sitting close to her, she whispered, 'Why did he do it?'

'He said I'd been with an Arab.' Phyllis's eyes were looking straight into Sarah's.

'But you hadn't, had you? Not an Arab.'

'He said I'd been WITH an Arab . . . not just speaking to one . . . WITH him.'

'But you've never even spoken to an Arab, have you?'

'Of course, I have.' Phyllis's eyes did not drop away. 'They come into the cafe every day, you've got to speak to them.'

'Yes I know, but not outside?'

'Yes, I've spoken to one outside.'

'Oh, Phyllis!'

'Don't say "Oh, Phyllis!" like that. He's a decent enough fellow; in fact he's better than them around these doors, I can tell you that.'

'Oh, Phyllis . . . but . . . but an Arab. You know you'll get your name up. You'll be hounded out of the place. Remember Betty Fuller? You mightn't, but I do. She married one, and when she came back to see her mother, Mrs Baxter emptied the chamberpot on her out of the upstairs window. I was only about ten, but I remember. The whole neighbourhood was raised.'

'What do I care? Anyway, I hadn't BEEN WITH him and I've only spoken to him twice outside the shop. Once, when I was crossing the ferry, Mr Benito had sent me to North Shields with an order and he was on the ferry and we got talkin', and I can tell you' – her voice now hissed at Sarah with a strength born of anger – 'I can tell you he spoke to me better than the lads around this quarter do. He talked just like any Geordie, but he had manners.'

Sarah did not say anything; she was bewildered, amazed. Phyllis talking to an Arab! Everybody knew what happened to girls who went with Arabs; they were ostracised, never again could they come back into the clan. Their families knew them no more – at least not around this quarter, they daren't. Most of the white girls who married Arabs lived in the Arab community in Costerfine Town and East Holborn way. Those who made a break and took houses in other parts of the town only stayed for a short time, the neighbours saw to that.

Even among their own kind Sarah knew that class distinction was strong. The top and the bottom of the Fifteen Streets knew their places; they didn't mix . . . or at least they hadn't until she had broken – or, more correctly, David Hetherington had broken – the hoodoo. But this distinction of class, which took its pattern from the even stronger sense of distinction that prevailed in Jarrow and Shields, even crippled as each town was with unemployment, was nothing to the distinction between a white girl of any class and an Arab.

At this point Phyllis's face screwed up with pain and she pressed her hands gently over her chest; then, turning her head slowly to Sarah, she said, 'You don't believe me?'

'Yes, yes, I do, Phyllis. But tell me, how did he' – she nodded towards the floor – 'get to know?'

'It was this afternoon; it was only the second time I'd spoken to him outside, as I told you. I'd just finished and I was comin' up into the market when I thought I would like to bring me ma something home; you know she likes mussels, and so I went to that shop, you know that sells the mussels and the brown bread and beer, and he was inside. He was having a plate of mussels and he asked me if I'd have one. I said no thanks, I'd just come in to take some home, and when I came out he came with me and we walked along the street and up into the market. I couldn't say "You can't walk along of me", could I?' Her eyes, painfilled yet rebellious, asked the question, and Sarah said, 'No. No, of course not . . . And that was all?'

'Aye, that was all; atween me and God that was all. But you know something?' Phyllis brought her face to Sarah's. 'It won't be all from now on. You bet your bottom dollar it won't be all. He's done something to me the night, broken something. He's belted me afore but not like the night, and I swear I'll get me own back. An' I know how I'll do it an' all. By God! Aye, I'll get me own back!'

'Oh, Phyllis, you're feelin' bad, don't talk like that.'

'Aye, I'm feelin' bad, I feel awful.' Phyllis now moved her head in a desperate fashion. 'I feel I'm gona die, but I'll not die.' Her head wagged quicker now. 'No, I'll not die, I'll live just to spite him. Oh God.' She joined her hands tightly together. 'Oh God, I'll get out of here and quick. You'll see, you'll see. I'll be gone afore you; you'll see, our Sarah.' She was talking as if Sarah was opposing her. And Sarah said, 'All right, all right, don't excite yourself. Go and lie down; let me put some of the cream on your back.'

Like a child now, Phyllis lay on her stomach, and when Sarah had treated her back she turned over slowly and said, 'I feel bad, Sarah; oh, I do feel bad.'

'You lie still, I'll go and get you something.'

Sarah smiled compassionately down at the slight figure, and her fingers touched the white cheek, the one without the weal.

But when she closed the bedroom door behind her she stood leaning against the wall for a moment. There was in her an overpowering feeling of rage. Such was its strength, it filled her with apprehension, for she had the desire to rush down the stairs, pick up the shaving strap that hung below the little mirror to the side of the fireplace and lash his thin body with it until he cringed for mercy; and she knew she could do it, she knew she was big enough and tough enough to do just that. Then why didn't she? Perhaps because she had never raised her hand to anyone in her life. She tried to force herself to carry out the urge, but all she did was to say, 'Holy Mary, Mother of God.' Then, as she groped her way down to the room below, she ground out at herself, 'You're big and soft. Why don't you do it? If you did he'd never use that belt again.'

There was only her mother in the kitchen, but a

signal from her indicated that her father was in the scullery. She said to her, 'I'm going to get the doctor.'

'What's that you say?' The small tousled head came round the scullery door.

'I said I'm going to get a doctor.'

'Be God y'are! You bring a doctor here and he'll be attendin' to two of you; I'll give you a taste of what I've given her. I intend to in any case, me lady. An' if I hadn't come across her the night with her chocolate-coloured fancy man you would have had it first. But it isn't too late.'

'I've told you I'm having no more of it.' Annie had moved towards her husband.

'You save your breath, woman. If you're satisfied to have a couple of tarts for daughters they're not staying under my roof.'

'Well, let them go!' Annie was shouting now.

'They'll go when I'm ready and not afore. But I'm not keeping a roof over a pair of bloody prostitutes.'

Sarah took two rapid steps and she stood leaning forward, gripping the edge of the table as she cried, 'Who you meanin'? You'd better be careful, because I'm telling you, after what I've seen upstairs it won't take much for me to turn the tables. You've had it your own way too long, everybody scared to death you've had. Well, it's finished. If you as much as raise your hand to me or anybody else in this house I'll use your belt on

you and flay you live I will! I will, I'm telling you!'
Sarah was yelling now, almost screaming the
words, and her mother was standing to the side of
her, pulling her away from the table by the
shoulders, as she tried to drown her voice by
shouting, 'Give over! Give over! Do you hear me?'

As if she had been galloping down the road,
Sarah leaned back, drawing in great gasps of air.
And this was the only sound for some moments,
then Pat Bradley, pushing the door back to its
fullest extent, came into the room. He began
talking, but his voice was low, even calm. 'Huh!
We're talkin' big now, aren't we, since we've
rubbed shoulders with the top end?'

'What about the top end?' Sarah was glaring at
him over her mother's shoulders. She watched
him saunter casually to the fireplace and stand
with his back to it, the palms of his hands pressed
against his small buttocks.

'Nothin'. Nothin' at all, if you know where you
stand. But when a fellow from Camelia Street
picks up someone from the midden end it's not
with the idea of turnin' her into a respectable
woman. Is it now? Plain thinkin', all round, is it
now?'

'Well, you're wrong then.' She was barking at
him again. 'You, with your sewer mind, you're
wrong then, because I'm going to be married,
see . . . SEE!'

She felt her mother's body start, and it acted like

56

an injection on her own. She slumped against the table. My God! What had she said?

There was silence in the kitchen again, until the alarm clock on the mantelpiece gave a rheumaticky whirring sound as it passed the hour.

'Well, well, we're movin' fast, aren't we? What's all the hurry for, eh? You haven't known him a month.'

She was gasping again. He had known all the time? No, no, he couldn't have; he would have been at her before if he had. But somebody had told him.

'Has he put one in your oven already.'

Before she realised what she was doing she had grabbed the teapot from the table. It was only Annie's strength against hers that forced her arm downwards and the big brown china pot fell with a dull thud on to the mat, where the lid rolled off and the tea spewed outwards.

This unusual retaliation coming from his stepdaughter seemed to tell Pat Bradley that he no longer had any domination over her – not physically, anyway. But he did not rely solely on physical force to gain his ends; he had other methods. And now he put them into action. Buttoning up his coat and pushing the knot of his muffler upwards towards his prominent Adam's apple, he hunched his shoulders and marched towards the scullery door, saying, 'Marriage is it, atween a Catholic and a chapelite? And him in the

57

dock office and his faather a boss there an' all. Don't make me laugh. Anyway, there's only one way to find out, and that's to go and ask him, isn't it?' He turned and faced them from the doorway, his thin features splitting into a wheedling grin. 'Will you kindly tell me your intentions towards me daughter, Mr Hetherington . . . sir?' He cut his mimicking short and ended, 'There's no time like the present for gettin' at the truth, is there, me girl?'

As the door banged behind him Sarah held her face tightly between her hands, repeating aloud, 'Oh no. Oh no. Oh no. Oh, my God, no!' Then she was gripping her mother's arms. 'He's going down there . . . stop him! Stop him, will you?'

'It's no use, lass. He may not go; when he gets outside he may think better of it. If I try an' stop him that's the one thing that'll send him pell-mell to their door.'

'Oh, no, no, no!' Sarah went to the mantelpiece and laid her brow against it. 'I want to die . . . I want to die. Oh God, I want to die.'

'Has he asked you?'

'No, no. I just said that.'

'A . . . aw, lass!'

'Yes, I know – aw, lass!'

'Well, you've cooked your own goose. You shouldn't have said a thing like that, not if the fellow hasn't said anything . . . he hasn't hinted?'

'No, no, not really. Even if he had this would

have killed it.' She brought her head slowly up and then, turning and facing her mother, she said dully, 'You've got to get a doctor to Phyllis, she's bad.'

'I'm not gettin' the doctor, lass. If a doctor was to see her it would mean the polis.'

'Well, don't you think it's time somebody took a hand?'

'I don't want no polis here. Anyway, I haven't paid his club for months; I'd have to pay on the nail and I can't. I'll go up and see to her. I'll bathe it in her own water, it's good for bruises.'

Sarah's nose wrinkled in distaste as her lips moved apart. She felt weak, tired and weak; all the verve had gone out of her. What was the use? She looked round the darkening kitchen. Well, she had known it couldn't last, hadn't she? But the shame of it . . . the shame of it. What would he think of her? And his mother and the rest of them? If she could only die. She stood looking down at her feet, her mind curiously blank now, numbed with pain. Then once again she opened the staircase door and pulled herself slowly up to the landing, and when she entered the bedroom the blind was down and her mother, by the light of a candle, was bathing Phyllis's back with a flannel rag that she was dipping into the chamber.

3

The round-faced stark-looking clock on the wall said one minute to twelve. David eyed the man at the end of the long-counter-like desk as he began quietly to clear his allotted portion. First, he closed two notebooks and put them into a drawer; next, he cleaned an ordinary narrow-pointed pen. This he returned to the groove next to the inkwell. The pointer on the clock had moved thirty seconds. Slowly he closed the ledger, screwed up some dirty blotting-paper, and dropped it into a basket where his feet were under the desk. Then, standing up, he pulled down his coat, adjusted his tie, pushed the legs of the stool over the wastepaper basket, then moved towards the man who was still writing in a ledger. The clock struck twelve.

'Will it be all right if I have a word with my father, Mr Batty?'

The man raised his eyes upwards, not towards David, but towards the clock, and his tone was significant as he said, 'Oh, it's twelve.'

The colour deepened around David's cheek-bones and his tones were apologetic as he answered, 'I've got a bit of business to do . . .' His voice trailed off.

'Aw, well, go on along . . . He won't be finished yet.'

This remark, with a stress on the he and a raising of the eyebrows, was a reprimand on clock watching, and as David went along the corridor he wondered what his reaction would be to old Batty if he weren't afraid of losing his job. Very likely the same as it was now, because he hated disturbances, rows, unpleasantness. He wished at times he had a bit of their John in him.

As he neared the door at the end of the corridor it opened and two men, one about his own age, and one well into his fifties, came out. The younger one said, 'Going to the match this afternoon, David?'

'No, not this afternoon, I can't make it.'

When he entered the room that held three desks his father looked up from a ledger in which he was writing and said, 'Hello there. Are you off?'

'Yes.' David stood in front of the desk looking down at his father, and he rubbed his hand across his chin before saying, 'Will you tell Mother that I won't be in for a while, not until about two?'

'You know what she is about spoilt dinners?'

'I can't help it.'

Stanley Hetherington took off his glasses and peered at his son. His eye was twitching rapidly. 'You're going through with it then?' he said.

'Yes. Yes, of course.'

'There's no of course about it, you've been rushed into this. I don't believe you asked that girl to marry you and neither does your mother. In fact, she's positive that you didn't. Bradley's a little snake of a man. I've known him for years; he'll neither work nor want. I knew him when he was in the docks here, a mischief-making little rat if ever there was one, and a toady into the bargain. The only thing he doesn't do is drink, and that makes it worse. You can forgive a man what he does in drink. But there's a bad streak in Bradley. Now look.' He wagged his finger slowly at his son. 'Don't you be driven into anything . . . Oh, I know.' He closed his eyes and flapped his hand before his face before going on, 'She's a fine looking lass, but if you marry her don't forget you're marrying her family, and is it fair . . . is it fair to your mother?'

'You know what my mother thinks, don't you? This is the lesser of two evils. Don't let's hoodwink ourselves about that.'

'Yes, yes, I suppose so.' The older man dropped his head; then, bringing it up sharply, he demanded, 'There's one thing you won't do, will you; you won't go over?'

'No, I won't go over. Yet I can't see, Father, why that should worry you.'

'My belief or lack of it has nothing to do with this present business really; all I know is, if they get you into the Catholic Church, under whatever pretext, you're finished, you won't be able to call your soul your own. No, my God, you won't.'

'But I'm not . . .'

'Yes, you say that now, but wait till the priests get at you. I've seen some of their tactics, I'm telling you. From all angles you've got to look at this thing with open eyes. She's from a bad home, she's a Catholic. Then there'll be the gossip; there's enough already, for, let's face it, David, to take up with somebody from the bottom end isn't the right thing to do. I can't see it working, although on the surface I must admit she's a nice enough lass, but she's got too many reins tied to her, holding her down to that end!'

'I'm going to marry her.'

Stanley closed his eyes; then, opening them again he wiped his glasses and put the wires slowly behind his ears before saying, 'Well, there's nothing more to be said, is there?'

'I'm sorry, Father.'

'Look, don't be sorry for hurting me or even your mother, although she's taken this better than ever I imagined . . .' He jerked his head. 'But, as you said, I suppose she's doing it because she can't bear the thought of anything coming of the other business. But it's yourself you've got to think about in this case. Marriage is a long and difficult business no matter which way you take it. You're in love with somebody one minute and you hate their guts the next . . . Aw, go on. Get yourself away or I'll say too much. Go on.'

David turned and went slowly from the room. He collected his raincoat and his trilby hat and went out of the main door of the dock office, and he stood for a moment on the pavement. The Saturday bustle was all around him; men coming out of the dock gates, those who were fortunate enough to be in work; men going into The Grapes, into The North-Eastern, into one after the other of the bars that lined the street opposite the dock wall and part of the bank that led to the station, the bank which always looked black, black with the figures of men standing against the railings or in groups on the pavement, waiting, waiting, and hoping, some cursing, some even praying to be set on, to get a few shifts in; even one a week would be something to help tide things over and take away the feeling of utter uselessness.

David never stepped on to this pavement but he imbibed this feeling that was sapping the moral fibre of the men of the docks, and of Jarrow, and of the whole Tyne, and many parts of the whole country. But today the feeling, although present, was subordinate. Covering his mind was the thought of Sarah and of getting to her and speaking to her, and comforting her.

He threaded his way across the road to where the tram was halted for its usual five-minute break, and as he went to mount the platform his arm was gripped and he was pulled round on to the road again.

'Where you off to?'

'Oh, I'm just going into Shields.'

'At this time? What about your dinner?'

David stepped back on to the pavement and looked at his brother in silence for a moment. John Hetherington was two inches shorter than David but he was almost twice his breadth. Like his uncle's, his face was nearly square, his eyes wide and of a deep brown colour, with a brooding quality in them. His mouth too was wide, as were his nostrils. His nose could be said to mar his face; it forbade the term handsome to be applied to it but made place for the word attractive, or perhaps arresting, for people always gave this man a second look. He now brought his heavy fringed lids together as he said, 'You look under the weather. Feeling off-colour?'

'No, no, I'm all right. I'd better tell you what's happening though . . .'

As David wetted his lips John said, 'Happening? Aye, well, go on then, but look slippy, I want to catch the tram.'

'I'm going to be married.'

'You're what?' The question was low, easy sounding and full of disbelief. Then, his tone changing swiftly, he said under his breath, 'Aw, no! You're not going to be such a bloody soft-headed fool. Man, it'll be suicide. And you know how me mother . . .'

'It's not Eileen.'

'Not Eileen.' The eyes were screwed tighter. 'O . . . h! No?' He thrust his fist out and punched

David in the shoulder. 'Not the missy from the bottom end that I've heard about? Why, man, you've only known her a couple of weeks.'

'I've known her longer than that, much longer.'

'Well, well!' John took a deep breath that pushed open his coat, 'Why all the hurry-burry?'

'Look, I've got to go. You'll hear all about it if you call in home . . . at least what happened last night.'

'Aye, aye, I suppose I will. But look here, Davie, don't let yourself be rushed into anything.' John's face was straight now, there was no lightness of any kind in the brown eyes. 'Look, lad, you be warned by me, and I'm speaking from experience. I've never said anything to you or anyone at home before, you know that, but I think you can put two and two together for yourself as far as my case is concerned. You make your bed and, by God, you have to lie on it! There's no truer saying than that in the whole world. Marriage can be hell, sheer bloody unadulterated hell. Oh, aye.' His voice was very low now. 'I know, I know there are wonderful marriages that go on for ten, twenty, thirty, forty, fifty years. You hear about them, in fact you see them; but, you know, you've got to ask yourself, have either of them done a day's thinking in their lives? Most of them are together because of the house and the sticks of furniture; they exist together, but they don't live. You know what most men are? A bread ticket . . .'

'Look, John, I'll have to go now; I want to catch

this tram.' He motioned to where the conductor was mounting the platform. 'I'll see you later.'

'All right, all right.'

They stared at each other a moment longer, then David swung round, leaped on to the platform, and took the stairs two at a time.

When their John started talking nobody could stop him; he could make an issue out of anything. He was always probing and dissecting the whys and wherefores of even the simplest things . . . But he had just said that marriage was hell. It had been his own marriage he was speaking of sure enough. He hadn't realised that he had felt about it like that. He had known that he and May went at it, but then May had a mind too. There was a pair of them in that way. May argued against politics and strikes and the dole, because, like half the women in the town, she was worried that the next pay-day might be the last.

Sheer bloody unadulterated hell.

He could never imagine his own life like that, not if he married Sarah . . . Sarah was no May. Yet what about his father saying you could love them one minute . . . Oh, my God! He wished they would all hold their tongues and let him do what he knew he must do . . .

Half an hour later he stood gazing into the shop window until there was only one customer left, then he went in.

Sarah saw him as she passed the woman her

change and she started visibly, and the woman, turning and looking at David, smiled knowingly to herself.

He stood facing her in the valley between the hills of glass jars. He saw immediately that she looked ill; her eyes, although not red, were puffy, and her face, which he held always in his mind as representing a bright light, looked dull, even brow-beaten. The fact that this girl, this well set-up girl who was going to be his wife – yes, she was going to be his wife – should show an emotion that held the ingredients of intimidation, raised in him a rare and answering emotion of anger; and so his voice sounded stiff to her ears when he said, 'What time do you finish?'

She could not look at him. More than ever now she wanted to die, just to sink through the earth and be swallowed up. Humiliation had stripped her of any small pride she had clung to in desperation to keep herself afloat in the bog of her section of the Fifteen Streets.

'Do you get out for dinner? Sarah, speak to me.'

'One o'clock.' It was a mumble coming from the region of her chest.

He whispered now with gentle insistence: 'Sarah, Sarah, look at me.'

She did not raise her head but turned it aside, and her hands did something with a box, pulling out pieces of crinkled paper and rolling them up into balls.

'It's ten minutes to, I'll wait outside . . .'

At three minutes to one Mrs Benton came downstairs from her flat above and Sarah, stacking empty boxes in the corner of the back room, said nervously, 'I've got a bit of shopping to do. I'll take me sandwiches and have them in the park the day, if you don't mind.'

Sarah felt Mrs Benton looking down at her. Mrs Benton didn't like serving in the shop. Sarah guessed that she thought it slightly beneath her, her being the owner, and it was rarely that she served the full hour. Very often at a quarter to two she would come into the back room and say, 'There's nothing doing; I'll just pop upstairs. Call me if the bell rings.' Sarah never called her. It was a good job and she wanted to keep it. Not many girls were getting eighteen and six a week and not soiling their hands. Of course a twelve-hour day was a long stretch, but she wasn't grumbling.

Without looking at her employer she knew she was annoyed. Mrs Benton was always annoyed when she didn't speak. Sarah grabbed up her coat and pulled her hat on without looking in the glass, and with a mumbled 'I won't be long' she went out of the side door and into the alley.

She had her head down and she did not stop in her walk as she saw David's legs coming towards her across the pavement but kept on moving down the road towards the sea and the park.

'Don't be like this.' He was walking close to her, his head bent down to hers.

'How should I be?' Her muttered words were not only a question but an answer in themselves.

They went on in silence until they entered the park and found a seat, which was easy, as the place was virtually empty at this time of the day. It was Sarah who spoke first, her head still down, looking at her fingers as they plucked at each other. She said, 'I'm sorry.'

'Sarah, look at me.' He had hold of her hands now, pulling at them with small tugging movements, trying to get her to raise her head, but she wouldn't, and he said, 'I've watched you for years going up and down the road, and I knew from the first night that I stood outside that shop that I was going to marry you. The only thing was I was too blooming shy to get it out, and you know you weren't very helpful.'

'Don't, don't.' The tears were raining down her face now from beneath her closed lids.

'Oh, Sarah, Sarah.' He pulled her forearm against his chest. 'Oh, my dear, my love. Oh, Sarah, dear, don't.' He took out his handkerchief and gently dried her face, all the while murmuring, 'Don't, Sarah, dear. Don't, Sarah, dear.'

'He . . . he said you were t-taken aback. He . . . he . . . said you got the surprise of . . . of your life.' She gasped out the words now as if wanting to be rid of the burden of them.

'Who did? You mean your father said that?'

'Yes.'

'Aye, well, I was taken aback. But just at the sight of him and the way he blurted it out. But I said straight off the bat that I wanted to marry you. I did, Sarah.' He shook her arm once. 'Believe me, I did.'

'Your mother was there an' all.'

'Yes, she was there. She came into the hall.'

Her head drooped lower as she put the question, 'Did he raise the house?'

'No.' David's voice was high. 'No. He was very quiet; in fact, I thought he was most reasonable. If I hadn't heard about him and was meeting him for the first time I would have thought he was a reasonable kind of man altogether. But things get about, you know, even as far as our end.'

'What did you say to him?' She had her head up now and was blinking away the still running tears.

'Well, when I opened the door . . . well, you see it was all so sudden. He said, "What's this I hear about you going to marry my daughter?" And quite honestly I couldn't say anything for the moment.' He gripped her hands tightly and once again brought them to his chest. 'He was putting into words something that's never been out of my mind since I met you, but at that moment it was such a surprise I couldn't say anything. And then he said, "Have you asked her?" It was then I sensed there was something wrong – I linked it up with what the boy said he was doing to your sister – so I said to him, "Will you come in?" And when he stood in the hall he repeated, "I asked you a question," and to that I said, "Yes . . . yes, I've asked her to marry me." It was then my mother joined us. He was very civil to her, very polite. He said, "I've just come round because my girl said that your son here asked her to marry him . . . " '

'And your mother didn't say anything did she?' Sarah licked the tears from her lips. 'She was so flabbergasted that she didn't say anything, for she knew if you had asked me you would have told her.'

'But listen, listen to me. I told her that I had asked you and that I was going to tell her . . . but later. I told her I had every intention of telling her and then bringing you round this evening for tea.'

'But she didn't believe you?'

'Why do you keep saying that?'

'Oh' – she screwed her body away from him, trying to pull her hands loose from his grip – 'I had it all word for word, nothing left out.' She shook her head slowly now and the scene of last night returned to her with all its ignominy; it returned for its hundredth showing in the few hours since it had been enacted. She had been lying in bed with Phyllis when the door had been kicked open and he stood on the threshold yelling into the darkness. 'Surprised to bloody death he was and frightened out of his bloody skin, an' all. Oh yes,

yes, he said, he had asked you . . . But he only said that because . . . because why? Because he knew I'd tell his mother what he'd bloody well been up to, an' I was right. No bloke like him is gonna be taken for a ride up the aisle by the likes of you unless he's gone in by the back door, you big-bellied sod, you!'

The street had been quiet; there was no sound coming from the Youngs' house or from the Radcliffes', for they were all listening and would be able to hear without any straining of their ears, as would the neighbours down the road. And those who had missed anything would be given it in detail, she knew, before the sun shone without shadow tomorrow.

Eternities of suffering later, when the flesh of her body seemed to have melted with shame and her large frame was twisted with the force of the humiliation that had beaten upon her, she heard the distant chimes of a clock, somewhere in the town, striking three. It was then that Phyllis, her own pain forgotten, her arms about her tightly, whispered, 'Don't let him take the gumption out of you. That's what he's after, to break your spirit, to have you crawl. You know why he's goin' for you, don't you? It's because he wants you himself.'

Her crumpled body had shuddered and straightened itself as if by an electric shock. But Phyllis still held her and went on whispering, fiercely, 'Me ma knows. What you want to do is to pack up an' get away. Don't think of how me ma'll manage, he'll have to stump up if there's nobody here . . . You know something? He had three pounds in the lining of his waistcoat yesterda' mornin'. He must have forgotten it, his waistcoat I mean, and left it on the chair downstairs. I went through the pockets when I was down early, and felt this paper in the lining. He's been running for a bookie this week. I'd like to bet he's got money tucked away somewhere . . . You stop worryin' about me ma and get yourself out of this, our Sarah, because I'm going to . . .'

'Sarah, look at me!'

She looked at him, into the eyes that were soft and glowing with love and kindliness, and her heart was sick at what she was losing.

'I love you, Sarah; I love you so much I just can't find words or ways or means of telling you . . . Now answer me one thing. If when we were going home last night I had asked you to marry me what would you have said? Truthfully, Sarah, what would you have said?'

'I'd . . . I'd have said yes.'

'Because you love me?'

'Yes.'

'Oh, Sarah, that's wonderful, wonderful. You know I just can't understand what you see in me. I've no push, no go.' He smiled. 'If you had fallen for someone like our John it would have been

understandable, but me! I'll never be anything.
I'm quite content to stay in my little rut until I die
. . . that is as long as I have you.'

He was changing the atmosphere, subtly
threading it with the description of his own
character, making it slightly jocular, ordinary; and
under this influence her bones seemed to
straighten and the flesh on them fill out again. Her
whole being was becoming saturated in enervating relief. She wanted to slump forward on to
him, lay her head on his shoulder and rest; that's
all she wanted to do for the moment, just rest. And
then she thought of his mother. She wouldn't be
able to face his mother; his father and his uncle,
yes, but not his mother. She said now with
candour borne of dead hope, 'There's your mother
. . . I couldn't face your mother, it's no use.'

'My mother!' He screwed up his face until it
looked comical. 'Why, she's the one who under-
stands most. Look, Sarah.' He had her by the
shoulders now. 'My mother wants me to marry
you; there's a particular reason why she wants me
to marry you. I won't tell you it now, but she wants
it in spite of your father.'

'My stepfather.' It was the only thing left she
had to be proud of, that there was no blood
relation between her and Pat Bradley.

'Your stepfather. I'm glad he's your stepfather.
Well, in spite of him and his barging in last
night . . . although I maintain he came in quietly

and left quietly; but in spite of all this she still wants me to marry you. You know, I think she's taken to you. She doesn't take to many people. She's what you would term a close woman, reticent, difficult, but she's been a very good mother, and, as I said, she's taken to you. I know her so well, better than my brother; better, I think, than my father, and I can vouch for what I say. Now . . .' He brought his hands from her shoulders to her cheeks, and, holding them, raised her face towards him. 'We were going to Newcastle tonight, remember? But instead we'll go home. I've told her I'm bringing you, and she's expecting you. I'll meet you when you're finished and we'll go straight there.'

'Oh, David . . . David!' She was leaning against him, her head in his neck, shaking both their bodies with the convulsion of her weeping.

Then once again he was drying her face – under her eyes, round her nose, round her lips. His eyes remained on her lips, fixed as if he had become lost in a dream. Then with a suddenness his hands were clamped to her ears, and when he pulled her face towards his her hat fell backwards on to the grass. And then they were kissing. In the open on a bench in the Marine Park and on a Saturday dinner-time, they were kissing. It was enough to get your name up. You could cry on a bench but not kiss. Something of this ran through her mind. But what did it matter? What odds? What odds?

Nothing, nothing in the world mattered at this moment except this man, this man David who wanted her.

4

His mother opened the door to them. 'Well, you've got here,' she said. She was smiling faintly.

David pressed Sarah before him up the two steps and into the hall. 'Give me your coat,' he said.

His mother opened the sitting-room door now. She put her head inside; then, withdrawing it, she looked at Sarah. 'There's a fire on; it gets chilly at nights, especially when it's drizzling.'

'Have we kept you waiting?' David was straightening his tie.

'No, no, they're all in the living-room. Tea isn't quite ready yet. Go on in.' She held out her hand and touched Sarah's arm with the tips of her fingers, halting her as she crossed the threshold into the room and adding quietly, 'There'll be plenty of time to talk later.'

When she turned away and walked across the small hall and into the room, from where came a buzz of voices, and the high gleeful shriek of a young child, Sarah, standing stock still, gazed after her. She felt unnerved; she didn't know if it was with relief because the talking had been put off, or because it was to come.

'Don't look so mesmerised.' David was pulling her into the room and towards the couch.

'Oh! If I get over the night I'll live to be a hundred.' It was her first attempt at jocularity, and he pulled her swiftly into his arms and held her tightly for a second. Then, releasing her as quickly, he whispered, 'They'll all be in in a minute.' And as if working along the lines that attack was the best form of defence, he said, 'Would you like to come into the living-room now and get it over with?'

'No, no.' Her tone was low and rapid. 'Give me a breather.'

'Do you mind if I leave you for a minute, then? I . . .'

He seemed hesitant to tell her why he had to leave her. It could be that he had to go to some place like the lavatory, she thought, then dismissed the idea. No, he wanted to have a word with them, or likely with his mother.

'Go on.' She pushed him gently, playfully. 'I've only got to die once.'

He laughed at this. His head back, in spite of his evident nervousness, he laughed. Then, clasping the palms of his hands for a second over her ears, an action of endearment she was to find that had its drawback, as it dimmed her hearing, he whis-

78

pered, 'We're going to have some times together, Sarah, good times; you were made to laugh, you know.'

He left her on this, and the sound rushed back into her ears again. She sat down on the edge of the couch thinking, I was made to laugh. Funny that; there's been so little laughter in me life. But he's right, I love a good laugh. Fancy him knowing that. She looked round the room. To her eyes it was a beautiful room, beautiful in its arrangement, in its prismatic brightness, and the absence of litter of any kind; not a paper or a book to be seen, nor clothes lying about, not a cap or a coat dropped carelessly. No packets of Woodbines on the mantelpiece. She looked at the gleaming white-painted wooden frame that surrounded the pale-blue tiles. She couldn't see anyone daring to lean a finger on that edifice, except to dust the marble clock and the two pink vases with the pictures on the front of ladies in old-fashioned dress. She turned her head and looked over the back of the couch to the piano. It wasn't cluttered either; it held only two photographs, one at each end. They were both of boys. One of them was David, when about six. His eyes hadn't changed, nor yet his smile. She sat gazing at it with a warmth of feeling that was yet threaded with awe. She was going to marry that boy. She was really going to marry that boy.

Her head jerked away as the door opened and

she looked at the man standing just within the room, and he looked at her. He still held the door in his hand, and after a second, when he went to close it, he did so without taking his eyes from her. Then he shook his head as he exclaimed, 'Good Lord! Fancy seeing you.'

Sarah had sidled to her feet. She couldn't remember seeing this man before. She guessed this was John, the brother. But he didn't look at all like David. Just as she was an oversize of a girl, he was certainly an outsize of a man.

'Well, well.' He was standing in front of her, holding out his hand now. 'I'm John, your future brother-in-law.'

His hand was hard, his grip was tight. 'I've seen you going up and down the road for years, but I didn't know it was you our David was after.' He jerked his head to the side. 'Well, I must say he knows when he's on a good thing.'

Sarah hadn't spoken. She was standing smiling weakly, as she thought, it's hard to believe they're brothers. The only thing she recognised as similar in both of them was their voices. Yet even these were different because this man used his words in a way that made his voice seem ordinary, in fact even like the voices of the people from her own end. Although he wasn't broad Geordie there was no refinement in his speech as there was in David's.

He dropped her hand and pointed to the couch

and said, 'Sit down and don't look so worried.'
The last words brought his chin out and his head
and shoulders towards her. He was speaking like
a kindly conspirator. 'In a few weeks you'll
wonder why you ever felt nervous and you'll kick
yourself.' He stood looking down at her, his hands
on his hips, and he brought the side of his face into
his hunched shoulder, which action laid stress on
the enquiry, 'You can talk; you're not deaf and
dumb, are you?'

'Yes . . . No.' Now they were laughing.

'I . . . I said to David if I get over the night I'll live
to be a hundred.'

He did not answer for some seconds; his broad
face took on an expression that puzzled her in its
implication of aggressiveness until his words
explained it when, bending down to her, his face
not more than six inches from hers, he said tersely,
'Look, you set out with the idea that you're not
going to be frightened of anybody, in this house or
anywhere else. If you think you're going to be
frightened you'll be frightened. If you let people
put the wind up you you've had it, you're
finished.'

'Yes, yes, you're right there.' What else could she
say. She could feel the heat from his face. She
looked at his mouth. It was well shaped, broad, but
not kind like David's. He was better looking in all
ways than David, handsome she would say, but he
wasn't like David. She was feeling disturbed,

nervous under the pressure of his eyes, when the door opened once again and Dan entered.

'Oh, hello there.' He looked past John towards Sarah, and Sarah took in a deep breath and smiled. There came a slackening of her muscles as if she had been relieved from an ordeal and answered 'Hello.'

'Oh, of course, you two have met before.' John cast his glance between Dan and Sarah, and Dan tossing his head and winking, said, 'Yes, I've got one up on you there, lad.'

'Mind, I'm going to tell you something.' John was standing on the hearthrug, his back to the fire, his hands rubbing his buttocks, his body bent forward towards her again. 'You look out for him there.' He motioned towards Dan with a sideways tilt of his eyebrows. 'A proper Casanova we've got in this family. It's a fact. He'll be after your blood.'

'Enough of that, John, enough of that.'

Sarah saw that Dan's face was slightly flushed and he looked put out, not really annoyed but just a little put out; she could almost have said a little hurt.

'You know he's my uncle?' John's arm went out and gripped Dan around the shoulders and they stood pressed together looking at Sarah.

'He doesn't look old enough to be your uncle.' Sarah looked at Dan as she spoke, and Dan said, 'I don't feel old enough to be their uncle. It's one of these odd situations, I was born late . . .'

'You said it, chum, you said it.' John rocked them backwards and forwards for a moment until Dan put in laughingly, 'Stop acting the goat, Sarah'll think you're barmy. She knows what I mean.' He nodded towards her. 'I was just a baby when Mary, their mother' – he indicated John – was married. We were all brought up together, so to speak. Mind you' – his voice dropped to a confidential whisper – 'they wouldn't have been my choice of relatives; but there, I didn't have any say in the matter . . . Davie's all right, but this one . . .' He tried to pull away from John, and now John's two arms were around him crushing him to his chest, and Dan was crying, 'Leave over, man. Look, you don't want to start a rough-and-tumble. You'll have your mother on us like a ton of bricks; leave o-ver.' With a sudden twisting jerk he freed himself and the two men stood apart, laughing at each other.

'See what I mean?' Dan sat down beside Sarah on the couch. 'Anyone would think by the look of him and the size of him he was grown-up, mature-like, but not him, he's still in the puppy stage.'

'Puppy stage! That's right, that's right.' John was standing on the hearthrug again, his hands once more behind his back and his expression and tone reverted with a suddenness to what it had been before Dan had entered the room. 'That's funny, that is. Not grown-up! When I'm the only one among the lot of you that sees straight. Davie with his head in the clouds . . . no offence meant, it's a compliment.' His tone was slow and flat, and he accompanied each word with a movement of his head towards Sarah, then went on, 'Father with the spunk beaten out of him.' He looked towards the door, then his eyes moved towards Dan, 'And you not caring a damn except . . .' He stopped abruptly and screwing up his eyes, asked loudly, 'Why did you set me off?'

'Aw! You don't need much setting off; and Sarah might as well know the worst from the beginning. What do you say, Sarah?'

Sarah turned and looked at the man sitting beside her, and before she answered she thought, this one could be David's brother, there's a kindliness about him. With sudden daring gaiety she replied, in broad Geordie dialect, 'Aa've summed him up, shockin' lot. He'd never get past the dock polis, him.'

This retort was daring in the extreme. She was joking as if with her equals, her equals down at the bottom end. Yet she had never thought of the inhabitants of the bottom end as her equals, and had rarely, if ever, joked with any of the neighbours and never with the men. But if she had done so her remark would have been similar to the one she had just made. And now she was amazed, and a little apprehensive at the reaction to it, for the two men, their heads back – this seemed to be a characteristic of the Hetherington family, to laugh with their heads back – were now filling the room with their laughter, and the sound seemed out of place in the atmosphere of gentility.

'Well, well! And what's all the noise about?' Mary Hetherington came into the room, followed by David and a thin dark young woman with a child in her arms.

'You know what? You've picked a cheeky monkey.' John's arm was out, the finger extended, stabbing in the direction of David, and David's face, with a bright relieved smile, said, not without pride, 'I have?'

'Yes.'

'Well, that's good.' He went and took up his place beside the couch, putting his hand on Sarah's shoulder. Sarah was looking at Mrs Hetherington now; fear and nervousness had leapt back into her system again. She hadn't liked it, coming into the room and finding them all laughing. Perhaps she thought she was being forward. But she was speaking to her now, stiffly.

'This is May, John's wife.' She nodded towards her son. 'And this is their child Paul.' She took the child's hand from its mother's shoulder as she spoke. The introduction had a formal sound and no one moved in the room while it was being made. Then Sarah attempted to rise to her feet, but Dan, heaving himself upwards, said, 'No, no, sit where you are; you come and sit here, May.'

May sat down, the child still in her arms. Neither she nor Sarah had spoken to acknowledge the introduction. The child was between their faces now, gurgling and bouncing, and as Sarah lifted a finger to touch it its plump hands shot out, and with startling suddenness and the power and demoniac tenacity, which in all infants is a contradiction to their helplessness, its fingers entwined themselves in Sarah's hair, dragging and pulling her sideways, bearing her head towards its mother's shoulder.

Although the diversion was painful, Sarah was thankful for it. The attention was on the child and amid cries of, 'Oh, you naughty boy, let go. Naughty Paul. Leave go, you rascal. Would you believe it, isn't he a little beggar?' she was eventually released.

Sarah laughed as she combed the thick waves of her long chestnut hair back into the bun with her fingers. 'It's all right; my sister used to do that. My scalp is tough.'

The baby was now in its father's arms, kicking its toes into his flat and seemingly unfeeling stomach, and as Sarah looked at him she became aware, as if she had not noticed it at the time, that they were his fingers which had prised the child's hands from her head.

'Well, now, that rumpus is over and we can have tea.' Mary Hetherington threaded her way through her family towards the door, adding as she went into the hall, 'Come on, Father is waiting.'

One after the other they followed her, David coming last, his hand extended, cupping Sarah's elbow. Before her went May, and with the perspicacity that lends itself to intuitiveness Sarah thought, I'm not going to like her, she's sour.

And when they were all seated round the tea-table and she found herself right opposite to May, she said to herself, 'She looks uppish and discontented.' Her eyes moved to John sitting to the right of his wife, the child on his knee, and she thought, What's she got to be discontented about? He seems a nice enough fellow, a bit noisy. And then she's got the child.

It was strange, and Sarah was aware of this, that all during tea her thoughts were on the slight, dark, thin girl opposite to her. Her mind was occupied so much with this new acquaintance that for the time being she forgot about Mrs Hetherington; and although she did not fail to notice that Mr Hetherington was very quiet and had hardly spoken to her, she did not worry about it. Perhaps he was always quiet. It was not until they were rising from the table to return once more to the sitting-room that it came to her that John's wife, as she thought of her rather than as May, had not opened her mouth at all during the meal; in fact she hadn't heard her speak at all. And yet nobody had seemed to notice it; nobody had remarked on her silence or pulled her leg about it.

'Let's have a sing-song. Come on, the occasion calls for it.' They were in transit between the living-room and the sitting-room when John, in a loud voice, made this announcement, but his mother's voice came quickly in answer, saying, 'Don't be so rowdy, John.'

'Look . . . my God, it's an occasion. Davie's going to be married . . . Oh, all right, I'm sorry.'

As John came into the sitting-room, his head lowered, he said in an aside to David, 'I wish she'd put a notice up, "No blasphemy, no swearing", then I'd remember.'

David turned to his brother, punching him gently in the back as he said, 'Come on, big fellow, forget about it. She's a bit up . . .' He pulled himself up abruptly, but not abruptly enough. Sarah knew he was going to say she's a bit upset.

She was again seated on the couch, and once more she was alone with the men. There were present now not only the brother and the uncle but Mr Hetherington. He was sitting to the side of her in an armchair, his hands resting idly on his knees. It was perhaps the idleness conveyed by his motionless hands that made her realise that not one of the men were smoking. That was strange, nearly all men smoked.

A rolling chord of notes brought her body twisting round towards the piano. She was looking at David's back; it was David who was playing, her David. The thought added dimension to her body.

'Oh, not Chopin, not tonight. Let's have something we can sing to . . . You don't want Chopin, do you, Sarah?' John's big head was turned towards her, then away again in a second before she would have been called upon to stammer her ignorance of Chopin.

' "Blue Heaven". Come on, let's have "Blue Heaven". Where's the music? That's appropriate: "Happy in my Blue Heaven".' John was singing now in a deep resounding bass voice. 'Here it is, and "All Alone on the Telephone", and "Yacky-hoo-lah, Hicky-doo-lah".'

Sarah wanted to get up and go to the piano. She knew the songs and she could sing them too. She was told she had a decent voice – she would have gone in for a singing competition before this if it hadn't been for her father. But she had better be careful. Yes, she had better be careful. She'd better not sing too loud, or push herself. At this point she thought, I should have asked her if she wanted any help with the washing-up. She leant forwards towards Mr Hetherington and said under the cover of David's playing and John's voice, 'Do you think Mrs Hetherington needs any help with the washing-up?'

For the first time Mr Hetherington smiled at her. He smiled slowly, a considered smile, as if it was the outcome of thought and a decision taken, and he brought his hands from his knees and joined them together as he leant towards her, saying, 'Mrs Hetherington can cope. And don't worry, don't be nervous any more. What has to be will be. I hope you'll be happy and make him happy.'

It was the first time that anyone had made any direct reference to her marrying David. It was in everybody's mind, but they were all doing different things, it would seem, so as not to have to mention it. She looked at the older man, his eye twitching every few seconds, and she had an almost uncontrollable urge to clasp his hands and bring them to her face and cry over them and pour out her thanks to him. She felt gratitude towards him equal to that she had for David. But all she could say was, 'Thank you, thank you, Mr Hetherington.' And then, her voice trembling and her eyes lowered, she finished, 'I'm very grateful.'

'Aw, lass.' He shook his head and his tone conveyed the same meaning as John's had done; it was telling her not to humble herself, not to crawl.

'Come on, up you get.' John's arms came over the couch under her oxters, pushing her upwards. Then, grabbing her hand, he pulled her round towards the piano stool and David, saying, 'Stand yourself there, next to your intended, and raise your voice in joyful song, something soft and harmonious. Come on: "Yacky-hoo-lah, Hicky-doo-lah".'

'Stop your clowning.' It was Dan speaking across David now. 'Go and fetch May in.'

'Aw, May knows the way. And, anyway, we're not speaking . . . There you are, there you are . . .' John was wagging his finger at Sarah. 'You're being let in on family secrets already: my wife and I are not speaking.'

The music stopped. David's hands became still on the keys, and, turning his head slowly upwards, he looked at his brother and said quietly, 'Stop it, John, and put the ego under lock and key for tonight, eh?'

Sarah watched the brothers. They were looking at each other, their faces strained, slightly tense. Put the ego under lock and key. What did David mean? What was an ego? Something to do with the way John was carrying on, but what was it? She must get a dictionary; she had always promised herself a dictionary.

'Sorry, let's sing. There . . . he's strapped down.' John's hands made the motion of tying a knot across his chest.

David touched the keys again and then they were singing. John and Dan and even Mr Hetherington. Mr Hetherington was singing with an odd-looking smile on his face as if he were laughing at himself. But Sarah found she could not join her voice to theirs; they were singing 'Blue Heaven' and she was finding it embarrassing.

Just Molly and me and baby makes three,
We're happy in my Blue Heaven.

She had a feeling almost of horror in case John should change the Molly to Sarah, but John was apparently behaving himself. The chorus finished, David's fingers changed the key almost imperceptibly into the ballad 'Parted', and at this her eyes brightened. Oh, she knew 'Parted' – she loved 'Parted'.

Dearest, the night is passing,
Endeth the dream divine,
You must go back to your life,
I must go back to mine.

She forgot her embarrassment. In a moment she was singing softly, as if to herself, and then, when David turned his glance towards her, nodding in approbation and encouragement, she let her voice rise. But not to its full extent; even so, it impressed them. She felt herself glow because of this, her one accomplishment: they liked her voice. She saw Dan signalling to John to stop, but John was already stopping, and when there was only her voice carrying the song she looked from one to the other and her words faltered and died away.

'I can't sing by my . . .'

'Come on, come on,' said John. 'Start again, David. You're going to sing that right through. You've got a voice, my girl.'

'Come on, Sarah, let's hear it right through from the beginning.' David's voice was quiet, even firm. It steadied her. He seemed, when sitting at the piano, masterful, in command as it were. Perhaps that's how he felt; he played beautifully, lovely.

She stood ready to sing, telling herself not to let her voice go . . . to do it gently.

> *Dearest, the night is passing,*
> *Endeth the dream divine.*

She was singing with only part of her mind, analysing the words with the other. She hoped . . . oh, she prayed that her dream divine would never end.

> *You must go back to your life,*
> *I must go back to mine.*

David and she would have no life separate from each other. She would love him until she died, she couldn't help it; even if only out of gratitude she would love him until she died. But she did not feel only grateful to him for wanting her; oh no, she loved him, she loved him because he was David, somebody different.

> *Back to the joyless duties,*
> *Back to the ceaseless cares;*
> *Living and loving parted,*
> *All through the empty years.*
> *How can I live without you,*

How can I let you go,
I whom you love so well, dear.
You whom I worship so . . .
You whom I worship so.

There was a short silence when she finished, and it was Mr Hetherington who broke it. He said, 'Very nice, very nice. You could do things with that voice, you know.'

David was looking at her, not speaking, his eyes tender and proud.

And Dan was looking at her. He was smiling with his head on one side, and he said, 'I would like to hear you let rip.'

But John was not looking at her, nor did he say anything. He was at the fireplace carefully lifting a piece of coal from the scuttle, carefully because one hand was poised underneath the coal in case it fell from the tongs. Sarah had not noticed him moving from the piano, but she did notice that he made no comment on her singing. Well, he can't have thought much of it, she said to herself; then added, he's a funny fellow, I can't really make him out.

'Play "Fur Elise".' Dan was sorting some music on a table by the side of the piano as he spoke, and then the front-door bell rang. 'Aw, who's this now?' His voice held a touch of impatience. It gave Sarah the impression that he was enjoying the present gathering and did not want it extended in any way.

She turned her head towards John. He was standing to the side of the bow window. It was the note of apprehension in his voice that brought her attention to him. He was squinting through the narrow aperture of the curtains looking into the street, and at the same time he was speaking directly to David. 'It's Eileen,' he said, 'and . . . and her mother.' Now his head turned quickly about and he looked over his shoulder to where David had moved from the piano stool to face him.

'Well, what about it? Let them come in, they've got to some time.'

'Not tonight, man.' Now all of them were looking at Dan. His head was still bent over the music. 'Here it is,' he went on as he lifted up a dog-eared doubled sheet and handed it to David, nodding at him. 'Go on, play.'

Whatever all this was about Sarah couldn't understand, but what impinged itself on her notice was that Mr Hetherington was sitting quietly in his chair and he had made no remark whatever. It could have been that he was stone-deaf.

David was now holding the music, and after rolling it backwards he placed it on the stand, manoeuvring it to keep it upright; and while he was doing this there was a movement in the passage and the front door was opened. There filtered into the room an exchange of voices, and then the room door was opened.

Instantly Sarah saw that all the men were disturbed, even Mr Hetherington, for he was now on his feet.

Standing to one side, with the door in her hand, was May, and past her came a short plump woman with fair hair. She was well dressed; as Sarah explained to herself, well put-on. Behind her came a tall girl. She was also fair and she had the most beautiful face that Sarah had ever seen, and it wasn't the first time that she had seen it. She had on occasions seen this girl when coming round the Stanhope Road way, and she had thought, By! She's beautiful, that girl.

Her skin was the colour of thick cream and her eyes were the deepest blue of any eyes that Sarah had looked at. Her features were perfect, too perfect. She looked – and Sarah was again colloquially explaining this to herself – the girl looked – too good to be true.

The two visitors were staring at Sarah, but before any remark could be made there appeared behind the girl the tall dominating figure of Mary Hetherington. Her face was flushed, her eyes bright, and her voice had lost the coolness that Sarah associated with this woman's whole demeanour. The tone was now brittle, nervous. She began talking straight away. 'Why, Ellen, I didn't expect you . . . And you, Eileen, how are you?'

'Oh, I'm very well, Auntie.'

'Well now, well now, you must come into the living-room and have a cup of tea. I was just making a fresh one. I never manage to get a decent cup when I'm looking after this hoard. Oh, by the way, this is Sarah, Sarah Bradley.' Mary Hetherington paused here, took a deep breath, then brought out in slow meaningful tones, 'She's David's young lady; they've become engaged today.'

Sarah was looking at the girl, and the girl was looking at David, and David was now looking at 'Fur Elise'.

'Oo . . . oh!' The sound seemed to be acting in reverse, as if it had started outside the elder woman and was sinking down into the depths of her stomach, for she held her arm across her waist as if in pain. She was looking at Sarah now with a look that made Sarah want to exclaim, Don't take it like that. The woman looked hurt, shocked, and angry, but most of all she looked hurt. Sarah watched her take hold of her daughter's arm and push her past Mrs Hetherington into the passage, and as May went to follow them and close the door, Mr Hetherington, his eye twitching at twice its usual rate, went hastily across the room, and, pulling the almost closed door out of May's grasp, went into the hall, from where the visitor's voice came clearly into the room, saying in broken tones, 'You're cruel, Mary, cruel. You've had everything and you're still not satisfied. You're cruel, cruel.'

As the door closed on the voice John seemed to spring across the room, and pulling it open, he thrust his arm outside, saying, 'Here a minute you.' And in the next second he had pulled May into the room.

'Leave go. What are you playing at?' May jerked her arm from his hand. It was the first time Sarah had heard her voice, and to her surprise it sounded refined.

'Why couldn't you have shown them into the other room?' John was hissing at his wife, his face hanging menacingly above her.

'Why should I?' Her voice was cool, aggravatingly cool. 'They always come in here, don't they?'

'You're a bloody mischief-making little bitch. You're never happy unless . . .'

'Here! Here! John, steady on!'

'Steady on?' John turned his head towards Dan. 'Steady on, you said?'

'Yes, that's what I said, steady on. And keep your domestic differences for your own hearth.'

'Now you're asking something.' May was nodding her head while her eyes stretched themselves into large circles. 'You're asking something, aren't you, Dan? Did you ever know him to use tact or discretion, the big fellow. The great I am.'

Sarah, standing apart, was experiencing a feeling of shock, and the shock in this case could almost be classed as severe. That the Hetherington family, this family from the top end who lived in

98

the best house in the Fifteen Streets, who were the best people among the two thousand or more who filled the houses, that they could quarrel, that one of their members could swear, could even look as if he was going to hit his wife, the wife who appeared as aggravating as any other working man's wife did when having a row, was a shock.

In this moment she saw all the Hetheringtons struggling in the mire beside her, and the effect was distressing in the extreme.

Only one thing was clear in her mind – and her reasoning on this point surprised her. She knew that she understood why John had lost his temper, and she could understand and even condone his attitude towards his wife. She watched him now screw up his eyes as if someone had suddenly thrown acid into them, clench his teeth as if the pain was unbearable, and with his head down, like a charging bull, dash from the room.

'Well! Nice conduct, isn't it?' May looked from Dan to David, then her eyes settling on Sarah, she spoke to her directly for the first time since they had met. 'You want to be thankful there are no two people alike in one family,' she said.

'Oh, May, May.' Dan moved towards her. 'You know what he's like; he'll be over it in no time.'

'Yes, I know what he's like, Dan. And as you say, he'll get over it in no time, but that will make no difference to me.' She tilted her chin on this statement and, turning slowly and deliberately about, she left the room, closing the door behind her, and this with quiet deliberation too.

David turned on the piano stool and, facing Sarah, he bowed his head as he said, 'I'm sorry about all this. I was going to explain it all to you later, but there's been so little time. It's all so very simple, Sarah.'

'It's all right, it's all right. It doesn't matter.'

But it did matter. Again Sarah was feeling afraid. Nothing ever went smooth in life, did it?'

'You go into the kitchen, David, and have a word with them, and then you and Sarah take yourselves out for a walk. Go on.' Dan pushed at David's shoulder. 'I'll do the explaining to Sarah.' He laughed here. 'I've an idea I can do it better than you. Go on now.'

'I won't be long.' David, his face tense-looking and sad, touched Sarah's hand, and again she said, 'It's all right.'

'Here, come and sit down.' Dan put the tips of his fingers lightly on her arm and drew her towards the couch, adding, 'And don't look so worried, there's nothing going to happen. Look, I'll make it brief and put you out of your misery.' He smiled again and patted her hand while she waited, sick with anxiety, to hear what he had to say.

'It's just like this. Eileen's always been sweet of Davie, but he's never returned the sentiments, if you follow me, not in the same way. Now her mother wanted to make a match of it. She had her own reasons.' He smiled widely here. 'You see, years ago her and Stan . . . you know, David's father . . .' He nodded towards the kitchen. 'Well, they were as good as promised to each other; nothing in the open or anything like that, but a sort of understanding between them. And then he goes and meets Mary and that was that. But Ellen's a nice woman, a forgiving woman, and over the years the two families have kept in touch, with the precise idea on Ellen's part that Eileen and David should make up for her lost romance. You see the pattern?' He raised his eyebrows at her. 'But then Mary didn't see it like that and she had every reason. And they were good ones, I must say that much, because . . . well' – he wagged his head – 'you would know, anyway, sooner or later; but Eileen's father's in Harton, in the mental block. He's had three trips inside these last few years, and Eileen, poor lass, has the curse of fits on her; not very bad, but nevertheless she has them. And she is also cursed, as you've seen for yourself, I'm sure, with a beautiful face. It's out of this world, isn't it . . . Now, look . . . look. You're not going to cry, are you?'

'No, no.' Sarah swallowed. 'But it's sad, very sad.'

'Yes, it is, I grant you. But you must believe this. Davie had never any intention of marrying her. Yet him being a soft-hearted chap . . . and you know he is soft-hearted, and it's nothing to be

101

ashamed of . . .' Again his eyebrows went up. 'Well, his mother was always a bit afraid that he would sink under the pressure both from Eileen, her mother, and Stan. And now . . . well, she's relieved. But I must tell you that his father doesn't see it in the same way as she does. In fact, I'm sure Stan would have welcomed Davie's match with Eileen. I think at the back of his mind' – he was whispering now – 'he thought that in some way it would make up for the dirty trick he had done on Ellen. You know, we're queer cattle, we humans. We'd sacrifice somebody else, our nearest and dearest, to our conscience. Anyway, there's the tale. And David picked for himself, and a very very good choice he's made, I'll say that for him.'

He was smiling at her, and she should have felt warmed by his evident sincerity and the fact that David had never any idea of marrying the girl, but instead she felt afraid because her thoughts were now taken up with Mary Hetherington . . . That was why she had been welcomed into this higher stratum; why she had been welcomed by this woman who evidently ruled and dominated her family. It was a case of any port in a storm. She thought of the little woman's voice saying, 'You're cruel, Mary, cruel. You've got everything . . .'

If things hadn't happened in such a whirlwind of hurry she would have asked herself before why this woman had stooped from her high perch and welcomed her. But she had the answer now: she was the lesser of two evils. Pehaps his mother had thought too that if she opposed her son's choice he might become more pliable under the silent pressure of his father and the desire of both the girl and her mother. It was as Dan had said.

'Don't look so sad. I've told you there's nothing more to it than that. Come on, smile . . . laugh.' He put his fingers out to touch her cheek but withheld them before they made contact. Then with an embarrassed laugh he withdrew his hand, saying, 'You know, you look the kind of lass that should laugh a lot.'

Everybody thought she should laugh, just because she was big. But he was nice, this young uncle of David's, so nice. He should have been the brother and John the odd man out. She smiled sadly at him now, saying, 'I've never had very much to laugh at.'

'We'll alter all that. You know, before John was married we used to have some good nights in this room. All except Sunday.' He pulled a face. 'David's a fine player, you know. He's passed all his exams and could teach if he liked, but there's nothing in it, he says. And his mother plays the fiddle; she's a grand hand with the fiddle is Mary.'

'Do you play anything?' she asked quietly.

'Me? Oh yes, yes.' He nodded his head quickly. 'I've got me diploma, first grade; mind you, it took some getting. There was a big do at Morgan's Hall the day it was presented.'

Morgan's Hall! That was at East Jarrow near the New Buildings, a big gaunt empty place. She never knew they presented prizes there. She asked politely, 'What do you play?'

'The comb. But mind' – he held his finger up – 'I have a special kind of paper on it.'

She was laughing; her body shaking, her hands pressed over her mouth, and her face turned into the corner of the couch. And Dan was laughing too; lying back, he too was holding his mouth.

'Oh!' Sarah groaned inside. He was funny, dry; he had her believing him. She slanted her wet eyes towards him and he was looking at her, his face alight.

'We needed that, didn't we?' His whisper was as one pal to another.

At this moment the door opened abruptly and David entered the room with Sarah's hat and coat in his hands. He looked to where she sat wiping her eyes and for a moment a lightness spread over his face and he drew in a long breath as if of relief. Then on a note he attempted to make jocular he said, 'What was it? Dan been telling you about the time he fell in the rain-barrel, or when Father was on the roof and he took the ladder away?'

'No.' Sarah shook her head. 'About him passing the examination for playing the comb.'

'Oh, that's a new one.' David nodded at Dan, then added, 'You are a fool, you know.'

Sarah was in her coat and hat now, and David

said, 'We won't bother going into the other room, we'll come back later.'

'Goodnight, Mr . . .' Sarah turned to Dan.

'Plain Dan, Sarah.'

'Goodnight, Dan.'

'Goodnight, Sarah.'

When she reached the front door she heard Dan's voice, soft sounding and careless, call, 'Here a minute, David.' And as she stood waiting she heard him say, his tone changed now, low and earnest, 'Macdonalds are moving from next door, they'll be out before Christmas. It mightn't be the most suitable place, so close, but empty houses up this end are few and far between as you know. I would get things settled as soon as possible, the wind might change at any time, understand?'

'Yes, Dan . . . thanks.'

Out in the dark street he took her arm. It was a firm possessive hold, and when they came to the main road he said, 'You heard what Dan said?'

'Yes.' Her voice was low and she kept her eyes ahead.

'Well?' The pressure tightened on her arm. 'Would you marry me before Christmas, Sarah?'

Her heart began thumping against her ribs, knocking like a small wooden mallet. It checked her answer for some seconds. Then she stopped and, looking fully at him in the dim lamplight, she said, 'I'll marry you any time you like, David.' Then she added. 'Thanks.' The last word had a silly sound. She wondered why she'd had to say it like that; it made her feel cheap, common. She didn't want to feel cheap or common. She thought of what John had said about being afraid of people. But she wasn't afraid of David, only grateful to him, so very grateful.

5

Sarah stood just within the kitchen door. She still wore her hat and coat. The kitchen was warm with the heat from a blazing fire piled high in the grate, but she still felt cold, and her body seemed to become stiffer as she looked at the priest, and he at her.

Father O'Malley was seated at one corner of the kitchen table, her father was seated at the opposite corner, and her mother at the corner nearest her. They formed the usual triangle of persuasion. One using threats – her father; one using cool fear-filled reason – the priest; one using the weapon of superstition – not the least strong of the three, her mother.

'Good evening, Sarah.'

'Well, don't stand there as if you were struck. You heard the Father speaking to you.'

'Yes, I heard, I'm not deaf.'

106

As she glared at Pat Bradley there arose in her, yet again, an acute feeling of hate. She had always hated this man, but the feeling had become stronger during the past weeks during which he had done everything in his power to break up her association with David and the family at the other end. The weapon he used was her religion, and his natural ally was the priest – at least this priest.

Father Bailey, on the other hand, had been understanding, even nice. He had asked her to bring David to see him, and David had gone and told him in a quiet way his reasons for not wishing to become a Catholic. He had pointed out to him that it wasn't a case of changing his religion because he wasn't of any particular denomination, he was an agnostic. She had felt proud that David was able to talk to the priest as he had done, and she felt that Father Bailey liked and respected him. He had said, 'Well, the Bishop, under certain circumstances, gives permission for a mixed marriage . . . they are not popular.' Father Bailey had smiled as he had said this. 'But nevertheless permission is given on the understanding that you will allow the children to be brought up in the Catholic faith.'

Sarah had felt embarrassed at this point, yet had waited eagerly for David's answer. It hadn't come immediately, but when he did speak she had let out a long slow breath, for he had said, 'Well, I'm no longer speaking for myself on this point . . . It won't be a matter of personal opinion but what Sarah thinks too. I'll leave it to her Father.'

He had buried deep into her heart when he had called the priest, Father. Oh, David was so reasonable, and Father Bailey was reasonable . . . Father O'Malley kept saying that he too was reasonable but he wasn't – he was adamant, fanatic. By the things he said anyone would think she was marrying a leper.

Yet this same priest spoke civilly to her father simply because he attended Mass every Sunday. It was a wonder, she thought, that the church didn't fall round about his ears. This undersized man who looked what he was: a dirty-minded swine.

'Have you thought over what I said last week Sarah?'

'Yes, Father.'

'Then you know you can expect no happiness or peace through a mixed marriage.'

Sarah remained silent.

'Can't you answer the Father?'

'Be quiet, Pat.' The priest lifted his hand in temperate admonition, then went on, 'I under stand from Father Bailey that this man has no intention of changing his views, now or at any other time.'

Still Sarah did not answer.

'So in that case you must see your position clearly. Surely you cannot contemplate damaging your immortal soul by joining in a union with this man . . . If you do you will be damned, and your children will be damned, and you will be held responsible. Do you understand that?'

Sarah's throat was swelling, her eyes were widening. All the pores in her body seemed to have taken on separate lives and were rubbing one against the other, jangling her whole being. Looking into the priest's eyes, she saw the loss of her immortal soul. It took the shape of agony brought on by misfortune after misfortune as he had prophesied during the past weeks. If she married David bad luck would dog her. The penance for her crime while she lived would come in the shape of every disaster . . . But no disaster that her brain could conceive would be equal to the loss of her immortal soul and the immortal souls of her children, so his eyes told her. She turned from their penetrating stare and the eyes of the others and, tearing open the stair-case door, she crawled frantically like some wild animal up to her room, there to find Phyllis waiting for her.

'What's the matter? What's he done?'

Sarah turned from her sister and, pressing her hands over her face, leant against the door.

'What is it, Sarah?' Phyllis was tugging at her. 'Look, what did he say?'

The hands still covering her face, Sarah whimpered, 'My immortal soul . . . He said . . .'

'Oh, my God!' Phyllis's sharp retort came as if from an older woman. 'Don't be a blasted fool, our Sarah, and let him scare the daylights out of you with that talk. Immortal soul! Tell him he can have your *immortal soul*, and stick it . . . Tell him to take my dear father's . . . there's an immortal soul for you. I bet if Father O'Malley hadn't taken up the priesthood he'd have been twin brother to Pat Bradley.'

'Ssh! Don't talk like that, Phyllis, not about the priest.'

'Look, our Sarah,' Phyllis was whispering again. 'I thought you had some guts. You don't mean to tell me you're going to let him get you down, not at this stage.'

'No, no, I'm not.' Sarah sat on the bed and, tearing off her hat, flung it into the corner of the room, repeating, 'No, I'm not! David's not going to turn and that's that. He's even willing to be married in the church, but he's not going to turn. No, they won't get me down.'

'Look, Sarah.' Phyllis was kneeling by Sarah's knees now, gripping her hands, looking up into her face with an urgency that seemed in excess of sisterly interest in this matter. 'Why don't you do what the uncle said, the Dan one? Why don't you get married in the registry office, then there would be neither Baptist chapel as his mother wants, nor the church?'

'I couldn't . . . No.' Sarah shook her head

wearily. 'Not in a registry office; I wouldn't feel married somehow.'

Phyllis pulled herself back on to her haunches and, looking up at Sarah, said, 'You know, our Sarah, you're a big softy; you let people play on your feelings, first one side then the other. When the only one you've got to think about is David. Now I'm telling you, our Sarah, things can happen, things that'll put the kibosh on you marrying him altogether.'

'Nothing'll stop me marrying him. The only thing I want is to be married in church, and he's for it.'

Phyllis looked at Sarah for a long moment now before turning and walking to the window. The paper blind was down but she stared at it as if she were looking through the glass, and her tone was fierce as she whispered, 'I expected you to be married afore this. Now I'm waiting no longer.'

'Afore this?' Sarah repeated in a harsh whisper. 'Well, we've only been going together just over two months. And what do you mean, you can wait no longer?'

Sarah was sitting on the edge of the bed now, her hands gripping the iron frame. Something that she had dreaded but forced down under the pressure of her own particular worries came rushing upwards. 'Our Phyllis! You're not going to do anything silly?'

'It all depends on what you call silly. An' don't say it that way.'

Sarah, getting up, went to Phyllis and pulled her round by the shoulders, peering into her face in the dim light.

'You're not going to live . . .'

'Yes, I am, but I'm goin' to marry him. I could have married him a month ago but I waited thinkin' that you would do something definite, stop being pushed around.'

'But . . . but you can't, our Phyllis. You just can't go down and live among the Arabs.' Sarah couldn't bring herself to say: live with an Arab, marry an Arab.

'Let me tell you somethin'.' Phyllis's voice was quiet now and her words deliberately slow. 'If half of them round these doors were as decent as them Arabs – not all, mind you, not all, I know that, I'm not daft – but taking them singularly and weighing them one against the other, this lot would lose hands down.'

'What's the good of cutting off your nose to spite your face?' Sarah was pleading now. 'You know what it'll mean going down there just to spite him?'

Phyllis shrugged herself from Sarah's hold, then, her voice still quiet, said, 'It was like that at first, but not any more. I like Ali and he can give me a home, and a decent one; they've got money.'

She jerked her head up. 'His father runs one of them boarding-houses and Ali helps. It'll be his one day and a lot more besides. His father's a name down there, and they have their own kind of stuckupness . . . Do you know something? He and some of the others are not very keen about Ali taking up with me. I thought everybody looked upon them as scum. Even from the bottom end here they do; but let me tell you, them Arabs have their own idea of scum, and we from this quarter are pretty well at the top of the list. I've had me eyes opened this last few weeks.'

'He won't let you do it.' Sarah's breast was heaving nearly as much now as when she had scrambled up the stairs a few minutes earlier. 'He'll go to the polis.'

'He can go where the bloody hell he likes . . .'

'Don't swear, our Phyllis . . .'

'Well, he can, and as far beyon't because once it's been signed and sealed he can do very little about it – nowt in fact. I was eighteen last week, an' I know him; it'll be such a slap in his dirty face that he won't be able to wipe it off, an' he'll want to keep mum about it.'

'Then you are doing it just to spite him.'

'No, I'm not; I've told you. But I can hear him: "Aa'va washed me hands off her, the trollop!" Ooh!' Phyllis lifted her face to the low ceiling, and there was a twisted smile on it as she exclaimed in tones that held even wonder, 'Won't it be lovely to be a trollop and get away from here, and him, and everything?'

Sarah sat down again. She felt sick, really sick as if she could vomit. This was the finish – the finish of her, anyway. Phyllis would go, but she would stay because when David's mother heard that her sister had gone down into Costerfine Town way to live with an Arab – even if she were married to him – that would be the finish.

And Mrs Hetherington had been rather strange lately, cool at times. She, of course, wanted them to be married in the Baptist chapel. Sarah had learned one thing about David's mother during the past weeks. She was a dominant, proud woman, proud of her family, proud of her station in the top end, of living in the best house – the only double house – in the whole place. When this knowledge of her future mother-in-law's character was added to that of her determination not to let David marry the girl Eileen, she appeared super-humanly strong. Sarah knew for certain now that if Mrs Hetherington hadn't been pushed for a substitute at a critical time she herself would never have got across the doorstep.

She swung her body round, straining it forward towards her sister, appealing with every fibre of it as she whispered, 'Wait till I'm settled, Phyllis; aw, wait till I'm settled.'

'I've been waitin', Sarah. I thought the way you

114

started it was all going to happen in a rush, you'd be married and settled afore now. Well, you started like that.' She shook her head at the silent denial from Sarah. 'I can't wait any longer, there's a reason. I'm . . . I'm leavin' here a week come Monday, it's all settled. I'm to be married then.'

'A reason?' Sarah's mouth was hanging open and the lashes of her upper lids were lying flat against the smooth skin of her eyes. 'A reason?' Her voice had sunk into deep emphasis.

'Yes, and it's no good going off the deep end, it's over and done.'

'Oh, my God!'

'Mine too.' This flippant remark would have at one time caused them to giggle helplessly even while Sarah reprimanded Phyllis for treating the name of God with lightness; but now she could only stare at the slight boyish-like figure of her sister. 'How far?' she asked.

'Six or seven weeks. It happened after he gave me the lathering. Ali saw me face and weals sticking up above the top of me blouse and he was kind to me. You know what?' Phyllis shook her head. 'He nearly cried. Can you believe that, he nearly cried. Well, it happened that night, and don't think I'm sorry 'cos I'm not, but you can see I've got to get away. An' you know it'll be just like gettin' out of prison. I've never been inside but I'd like to bet me bottom dollar that this place is ten degrees worse than any prison. D'you know, I've had to come straight up here every night for weeks to get out of his sight, for his hands 'ave been itching to leather me again. He can manage me, you see; even if I kick and tear he can manage me. He couldn't you; that's why he's never started on you, only that once when you first went to work and that lad set you home. But me, I'm smaller than him, something that he can handle in the way he wants, and me mother's let him get away with it. She's putting her foot down now when it's too late 'cos she knows we can both skedaddle. She's as much to blame as he is. She could have managed him with her bulk, but now he's got her as frightened as he thinks he's got me. But he doesn't know he's made a mistake. Oh lad, I wish I could be in two places at once next week when I post them me news. An' you know how I'm goin' to end it?' She cocked her head up defiantly. 'I've been goin' over it in me mind for days. I'm goin' to say, after the bit about me being married, I'm goin' to say, "You can come to the christenin' if yer like, it'll be in about seven months' time".'

'Oh, our Phyllis!' Sarah lowered her head in a series of low swings until her chin lay on her breast.

'Listen!' Phyllis had raised her hand. 'He's goin' out. He's likely settin' the priest down the road, and on his way back he'll do a bit of his snooping on the courtin' couples. Oh, I wish some fellow would catch him at it and take him by the legs and swing him face forward against a coal hatch.'

Sarah put her fingers to her lips and stared at the tiny iron grate opposite her. Then, jumping to her feet, she asked, 'What time do you think it is?' She was standing at the foot of the bed buttoning her coat up now.

'About quarter to ten I should say. Where you goin'?'

'To see David. I've got to.'

'You goin' to the house?'

'Yes.'

'What will his mother say?'

'I don't suppose she'll be there. The grandchild ... John's boy's ill, it's whooping cough, and bad. David said his mother was taking a turn over there tonight, but if she isn't I'll just have to make some excuse, I don't know what yet.' She was gabbling now.

'But how'll you get back ... in I mean?'

'I'll take the back-door key and get me mother to leave the bolt loose. I'll sleep on the couch until the mornin'.'

'If he finds out he won't let you in.'

'I'll have to risk that; I've got to see David. I can't wait until tomorrow night, I'll go mad.'

'You're goin' to tell him you're going to be married in the Baptist?'

'No, no.' Sarah shook her head violently.

'What, then?'

'Oh, I don't know. I just don't know. I just want to talk to him.'

117

'An' tell him what a wicked girl you've got for a sister?'

'Aw, our Phyllis, I won't do any such thing, you know I won't.'

'I know you won't, Sarah. You're soft, our Sarah, soft. But go on. Go on and get back as quick as you can, I'll keep awake.'

Down in the kitchen Annie said, 'For God's sake don't make a noise when you come in.' She pulled the big key from the lock of the back door. 'I'll stay down as long as I can.' Then she added, 'What's got into you? Why do you want to go out at this time? Are you going to the top end?'

'Yes.'

'Is it about the priest?'

Sarah hesitated. She would have to give some reason for going, so she nodded abruptly before slipping out of the door.

There was a moon shining, caressing the grey slate roofs of the long street, casting deep shadows over the rows of small windows on one side and lighting them up on the other, showing them as elongated eyes in an elongated face of dirty reddy-brown brick. But the moon was kind. The streets were mellowed. The grimness of the poorer houses was dimmed, and where the streets began to improve the moon lent a touch of enchantment. In Camelia Street everything was bright and gleaming. The houses looked like smiling faces. The bow-windows were glistening eyes and the bath-bricked steps large white teeth sticking out of flushed faces. All the doors in Camelia Street were painted every year.

Sarah stood with her arm raised towards the knocker of number one, and before she grasped it she doubled her hand into a fist and punched her cheek as she asked herself, 'What will I say? How will I begin?'

It seemed to her that the knocker had hardly touched the door when it was pulled open, and there stood Dan.

'Why, Sarah, come in, come in. What are you after at this time of night? David said he had packed you off home because of your . . .' He looked down at her ankles. 'Because you were tired.'

'Is he in, Dan?'

'Yes, yes. He'd have been here waiting on the step if he'd thought you were coming back. Come on, come in.' He pulled her aside so that he could close the door; then, peering at her through the hall light, he whispered, 'Anything wrong?'

She did not answer his question but whispered back, 'Is . . . is his mother in?'

'No, she's over the road. The young 'un is pretty bad. There's only Davie and me in. His dad's over there an' all . . . Come on.'

When Dan opened the living-room door he pushed Sarah before him, saying, 'Look what the moon's flushed up, Davie.'

119

David was on his feet. 'What's the matter?' He was holding her hands now, looking into her face. 'Is anything wrong?'

'Yes. Can I sit down?'

'Can you sit down!' It was Dan who pressed her into the chair while David still held her hand. 'What is it?' David asked gently.

'Look, I'll be off to bed now, I'll say goodnight.'

'No, no.' Sarah looked up at Dan. Somehow she felt that Dan's cool head, his easy unaffected way of seeing things, might help. 'You might as well know.' She turned her face to David. 'I had to come straight away an' tell you. It's about our Phyllis. I know it's going to make all the difference, but I had to come and tell you. It isn't her fault really, but she's marrying an Arab . . . A week come Monday.'

When she felt her fingers slide from David's she cried wildly inside herself. 'Oh no! no! Hold me hands.' She turned her eyes from his startled face and looked at Dan. His face too was wearing almost the same expression as David's, and the two men were looking at each other now. David's lips were moving; it was as if he were saying something to Dan yet no sound came.

The thoughts flowing between the two men were like hot wires passing through her body, vibrating pain. She couldn't bear to look at them any more. She wanted to rise from the chair and rush out of the house, but she hadn't the strength;

she hadn't even the strength to keep her body upright. It was bending over as if beaten. From her downcast lids she saw David's legs move. He swung a chair round and then his knees were touching hers and there was promise of life when once again her hands were in his and he was asking, 'When did you say she was going to be married?'

'A . . . a week come Monday.' Her voice cracked on the last word and she cleared her throat.

'There's not much time.' Dan had turned another chair round and he too was sitting, almost in a line with David and in front of her. 'Look, Sarah.' David was shaking her hands as if bringing her awake, and he began to talk rapidly, his words crisp, decisive. 'You won't countenance the Baptist chapel, and this business of your church is going to take weeks. There's only one thing for it: the registry office.'

The words jerked Sarah. It was as if the wires had twanged against a patch of fear, disturbing it, sending it flowing in all directions through her body.

'I know you don't want to be married in a registry office, and neither do I, but it's like this, Sarah. Well . . .'

He stopped and closed his eyes, and Dan, putting his hand out and gripping his knee, said, 'I'd better finish for you. It's his mother, Sarah. You know how things are, you're no fool. When this business of your sister's is made public, it isn't only God alone who will know what her reactions will be, we'll all know. She's a very proud woman is Mary, and she can be hard, unmoving . . . Now, what you've got to do is to create a *fait accompli.*' He smiled here, then went on. 'I mean, you've got to do the trick, get married. The thing is then done, achieved, and she'll have to face it. But, on the other hand, if she gets wind of your sister marrying . . . an Arab . . . ' He wagged his hand at Sarah. 'I'm not saying that there aren't decent Arabs . . . they would be bad if they weren't as good as some of the whites; but you know how it's taken, don't you?'

Into the silence David said, 'Will you, Sarah? Will you get married in the registry office?'

Sarah stared into David's eyes. If she didn't marry this man in the registry office she wouldn't get the chance to marry him at all, of that she was certain. Between the pressure of the priest and the power of Mrs Hetherington, David and she would be torn apart, the battle would be too much for them. It mustn't be. Never again would she meet a man of David's standing, not one who would want to marry her. Not one so lacking in side, not one who was the antithesis of his mother, of all proud mothers. But that she would suffer if she was married in a registry office she also knew . . . Her immortal soul would be in jeopardy, and her actions would make her responsible for the souls of her children – the priest had said. Even so, she must do it. She must marry David, if not in the sight of God, then in the sight of man.

Thinking along these lines, she was surprised that she should openly show the extent of her relief in the way she did; for she cried, 'Yes. Oh yes, David . . . any place . . . any place.'

David pulled her hands up under his chin and held them there, and Dan rose to his feet with the comment, 'Well, now, we'll drink on that, the kettle's on. And don't let's waste any time. How soon can this thing be got through – in the registry office, I mean?'

'About a week.' David was not looking at Dan, he was looking at Sarah.

'Well, if you give the notice in tomorrow you should be able to do the deed in a week to a fortnight. And if you make it a Wednesday I can get the morning off. Look.' He turned round the teapot in his hand. 'I tell you what I'll do. I'll stand the wedding breakfast, eh?'

'Aw, Dan, man, there's no need for that.'

'No need? Of course there's no need, but I'll do it all the same. It'll be a bit of a wedding present. And look.' He came eagerly towards them, the teapot outstretched in the direction of the wall. 'The Macdonalds are moving on Friday, it couldn't be better. Everything will work out. And you can spend your honeymoon doing the place up. You've got a week to come, haven't you?' He now dug the spout of the teapot into David's shoulder, and David smiled up at him without answering. 'Well, there you are, everything fixed.' He was looking at Sarah as he spoke, his voice and manner sweeping away all obstacles. But there was one obstacle it was impossible for him to remove from her path, and it wasn't her religion she was thinking about now, it was Mary Hetherington. Her face straight, she looked at David and said, 'Your mother will never forgive me.'

'Oh yes she will. I'll take the blame.'

She moved her head in small jerks. 'She'll never forgive me. She'll even hate me.'

'Now don't be silly.' Dan was bending over her, his face on a level with David's. He spoke sternly as if to a recalcitrant child. 'That's nonsense. Get the thing done and stop shilly-shallying. I'm glad this has happened, you know, for you could both have gone on between church and chapel, between turning and not turning for the next two years and then finished up' – he straightened his broad shoulders, and spread his arms wide, the teapot still in his hand – 'not getting married at all.'

'You're wrong there, Dan. Sarah and me will be married whether it's next week, or next year, or the year after. But for my money it's next week . . . That's it, isn't it, Sarah?'

She was about to nod when the latch of the back

oor clicked and they all turned their eyes in the
irection of the kitchen.

'What can I say?' She was on her feet whis-
ering.

'Nothing, nothing.' David was patting her
ands. 'I brought you in, that's all. We'd just come
ick.' That meant his mother had been out when
e returned home.

When the living-room door opened and John
ntered their combined sigh brought his gaze
om one to the other. 'Aye, aye! What's up here?
ou all look as if you'd been caught in the act of
reaking and entering.'

Dan cast a quick glance at David, wanting to
now whether he was going to confide in his
rother and David answered him by looking at
hn and saying, 'A little crisis has arisen. Good in
way, in fact for my part I'd say splendid. Sarah
id I are going to be married next week . . . in the
gistry office.'

John stared at his brother. 'Sudden!' he said
uietly.

'Yes, it is. But things are better that way.'

'Mother know?'

'No, and I don't want her to.'

'Dad?'

'Nor him either. Nobody, only Dan here and
ou.'

'Do you want a best man?' His lips smiled.

'Would you?' David moved towards him.

'It's as little as I can do.'

'Thanks, John.' David thumped his brother[
broad chest without causing him to move in th[
slightest. 'And Dan's seeing to the breakfast.[
couldn't feel happier about it.'

'Well, she doesn't think she's going to get yo[
without taking the rest of us on, does she?' Joh[
was looking over David's shoulder, holdin[
Sarah's eyes now. 'She takes one, she takes the l[
– the Three Musketeers, one for all and all for on[
isn't that it, Dan?'

'You're a fool. Take no heed of him, Sarah,' sai[
Dan.

'Well, we've always hung together, haven't w[
against authority . . . politics, religion, and . .[
women?' He smiled broadly as he said the la[
word. Then, coming towards Sarah, he held o[
his hand. She placed hers in it, and when h[
covered it with his other large square palm an[
said gallantly, 'But not – not this one,' she had th[
strange desire to fall against him, to put her arn[
around his thick neck and cry and cry and cry an[
cry.

This feeling, unheralded, springing upon he[
from nowhere, was as frightening as the hat[
which had attacked her in the bedroom a sho[
while ago, and again, as on that occasion, she wa[
trembling, every pore in her body was movin[
Her breath quickened; her neck swelled and th[
pain in it became so unbearable that it forced itse[

126

up the back of her throat and into her eyes. She closed them tightly to stop the flood escaping, but it was no use.

'Oh! Oh! Don't, don't, Sarah. Aw! What is it? Come now, come now.' Their voices were floating around her, exclaiming, soothing. Their hands were touching her, her arms, her shoulders, her head, patting, patting. Her feelings changed now into panic; she wanted to push them off, all of them, and fly from the house. It was only a momentary feeling; it was gone as quickly as it had come.

Through her blurred vision she put out her hands and grasped those of David. His hands were different altogether from anyone else's. She gripped them and turned her face into his shoulder, and the others melted away.

The room became quiet, there was only David and her. There would always be only David and her. The rage, the fears, the strange emotions, were things of the past. There came upon her spirit a quietness which even the thought of Mary Hetherington or the loss of her immortal soul could not dispel: she had David. Next week she would have him for life and she would know peace.

6

'Well, how do you feel?' Dan leant his big head across the table towards Sarah as he whispered the question.

'Fu . . . funny.'

'Not f . . . funny-daft, funny-nice, eh?'

'Stop acting the goat, here's the waiter.' David, the red veins on his cheeks seeming more prominent because his skin was a shade paler, pushed Dan upwards by the shoulder.

The waiter had a bottle in his hand which he presented to Dan as if for him to read the label, saying, 'All right, sir?'

'All right.' Dan nodded. The waiter tore off the lead cap, pulled out the stubby-headed cork and proceeded with practised art to fill the four glasses with the sparkling wine.

When the waiter had departed and they had the glasses in their hands David said under his breath, 'Either you're loopy or you've come into money . . . Champagne! You're daft, man.'

'Drink it up and stop your nattering . . . Here's to you both.' Dan held out his glass. It was on a level with John's, but John did not speak, he merely inclined his head.

The wine had very little taste, Sarah thought. Its only noticeable effect was the gas which pricked her nostrils. But it was champagne. Fancy her drinking champagne! Oh, Dan was kind. He was a nice man was Dan.

'This is the life.' Dan was sitting back in his chair beaming. 'Wednesday morning and me not at work. It's never happened before. Every Wednesday morning at this time' – he looked at his watch – 'quarter to twelve, in comes Mrs Flaherty, and we have the same performance, it never varies. If her old man's had the dole or not the programme is as usual. "What's your ham, the day, Mr Hetherington?" she says. Give her her due, she's about the only one that gives me me title. "Wan and two, Mrs Flaherty." I'm very deferential to her; we're both deferential to each other, and she has me talkin' the Irish as broad as herself.'

Dan was addressing himself solely to Sarah and she was smiling at him. She knew he was doing his stuff to put them at their ease . . . oh, Dan was nice.

' "Wan an' two, Mr Hetherington. Aw, dear God, Aa couldn't go for that, not this smorin'. An' what's your back?"

' "The short is a shillin', Mrs Flaherty, and the long is eightpence."

' "Begod! it gets dearer . . . " And us the cheapest shop in the town, cutting everybody else's throat.' Dan made this quick aside to David, and David choked on his drink.

' "What about a bit of collar, Mrs Flaherty?"

' "Aw, it's always too lean an' it kizzles up in the

pan. Like the top of his boots he says it is; he'd throw it at me he would . . . collar!"

' "Well, I've some nice streaky here, now how about that? There, look, that's a nice lean piece, an inch or more running through its middle!" ' Dan held out the table napkin and Sarah could believe it was streaky bacon she was looking at. 'I tell you I'm talkin' as thick as she is by this time. And this happens every Wednesday in life.'

They were all laughing now, even John; and with the bubbles from another sip of champagne making her screw up her face, Sarah asked, 'What did she have in the end?'

'Pieces.'

Their laughter turned into a roar and they made individual efforts to stifle it while glancing round the half-empty hotel dining-room. And they were returning to normal when Dan finished laconically, 'Three pennorth.' His accent was exaggerated now into broad Geordie, the inflexion high on the last syllable. They were off again, unrestrained now, and Sarah thought wistfully, Oh, if we could go on like this all day right till the night, just laughing and carrying on.

There was no doubt in her mind that Dan could have kept them laughing for a week, but within the next hour or so she would have to face Mary Hetherington, and the prospect, when she let herself think about it, was terrifying.

The meal began with sole, and when the main

ourse turned out to be duck, and this accom-
anied by another wine, David, looking at Dan,
nook his head reprovingly, 'You shouldn't have
one to this, man.'

'Why not? You mind your own business and
ick in, that's all you've got to do.'

'Don't worry about him throwing his money
bout.' John was looking at Dan. 'It'll take a little
eight out of the stocking leg and he's got stacks
 them piled away, and not even Mrs Flaherty
ould get her big toe into one of them.'

Sarah, laughing with the rest, looked at John
nd realised that it was the first time he had
pened his mouth since they had left the registry
ffice. He looked slightly off colour, and his
anner was not so boisterous as usual. He was not
riding ahead as though the world were a football
 his feet. That was how she saw John, this brother
 David's, who was so totally unlike him. Perhaps
e thought he was worrying about the child, but
e boy was getting better now; or perhaps he'd
ad another row with his wife.

It wasn't until an hour later, when they stood in
ng Street, outside the hotel, that she felt she had
en given the reason for John's quiet manner and
m looking so off colour.

David had just said, 'I don't know how to thank
u, Dan. Do we Sarah?' And she had shaken her
ad dumbly.

'Look,' said Dan, 'it's nothing. Anyway, it's only

131

half your wedding present . . . I'm opening anoth
stocking leg.' He thrust his hand out towards Joh
on this remark.

David too had turned to John, and he aske
'Where you going? You coming back home?'

'No,' said John, 'I'm off to the Labour Ex . . .' H
bit sharply down on his lip.

'So that's it?' Dan was standing with his ch
pulled in. 'I was wondering what was up wi
you. You're out?' His face was screwed up. 'Whe
did this happen?'

'Aw, my big mouth. I was off me guard . . . O
for over a week.'

'For over a week? And you've never sa
anything?' David's voice held a reproach. 'Do
May know?'

'No, nobody knows; at least they didn't.' Johr
head was wagging as if it had been snapped at tl
nape. 'I thought I'd be set on afore this, it's just or
of those things.' His head bounced up now. 'Dor
start being sorry for me, either of you.' His ey
were round and bright, his face and mann
aggressive. 'Look, they're not getting me on tl
scrap-heap, I'll be in work next week.'

'What happened?' Dan asked quietly. 'I thoug
it would be the last place to pay off, and you tl
last one.'

'Well, there was no more orders for boats; bi
little, tall, or small.'

'But your place only dealt with small craft

132

thought there was still a market for them from the south, and for lifeboats.'

'Aye, well, so did everybody else, but they seem to have all the boats they need in the south. And nobody seems to be getting drowned now as there's fewer ships on the water so nobody wants any more lifeboats. And that's something to be thankful for, isn't it, nobody getting drowned?' He was grinning now, a false grin. 'Look.' He took them all in with a swing of his head. 'Don't let it be on my conscience that I've put a damper on the proceedings. Don't be sorry for me, for God's sake. I'm all right. For weeks ahead, I'm not broke, but I'm not going to let the blasted government get off with anything. No, by God, I'm going to get some dole out of them.'

'You won't get any for a fortnight, anyway; they don't recognise the first week and then there's three days lying on.' Dan was still talking quietly.

'Tell me something I don't know, man. Anyway, I told you I'll be at it again next week and I'll tell them what to do with their dole. But look.' His manner changed abruptly and his voice became serious as he turned to David. 'Don't let on to me mother, mind.'

'No, no, of course not. Although' – David was now smiling wryly from one to the other and his eyes came to rest on Sarah as he finished – 'I think it would be really the best time to tell her, for she'll be going at us two so much it'll pass over her head.'

His words were meant to reassure Sarah but they failed, and it was evident to the three men. Dan said briskly, 'It'll be all right, never fear . . . Well, I'm off to . . . Westoe.' It seemed as if the name had brought a self-consciousness to him, for his laugh was sheepish.

'Go on, you old roué.' Sarah could not understand this remark of John's. She did not know what a roué was but she could gauge that it was something not quite nice, for as Dan looked at her there was a pink tinge under his skin. The next moment he was holding her hand, saying, 'I wish you all the happiness in the world, Sarah.'

'Thanks, Dan.' Her voice had a cracked sound.

'And mind you, you make the best of those three days in Newcastle and when you come back I'll have one room cleaned out at least, if not papered . . . I'll put the big fellow on here.' He grabbed at John's arm. 'You know what he is when he gets started, skull, hair, and white-wash flying . . . God bless you.' The last was soft as a benediction and it was almost too much for Sarah. That is what the priest would have said, God bless you – at least Father Bailey would have said it.

Now John was standing in front of her. He did not touch her, not even to take her hand, but he looked deep into her eyes, past the worried surface of her mind, past the deeper level where lay the love she had for David, down, down, until his gaze reached a depth in her she did not know existed. She did not retreat from the return of the strange feeling, but wide-eyed watched his lids droop, the short black thick lashes creating a shadow on the broad high cheek-bones. She was married and safe, she had nothing to fear from strange feelings or anything else . . . except perhaps David's mother.

'All the best.' It was an ordinary, trite remark, used on such occasions. It was intended to mean everything, it usually meant nothing. Again John repeated this as he now shook hands with David. 'All the best, man,' he said. And David, gripping his shoulder with his free hand, answered, 'Thanks, John, thanks.'

David now took Sarah's arm and turned her about and across the road to where the tram was, the same tram that had carried her part of the way home during all her working days. Now she would use it no more – not as Sarah Bradley, anyway. She was Mrs David Hetherington. She made an effort and forced her shoulders back and lifted her head. What could they do? What could any of them do? Her father, his mother. She was married, legally married . . .

Dan and John stood still on the pavement watching them until they boarded the tram, then they waved.

'Better them than me.' Dan's voice was low. 'Your mother's going to play merry hell. That lass is going to have a time of it. We'll all have to stand by her. Davie alone won't be able to screen her. You know what your mother is when she gets her fangs in, and she hasn't had a target for a long time. We'll all have to act as a buffer in one way or another, she's too nice to be nooled.'

'I can't see anybody nooling her.' John spoke as he looked ahead to where the tram was disappearing into the distance. 'I mean, I can't see anybody wanting to nool her. And me mother puts up with May.' John now turned and glanced at Dan, a quizzical smile twisting his lips.

'Yes, but May married you, she didn't marry Davie. The truth is, your mother didn't ever have any intention of anybody marrying Davie, at least that's how I figure it. She pretended to accept the lass knowing that the scales were weighed heavily against her, her coming from the bottom end and all that, and she was hoping that the weight would gradually tell on Davie – religion, background, the lot. Of course, I might be wrong.'

'You're never very wrong, Dan.'

Dan turned and looked at his nephew. There was six years between them, but this was in no way apparent, they had always looked and felt equal. Dan said now, 'You look off colour. Are you worrying about being out?'

'No, no, I told you . . . No, by God.' He turned his head round on his shoulder as if looking at someone behind him. 'No. They're not getting me to rot at the street corner. Don't you worry about me, Dan. I'll fall on me feet, I always have. Now, I'm off . . . And by the way, thanks for the meal. You went to town, didn't you, and it was decent of you. I thought about making them a dining table and chairs. I can get the wood at cost.'

'Oh, they'd be tickled pink at that; that's a good idea, John.'

'Well, I'll be off. So long, Dan.'

'So long, John. See you the night.'

'Yes, see you the night.'

Dan crossed the road, and John turned the corner and went in the direction of the station, his stride long and quick. He reached the yard and made for the urinal, and there with his body bent double and his hand against the wall he retched.

'You feeling bad, mate?'

John wiped his face with his handkerchief. The sweat was running in rivulets down from his hair. After nodding at the man he said, 'Eating too well . . . duck and champagne.'

'Aye, begod, you'll get sick on duck and champagne these days, on seventeen bob a week. Aye, you'll get sick on that. Sick for the want of a good feed. You all right now?'

The man's reaction to John's remark had been what he had intended, and after he had nodded at him the man went on, 'Duck and champagne. You'd have to be in Parliament to have duck and champagne these days. Even the mayoral banquets wouldn't sport that the day in case the

137

smell got into the streets and sent people mad. Something should be done . . . it'll have to be done.' The man pointed his thin dirty finger at John. 'We'll have to hang together, that's the solution. The bloody unions will have to find out whose side they're on. Why aren't they up in London doing somethin'? There'll be riots afore long, you'll see.'

If the fool didn't shut up he would push him on his back. He turned away from the man and kept his face to the wall, and the voice coming from a distance now said, 'That's it, get it up. It's better out than in, whatever it is.'

Left alone, John again turned and leaned against the wall. 'Get it up,' the man had said. 'Better out than in.' But the man didn't know that he was sick in two ways.

A mixture of sauterne and champagne and duck had been too much for his stomach which had grown accustomed to the dull diets of an in-different cook. But this was a kind of sickness you could get rid of. He wished to God the other could be vomited up in the same way. What had Dan said? They would all have to act as a buffer between her and his mother. That was funny that was, damned funny, for Dan didn't know that from the minute he had seen her that night in the front room he had wanted to act as a buffer between her and the world.

Before he'd had May he'd had his practice. He

knew all about women. From when he was fourteen and looked seventeen, and the lasses had made a bee line for him, he'd had them; he couldn't help but have them, for they had tripped over themselves to get him to touch them. He'd had his first lass when he was fifteen. His mother would have had a seizure if she had known. Yes, he knew all about women, but he had never loved any of them. Wanted them? Oh, aye, wanted them until he couldn't bear himself. Lusted after them was the phrase. He had wanted May but he hadn't loved her, but he had taken her and she had seen that he damned well paid for that bit of frisking. She was the only one, at least to his knowledge, whom, as his mother would have said, he had got with child. Paul had been born prematurely. He had laughed at that. He wondered if the midwife had laughed too. If she had, she hadn't done it in front of him or his mother. Everything that had happened to the child since had been put down to his premature birth. Did a child ever become aware that he had been born of lust and not love? He had told himself that as long as you had the other thing you could live without love. That's what he had told himself. Until the night he had walked into the front room to see the lass their David was going to marry. That night he had said to himself, Don't be a blasted fool, it couldn't happen as quickly as that. But the passing days had proved him wrong. He was known as the big fellow, he liked the title. But the bigger the weight the harder the fall, and by God his fall had been hard.

He pulled himself from the wall and wiped his face, then straightened his hat and buttoned up his coat. Well, it was done. Two hours ago she had become Davie's wife. If it had been anybody else but Davie, Dan even, he would have gone all out, full sails set, and caught her up like a demon of wind, all the magnificent size of her, all her unconscious, unaffected loveliness. He would have cried, To hell, let's get out of here. What did it matter about a wife and a bairn, about a mother who was so stiff-necked with pride and a sense of security it became painful at times for him to look, or listen, to her. He knew that if he had let himself sail before the wind of his passion, Sarah, whether she wanted to or not, would have been borne along with him. But it was Davie she had married, Davie she wanted. Or, did she? . . . Anyway, Davie had wanted her, and the only decent thing that had been in his life had been the love for his brother.

PART TWO

Sarah alighted from the tram at the Market Place and made her way to the ferry. Her step was light, for there was no swelling around her ankles. Three men, coming up the bank from the landing, turned their heads towards her and one of them whistled as he winked at her.

Cheeky thing. She moved her body slightly, expressing indignation that she did not feel. That's what new clothes did, she told herself, made men cheeky.

But as she bought her ticket the pleasure that the men's admiration aroused in her vanished, to be replaced with the feeling of being slightly ashamed, slightly anxious and apprehensive.

Before boarding the ferry, she thought, What if she hasn't turned up? Well, I'll only have to come across again. But she said the two-thirty.

She stepped on to the boat and moved quickly around the engine-house, and there in the bows, her back to the rail, stood Phyllis. In a moment they were together, their hands joined, exchanging smiles and gabbled greetings.

'I thought you weren't comin'. You got me letter?'

'Well, I wouldn't be here else, would I?'

'Don't be silly.'

They laughed at each other as they moved back to the rail, and Phyllis, leaning her side against it, examined Sarah, and her verdict was, 'By! You look bonny. I've never seen you look like this. All new things?' She flicked Sarah's coat with her finger.

'Yes.' Sarah smiled shyly. 'I've got two complete rigouts right through ... But never mind me. What about you? Are you in trouble?'

'Trouble?' Phyllis drew her chin in. 'No, no. I'm in no trouble.'

'Oh?' Sarah paused. 'I thought when I got your letter ...'

'I just wanted to see you. I felt I had to see you. An' I wanted to hear about me mother an' all.'

Phyllis turned and leant her forearms on the rail; and bending over it and looking down to where the water was beginning to froth as the boat moved from the quay, she added, 'I would have come up to see her.' She swung her head quickly up and sideways. 'I'm not afraid of that lot up there. They couldn't do anything to me. I'm not afraid of any of them, but it was him. I didn't want to run into him. You understand?'

Yes, Sarah understood. She, too, looked over the side of the boat, but without leaning her arm on the rail because it was grubby and would soil her new coat. She looked for some time at the waves dashing themselves against the bows before she said, 'I've missed you an' all, Phyllis. I've thought about you nearly all the time. I've wanted to write but didn't know where to . . . How's things?'

'Oh, fine.' Phyllis now turned her back again to the river, and, supporting herself with her elbows against the rail, she nodded slowly at Sarah as she said, 'An' it's the truth, things are fine, better than I thought. I can hardly believe it, mind.' She flicked her eyes downwards. 'Still, things isn't all jam.'

'He's all right to you?'

'All? Oh, Ali's all right! I've got him there.' She twisted the forefinger of her left hand around the little finger of her right. 'I can manage him. Course he's a bit rough at times.' She pulled a knowing face. 'You know what I mean.' Noting Sarah's flushed face she laughed, and said, 'Aw, our Sarah, come off it, man, you're married . . . An' when we're on, how's things with you? Is he all right?'

Sarah wanted to say wonderful, wonderful, but she felt that her enthusiasm might in some way hurt Phyllis. Yet she seemed happy enough. But still it might, so she answered almost flippantly, 'Oh, you know, could be worse.'

'You've got your own house?'

'Yes, next door. You know, the one I told you about. We've got the kitchen and one bedroom furnished and are getting at the front room now. John, David's brother, is making us some furniture.'

'I thought he was a joiner . . . a boat joiner?'

'He is, but he can do anything with his hands and wood, it's a hobby. And he's got plenty of time now, he's on the dole.'

'On the dole! . . . One of the Hetheringtons out of work?' Phyllis was evidently surprised. 'My! I didn't think it would touch them. Anyway, how you findin' them all?'

'Oh, they're lovely. At least . . .' She pulled a face at Phyllis. 'The male members are.'

'His mother still sticky?'

'Oh, Phyllis.' Sarah now covered her mouth with her hand and closed her eyes for a second. 'I don't think I'll ever forget the day we were married and we went back and told her. Honestly . . . You know she's a quiet woman, I told you; you wouldn't think she would ever lose her temper, all dignified like, you know. Well, you know something?' She leaned towards her sister, and it was as if they were on the bed again in the back bedroom. 'I thought she was going to hit me, I did, honest. I've never seen anyone get into such a rage. You know how Mrs Cartwell used to go mad and break things around the house and throw them into the yard. Well, she went on just like her. It was an eye-opener. I thought she would be stiff, and cold and on her high-horse, but I never dreamed she'd act like that. I think she shocked

146

David an' all. He looked flabbergasted. He expected her to go off the deep end an' all but not in that way. It put the damper on our time in Newcastle, and she never spoke to me for a fortnight. I don't think she would have spoken even yet if David hadn't stopped going in; that made her come round.'

'Is she all right now?'

'She is, on the surface. But you know, Phyllis, somehow I think she'll never forgive me. I've got to be so careful. You see, when David stopped going in, the men started to come into our place, Dan, and John, and even the father; but now that things are all right – at least, as I said, on the surface – they still keep coming in . . . Oh, I like it.' She smiled at Phyllis. 'It's lovely to have them all there, and Dan's a lad, he keeps us in stitches. But the awful thing is now, she's started to knock through. You see, our kitchen fireplace and their living-room fireplace are back to back and she must have heard us all laughing the other night, for there came a rat-tat on the back of the grate. Oh, Mr Hetherington was vexed. I've never seen him so vexed. And you know, one night last week he said to me, "Can I smoke, Sarah?" Just like that, he asked me could he smoke. Do you know where he's got to smoke?'

'In the lav!'

'No. She won't allow it there; he's got to use the shed at the bottom of the yard. She's never let him smoke in the house. That's why David or Dan don't smoke. John does, in his own place. When he asked me I said, "Of course, fancy asking." And when he said to me, "I shan't make a habit of it, only now and again," do you know, I could have cried, Phyllis. I like him, I like him better than I did at first. The twitch in his eyes got on my nerves, but now I don't notice it.'

'Her and Ali's father would make a pair. He tried to put me there.' Phyllis pressed her thumb into the palm of her hand. 'But I let him see just how far he could go. He runs a boardin' house, you know, and he thought he'd got some cheap labour in me, but he found his mistake out. He's as mean as muck. But Ali's got ideas . . . What d'you think we're going to do, Sarah? . . . Start a shop. Oh, I wish this wasn't comin'.' She patted the front of her coat, and Sarah exclaimed, 'Oh, I'd forgotten. You're not showing, how are you feeling?'

'All right now. I felt lousy at first.'

'But this shop, what kind? Oh, it would be lovely if you could start a shop.'

'Well, it'll be a sort of café. There's money in it, 'cause even if it's only tea and buns people've got to eat. Eeh, the men that's out of work around us, from the boats, it makes you frightened. It's worse down here than our end was, and that was bad enough, God knows . . . That's why' – her voice was excited – 'I'd love a café, 'cos food's the most important thing in life. It is, you know; you've only got to see them looking hungry and you know damn well just how import . . .'

As the ferry bumped against the North Shields pier Phyllis stopped talking, and for the first time looked rather helplessly at Sarah and asked, 'What we going to do? Have you got to get back?'

'No, not until tea-time. Let's go for a walk and have a cup of tea somewhere.'

'Aw, I'd like that.'

In the murky half-light of the December afternoon they walked through the dull streets talking, talking, talking. When in the main thoroughfare they came across a cafe that looked a . . . bit posh, they went shyly in, and over the elegance of a set tea with toasted tea-cakes and cream buns they laughed and giggled with the excitement of two girls let out on their own for the first time.

It wasn't until the ferry was half-way across the darkened water nearing South Shields again that their chatter trailed away, and they stood silently side by side, their arms touching, looking towards the unseen waterfront picked out with meagre lighting along its jumble-scarred length.

'Look.' Phyllis was fumbling in her bag now. 'I want you to give this to me mother for Christmas.' She handed Sarah two pound notes, and Sarah said, 'All that? Can you afford it?'

'Oh, aye. I look after number one.' The remark sounded as if it came from a woman versed in the ways of handling men, or riddling pockets, of demanding pay packets. But Phyllis wasn't like that; she was still a young girl, at least so she looked to Sarah, a short pink-and-white, doll-faced young girl.

'She'll be grateful for it, Phyllis.'

'Tell her it's for herself, mind. I'd burn it if I thought he'd get his chaps on it . . . Do you know how much Ali gives me a week, just to run the house with odds and ends, because we mainly feed downstairs?'

Sarah shook her head now.

'Three pounds. He said once we get the café going he'll double it.'

'Three pounds!' Sarah exclaimed.

Three pounds for odds and ends. Why, David's whole wage was only two pounds seventeen and she had thought that marvellous. She said to Phyllis, 'By! You're lucky!'

In the darkness Phyllis turned from her towards the rail, and her voice had a flat far-away sound as she said, 'Yes, yes, I'm lucky. An' I'm all right, Aye, I'm all right.' It was as if she was confirming a statement in her own mind. 'There's only one thing I can't stand.' In the darkness she swung round to Sarah and caught at her hand, and her voice cracked as she said, 'I feel a beast, Sarah, a proper swine 'cos Ali's good. He's better than any of them up there. I know that, I do. But . . . but it turns me stomach up when we walk down King

Street or through the market. It's all right in our quarter, it doesn't matter, 'cos there's other white girls there. Some of them's tarts, but one or two's nice. One girl's from High Jarrow. So it doesn't matter there. But going down King Street I want to yell at them . . . people who look at me: "Keep your pity for yoursel', missus!" I want to say. You know something, Sarah? You know the Howards that live in Duxham Street, you know when all the schemozzle was on a few years ago about the girl having a bairn to her brother . . . well, she didn't know whether it was her brother or her father, you remember? Well, you know, I always felt sorry for her and I've always spoken to her on the road when we passed. Well, what do you think the bitch did? We were in the market and she cut me as dead as a doornail. Do you know, I almost threw me basket at her. I was so flaming mad.'

'Oh, Phyllis! Perhaps you imagined it. Oh, our Phyllis!' Sarah's compassion brought the tears into her voice.

'Don't be daft; you don't imagine things like that. An' the others told me they've all had to go through it. But most of 'em can go back and see their folks . . . Oh, Sarah!' She was holding tightly to Sarah's hands. 'I wish we could be together, or we lived nearer, so I could pop in.'

There was a new kind of pain tearing through Sarah now. She wanted to say wholeheartedly, 'Well, don't you be daft. Come whenever you like;

151

you'll be welcome, you know that.' And if she was speaking for herself Phyllis would be welcome. She would have even let her bring the Arab with her – she couldn't think of the man as Phyllis's husband. But there was David to think of. No, it wasn't David she was thinking about – David had said everybody must do what they felt driven to do. He had added lovingly at this point that he had felt driven to marry her. No, it wasn't David she was thinking about, it was his mother. She had hurt his mother very much, she realised that. Deep within herself she felt guilty. She felt she had forced herself into her family, and Mrs Hetherington fed this impression. So she couldn't make matters worse at this stage by asking her sister into her house. If they hadn't lived next door to David's mother she would have managed it somehow, but asking Phyllis up would be like asking her into the Hetheringtons' living-room. She couldn't do it – but oh, she wished she could. She gripped Phyllis's hands as she said, 'Look, we'll get together, make a habit of meeting, and I'll bring me mother with me sometime. What do you say?'

'I'd love that . . . You know, Sarah, you can come to our place if you wouldn't mind. I've the two rooms at the top done nice. You'd be surprised at the things I've got. But . . . but don't come on a Friday.' It was as if Sarah had already accepted the invitation. 'Friday's their Sunday, you know. You wouldn't believe it, you talk about the Catholics being religious . . . Coo! They couldn't hold a candle to Ali's people. His father's a big noise in their kind of church . . . they're Moslems. They're always prayin' all times of the day, you wouldn't believe it, an' yet the old devil – Ali's father, I mean – bleeds his own folk white!' She pushed at Sarah. That's funny, isn't it? Bleeding them white! . . . They want me to become a Moslem.'

Sarah was aghast, 'But you're not!'

'No, I'll not. Not that it makes any difference; I was never affected by our church as you were, it just slid off me. Hell fire if you missed mass on Sunday. Who do they think they're kiddin'! You know, Sarah, you learn a lot by mixin' with other people. Still, I'd have to learn a lot more afore I became a Moslem.' She was laughing now and punching Sarah on the arm. And her laughter began to rise until Sarah said, 'Be quiet, our Phyllis, you'll raise the boat.' She wanted to slap her sister to stop her laughing because the sound was painful, it wasn't real laughter; it was the kind of laugh you laugh to stop crying.

As the boat once again bumped against the quay she gripped Phyllis by the arm and together they walked over the gangway and up the rough road to the market-place.

As the clock struck five Sarah exclaimed, 'Eeh! David will be in and he'll wonder what on earth's happened to me. No tea ready.'

'You didn't tell him you were meetin' me?'

'Yes, yes, I did.' Sarah made the lie sound convincing. 'But you know what they are for their tea. There's the tram in, Phyllis, I'd better catch it.'

They stood peering at each other in the dim light; then, their arms around each other, they held together tightly for a moment before turning away without further words . . .

All the way home Sarah wanted to cry. She kept saying over and over in her mind, Oh, our Phyllis. Oh, our Phyllis.

When she alighted at the bottom of the street there was David standing waiting for her. He came forward at a bound, saying, 'Where on earth have you been? I've been worried stiff. Look, it's quarter to six, the house all in darkness. Where've you been?'

'Oh, I'm sorry I am, David. I'll get your tea directly.'

He had her by the arm hurrying her up the street. 'It's not my tea I'm worrying about woman.' He shook her. 'You've never been out before and there was no note or anything; I didn' know what to think.'

Sarah suddenly felt warm, wanted . . . she belonged. She dropped her head on to her shoulder and hunched it up against him as she said, 'Don't worry, I'll never run away.'

He patted her cheek before saying, 'But I do worry . . . and about you running away.'

'You're joking.'

'No, no I'm not.'

They were at the front door now. 'But you must be, David.'

'Get yourself in.' He pushed her playfully from behind. Then when the door was closed and they stood in the black darkness of the passage he groped at her and, pulling her into his arms, kissed her. It was a long hard kiss, and when he was finished he said, 'Always leave a note, will you?'

'Yes, David.' His deep concern at her absence puzzled her, she couldn't fully understand it. If he had been a little irritable, or chastised her in a jocular way, or even sulked, not that David would ever sulk, but if he had taken any of these attitudes she would have understood it, but that he was really frightened that she wouldn't come back was something that she couldn't take in because it put value on her beyond her worth, at least the worth she placed on herself. Now if the boot were on the other foot and she was concerned about him walking out on her, well she could have understood that plainly, because she knew that compared to David she was very ignorant. She wondered sometimes how he put up with her ignorance. She was doing her best to improve, she had even asked him to get her books, but she could never see herself conversing with David other than on personal topics. She would never be like

May, able to hold her own, even argue with John or Dan about unemployment and politics. Yes, she could have understood it if the boot were on the other foot.

When the gas was lit in the kitchen it showed the fire banked down and almost out, and she hurried forward, saying, 'Eeh! I'll never let this happen again. I don't know what I was thinking about.'

'Don't worry.'

'But I am. And no tea ready for you. The time just flew.' She straightened her back from the fire, and turning to him, said, 'I haven't told you where I've been.'

'It doesn't matter.'

'I've been to see our Phyllis.'

He swung round towards her. 'You've been into Costerfine Town . . . to the house?' His voice held concern again.

'No, no, I got a letter from her by the second post. She asked me to meet her on the ferry. We went across to North Shields. I didn't know whether to tell you or not.' She drooped her head. 'I thought if I did you might stop me, and I wanted to see her because . . . because she's a good girl really. She's not bad, our Phyllis, she's only a child yet.'

'Oh, Sarah.' He was enfolding her again now. 'I wouldn't have stopped you. The only thing is I hate you going around the lower docks and that quarter on your own. It's pretty rough round there, you know, at all times, and' – he pummelled gently round her chin with his fist – 'you're an eyecatcher in any port.'

'Oh, David, I'm not. You stretch it.' She laughed, raising her brows at him. 'You forget I've been going back and forwards into Shields since I was fourteen.'

'Perhaps, but you didn't look . . . well . . . like you do now . . . happy. You're more than fetching, Mrs Hetherington, when you're happy.'

'Am I?' She slanted her eyes up to the ceiling as if thinking. 'Well, I'm not to blame, it's all your fault . . . Oh, David. Darlin' . . .'

They sprung apart as if cleaved by a chopper when there came a voice from the backyard and a knocking on the back door. 'Are you in?'

As David withdrew the bolt Sarah applied herself madly to the fire. No fire on, no tea ready . . . his mother would have to come in at this minute.

'I've been round three times this afternoon. You've just got in?'

Sarah turned from the fire. She was still wearing her outdoor coat and she muttered hastily, 'Yes, yes, I was held up.'

'She's been looking round the shops for Christmas boxes, got fascinated with the bargains and forgot the time.'

Mary Hetherington was looking at the table covered with a chenille cloth and no sign of food on it. Then, looking at the fire, she remarked coolly, 'It'll be some time before you'll get anything going on that; the tea's still on the table indoors, you'd better come in and have it.' Then, looking at David she added, 'I suppose you're ready for it with not a bite since dinner-time.' On this she went quietly out.

Sarah and David exchanged glances, and as Sarah saw him make a gesture towards his mother's back that meant refusal she quickly raised her hand, then called, 'We'll be in in a minute.' She pushed at David as she whispered now, 'You go on. I'll just put some sticks on and get it going. I'll follow you.'

'No, no, I'll see to it. I'm not going to be . . .'

She swung him about and pushed him out of the kitchen, saying, 'Go on. Go on.'

When she had closed the door on him she stood with her back to it looking towards the dead fire, but she felt as warm as if it was ablaze and its flames were lapping the heat towards her. If David had to choose between her and his mother there was no doubt which side he would be on. She knew that when a man married the cord was not always cut between him and his mother, and if the wife went to snap it she was in for trouble. But in this case it was his mother who had snapped the cord. Yet there was a part of her that felt sorry about the severance. She didn't want any upset. She didn't want David to have to take sides.

She wanted him to want his mother; not as much as he wanted her, but to want her nevertheless. She wanted them all to be happy and jolly together because she was happy. Life was being wonderful to her, and, oh God, she was thankful. As her mind uttered the word God she turned her glance quickly round the kitchen as if to reassure herself she was alone, then, dropping quickly on to her knees by the side of David's chair, she buried her face in her hands and began to pray, asking God, as always, to overlook her past sins and to recognise her marriage. She followed this up with a prayer of thanksgiving, praying in her own way, her words bereft of any supplication. She made no pleas for future happiness, she only thanked God for giving her David.

And as she rose from her knees she thought of Sunday morning and muttered aloud, 'I'll go to Jarrow mass, early. They know nothing about me there.'

Only once since her marriage had she been to Tyne Dock church and she had come out feeling like the scarlet woman herself, and she knew that she couldn't sit under the gaze of Father O'Malley ever again.

She turned down the gas and was about to move out of the kitchen when she stopped and looked around. It had been a funny day. Funny things happened to people, perhaps they always had. But as you got older you became more aware of them. She had been to North Shields with Phyllis and walked countless streets, talking, talking, talking. David had met her off the tram and had nearly carried her into the house and had wanted to make love to her in the passage. Her body shivered deliciously at the thought. And then his mother had come in and brought with her bleak condemnation. And just a minute ago she had gone on her knees and prayed. She had never gone on her knees in the day-time before, unless she was in church . . . Yes, it had been a funny day.

She locked the door leading into the yard, and when she went to open the back door into the lane it was pushed inwards and she was confronted with John's broad back. He swung round towards her, his bulk only discernible in the reflection of the lamp from the bottom of the lane. His body stood within the shadow of the wall, but she could make out the chair he held in front of him.

'I've just finished this one,' he said.

'Oh, I've been out. There was no tea ready. Your mother came round and said we must go in for tea. I've locked up; will I let you in?' She was gabbling.

'Well, I'll only have to take it back, I'm not leaving it in the yard. Don't you want to see it?'

'Oh yes, yes, John.' She rushed back up the yard, unlocked the door and held it open for him, and he moved past her into the kitchen and placed the chair by the side of the table.

'There, what do you think?' He was looking at her.

'Oh, it's lovely.' The words were slow in admiration. 'I've never seen any like it, with a carved back.'

'Sit in it and see how it feels.'

She sat down and moved her ribs into the curve, then wriggled her body in the seat. 'It's lovely, and so comfortable. Oh, thanks, John. But you shouldn't go on wasting your time making these. You've done us the table, that's enough.' She got to her feet and put her hand on the top rail.

'I don't think it's a waste of time.' He was looking at the chair. 'Chairs are the most difficult things to do, more so than a table. A chair knows it's going to be sat on; it's a personal thing, a chair.' He touched its back and moved his fingers across the grained wood to within an inch of hers.

'Nice feel wood, hasn't it? Clean, nothing underhand about wood.'

She looked at him. He was waiting for her eyes. They hadn't been alone together but once since she was married. She felt nervous, even slightly afraid, of what she couldn't say. There came to her the memory of the night when she had wanted to fall on his breast and cry. She moved quickly and said, 'Eeh! I'll have to be getting next door or I'll be in the black books. Are you staying?'

'If you don't mind.' His eyes were still on her.

'Have you had your tea?'

'Yes, I've had my tea, but I'll stay until you come back. I want to have a talk with Davie. But don't let on to the old lady I'm here.' He smiled. 'It wouldn't do, would it?'

She shook her head. They were like conspirators now. She moved towards the door, but felt compelled to turn and look at him again. His eyes never seemed to have left her. She said quietly, 'Thanks for the chairs, John.'

'It's nothing,' he said. As she turned away again his voice came at her. 'You know what I'm going to do when I get me dole this week?' She looked over her shoulder waiting. 'I'm going to get blind drunk. I'm going to bust the lot, every penny, and I'm going to roll in next door and lie on the couch snoring.'

She couldn't laugh. She knew that he wouldn't get drunk on his dole. She knew that he would never lie on his mother's couch snoring, as much as he might want to. He just said these things, he said them to her often, these things, apropos of nothing that had gone before, to hold her attention, to keep her looking at him. At first she had not known how to meet these moods – they were like the tantrums of a precocious child – and she had remained silent and embarrassed on the spate of his words, but on this occasion she put them in their place by saying, 'A raw egg in tea is a very good thing for a hangover.'

She was closing the back gate as she heard his

laugh. It was high and mirthless, of the same quality as Phyllis's had been on the ferry.

It had been an odd day.

2

'Have you tried Palmers' lately?' said Dan.

'Aye.' John lowered himself further into the couch by letting out a deep breath.

'No good?'

'No good.'

'I thought since the N.S.S. had taken it over things had looked up. I heard they had a number of ships ordered.'

'Aye, they have; and they've got a number of men to do the work and they're sitting tight. They'll drop down dead on the job before they'll take a day off sick, that's what fear will do to you . . . But, look, don't worry about me, Dan. Stop it, man, will you?' John hoisted himself up straight again. 'You're like an old hen. Isn't he, Sarah?'

Sarah was working at a side table, her arms deep in a batch of dough, mixing, turning, kneading. She looked relaxed, completely at ease. She turned and smiled, not at John in particular but at the three men sitting around the fire. Her eyes coming to rest on David, his long legs stretched out on the fender, her smile widened, and he said to her, 'Are you ready for more water?'

'No, I've got enough, I don't want to drown the miller.'

'You can't kid me,' said Dan, 'you're worried. Why not admit it and stop acting the big fellow. It stands to reason, everybody's worried. Even with the Palmers' little boom on, people are not spending like they used to, they're frightened. And who's to blame them? You know, some of them on the dole are spending as much on groceries as those in work. I had a talk about this to a woman, a Mrs Robinson – she's been a customer of ours for years. She admitted it. She said they were clearing up the rent and clubs and things because when the next bad spell comes they'd be able to run up again. But if they didn't pay up now they'd get short shrift if they ever wanted tick again. And, as she said, you may be sure they'd want it again. It's an awful look-out, you know.'

'Don't,' said John bitterly now. 'It makes me want to go berserk. We're back a hundred years ago, man. There's riots breaking out all over the country, and fellows being jailed. Nothing changed in a hundred years. The men marched from Hebburn and Shields to Jarrow in those days to be at a Trade Union meeting and what happened? Seven of 'em were sentenced to death. It was changed to transportation. Lads who were

God-fearing, peace-loving individuals, Primitive Methodists . . . Not that I carry any flag for Primitive Methodists, but all they and the others wanted to do was to work and eat.'

John was sitting forward now addressing Dan loudly as if this young uncle of his was the cause of all the past and present trouble. 'Young lads under twelve kept at work for twenty-four hours at a stretch they were then.'

'But that was in the pits . . .' Dan began, but was shouted down again by John crying, 'Pits or shipyards or steel mills or puddling mills, what does it matter on a twenty-four hour-stretch? It shouldn't 'ave been tolerated. And it's as bad today in a way. How do they expect a man to live? Twenty-six shillings to keep three of us. Two shillings to keep a child! Did you ever hear anything like it? And if I hadn't been working full time these last years I wouldn't be getting that. How about the poor devils who haven't had thirty contributions on their cards in the last two years or so. I tell you it's a bloody scandal.'

'Look, John, calm down and fight your own battles for the moment. As you stand now you could be off for seventy-four weeks and still get benefit . . .'

'Seventy-four weeks! My God, man, do you want me to land up in the loony bin in the Institution . . . Look, Dan. Don't you start talking as if they were being kind to me. Every man Jack of us is up afore them every eleven weeks and our money could be stopped like that.' He cracked his thick fingers and the sound was like the meeting of drumsticks. 'There's a clause called "the not genuinely seeking work clause". Have you heard of it?' His voice was sarcastic. 'You want to get into that queue, Dan, and hear just how those boys behind the wire grids with their smug gobs can manoeuvre it.'

'They're not to blame, John. They're just doing their job.'

They all turned and looked at David now. He was speaking quietly, his eyes directed towards the fire. 'Phil Taggart in the Exchange said he would be out of it tomorrow, but it would just mean him standing on the other side of the grid.'

'Phil Taggart!' John's voice was scornful. 'He's just one; you want to see the attitude of most of those swine. They look at you as if you'd just crawled up the wire. "Stand aside." "Come back this afternoon." "What did you say your number was?" ' John's voice had taken up a haughty tone. Then it changed abruptly back as he said, 'There'll be riots I tell you, men can only stand so much.'

Yes, there would be riots. If all the men were like John there would be riots all the time, Sarah thought as she turned the dough over for the last time. Lack of work, resulting in enforced idleness, broken only by miles of tramping in search of the elusive job, had taken the spunk out of most of the men. She remembered the men two or three years ago standing at the corners, talking loudly, protest oozing out of them, aggressive against misfortune. Now they still stood at the corners, but they were more quiet, their talk intermittent. Some of them walked slower. Their faces had a pale-yellow tinge. They hoarded Woodbine ends in small tin boxes. Some of them pushed home-made barrows down to the tip at the bottom of Simonside Bank and scraped there for cinders and came around the doors selling them; a shilling they would ask for a barrow-load. She always bought a load. There were six buckets to the barrow. They were burnt-out cinders and wouldn't burn on their own, but they did all right for banking down. One man had called twice last week. He did not ask her to buy the second time, he just stood looking helplessly at her. She hadn't wanted the second load but she had taken it and said, 'Would you like a flat cake? It's just out of the oven?' 'Oh, missis!' was all he had said, but his lips became soft with saliva. It was the first time she had been addressed as 'missis', and it made her feel married and very adult.

Then there was David. David worried about the unemployed. He always had apparently, but now his concern was centred around John. He was very fond of John. He didn't agree with half he said and argued with him, but nevertheless she knew from the way he talked that he thought a lot of his elder brother. He said John was the last person on earth who should be out of work, it would do something to him. Unemployment was like a personal insult to a man of his calibre. John, he said, would die protesting. He was made like that . . .

Tomorrow was New Year's Eve, the last day of nineteen twenty-nine. She had decided to get her baking done tonight so that tomorrow she would only have the cleaning to do. Everything must be polished and shining with an extra brightness to greet the New Year. Everybody everywhere – to her everywhere was a synonym for the North – cleared up for New Year's Day. She wanted to be all done before tea-time because they were going to spend the evening next door. Apparently they had a lot of jollification on New Year's Eve, and also apparently without getting drunk. But this was the one night, she understood, when David's mother allowed wine in the house. Also for this night she brewed a batch of home-brewed beer, the recipe for which she would tell no one, and which had a kick Dan said that was better than any Burton and as good as some whiskies. She was a strange woman was David's mother, Sarah thought, and a frightening woman in some ways. She had decided on one thing: she wouldn't sing tomorrow night, not even if they pressed her, because she knew that her mother-in-law didn't like her to sing – not on her own. She had gone out of the room when she had sang last time. It was

'Where my caravan has rested', and they had all praised her – all except David's mother.

As she put a cloth over the dough David rose from his chair and lifted the heavy earthenware dish down on to the fender. John was still at it; he was thrusting his finger at Dan now and saying, 'We'll be marching from here, you'll see. It's the only way to get things done. The Scots did it last year, they're not the blokes to sit down under injustice. They've been marching and protesting since nineteen twenty-two.'

'The N.U.W.M. got up the national march last year, don't forget that,' said Dan. 'You don't have to be a dour Scot to get things done. They made the Tories consider the "Not genuinely seeking work clause" that you're on about; they didn't get it abolished but they got another year's grace. And it was prophetic that only a few weeks later the Tories were out . . .'

'Well, for all the good the change has done they might as well have stayed in, for Ramsay MacDonald and Snowdon are still carrying on the same policy; they make my belly heave. Once the Labour Government got in it was going to play hell with a big stick. And it's done bug . . .' On a warning look from David, John just suppressed the adjective and substituted 'damn all' in its place.

The little incident caught at Dan's sense of humour. The heat of the discourse, the added

169

colour that rose to John's face with the suppression of the word bugger was too much; he put his head back and let out a bellow of a laugh.

'You . . . you big stiff!' John's great arm knocked Dan sideways on the couch. 'You can laugh.' But now John's laughter had joined Dan's. And Dan's finger came out and wagged itself in John's face while with the other arm he gripped himself around the waist to ease the pain that his merriment was causing. The next moment the two men were locked together sparring like irrepressible schoolboys.

'Give over, give over, you fools!' David was standing above them. 'You'll break the couch, the pair of you.' He jumped aside as they fell sideways on to the floor and there, locked together, they lay panting and still laughing.

'You pair of fools!' David, himself laughing now, was staring down at them where they both sat with their backs to the seat of the couch, their legs stretched out on the mat.

'That takes us back some years.' John had his head turned to Dan, and Dan, rubbing his wet face with his hand, said, 'By! It does that. We used to have some fun and games, didn't we?' As they hitched themselves back on to the couch, Dan took a fit of coughing which caused him to press his hand across his chest.

David, turning now to where Sarah was rubbing fat into flour preparatory to making pastry, and herself laughing at the antics of these men acting like young lads, said eagerly, 'What about us throwing a bit of a party, eh, Sarah?'

Her hands stopped their rubbing. 'A party! Oh, yes. Oh yes, I'd like that. When?' They were all looking at her. 'What about Thursday?' she said. They continued to look at her but no one spoke. John was the first to look away. He cast his eyes sideways towards Dan and then said on a small laugh, 'Well, what about Thursday?'

Dan got to his feet, pulling his coat straight, saying as he did so, 'Not Thursday, Sarah.'

'Oh no.' She nodded her head. She had forgotten, Dan always went to stay with a friend of his on Thursday. She could understand Dan having lots of friends. She had never seen this friend. Apparently he lived at yon side of Westoe village. Perhaps he had a wife, she didn't know. David hadn't seemed to know much about it when she had asked him about Dan's friend some time ago. Impetuously she said now, 'Why don't you bring your friend along, Dan? Shouldn't he, David?'

Dan's head came up quickly. He had been dusting the legs of his trousers and now his hands were held outwards as if the question had fixed him in one position. There was a look of perplexity on his face, until he turned his gaze full on David and smiled at him. Then, moving towards the scullery door and coming abreast of Sarah, he

171

said quietly, 'Make it Friday and we'll have a night of it.'

When the door closed quietly John turned to David, and speaking below his breath, he said, 'Do you mean to say you haven't told her?'

'I didn't see the need.' There was an unusually sharp note in David's reply.

John turned his head and looked at Sarah now, and she looked at him as he said, 'Well, she's a married woman and she won't faint, and, being Sarah, she'll understand, won't you, Sarah?'

'Understand what?'

'About Dan. You see . . .'

'I'll tell her, John. If it's necessary, I'll tell her.'

'All right, have it your own way, but it would have saved an embarrassing situation if she had known already, wouldn't it? But that's you.' He brought his fist in a quick flick past the end of David's nose. Then he screwed his face up at him and moved across the room. 'Goodnight, Sarah.' His voice was quiet now.

'Goodnight, John.'

When the back door had closed, Sarah, scraping the flour and fat from her hands, looked over her shoulder and asked, 'What was all that about, about Dan? Is there something wrong?'

'Really it's none of our business, it's Dan's business.'

'Did I put my foot in it in some way?'

'No.' He caught at her floured hand and pulled

172

her towards him, pressing her down into the big leather chair at the side of the fireplace. Then, seated himself on a cracket close to her knee and looking to where the rising dough was pushing against the cloth, he said, 'Dan's got a woman.'

Dan with a woman! Sarah couldn't believe it. Dan the kindly, jocular, nice man, carrying on with a woman! He wasn't the type. She made David look at her as she said, 'I just can't take that in.'

'It's true. But it's his own business; it's Dan's own life and he can do what he likes with it.'

'Yes, yes, I know, David. Yes.' She was quick to agree with him. 'But somehow – well, Dan just doesn't seem . . . Is she married?'

'No.'

'She's not? Well, why doesn't he marry her?'

'It's very difficult to explain.' David took hold of her hand again. 'It sounds a bit fantastic, but you know different people think in different ways and some people think for themselves. Dan does, and apparently this woman does too. She's a widow and as far as I can gather she's glad to be a widow, as she had a pretty rough time during the six years she was married to her husband. He was killed by a lorry and the firm was found to be at fault and she gets a small pension. Perhaps this is a bit of the reason for her independence. Well, anyway, she doesn't want to marry and neither does Dan.'

'Dan doesn't want to marry her?'

'No, nor nobody else. I mean Dan doesn't want to marry anybody. Dan's been serving in a shop since he was twelve. He started running errands then and he's had a sort of education against marriage through listening to women . . . at least that's how he laughingly put it to me. But he just doesn't want to marry. Anyway, he met this woman. How, I don't know, he never told me; I only know that she's got a decent kind of house and that one night in the week, Thursday night – it has never varied over the last four years – he goes and sees her.'

'But your mother . . . ?'

'Oh! There was the devil to pay. Being Dan, he was quite straight about it. But fancy having to tell a thing like that to my mother; imagine the scene; especially when she looked on him almost as a son and not a brother. You see, she had the business of bringing him up when her own mother died. Anyway, he gave her the option; he was quite willing, he said, to go and get lodgings elsewhere. He emphasised to her that he was not going to live with the woman, only see her that one night a week. Lord, he had some pluck. It all sounded fantastic and I can see how my mother thought he was going up the pole. But, anyway, she didn't tell him to get out and take his life of sin with him. And for two reasons. First, she's a saver, and a very careful housekeeper as you have gathered. She's nearly always had twice as much coming in each week as what she's spent. She could teach Micawber a thing or two.'

'Micawber?'

'Oh, he's a character in Dickens. I must get you Dickens, you'll like him . . . And then there was the fact that if she ordered Dan out he might, although he said he wouldn't, go and live with the woman, whereas if she kept him under her eye she might manage to convert him from his sinful ways. But up to date she hasn't made any impression on him. The atmosphere in the house on a Thursday morning is always painful.'

'But it's fantastic. I can't see . . . well, I can't see Dan doing it. And if he's living with her part of the time what's the difference, why doesn't he live with her all the time?'

'Don't ask me, Sarah, I just don't know. Dan has arranged his life and he has found someone to arrange it with.'

'I liked Dan.'

'Don't say it like that in the past tense, Sarah. Surely this won't stop you going on liking him. Dan's a fine fellow.'

'But it's a bit of a shock. Dan doesn't look . . .'

'You can never tell by people's looks, Sarah. And see here.' He tilted her chin upwards, his voice holding a note which she had never heard before. 'You are not going to make any difference to Dan, I mean in your manner; I wouldn't like that, Sarah.'

'No, no, of course not.' She smiled at him now. 'It was just . . . well, just as I said. I . . . I couldn't see Dan doing anything like that. But don't worry, I'll be the same to him. And why should I make any difference?' She shook her head. 'I've got no room to speak. Look at our Phyllis. And she's nice and all. I've always told you our Phyllis is nice.'

'There you are then.' They were smiling at each other. He leant towards her now. 'And you're nice, too, Mrs Hetherington. Very, very, very nice. Do you know that, Mrs Hetherington?'

The niceness was inside her, she could feel it. David could make her feel that she was nice. She felt a different person when she was with David, soft inside, even refined. Yes, even refined. She had always longed to be refined, to know what to say, to know what to do. She had always felt she would never reach this desired pinnacle, not only because she was ignorant but because she didn't look refined, at least her body didn't, it was too big – the word was voluptuous. She had looked that up in the dictionary David had bought her. He bought it for her the very next day after she had told him she had always wanted a dictionary. He had seemed very pleased that she had wanted a dictionary.

David was looking at her now. She knew the look and she became quiet. She remained quiet when he rose swiftly from the cracket and went

nd put the bolt in the back door. She hitched her
lips to one side and made room for him when he
returned, and he lay with his head on her
shoulder, his fingers slowly outlining her breasts.
Her lips dropped apart; they were trembling
lightly and moist. 'I've got the bread to do,' she
said in a whisper. 'I've got all my baking to get
through.'

He opened her blouse, and, supporting the large
cup of her breast on the palm of his hand, he said,
'I wish all men joy because of you.'

She felt more than nice; more than refined, she
felt wonderful, honoured, like a queen must feel.

3

New Year's Eve was typical, the day being made
up of a number of small busy-busy issues leading
to the climax. But when Sarah looked back on this
particular day she saw that everything she had
done had a bearing on what was to come. Like
threads of a tapestry, on which was worked the
outline pattern of her life, they began to work
inwards to the central point.

It was when she finished scrubbing the scullery
and had returned to the snug warmth of the
kitchen that she thought, I wonder how me

mother is. I should slip across, it being New Year' Eve. She'll feel it, being all on her own. And he'l be out this morning, signing on. Yes, I should sli across.

Ten minutes later she locked the scullery doo and went down the back-yard and out into th lane. The back lane was clean and empty – you very rarely saw the women of Camelia Stree standing gossiping at their back doors; it was sign of their raised status, that any gossiping the did was over a cup of tea in the afternoon afte they had . . . got the men off.

The morning was biting cold; there was a hig wind blowing that spoke of snow. Sarah felt sh could smell it. She pulled the collar of her new coa up around her ears and kept her gloved hands u under its warmth as she walked. She loved thi coat, she had never had anything like it; it wa David's Christmas box. He had paid five pound ten for it. She had played war with him. It wa dove grey, trimmed with brown fur, and it fitte her as if it had been made to measure.

Perhaps it was because her life was now spen between the sparkling cleanliness of her mother in-law's house and her own home, that the street through which she was now passing seeme dirtier than she had ever noticed them before, an the houses, although the same size as those i Camelia Street except for number one, looke smaller.

There were three men standing at the bottom of Howard Street and they looked at her but seemed shy of acknowledging her, until she remarked breezily, 'By! It's a stinger, isn't it?'

'Aye, aye, it is that. How are you getting on, Sarah?'

'Oh, fine, Mr Prideau.'

'That's the ticket, Sarah. You're looking well . . . Bonny.'

She turned her head as she passed them, smiling widely on them. People were nice, people were kind.

'Happy New Year, Sarah. Happy New Year.'

The combined voices turned her head towards them again and she called back, her mouth wide and laughing, 'Happy New Year to you an' all. Happy New Year.'

Mrs West from number seven was doing her windows, and Mrs Young was doing her step. It was late to do steps this time in the morning; still it was New Year's Eve and all the work was topsy-turvy.

The two women stopped what they were doing and waited for her approach. 'Hello, Sarah. Goin' to see your mother?' Mrs West nodded her head at her.

'Yes.' She nodded back, then turned to Mrs Young. 'Hello, Mrs Young.'

'Hello, Sarah, lass. By! Isn't it cold!'

'Freezing.'

'How's things going?' Mrs West was poking her head forward, speaking in a confidential whisper

'Oh, fine, Mrs West, fine.'

'You like it up there?'

'I couldn't help but, could I?'

'No, I suppose not. Anyway, I'm glad to see you've fallen on your feet. Your mother can be proud of you, at least.'

Sarah turned from Mrs West again. She would have to say that, digging at their Phyllis. She said quickly, 'How are you keeping, Mrs Young?'

'Fine, lass, fine. But I won't say I wouldn't be better if they were at work. Still, you never know what the New Year'll bring, do you?'

'No, Mrs Young.' Sarah knocked on the front door, and as she heard the steps approaching on the other side she said, 'I wish you a Happy New Year in case I don't see you again.'

'The same to you, lass.'

'A Happy New Year, Mrs West.' She nodded to the other woman.

'The same to you, Sarah. The same to you.'

Annie was surprised to see her, but the light that spread over her face showed her pleasure. 'Why, lass, I didn't expect you across the day.' She spoke as if Sarah was in the habit of visiting every day. She went before her through the front room and into the kitchen, talking quickly. 'I've just made a cup of tea, I must have known you were comin'. haven't done me baking yet, I was just about to

180

start. Sit down, sit down, lass. By! You're looking well. Is that a new coat? It's bonny . . . a beauty.'

'David brought it for my Christmas box.'

She hadn't seen her mother since three days before Christmas when she had given her Phyllis's money and a pound of her own.

Sarah watched her mother pouring the tea out. Her hands were shaking slightly, and she spilled the tea into the saucers, exclaiming on her awkwardness as she did so. Sarah glanced around the kitchen. Everything looked clean but not with the sparkle of her own house. She said, 'You're all done, I see.'

'Yes. Yes, I thought I might as well get it over with. Yet I ask meself, what for?' Annie sat down suddenly opposite to Sarah. Her hand was still on the teapot. She looked at her daughter for a long moment before saying, 'Oh, I'm glad to see you; I felt the house would be empty all the day. You notice it more on New Year's Eve and I was dreading twelve o'clock. We always sat up, didn't we, me and you and Phyllis, and saw the New Year in. But it'll be different this year.'

Sarah felt a lump rise to her throat. Yes, it would be different for them both. As her mother had said, they had always seen the New Year in; their father never sat up. Not given to drink or merriment of any kind, he saw no point in it. His logic on the matter had always been: it's just another day so why kid yourself? And he had usually left them with this sentiment, but slightly more embellished.

She said to her mother now, 'Are you going to sit up?'

'Well, I always have, lass. It's like a habit. Mrs Young has asked me next door but I don't think I'll go.'

'Why not? Go on.'

'I like me own fireside. You know what it is on a New Year's Eve. Everybody should be at their own fireside.'

Sarah hesitated only a moment, then she said, 'Why don't you come across to us? You've never been. You'll have to come some time. Come on.' She leant forward and caught her mother's hands.

'Ooh, no, lass, no, I wouldn't dream of it. I don't know them.'

'But you've met David that once, and you said you liked him.'

'Yes, yes, I do. I think he's a fine fellow. But no, no, lass. But mind' – she nodded her head at her daughter – 'I'm glad you asked me, and I won't forget it. But don't worry about me.' She straightened herself up in the chair. 'I'm all right now that I've seen you.'

'I tell you what.' Sarah's voice was eager, her attitude like that of an excited child. 'Are you sure you're going to sit up?'

'Yes, lass, yes, I'll sit up.'

'Then I'll come across about half-past twelve

and wish you a Happy New Year.' Their hands were joined again. It was as if some great problem had been solved. Their hands still holding, they got to their feet and Sarah said, 'That's what I'll do.'

'But, look, you haven't drunk your tea.'

'Oh no.' Sarah took up the cup.

'Oh, I'd love that, lass. Do you think you'd be able to get away?'

'Oh yes. David will run over with me.'

In the middle of the front room Sarah stopped and, turning to her mother, asked quietly, 'But what if he stays up the night, you being on your own?'

'There's very little possibility of that, lass. But if he does, well . . .' She looked around as if searching for a solution. Then she said quickly, 'Well, if he's up or if we're in next door – he was asked an' all and you never know with him – well, if that happens I'll leave the front room blind up. All right?'

'All right.' They nodded at each other then moved towards the door, but there stopped again, and Sarah, looking down at the handle round which her fingers were curved, said, 'I do miss our Phyllis. With everything I've got I still miss seeing our Phyllis . . . Oh, I'm sorry.' She looked at her mother's bent head. 'I shouldn't have mentioned her again.'

'Aw, lass, I'm glad you did. I think of her all the

time. And you know what?' Annie thrust her head forward. 'In the New Year I'm going to start going out, I'm going to take trips into Shields.' She spoke as if Shields was a long distance away instead of three miles to its centre. 'And then I'm going to look in on our Phyllis. I don't care, I'm going to look in on her. He needn't know anything about it. But now and again I'll look in on her.'

'Oh, Mother, I'm glad. Oh, I'm glad of that.'

'Well, something must be done, she can't come up here.'

'No, no, that's true. Oh, I'm glad you're going to see her.' She leant quickly foward and they kissed and clung together, not close, just holding each other's arms. Annie was crying gently now, and Sarah, fumbling with the lock, let herself out and hurried down the street. She felt sad and happy at the same time, and overall a feeling of relief. Her mother was going to see Phyllis and she too was going to see Phyllis. Yes, she would in the New Year on the quiet. She would tell David. Oh yes, she would tell David. He wouldn't stop her, but she must do it on the quiet. His mother would never forgive her if she knew she was going into a house in Costerfine Town . . .

The second thread was the arrival of Dan through her back door around twelve o'clock, long before his usual dinner hour. His face looked peaked and his voice was husky as he said, 'Oh, I'm glad you're in, Sarah. I wouldn't have known what to do with this except put it in your coal-house.' He pulled from the inside pocket of his coat a flat flask of whisky. 'It's about the only sure cure for this.' He pointed to his chest. 'It's settling here. If I have this hot and stay by the fire for half an hour or so it'll do the trick. You don't mind?'

'No, no, of course not.' She looked hard at him. But she was not seeing him as the man whose goings-on had shocked her last night in spite of her denial. She did not see him as the man who was keeping a woman, and in a very odd way. He was just Dan, who was nice. She said, 'Sit yourself down, I'll get the fire going. You've had this cold coming on for nearly a week, why haven't you done something about it?'

'Oh, Mary wanted to put me to bed, but I thought I could work it off. I hate to be away from the shop. Young George is all right, he can carry on, but the girl and the lad are new to it. Just started this past month, and Friday and Saturday are our busiest days. But I felt I had to come away this morning, I thought I was going to pass out. I told the old man.'

'You should be in bed.' She was bustling around filling the kettle, bringing in a mug and sugar, putting more coals on the fire. 'Take your coat off,' she said, 'and I'll fill a bottle.' She bent down to the bottom cupboard and brought out a stone water-bottle.

'No, no, Sarah, I'd better not get too hot. I'll be

all right. If I'd had a hot whisky going to bed each night it would have done the trick. But you know Mary.' He sighed. 'And yet the stuff she brewed yesterday is more deadly than raw Scotch.'

She was pouring the boiling water on to the generous portion of whisky when the back door opened and a voice called, 'Are you in, Sarah?'

'Yes, yes.' She glanced quickly at Dan. 'It's May.'

'Oh, May's all right.' Dan smiled wearily.

May stood within the kitchen door. She looked smart, yet cool and distant as always. She wrinkled her nose as she said, 'What's this? Whisky?'

'Help yourself,' said Dan, pointing to the bottle. 'I had to get something for this stinking cold.'

'Well, well.' May came and sat down by the table, and, lifting up the bottle, she looked at it. 'I won't say no.' She glanced at Sarah and smiled.

It was rarely May smiled and that was a pity, Sarah thought, because she looked attractive when she smiled. And softer, oh so much softer. She said, 'You really want a drop?'

'Yes, of course. Why not? We often used to have a toddy when we were first married, late at night . . . so the smell wouldn't carry . . . How you going to get over that, Dan? She'll smell it off you.'

'I brought some mints . . . Provided for everything.' He smiled weakly.

As Sarah watched May pouring herself out a good measure of the whisky her mind lifted to the

186

room on the other side of the fireplace and it came to her with a strange feeling of sadness that Mary Hetherington was ruling an imaginary world. Within the confines of her four walls she dictated and claimed obedience, and was satisfied, at least apparently, that her family were subject to her. But did she guess, even faintly, that all of them threw off her domination once they crossed the threshold into the street? Dan with his women and his whisky – he likely had his whisky when he was with her; John with May and their toddies at night. This was only a small thing, the bigger issue there was the separate turbulent life that John and his wife led away from the narrow confines of number one. Then there was David. David most of all, she thought, had moved away from his mother's domination. Although he was still nice to her, gentle with her because that was David's nature, there was a part in him that had been set free when he had taken herself from the bottom end and married her. The only one who could not escape was the father. Yet even he tried. Yes, she could see that her mother-in-law was ruling a world that existed only within her own mind, and a part of her was unhappy for the dominant, self-satisfied woman, for this woman who would never like her.

An exclamation from May broke the trend of her thoughts and brought her eyes to the kitchen window and the dark shadow passing it.

'It's the big fellow himself, he must have smelt it.' May sniffed disdainfully, and as John entered the room she looked at her husband and said, 'Altogether like the folks of Shields. Did you smell it?'

John did not answer his wife but looked to where Dan was crouched over the fire. 'You've got it bad,' he said. 'You should be in bed.'

'This'll put me right.' Dan held up the mug.

'It'll do no such thing unless you can sweat it out of you. You'll be a damn sight worse drinking that and then going out into the blast. Have some sense, man; go on, get into bed.'

'Yes, it's the wisest thing,' said May. 'He's right. You should get yourself to bed, Dan.'

'What! On a New Year's Eve and the jollification coming up? What'll they do without me?' He grinned and inclined his head towards the back of the fireplace.

'Aw, you think too much of yourself,' said John. 'You won't be missed as long as there's Davie to play the piano. That's all that she'll want. That's all that'll be necessary.'

Dan, taking the remark the way it was meant, said, 'True, true. But all the same, I'm not going to bed. I've never been to bed on a New Year's Eve yet and I'm not going to start now. And' – his grin widened – 'what do you think I am, to miss the home brew and the port at three shillings a bottle, mind you. You must think I'm barmy!'

As they laughed, Dan, thumbing the whisky bottle, said, 'Help yourself; I'm bringing another down later. I've got to have them in flat halves so they won't bulge my coat. You never know, she could have run into me coming round the back way.'

The air of conspiracy was again to the fore. The feeling was always strong when the family were together – outside the parents' home.

May, like a practised hand, threw off the last of her whisky, then, looking up at Sarah, said, 'I just popped over to see if you would have Paul this afternoon. I want to go over to my mother's and it's too cold to take him, crossing the water and all.'

Before Sarah could reply John put in, 'I'll stay with him, I told you.'

'You're doing nothing of the sort, you're coming to my mother's. You never show your face there from one year's end to the other; in fact my family . . .' May now looked from Sarah to Dan. 'My family don't believe I've a husband.'

John's head was lowered in a bull-like attitude. He was biting on his lip but he said nothing.

Sarah said quickly, 'Oh, I'd love to have him, May. Oh yes, leave him with me.'

May rose to her feet. 'Thanks.' She smiled at Sarah. 'He likes coming over here. You wouldn't believe I found him up the back lane the other day. He was crawling on his hands and knees over Mrs

Barrett's step. He had gone to the wrong end, but he knew the house was near the end . . . Come on, big boy.' She pushed her husband sharply on the shoulder. 'Finish that up and get on your feet.' She spoke to him as if he were drunk and incapable; her tone held a deriding note. It made Sarah think, Why does she do it? She could handle him if she didn't use that voice and manner.

She watched John rise to his feet as if obedient to his wife's summons. She could not see the expression in his eyes, for his lids were lowered. He nodded towards Dan, saying abruptly, 'You look after that cold or it'll mean trouble.' Then he followed May out. He had not, Sarah noticed, said one word to her, neither hello nor goodbye. He must be in a state inside, she thought. It wasn't only not having a pay packet; it was, as David said, John needed to work.

Dan was laughing now, and his voice cracking, he said, 'That's a funny remark, you know, and everybody makes it. Take care of that cold, they say, as if it was something tender to be cherished. People say funny things.' Then, turning his body half from the fire, he asked quietly and abruptly, 'David tell you about me last night?'

The suddenness of the question took Sarah aback. She blinked and moved her head, then she made a gesture with one hand as if flapping something aside and answered, 'Yes, yes, Dan, but that's all right.'

190

'You weren't shocked?'

'No, Dan, no. That's your business. As David says, it's your business.'

'Aye, David says that, but what do you say?'

'Well' – again her hand flapped outwards – 'if you want it that way, and it's good for you . . . well then.' She paused and finished inanely, 'It's your life.'

'Yes, it's my life.' He turned towards the fire again. 'And I've arranged it as I want it. Though, let me tell you . . .' His voice was cracking more now. 'Eva wants it like that too. I'm not taking any young lass down, believe me, nor wrecking a home or spoiling a married woman's life. She's a widow, a very quiet sort, and wants no ties no more than I do.'

'All right, all right, Dan, now don't get upset. Look, it's like John said. I should go to bed if I were you.'

'I'll be all right, I'll be all right.' He lay back in the chair holding the stone water-bottle to him and closed his eyes. Sarah stood looking at him. His face looked drawn and weary, but still there was about him an attractiveness. She could understand any woman going for Dan, but she couldn't understand her not wanting to marry him. All the Hetherington men had something about them, in different ways. Yet Dan wasn't a Hetherington, was he? His name was Blyth.

A few minutes later, when the back door

opened again and David entered the house, she was scrambling round setting the table. The dinner, a hotpot, was already in the oven. She greeted David in the scullery. They held each other for a moment while they kissed, and then she whispered swiftly, 'Dan's inside. He's not well, he should be in bed. It's his cold.'

When she entered the kitchen with the dish in her hands Dan was saying, 'It's only a cold, don't worry your head. I'm sweating it out. Look, it's running down me. I've got over half an hour before I need go next door, I'll be all right. Help yourself.' He pointed.

David did not reply. He just continued to look at Dan and shake his head. Then, turning to the table, he picked up the bottle, went to the cupboard and got himself a glass and poured himself out a measure of the whisky.

She hadn't known David drank whisky. Again her thoughts turned towards the woman in the room behind the fireplace, and again she felt sad for her, sad in a strange inexplicable way.

The jollification had begun. It had got on its way around ten o'clock. Besides the family there were additions to the party. Mr and Mrs Riley from number fourteen. Mr Riley was one of the two men who worked under Mr Hetherington. And there was Mrs Riley's sister and her husband who had come down from Hartlepool for the New

Year. Then there was Mr and Mrs Ramsay from next door to Sarah. The sitting-room was crowded, and laughter filled the house, and the passage between the front room and the living-room was as busy as Newcastle station.

Already Mary Hetherington had doled out the first taste of her brew, and as usual it had been acclaimed with high praise and requests from the visitors to know the recipe. But, 'Ah! Ah!' said Mary. No-one was getting that, it would die with her. No, not even her husband knew how the brew was concocted. Nor did her brother either. Her mother had passed the recipe on to her; men had never had anything to do with it. There was high laughter at this point.

Sarah was in the kitchen beating up tinned salmon with mustard and vinegar to make up another batch of sandwiches; the first lot had vanished quicker than snow under the sun. She lifted her head from her task, her face bright and flushed with happiness, and looked at her mother-in-law who was entering the room. Mary Hetherington's face too was bright and flushed, and for the first time since she had come to know her, Sarah saw her smiling, really smiling. She looked relaxed and happy . . . in her element, as Sarah put it to herself. She said to her, 'These won't be a minute, I've got all the bread buttered.'

'That's good of you, Sarah. May could have

given you a hand, but no, May's not like that.' There returned to her face a reflection of the primness that was usual to it, and then it was gone as she asked, 'How did you like my ale?'

'Oh, I thought it was wonderful, lovely. I've never tasted anything like it. I'm not going to ask you how you make it because David said it was a secret, but oh, I wouldn't mind a drop of that every day.'

'No, no.' The tone held laughter. 'It's not for every day, it's just for special occasions. I make it once a year as my mother did, and her mother afore her. You know, my mother was a farmer's daughter from near Blanchland. Lovely country that, lovely. It was a big farm, quite an estate. She took me once to see it when I was a little girl. She knew lots of country secrets did my mother, and . . . well, my ale is one of them. I could tell anyone what I put in it but they couldn't make it. It's just wheat and barley and hops and horehound, and odds and ends, but it's the quantities and how you use them. It's like cooking; some cooks can turn cream sour.'

As if she had uttered a great witticism they both laughed. Then their laughter stopping suddenly, they looked at each other, and Mary Hetherington said, 'Don't you think it's about time you had a name for me, Sarah?'

'Oh! Oh!' Sarah wagged her head in embarrassment. She had always addressed this woman as

'Mrs Hetherington', she had not dared say, 'mother'.

Mary Hetherington turned away and began to transfer mince-pies from a tray on to a plate and her hand moved swiftly and her words kept pace with it as she said, 'Mam would be nice I think, don't you? We can't go on for ever being addressed as "Mrs Hetherington", can we? Yes, I think mam will do.' Her hand and her voice halted abruptly and she turned her head and looked at Sarah.

Sarah remained very still as she said softly, 'Yes. Oh yes, I'd like that.' It was as if an honour had been bestowed on her.

And Mary Hetherington, acting in the manner of one who had bestowed the great gift, inclined her head downwards. Then adding one more mince-pie to the plate, she said, 'Well, that's that settled,' and left the kitchen.

Sarah sighed. A smile spread slowly over her happy face; she felt her ears moving backwards with it. Wouldn't David be tickled to death. Oh, his mother . . . Mam . . . should make her brew every week. Oh, she should! She'd had a glass or two, that was evident, she was a different woman the night. Sarah gripped the bowl with her two hands and had the desire to throw it towards the ceiling. Then her body shaking with inward laughter, she applied herself frantically to the sandwiches. It was a lovely New Year's Eve, lovely.

Sarah had become conscious that David had stopped playing the piano some time before she took the two plates of sandwiches into the room. As she pushed at the door with her hip, John, standing behind it, pulled it open and, relieving her of one of the plates, whispered, 'The old man's on his feet.'

Sarah looked to where Mr Hetherington was standing on the hearth rug, his back towards the blazing fire. He had a glass in his hand and was motioning with it down to his subordinate Mr Riley, saying, 'It's true, you'll endorse it, Bill. Hope can be as dead as a doornail, but come this night and it's injected with a spark of life. Even those who have been out for years, the night they'll be thinking next year's bound to be different. Am I right?'

Mr Riley made a deep obeisance with his head. 'Yes, you're right, Stan.' There followed a rustle through the room, then silence again as they all looked towards their host. And Stan went on, 'New Year's Eve, as I said, is not an ending, it's merely a day afore a beginning, a day when you clean inside and out, a day when you see your assets mounting. This affects every man Jack the same up till the moment the clock strikes twelve. You know, nobody, at least no northerner, can be without hope on New Year's Eve; we've proved it again and again, haven't we?'

His thin chin thrust forward, Stan looked

around the company and was greeted with, 'Yes, you're right there, Stan. Aye, aye, never a truer word spoken.' And then they waited once again for him to go on as if they were enjoying it.

It seemed to Sarah as if Mr Hetherington was doing a turn. She looked towards David, but he was looking at his father. She looked quickly towards John, and John was looking towards her and he indicated with a swift downward glance the bottles on the sideboard, and Sarah, picking up his meaning, nodded and smiled, then turned to listen to her father-in-law again.

'The North is a separate world, you know, and it breeds a separate kind of man.' Stan was waxing eloquent now. 'Men who are anathema to men of softer tones, to men whose egos are of a normal size and who argue only with knowledge . . . for let's face the facts, we are an aggressive pig-headed lot. And I say thank God for it . . . What do you say?'

'Hear, Hear! Stan. Hear, hear! Carry on. Carry on.'

'Well, as I was saying, the Tynesider, right back to Bede, has had to push himself up through the mire for both bread and learning, and always on this particular night he dons the cloak of hope, and he throws his head back and looks to the coming year, to the set number of days, days in which he sees himself working hard, eating well, and sleeping soundly. And why not, why not?'

At this point Stan dramatically raised his glass, crying, 'Let's drink to the Northerner!' There was a rising to the feet and cries of 'Well spoken, Stan!'

John, turning to Sarah, whispered loudly, 'He should have been in Parliament, he could give MacDonald points . . . That's if me mother brewed every day.'

Their laughter was lost amidst the noise and chatter now filling the room, and Sarah, looking towards her father-in-law, thought, It's funny to hear him lead off like that. He must think that way all the time. He's like David, or David's like him. They both think alike, but it takes the drink to bring it out. And his eye has hardly twitched at all the night.

'It happens twice a year,' said John, still whispering. 'New Year's Eve and Armistice Day. He generally gets blotto then, on Armistice Day.'

'Really!' This surprised Sarah.

'It's a kind of protest against the War and . . .' He moved his finger unobtrusively towards his eyes.

Sarah couldn't imagine Mr Hetherington getting really drunk, but she remembered back to Armistice Day just a few weeks ago when he had been in bed for two days with a cold. She smiled to herself, and shook her head. Funny the things you didn't know.

'Look, it's three minutes to. Get the glasses filled there, Mary.' Mr Hetherington was addressing his wife as if he was master in his own house, and obediently she went to the sideboard and began refilling the glasses. She looked proud and happy.

Sarah was standing with David now, an arm around each other. They were behind Dan, who was sitting to the side of the fireplace, and they each had a hand on his shoulder. Dan, Sarah thought, was in a bad way, he should be in bed.

David bent down towards Dan, pulling Sarah with him as he said under his breath, 'Why don't you go up, man?'

'I will as soon as it's in.'

Sarah and David raised their heads, then looked at each other and for a moment pressed closer together. The room became full of bustle. Mr Riley, who was to be first-foot, had left by the back door laden with coal and bread – Mary Hetherington had never added a bottle to the ritual as was the rule – and now as many of the company as could manage it were in the passageway.

The ship's hooters were blowing. The church bells were ringing. The whole world outside of the house seemed to be alive with sound. In contrast the house appeared quiet, almost empty for all the voices had died away. Each member of the party was waiting, all touched in this moment with a feeling of awe, touched with the elemental feeling of mystery and of sadness. One woman, Mrs Riley's sister-in-law, was crying quietly. All the expressions were touched with tenderness. It was as if the essence of this quality had been brushed swiftly over them all. Not one of them at this moment held within himself bitterness or anger. Not one of them remembered past grievances. At the death-bed of the year their souls shone out from their eyes.

The wind was blowing high and hard and it brought the first booms from the clock in the centre of the town right to the door itself, and the sound split them apart. The faces returned to normal, mouths opened and cried in different ways: 'It's here. It's here.' As the clock struck for the twelfth time the rapper on the front door banged, and borne in on the wind came Mr Riley.

'Happy New Year. Happy New Year.'

'Happy New Year. Happy New Year.'

They shook hands; they embraced each other, they all pressed back into the sitting-room, still shaking hands, still embracing. Sarah found herself being held by her father-in-law.

'A Happy New Year, a Happy New Year, Sarah. And I mean that, I mean that.' He leant towards her and his moustache pressed tight against the side of her mouth.

'Happy New Year,' she cried. 'Happy New Year . . . Dad.'

At this Stan let out a bellow of laughter and for a moment they hugged each other. Then she was standing over Dan.

'Don't kiss me unless you want this cold. Happy

New Year, Sarah. Oh, that's what I wish you, a very Happy New Year. Indeed I do.'

'The same to you, Dan. The same to you.' They were holding hands, shaking them up and down like children.

The three strange men kissed her, great smacks on the side of her cheek.

She stood before May for a moment exclaiming a Happy New Year, then such was the power of this night they leant swiftly to each other and embraced.

And Mary Hetherington kissed her. Her lips touched her cheek, and she said, 'A Happy New Year, Sarah.'

'A Happy New Year, Mam.' Again they laughed together.

People were passing from one to the other, and then she was standing in the passage opposite John.

'A Happy New Year, Sarah.'

'A Happy New Year, John.' They looked at each other, but they did not even touch hands. He smiled, and his smile still held something of the gentleness of the moment before twelve. He said again, 'A very Happy New Year.'

When he passed her and went into the room the laughter slid from her face for a moment; she felt slightly disturbed, even slighted. Then, tossing her head up, she almost ran into the living-room. That was John – she never knew how to take him.

And now she began whipping up plates of mince-pies, and rice loaf, and bacon and egg tart, on to a large tray. As she turned to leave the room May came into the kitchen, saying, 'Dan wants a strong cup of tea.'

'I'll make it for him in a jiffy.'

'No, you carry on with what you are doing. I'll see to it.' May sounded pleasant, nice. Everybody was nice . . .

And then it was quarter-to-one.

David was playing the piano. Everybody was singing. Sticking to her decision she had refused to be persuaded to sing alone; nothing must mar the new-found harmony between herself and her mother-in-law. It was at this point she thought, I must slip across now. As she went from the room she whispered quietly to Mary Hetherington, who was still busy at the sideboard, 'I'm just going to slip across to wish me mother a Happy New Year.'

'Will you be all right?'

The concern was warming, heartening. She nodded briskly. 'Yes, yes, I'll be all right.'

May was standing near the door and she touched her arm, saying, 'You're not going across there on your own, surely?'

'Oh, I'll be all right, I'm used to it.'

'Well, I wouldn't take a gold watch and go through the streets at this time of the morning.'

'There'll be plenty of people about.'

Oh, everybody was nice. Fancy May being concerned about her.

May followed her into the passage, saying, 'You should have somebody with you. Tell Davie.'

'No, no. It will spoil things, they want him to play. I'll be all right, May, honest.'

'Wait until John comes back, then; he's just gone over to see to the fire, and he's going to look in on old Mrs Watson next door. He won't be long.'

'No, I won't wait, May. I'll be back before you know I'm gone. You see' – she smiled broadly – 'I'm used to going about the streets in the dark. I had to do it every night for years coming from work.' She nodded at May, then hurried into the living-room, and from a cupboard under the stairs she took out her coat and wrapped a scarf around her head, then went out of the kitchen door.

It was as she entered the back lane that she bumped into John. He gripped her arm to steady her and peered at her in the dim light from the lamp at the bottom of the lane, saying, 'Where on earth are you off to?'

'Oh . . . oh!' she laughed. It was a nervous laugh. 'I'm just going to run across and wish me mother a Happy New Year. I won't be long.'

'You're not going on your own? Where's Davie?'

'He's playing, I didn't want to stop him.'

'Well, you're not going across there on your

own at this time of the night, I'll come along with you.'

'No, no.' She was standing stiff, talking stiff. 'I'm all right I tell you. There's no need, I won't be a minute.'

'A minute or half an hour, what do you think I am? What would Davie think if he knew I let you go across the streets, especially at this time, on your own? There'll be drunks all over the place; it doesn't take much to knock them out these days.'

'No, no.' She was protesting now, with her eyes closed.

'All right then . . .' His voice sounded sulky. 'If you don't want me to go with you come back in and get Davie, but I'm not letting you go over there on your own. If anything was to happen to you, what would they say? Fancy him doing that, letting her go across there on New Year's morning by herself.'

Yes, she knew. That's just what they would say. But nothing was going to happen to her and she didn't want him to come with her. She didn't. She didn't. She felt herself jerked around. He had hold of her arm, laughing as he pulled her forward, but his voice was gentle, very gentle as he said, 'It's New Year's Day, Sarah, New Year's Day. Everybody's nice to everybody on New Year's Day, remember?'

They met the full force of the wind as they came out of the lane and into the main road.

'By! It's blowing itself in all right. And look at that moon riding up there. It looks as if it's training for the Derby.'

Sarah looked up through the scudding clouds. David said it was the clouds that moved not the moon, at least not quickly. David had learned her lots of things . . . Eeh, that was one of the things he had taught her, that nobody can learn you, only yourself. They teach and you learn, David knew more than John, at least about some things, about the nice things. John was eaten up with politics and such . . . Eeh! The exclamation burst from her now as her hand was gripped and she was forced into a run.

John was running against the wind like a great lolloping bear. She tried to shake herself free, but his grip was like iron, and she could no nothing but run with him.

'We'll race him.' He was yelling like a lad and pointing upwards. He was daft. Mad. They fled past two groups of people all singing, and mingled laughter and song followed them on the wind.

'J-o-h-n . . . stop!' She pressed her body back from him and strained at his hand, and gradually they came to a stop, just three streets from her own. She leant against the wall now, her two hands under her breasts pressing against her ribs. She was gasping and laughing. It was either laugh or get into a temper and this was a New Year's morning.

'You . . . You are a fool, John. You're mad.'

' Perhaps I am. But have you never raced the moon afore?'

She shook her head at him. He was standing with the palm of one hand against the wall, the arm straight; the coat sleeve touched her shoulder. His face, looking upwards, appeared young and boyish. As he turned his head towards her the moon disappeared behind a bank of cloud and she could no longer see his face. As she pulled herself from the wall, she said, 'I'm all out of puff, I've never run like that since I was at school.'

'You've missed something then.' His voice was even now, and his tone ordinary. 'Up to the last few years I used to run every morning before breakfast, I was in the harriers. Six miles sometimes, and more; and then I cycled to work. And on a Sunday a hundred miles with the Cycling Club was nothing. I felt fit in those days.' His voice trailed away and they walked a few steps before he said, 'Is this your street?'

'No, the last one.'

Everything seemed very ordinary. He was David's brother. Why had she made such a fuss about him bringing her over? He was just like a young lad. He might be older than David in years but in his mind he was younger. That was because he did sillier things, and said sillier things; and although at times he was surly, he had, she thought, something of Dan's sense of fun. She turned to him now, saying, 'This is it. Look, I won't be more than five minutes. I won't keep you waiting.'

'Stay as long as you like, I'll do some skipping until you come out.' He lifted his big frame from the ground with a lightness that surprised her and began skipping in an imaginary rope.

'You are daft, you know.' She was laughing freely. Then, 'I won't be long,' she said again, and hurried from him.

When she reached the house and found the blind up she felt a sense of disappointment. Her mother had gone to Mrs Young's then, or perhaps to bed. No, she wouldn't have gone to bed. She must have gone next door to bring the New Year in. There came to her the sound of laughter and voices from the Youngs' kitchen and as she turned away she thought, 'Well, I'm glad she's having a bit of enjoyment.'

'By! That was quick.' John was standing against the wall, not jumping up or down any longer.

'She's not in. She's next door, by the sound of it. Anyway, we'll get back all the sooner.'

She had turned to walk down the road when he said, 'Let's cut down the back end, we'll escape the wind that way. We won't have it in our faces then.'

'All right.'

They went across the road and through Walham Street. 'We can cut through Fanny's Alley here,' he said.

She turned to him, her mouth wide. 'You know Fanny's Alley?'

'Of course! Why do you sound so surprised? I know every bit of the streets.'

'I didn't think you'd know about this end, and Fanny's Alley.'

'Why?' There was a slight argumentative note in his voice now that put her on her guard, and her tone was placating when she answered, 'Oh, well, you know, the top end never came down to the bottom end . . . that was until Davie came for me.' Her voice was soft as she finished speaking.

They had entered a cut between two houses, Fanny's Alley. He went first and they came out on to a piece of wind-torn waste ground that had on it a number of corrugated iron huts – the tool sheds of the allotments. They were in the black shadow of the gable-end wall of the last house and the first of the sheds when he turned on her bringing her to a halt, saying fiercely, 'Don't talk like that . . . humble . . . Why must you eat humble pie all the time? What's the matter with you?'

'What do you mean? What are you on about now?' She sounded both surprised and frightened.

'I'm on about you bending the knee so much . . .'

'I don't.'

'Yes you do, and you know it. My God! Where do you think you've landed, anyway? In Lord Redhead's or with the Percy family? Look, Sarah, get it into your head that you're still in the Fifteen Streets. We're in the Fifteen Streets . . . we're all in the Fifteen Streets. I tell you it makes me flaming mad to see you acting as if somebody had picked you up out of the gutter . . . And when you're with my mother . . . oh my God!'

He stopped, and in the darkness she felt his arm going up as he put his hand to his head, and she retreated a step from him. She was shivering inside with a feeling which his words were forcing into life, the feeling that had come unbidden into her body when she had first looked at him. She fought it now in the only way she knew. She said, 'Don't be silly, going on like that; it's the beer you've had.' She laughed nervously.

'Beer! Huh! It might knock them over, but it doesn't touch me. It'll take something stronger than that. I've had very little the night. Look, don't evade the question. I've been wanting to get at you about this for some time . . . Sarah.'

She felt her body jerk upwards as his hands came down on her shoulders covering them like clamps. 'Don't you realise your worth, woman? They . . . I mean our family isn't bestowing any honour on you; you're doing the honours, if it comes to talking about honours. Aye, you've given them life. You've brought the old man alive. You've made Davie into a man, and you've done something for Dan . . . aye, Dan, who doesn't need any lessons. Don't you know what you've done,

209

woman?' He was shaking her now. 'Don't you know what you've done?' His voice was a hoarse whisper. His words were sending gusts of hot breath over her face. He still had hold of her shoulders, but his elbows were bent now, his body touching hers, but lightly, just their clothes.

'Sarah! Sarah!' The wind was whirling her name about her head. 'You know what you've done to me, don't you? You know it, that's why you've kept out of my way . . . Oh my God, Sarah.'

'No! No!' She thought she was screaming, but the scream was only inside her. Her words came out on a low hiss. 'No! No!' And then she was lost between his body and the corrugated iron hut. Through the thickness of their clothes she felt him, every inch of him; his knees, his thighs, his belly, his breast, they were all picking out the counterparts in her and she was gasping under the pressure of them.

'No, no, leave go of me. You're mad, mad . . . David!'

'Aye, David.' His mouth was against her ear; his words dropping into it like molten lead, burning her. 'There's David. You've got no need to remind me there's David. If it wasn't for David I would have tipped you up from the start. Didn't you feel it the first time we met in the front room? I knew then, in an instant.'

'Let me go! I tell you let me go! What if David found . . .'

'Don't worry, he'll not find out.'

'I'd rather die than hurt David, do you hear? Do you hear?' She was speaking through her teeth. 'Let me go.'

'Just a moment longer. Let's be like this a minute longer. It might have to last a lifetime. Oh, Sarah, Sarah.' His mouth was covering her ear.

She screwed her head into her shoulder and struggled with all her might to free herself from his arms, but he held her fast. As big as she was, he held her as if she were a child. Then with a suddenness that made her feel sick she felt her body go limp against him and she spluttered as she cried, 'I'm happy, I'm happy, leave me be, don't spoil it. I've never been so happy in me life, it's all I want, Davie and the home . . . A place of me own.'

'You're not happy. You don't know what it means. Davie rescued you. He was the first plank thrust out to the bottom end and you grabbed it, and now you're breaking your neck with gratitude.'

'I'm not, I'm not.'

'How does he love you, eh? How does he? Gentle, considerate, kindly, as if asking a favour? He doesn't take you, he couldn't.'

'Shut up, you! David's good . . . good.'

'Aye, he's good. Davie's a good fellow, a fine fellow. I'm his brother. Aye, aye, I'm his brother, and I wouldn't hurt him for the world either, so

211

you have it, you needn't worry, but he hasn't got it in him to love you. Not like this . . . and this!' He jerked his loins into her. His mouth almost covered the lower part of her face and for as long as it took her to realise that he was right, every word he had said was right, she submitted to him, and then she was thumping and pushing and kicking his body from hers.

They were standing apart now, breathing like two great animals lost in the wind and darkness, still alone in a world that had been created when she had submitted for an instant to him. It made no difference that there was no contact of flesh, they knew each other as if they had sported stark naked on an open moor.

Then her limbs became weak, all strength left her and she had to lean against the shed again for support. Her whole body was shaking as if with St Virus's dance. Her bones seemed to be strung on jangling wires. She had no power to move, nor did she want to; she had no urge to get away from him. No desire to run, nor did she wish she were dead, or that he had never been born. The only coherent thought in her turbulent brain was that David must not be hurt.

So close were they at this moment, even spiritually, that he picked up her thought and said, 'Stop worrying.' His tone was flat now. 'Davie won't be hurt. You would never hurt him, not with your sense of gratitude. And I don't want to hurt him either, I've told you . . . But I'm not in a position to hurt anybody, am I? You don't say "Come fly with me and be my love" when you're on the dole, do you? But everything apart, this is between you and me, so don't worry. Me madness is under lock and key and I'll try to see it doesn't break out again. Not in that way, anyhow . . .' He groped now and found her hands, and she did not resist him and he said softly and sadly, 'But, by God, how I could have loved you, Sarah.'

When she heard her voice answering him it sounded strange to her, she couldn't recognise herself, for it was a woman who was speaking, speaking the thoughts of a woman, slow and flat, 'It all depends on what you call love. David's kind of love takes in even me feet, and they aren't lovely. They swell and go shapeless and look like big white puddings, but he takes me shoes off and pulls me stockings away from me soles after I've walked back from the docks, or shopping. He's even washed me feet in hot water and soda – you wouldn't do that, would you?'

Except for their heavy breathing, which was caught and whirled away by the wind, there was no sound between them for some minutes, then he said, 'What you talking about? . . . I was talking about loving you.' His voice was hoarse and there was a note of perplexity in it.

'Loving me?' She experienced a weird urge to laugh, long and loud. She was afraid of the feeling.

She was afraid of herself altogether at this moment, and she was actually shocked at the rawness of her next words, but still in that slow flat grown-up woman's tone, she said then, 'I know your kind of loving, you'd take me clothes off but not me shoes . . . Oh, I know, I'm no fool . . . Leave go me hands.'

She was shaking herself roughly, violently, to try to get away from him when with his voice, urgent and tender, now he appealed to her, 'Don't shut me out, Sarah . . . don't. And don't be frightened of me, ever. I won't do anything, try anything, I promise you. Just let me talk to you now and again and look at you. Give me this much . . . Say something to me, at times, something kind, Sarah. I need kindness, I do. You just don't know what it's like to be without kindness. And you're kind. The first minute I saw you, I saw your big heart shining from every part of you . . . You're big, Sarah, in every way. You're big and kind . . .'

Normality was rushing back into her body, the normality of fear, fear against the softening effect of his pleading. She almost whimpered now, speaking as if to herself. 'If I bring trouble on the house I'll kill meself, I will, I will. I couldn't bear it . . . Your mother . . .'

It was as if the mention of his mother's name broke the spell, for now he burst out, 'Oh, for God's sake! I've told you to stop being afraid of me mother, and of any of them. I think that's about the only thing that could make me really mad with you. It drives me crazy when I see you bending before them. And when May, the upstart, looks down her nose . . .'

'M . . . ay?' she put in stammering. 'M . . . ay? May looks down her nose at me?'

'Can't you see it? And she's not fit to wipe your shoes. May's a prig; a cold, bloodless prig. She's got as much of a woman in her as Leslie Waters next door, and he doesn't know what he is. But you've only yourself to blame, you're so damned humble . . . humble and kindly. Kindly, that's you, Sarah, when you should be haughty and proud, because you've got something to be proud of . . . You're beautiful. My God, you're beautiful . . . your face . . . your body . . . everything . . . Oh, it's all right, don't worry; I'm not going to start again.'

Above her own gasping breath she could hear the quick intake of his as if he were sucking it in and out through his teeth. They stood quiet and without words for some minutes, and then he asked, 'Is it a deal?'

There was another moment of silence before she said, 'What do you mean?'

'That you'll not ignore me, not push me aside as if I didn't matter. I won't ask anything of you, I promise you, and I mean it . . . Mind, I wouldn't say I'd be talking like this if there wasn't somebody like Davie with a claim on you. But that's the throw of the dice. It is Davie and that's that . . . Come on.' He pulled her sharply from the support of the shed and, holding her arm, he said softly, 'Stop trembling. You can't go in like that. Come on, walk briskly.' He led her forward, supporting her, and she walked like someone slightly drunk.

They went across the waste land above the bottom ends of the streets until they came to Camelia Street back lane. Neither of them had spoken since they started to walk, but now she halted and with her head down she muttered, 'You'd better go on, I'm going in our house for a minute.'

He went to take her hand again, but she pulled it aside, saying under her breath, 'Don't! My God, don't! Not here. You don't know who's out the night.'

He stood looking at her bent head for not more than a few seconds, then, without further words, he turned abruptly and walked down the back lane.

She stood, with her back arched, leaning against the wind, and not until she heard the dull thud of the back door banging did she go down the lane, and through her own back door and up the yard.

Once in the kitchen she didn't light the gas, but, crouching down on the mat beside the fender, rested her arm on the seat of David's chair, and twisting her hands together, she stared into the dying embers of the fire, crying, 'Oh, David! Oh,

David! Oh, David!' Then jerking herself around she enfolded the chair in her arms as if it was the kindly gentle loving David himself. And her mind kept reiterating, Oh, David! Oh, David! Oh, David! and she told herself that she only wanted David, and David's kind of loving. She didn't want that other kind, not John's kind. No, no, she didn't want that, she didn't.

She became still, quite still, her body and her mind, and in the stillness she recaptured again the moment of terrifying intensity when she had grappled and strained and writhed to answer his body's demands and now she extended it. She could feel them struggling together like two savages, their bodies joined at every point possible, striving towards a climax of unearthly rapture, receiving and inflicting pain that created laughter, and the laughter did not escape from them but flowed back and forth through their beings as if through one body. The chair moved under her across the line and its motion brought her heaving body to stillness again and her mind to the present.

She became aware for the first time since entering the kitchen that they were still singing next door and she turned her face slowly towards the fireplace and whispered aloud, 'I can't help it. It wasn't my fault.' And it was as if in answer Mary Hetherington came walking through the wall and stood before her, saying, as she had done on the day of the wedding, 'A mixed marriage is bad enough, but to have it unsanctified in a registry office . . . Well, I only hope some good will come of it.'

Then she saw her mother-in-law joined by the priest, and Father O'Malley said, 'I told you mixed marriages have their penalties and this is only the beginning.'

Her greatest fear from a mixed marriage had been the loss of her immortal soul, but now even the phrase seemed meaningless. It was something that might or might not happen, something that wouldn't be proven until she was dead. What had come upon her tonight was something of the now – and it was tangible, this thing, this other love.

'No, no, I don't love him.' She was on her feet, speaking her denial aloud. She pressed her hand over her mouth and stood looking through the dark towards the wall. Then, heaving a great sigh that swelled and deflated her body, she said helplessly to herself, 'You'd better get in.'

They'd be wondering next door and they mustn't wonder, they mustn't ask questions. Nothing had happened, nothing ever would. As she had said, she would die rather than hurt David. David had pulled her up out of the mire . . . All right, what if he was a plank, he was a plank that she was going to cling to all her life. She would manage this thing, this wild-beast thing. She would have to. She straightened her shoulders, gulped spittle into her dry mouth, pulled the bolt out of the door, and went into the yard.

4

Sarah came quietly down the stairs and into the living-room. Mary Hetherington was sitting in the armchair near the fire, her eyes closed, and as Sarah tiptoed past she opened them and said, 'I'm not asleep.'

'Oh, I thought you might have dropped off. You should, you know, you're worn out. He's asleep now; it seems sound, not like it's been.'

'I've made some tea. Would you like to pour it out, Sarah?'

Sarah poured out two cups of tea and took one to her mother-in-law, then sat near the end of the table drinking hers.

Mary Hetherington sipped at her tea, then, looking down into the cup, she said, 'It's been a time, hasn't it? All that jollification on New Year's Eve and since then we've never stopped running, three weeks of it.' She looked up and towards Sarah, and added, 'You've been very good, Sarah. I don't know what I'd have done without you.

May is very little use in sickness, and she hasn't the lifting power of a mouse.'

'Well, I'm about twice her size. And she's been very good with the shopping and getting the medicine and that.' Sarah felt that she had to defend May, as if she owed her something. She didn't like this feeling and the only way she could ease it was to say something nice about May.

'I don't know what we'd have done if John hadn't been off work. Everything has its other side, hasn't it? He's been so good sitting up too, because David and his father couldn't have kept it up. With having to go to work they need their sleep . . . Ah, well.' She took another sip from her cup. 'He's past the worst but I never thought he'd get over it.'

'Nor did I.' Sarah shook her head. No, she never had thought Dan would get over it. His cold had resulted in double pneumonia and he had at one point seemed almost sure to die.

'Oh!' The cup wobbled in the saucer as Mary Hetherington brought herself upwards in the chair and, leaning towards Sarah, said, 'I'm awfully sorry, I forgot to tell you. I hope it isn't important, but your father called round this morning to see you. It was when you were out.'

'Me – my father!' Sarah screwed her face up in disbelief. 'My father called here?' Her lips were spread wide from her teeth.

'Yes.' Mary Hetherington's voice was soft. 'And

he was very nice and civil. He asked if you were in and I told him you had gone out shopping for me. He said he was very sorry to hear about my brother. He asked if he could do anything.'

'My father!'

'Yes, your father. Now you musn't be vindictive.' Mary Hetherington's Christianity was to the fore at the moment. 'Although I'd be the last person to tell you to encourage him, you mustn't bear malice or bitterness. It's never worth it. As I said, he was very civil and he looked very clean and tidy.'

'Did he say what he wanted?'

'No, no, he didn't say.'

'Perhaps my mother isn't very well?'

'I shouldn't think so. He said he called at the back door once or twice last week but got no reply; he wondered if you were all right.'

Again Sarah's face screwed up, but she said nothing this time. Her father calling on her? What was he after? Likely on the cadge. He was having to stump up his dole now that her mother hadn't got Phyllis's and her own money coming in. Yet he was no fool was her father, he knew the feeling that existed between them. He had never asked her for any money in his life, he had just taken it – that is, everything he could get his hands on. But was it likely that he would come cadging from her now? She couldn't understand it. Still, she would likely know what he was after when he turned up again. She said now, 'I'll take the washing round and put it in soak while there's still light.'

'No, no, no, Sarah, it's far too much; you've done it for weeks now. I'll get Mrs Watson to come in. She used to, you know.'

'There's no need when I can do it. I'm doing our own, and I'm as strong as a bull, anyway.' She flexed the muscles of her arm and smiled, and Mary Hetherington returned the smile, saying, 'Well, have it your own way.'

Sarah went out of the scullery and down the yard into the washhouse, and, gathering up the dirty linen from the poss tub, made it into a bundle and carried it next door, and placed it in her own washhouse.

In a way, if she could put it like this, she felt grateful to Dan for being ill. It had helped her to be of use to Mary Hetherington, really of use, and it had broken down some of the older woman's reserve . . . it had also given herself less time to think.

She began now to carry buckets of water from the tap at the bottom of the yard and fill the poss tub, then she placed in the ice-cold water all the white linen, sousing them, with her arms up to the elbows, until they were all wet. They would be ready for her early start in the morning.

The twilight was deepening when she went into the kitchen, but she didn't light the gas straight away, she was practising economy. Over the past three weeks she had learned more of the running of a house from her mother-in-law than she had in all the first weeks of her marriage. Mary Hetherington had unbent enough to give advice, such as, 'You can save so much by doing a thing the right way; you needn't be mean, you know. For instance, if you riddle your cinders every day you'd save a bucket of coal a week, four buckets a month and fifty-two a year. Reckon that up; the saving would buy you something for the house, wouldn't it? And then there's the men's clothes. Now when I buy a new shirt I always cut three inches off the tail straight away. This piece will give you a new collar and cuff facings later on.'

Yes, Sarah was learning a lot, and she had already started to save and with an object in view . . . she was going to get David a second-hand piano. She hadn't told anyone about this, not even David, and certainly not his mother, for she didn't think the purchase would be looked upon favourably; it would mean that David wouldn't be such a frequent visitor next door. Not that she minded him going to his mother's, but she knew that he would like a piano of his own.

But with regards to saving through economy Sarah found it was difficult to economise on food, because she and David went down to Shields Market on a Saturday afternoon. When they had first married it had been a sort of hilarious excursion and they had come back laden. That was, until the day they passed the men standing in the roadway, when one of them, looking at the top-heavy baskets, had remarked with sadness but without envy, 'By! That's a sight for sore eyes. There's not a better sight in the world than a basket laden with grub.'

On that Saturday David had said, 'We mustn't buy so much altogether, we'll just get what we need for the weekend and you can get the rest in the middle of the week.' So she did that, but she found it was dearer buying in bits and pieces.

After she had set the table for the tea she sat down for a moment by the fire, in the now darkening room. She had had little time to sit in the past three weeks and that was just as well. Sometimes she thought that what had happened in the wind-maddened first hour of the New Year was a figment of her imagination, and she could at times actually believe this, for neither by look nor sign had John reminded her that he had been party to the madness . . . the instigator of the madness. If there was any noticeable change in his manner towards her it was evident in an unusual gentleness of manner, like the gentleness he used towards Dan, but in Dan's case the gentleness was charged with power, and authority even to ward off death. John had literally fought with death to keep Dan alive, seeming almost to breathe for him when this became almost an agony. Only once had she seen the old John come rearing through this new gentleness. It was one evening down in the living-room when May said, 'Why don't you put in for a job of male nurse? They're going at Harton, you'd be in your element. They are always wanting them on the mental block . . .'

When she heard the knock on the front door she thought, Oh dear, somebody selling something again. But she was half through the front room when she remembered Mary Hetherington saying, 'Your father called.' She stopped for a moment. What if it was him?

Her approach to the door was slow, and when she opened it her face was set, almost grim, and it didn't change when she saw Father O'Malley standing below her on the pavement.

'Good afternoon, Sarah.'

'Good afternoon, Father.' They stared at each other.

'Well, aren't you going to ask me in?' This was no jocular request, it was made in the form of a command.

Without answering, Sarah stood aside and the priest moved past her and into the passage, where he waited for her to close the door. She seemed to take some time over this, but when she at last passed him she said, 'Will you come this way, Father. I'll light the gas.'

After the gas plopped and fluttered, then filled the mantle, its rays, through the pink porcelain globe, softened both their expressions. The priest was looking round the room and his gaze moved from the low-backed oak chairs to the legs of the table that had a stretcher joining them; then his hand going slowly out, he turned one of the chairs away from the table and without an invitation sat down.

'You've got this very nice.'

'Thank you, Father.' Sarah remained standing and he looked up at her, saying, 'Sit down, sit down; we'll talk more comfortably then.' He was entirely in command of the situation . . . and her. She could have been the visitor. His features moved into what was for him a smile, but it didn't lessen the agitation that was filling her.

The priest began drumming his fingers in a rhythmic beat on the corner of the table, and he looked at them for a full moment before saying, 'You are going to tell me that you are very happy?'

Her body was stiff, yet her chin trembled as she answered, 'I can say that, Father, and it's true.'

'The days are young yet, your life hasn't begun. It would be disastrous at this stage if you found yourself unhappy.' He paused. 'The awareness of conscience is a slow processs.'

'I've got nothing on my conscience, Father.' Her voice was trembling now, her agitation visible.

'Well, that's a matter of opinion, and time will prove which of us is right or wrong. God works in strange ways, sometimes through a series of disasters.' The priest turned towards the fire as if he were actually seeing the events passing before his eyes. 'Sometimes by withholding His hand until the eleventh hour, His ways are strange and it is not for us to question them . . . But it is our duty . . .' Now his voice was stern and his eyes were riveted on her, and he repeated, 'It is our duty not to bring His wrath upon us, not to aggravate Him too much.'

Sarah swallowed. At least she made an effort, for she felt that she was choking. She felt as she had done when a child, that God was a man who lived up in Newcastle, a big pot of big pots. Someone who could order you, through the medium of the priest, to be condemned to hell. Hell to her then was the blast furnace, the blast furnace that illuminated the sky all over Jarrow when the residue was poured on to the slag heap. That was hell: hell was fire, and hell was in Jarrow, administered from Newcastle . . . such were the narrow boundaries of her world. She had been twelve before she could grope with the fact that hell was not directly connected with Newcastle, nor yet the blast furnace. But she still believed in hell, then, and now, and she still believed it was administered by God. And she still believed that people paid for their sins. But at the same time she knew that she didn't want to believe it, and it wasn't only since she met David that she had kicked against these beliefs. Her rebellion had begun to stir much earlier . . . yet not against her religion. No, it was against Father O'Malley's delivered conception of God and of his own vindictive power that she had dared set her puny mind.

'Why haven't you been to Mass, lately?'

'I have, Father.'

The priest's eyes narrowed. 'I haven't seen you, nor has Father Bailey.'

'I go to Jarrow, first Mass.'

'Why to Jarrow? All your life you have attended my church, so why to Jarrow?'

She wetted her lips and cast her eyes downwards but did not lower her head because the thoughts in it tended to thrust her chin out and upwards. She didn't go because of him. She didn't go because they all looked at her. The girls she had gone to school with, their mothers and fathers, they all knew she had married a Protestant; and if that wasn't bad enough, she had got married in a registry office. So to them she wasn't married at all. That's why she didn't go.

'It wouldn't be because you're ashamed of what you've done?'

'No, I'm not ashamed.' She was on her feet now, 'I've got nothing to be ashamed of, Father. I've married a good man, a very good man.'

The priest slowly drew himself upwards; he buttoned the top button of his black coat, took from the pocket his black gloves and put them on before saying, 'You know as well as I do, Sarah,

228

that in the sight of God and His Holy Church you are not married, in fact you are living in sin . . . Well, I'll leave you with that thought, I'm always in the Presbytery any time you want to see me to make arrangements for the ceremony.' He turned and walked into the dark room, and from there he said, 'Tell your husband I've called.'

She heard him fumbling at the front door, but she could not go to his assistance.

She heard the door open and then close, and slowly she lowered herself into David's chair. 'I'll see you in hell first.' She did not recognise the sound of her own voice; it wasn't a young girl's voice, it was again the voice of a woman, the woman who had spoken to John on New Year's morning. He was cruel, cruel. She was married, she was. He was a pig of a man, a swine. She shuddered at her daring, at the blasphemy of calling a priest a pig, a swine. Well, she didn't care, she didn't care if she was struck down dead this minute . . . he was. He was a priest, a Christian, and he had sat there prophesying disasters, wishing them on her; yes, wishing them on her to prove himself right . . . The awareness of conscience . . . God works slowly.

She leaned back in the chair, feeling faint of a sudden. The fight seeped out of her. She felt funny, odd, and she asked herself was she frightened. Yes, she supposed she was. He had the name of being able to put the fear of God into anybody.

Yet this was an odd feeling she had, a sickly odd feeling. She found that her stomach was acting in a strange way.

She wished David was in, just to look at him, to feel his hands holding hers, to know that she was secure. She lay with her eyes closed and gradually the feeling passed. It was funny to feel like this, weak . . . she had said to David's mother she felt as strong as a horse. Well, at this moment she felt as weak as a kitten, like a baby. The word brought her sitting straight up in the chair, a great question mark filling the room. She looked round as if for the answer. Then her eyes slowly came to rest on her stomach. She put her two hands across it and stroked it slowly, then whispered aloud, 'Oh . . . oh . . . but I'd better be sure before I say anything . . . Yes. Yes. I'd better. It might only be fright through him . . .'

When David came in, even before he changed his shoes or sat down and had a cup of tea, he took her in his arms. He looked at her, he kissed her. Then, holding her at arm's length, he said, 'Hello, Mrs Hetherington.'

It was a game, a playful routine, but it was also something that set their marriage apart from other marriages. Marriages, everybody knew, sank into mundane ordinariness after a wedding. Life became a routine. Even a battleground of wills, of warring temperaments, of hitherto unrevealed personal habits, irritating, maddening personal habits which became obnoxious to the other party. Sarah knew all about marriage from this angle. She had witnessed the process around the doors. She had heard it discussed among women in the kitchen. She had seen it enacted between her mother and father. Their first flush of love had not reached even the pale pink tinted stage before reality had hit them. Terms such as, 'Anybody seen that old cow of mine?' were thought funny and even a sign that a man loved his wife. That's how marriage went in the bottom end. And people and attitudes weren't all that different in the top end. Sarah was coming to this knowledge painfully. The upper stratum was only a bath-bricked step from the lower stratum. John had been right there.

But her marriage was different. She had been married for weeks now and David seemed to get more loving and gentle every day . . . John had been right there too . . . Damn John! Damn the priest!

'I said hello, Mrs Hetherington.'

'Hello, Mr Hethrington.' She rubbed her nose against his.

'What's the matter? You look peaked. Are you all right?'

'Yes, yes, I'm fine. Of course, I'm all right.'

'Have you been washing, doing all the lot? I told you last week that you hadn't to do it, Mother can get Mrs Watson. She's had her before . . .'

She had her fingers over his lips. 'You're wasting your breath; I haven't been washing, I've been sitting most of the afternoon with Dan.'

'Well, that's not good for you either. You've been up there too much. You've got no colour in your face . . . How is he?'

'Oh, much better. He seems to have improved a ton today.'

He turned from her now and, going to his chair and sitting down to change his shoes, he said, 'I want to talk to you, Sarah, about Dan. You know what I told you about his friend . . . the woman down Westoe?' He cast his eyes at her and she nodded. 'Well, he hasn't seen her for over a month, and on New Year's day, as bad as he was feeling, he wrote her a note, but he's received no reply. He wrote another after he got over the crisis, and when he had no reply to that either it dawned on him that they hadn't been posted; my mother just hadn't posted them. Naturally he was worried. He didn't know what she'd be thinking. From what I can gather – he did some talking to me when he wasn't quite himself – things haven't been running too smoothly lately in that direction. Surprisingly, he has asked her to marry him and she won't. Anyway, to ease his mind I wrote to her and told her what's happened. And I've talked the matter over with John, and he says that she should be allowed to come and see him if she wants to. It would likely get Dan on to his feet quicker than anything, for he's very low at present and it's not like him – he could joke with a gun at his head, could Dan.'

Sarah, her mouth hanging slightly open, said, 'Her come up here? Your mother would go mad.'

'Yes, if she knew, but she needn't. Dan's likely to be confined to the house for weeks yet, so we thought that if Mother could be persuaded to go to the chapel meeting as usual on Wednesday afternoon the woman could come in here, and when Mother's gone she could slip next door for half an hour, no one would be any the wiser.'

'But, David, what if your mother didn't go out?'

'Well, that would be just too bad. But look.' He reached out and grabbed her hand. 'There's no need to get worried. We're not planning a bank robbery or anything like that.'

'A bank robbery would be safer. What if she was to find out?'

'But she won't. Nothing will happen if she doesn't go to the chapel meeting, that's all there is about it. But don't you see.' He pulled her towards him. 'It would please Dan, and I want to please Dan. He's a good fellow is Dan. I've always known that, but I didn't realise how much I'd miss him until I thought he was a goner. Come on, come on.' He shook her hands. 'Don't look so frightened. If me mother found out, and she wanted to kill anyone, it would be me or John.'

Sarah looked down at him in silence. She made

a small motion with her head but she did not reply, except to herself, and she said, 'No, no, she wouldn't kill either of you, it would be me she would kill.' And the knowledge brought a feeling of dread into her being.

5

Sarah liked the woman from the moment she opened the door to her, but at the same time she wondered what Dan saw in her. She was quite well-dressed and she spoke nicely. Her manner was shy, quiet. She had about her a quality of refinement, but the impression she imparted to Sarah almost at once was that she looked nooled. Perhaps this was because she'd had a disastrous marriage, but still, that was over and she had Dan now and Dan wanted to marry her. And there was a timidness about her; she was like – Sarah searched in her mind to describe what the woman was like and, when the thought came to her . . . she looks like a superior mouse. She was pleased with herself because it was an indication that she was learning, that she was picking these things up from David.

The woman's name was Mrs Mount, Eva Mount. Sarah addressed her as Mrs Mount. She offered her tea and biscuits and tried to make conversation, but it was hard going.

'Are you sure it's convenient?' The woman asked for at least the third time since her arrival, and Sarah assured her that it was, or it would be. 'My husband did explain to you about his mother?' She said this gently.

'Yes, he did.' Mrs Mount's voice was small, high. She spoke in monosyllables most of the time. Only once more did she break away from yes, and no, to ask, 'Dan has told you about me?' And Sarah answered, 'Yes.' And added, 'Dan's nice.'

Following this there was another silence, and Sarah, glancing at the clock, said, 'It's half-past two. She's likely gone now, I'll go in and see.'

Mary Hetherington had gone. John was in charge in the bedroom, and when she entered he looked quickly towards her and said, 'All set?'

She nodded, but towards Dan, an older-looking much thinner Dan now, and he smiled at her and said, 'You're like a lot of conspirators. By! If this was to come out it would be the end of the world.'

'I'll go and get her.' As she turned away John said, 'I'll make myself scarce an' all. I'll go over home for an hour. I'll be back.' He punched the air in the direction of Dan, and for answer Dan smiled weakly, saying, 'Thanks for everything. If ever a war comes they'll make you a general.'

'Roll on a war.' John was coming down the

stairs behind Sarah now, and he added, 'That's what we want, a war.'

Sarah wanted to say, 'Don't be silly.' But, as always, she prevented herself from making any retort to John's provocative remarks. She didn't want to get him going in any way, she told herself. Like a dangerous dog, he was better left sleeping.

They were in the living-room now, alone, and as she went to pass him she looked at him because he willed that she should. She was an arm's length from him and for a second or so they stared at each other until he asked quietly, 'Not mad at me any more, Sarah?'

And just as quietly, even gently, she replied, 'No.'

'Good.' He turned abruptly and preceded her into the scullery, and as he opened the door to let her pass he said, 'You'd better tell her to keep it to half an hour, just in case.' And as he closed the door on them he said under his breath, with a laugh that was both sad and bitter, 'The things we do for love.'

Then they went down the yard and parted in the back lane without looking at each other again, but she was trembling. He could always make her tremble.

Almost moving on tiptoe, Sarah led the woman from her house and into Mary Hetherington's. She never thought of her mother-in-law as mam although she now called her by this name; she thought of her as she, or David's mother.

As she opened the kitchen door the very house itself seemed aghast at the act she was perpetrating. She said hastily to the woman, 'Give me your coat and hat. You'll need them when you go out, it's so cold.'

But the woman said, 'I'll keep them on, if you don't mind.'

Without further ado Sarah led the way out of the room and up the stairs. Then, tapping gently on Dan's door, she went in. She smiled at him, let the woman pass her, then went quickly out and down the stairs again.

As she stood in the living-room looking at the clock her heart began to beat uncomfortably fast. Just supposing what would happen, just supposing she walked in that door at this minute. Just supposing! . . . She gave a violent shake of her head. Why was she so frightened of her mother-in-law? John was right: she shouldn't be frightened of anybody. She was big and strong enough to face ten Mary Hetheringtons, yet . . . She looked at the clock. Only five minutes gone. She wished, oh, she wished somebody would come. Oh, she'd better be careful and state her wishes precisely, else who knew but his mother herself might walk in the door. She wished John would come back. She didn't feel half so afraid when he was about; not of other people anyway, only of him, but that was a different kind of fear.

She filled the kettle and set Dan's tea-tray. She took the chenille cloth off the dining-table and put on the lace-edged one, the second best, and set the table for two.

She looked at the clock again. The woman had been up there twenty minutes. Oh, she wished she had said a quarter of an hour instead of half an hour.

There were two pairs of shoes by the door with mud on them; she cleaned them. The woman had been upstairs now twenty-seven minutes. She gazed up towards the ceiling, and as if her anxiety had prised through the floor she heard footsteps walking towards the bedroom door. She heard it open and close, then she herself moved towards the living-room door. She was two steps from it when the key turned in the front door and she let out an agonised exclamation that was also a prayer. 'Oh God in Heaven!' she groaned.

The woman was on the last stair but one when Mary Hetherington saw her. She had the door in her hand, but she didn't close it. Slowly she pushed it behind her and slowly she walked forward. She brought her eyes for a second from the woman to Sarah's red and agitated face, then looked back towards the woman again.

'Who are you? What are you doing here?'

The woman opened her mouth to speak, then, glancing fearfully at Sarah, she closed it again, and as she did so Mary Hetherington looked over her head towards the top of the stairs and the bedroom. Then, speaking below her breath, in a voice so deep that it seemed to be that of a man's, she growled, 'How dare you! Get out of here.'

'I've done nothing. Wh . . .'

'Get out of here!' Mary Hetherington seemed to leap backwards towards the door and, pulling it wide, she pointed dramatically towards the street.

The little woman, very, very like a mouse now, a trembling pathetic mouse, gave Sarah one piteous glance, then made her exit on the point of a run. As Sarah watched her scrambling ignominiously down the steps into the street, the reason why Dan had taken up with her became clear: it was because the poles of the earth were not more apart than she and his sister. In spite of being brought up under the domination of Mary Hetherington, he had survived and had become a man with a mind of his own, but Mary's dominance had coloured his choice of a woman.

As Sarah watched her mother-in-law come towards her she said to herself, Stand up to her, don't let her frighten you. But the admonition did not prevent her retreating into the living-room, where she stood at the far side of the table not daring to look into the outraged face before her. She had only seen this woman in a temper once before, that was on the day she and David had returned from the registry office, and, as she had told Phyllis, she had been frightening. During that particular scene she had raised her voice – if she had not actually shouted she had talked loudly – but now her voice was not raised, it was very low and it made her much more frightening than any wild burst of temper could.

'You . . . you knew about this, didn't you?'

'No, I didn't.'

'You arranged it.'

'No! No, I didn't.'

'You're a liar . . . a big blowsy, lazy liar.'

The attack widened Sarah's eyes. This was how the women of the bottom end talked. Moreover, this was an attack on her. It had really nothing to do with Dan or the woman, it was directed against her. She felt it. She knew it.

'Dan would never have dared, he knows how far he can go. But you . . . do you know what you've done?' She had her hands flat on the table and the edge of it was pressing her clothes into her thighs, her stomach, surprisingly large for one so thin, was covering inches of the table, and she was leaning at an angle that brought her head and shoulders half-way across it. 'You've wrecked my home, that's what you've done.'

'You don't know what you're talking about. I've done nothing. It wasn't me who . . .'

'Shut up! You could talk until you're black in the face and I'd never believe you. You're sly, cunning . . . using your lumps of flesh . . .' She released one white-knuckled hand from the table and flicked it within an inch of Sarah's breasts. 'You don't need any sign outside the door saying "All men welcome", you've just got to show yourself . . . You – you young hussy – setting your cap for my menfolk! And you've taken them, haven't you . . . my menfolk. That's what you've done. And you meant to, didn't you?'

'I . . . I . . . What are you talking about? You must be mad!' Sarah shook her head slowly. Her mouth hung open and her tongue hung slack on her teeth with amazement.

'Go on, play the innocent, first David and then Dan. Oh, he has his woman on the side but he can't keep away from your kitchen. And then my own husband . . . what did you do to him? Encourage him in . . . "You can smoke in here, Dad" . . .' She was mimicking Sarah's voice. 'You think I don't know your little game. I wasn't born yesterday. And John, running round making your furniture when he won't knock a nail in for me, or May either.' She took a great intake of breath now. The beads of sweat were ringing her upper lip. She straightened her back, breathed hard again, then with her eyes still riveted in patent hate on Sarah, she went on, 'You should be in Costerfine Town with your sister. There's not a pin to choose between you. I must have been crazy to think that you were the lesser of two evils. Ellen said I'd be paid back, and how true her words have come. But

241

I realised it from the beginning. And it wouldn't have happened if you hadn't sneaked off to the registry office. There are worse things than a taint of insanity. Well, God has punished me. Sure enough. He's punished me. I've lost a good friend in Ellen, I've lost a girl who'd have been a daughter to me, and what have I got? . . . You . . . who've split my family apart.'

'It's not true.' Sarah was standing straight now, her breathing sharp. 'Not a word you've said is true. I've never asked any of them into the house. If they come next door it's not to see me but for a bit of peace, do you hear? Do you hear that? For a bit of peace!' Although she was still trembling, still afraid of this woman, there came to her aid retaliation born of a sense of injustice. This feeling came boiling up in her when dealing with her father, or the priest, and it now enabled her to thrust back at her mother-in-law the truth, the truth that was going to sever their connection for all time. Her voice spitting out the words, she cried, 'And if they do come into my house who's to blame them? What is there for them here?' She flung one arm wide. 'Is there any real comfort or happiness? This isn't a home, it's your show-place, and you're the big boss. Dan is the only one who has kicked over the traces, but it's a wonder to me they're not all regular visitors at Maggie Conaman's . . . There, you've asked for it, and you've got it . . . You never intended I should have David, did you? No, you didn't. As you said, it wouldn't have happened if we hadn't sneaked off to the registry office. Well, you were foxed, weren't you? I've got David, and I'm going to keep him, and you can't do a thing about it. Now you've really got something to get your teeth into, so bite hard. You can't hurt me, do you hear? You can't hurt me.'

She turned away from the livid countenance and went out of the house, not rushing, just walking, walking steadily. Although fearful at her temerity and amazed at her daring, she was possessed of the knowledge that she was indeed a woman, all of her and for ever. The girl in her was gone completely.

Maggie Conaman was a notorious character of the docks and Sarah would have denied any knowledge of her existence if the question had been put to her, but now she had used her knowledgeably and thrown her into her mother-in-law's chapel-going sanctimonious teeth.

A few minutes later, as she stood in her own kitchen, her hands above her shoulders gripping the mantelpiece as she stared down into the fire, she seemed to see there her values being melted and reshaped. What were this family, anyway? What were they? They were no better than those at the bottom end. When she thought of the family she was not including the men. There was one figure only who represented the family: her mother-in-law. She had talked and gone on like any woman from Baxter Street or Poltar's Row. And only yesterday she had said one mustn't bear malice or bitterness. That was funny, that was. Anyway, who did she think she was, anyway? WHO? She grabbed at the poker and rammed it into the fire, stirring it vigorously, sending the ash over her shining black-leaded hob. A big, blowsy, lazy liar. She dropped the poker with a clatter on to the hearth, then, throwing herself into David's chair, she turned her face into the corner and began to cry, slow painful tears. There was always someone or something to spoil things, always, always.

'Don't worry yourself.' They both said it at once, John and David. They were standing in front of her and she looked up at them as she said, 'You're wasting your time. She blames me for it all. So let her go on thinking that. You're not going to make things any better by telling her the truth. In fact you'll make them worse.'

'We'll see about that.' David nodded his head down sharply at her. 'Come on.' He beckoned to John. 'This is one thing we can get straightened out and waste no time about it.'

'Have your tea first,' she said.

'Tea be damned!'

That was the first time she had heard David say damn; he was very upset for her. As she heard their combined footsteps going down the yard she joined her hands in her lap and sat waiting. Within a matter of minutes she heard the sound of voices, low and muffled, coming through the wall.

Five minutes later she raised her eyes towards the kitchen door as she heard the back door open. She was surprised to see John coming in alone. 'I've left him,' he said, jerking his head towards the fireplace, 'pouring buckets of oil on the troubled waters. Not that it will do much good. You were right.' He came close to her, and, bending towards her, his hands cupping his knees, he asked quietly, 'Did you say we should all have gone down to Maggie Conaman's for diversion?'

She dropped her eyes from his and after a moment said, 'Something like that.'

'Good for you.'

She looked up at him. His eyes were twinkling, his face twisted into a wry grin. 'You certainly rent the temple asunder with that salvo. And the funny thing is, you know' – he wagged his finger slowly in front of her face – 'many's the time I nearly did just that.'

She lowered her eyes again and looked down at his feet. They were an extra large size. His boots were highly polished; he always took pride in his appearance. She liked that about him; he would never look down and out if he was out of work for ten years, she thought. She was wondering why she was thinking this way at this particular moment when his voice came at her again, saying,

'You know, some people think your church is the last word in domination. Well, it might be, but with it neck and neck at the post are the Baptists, ones like my mother. Humbugs who condemn drinking yet make a brew with a kick in it . . . Oh, I know I said it didn't affect me, but then I can stand a good deal . . . You know, I once believed in God. But no smoking, no drinking, no swearing, no taking the Lord's name in vain, no reading books on a Sunday other than . . . the Book; no playing the piano on a Sunday unless hymns, these things changed my opinion pretty early on about God, and chapel, and living the good life. And if they hadn't, the face of the bolster atween her and Dad would have done it in any case.'

'What?' She did not quite follow him. 'A bolster?'

'It's a fact. After Davie was born no more of . . . THAT, she said. I wasn't five at the time, but I remember as if it was yesterday, and getting out of bed because something disturbed me, I didn't know what, and opened the bedroom door. There she was standing on the landing in her nightie saying, "I want no more of that." The word THAT stuck in my mind for years. I was about ten when I discovered what THAT was and just turned thirteen when I learned about the bolster. It was the first of Dad's Armistice celebrations. You know, he always gets tight the day before Armistice Day and he told me – he was crying just like a kid – and

246

he told me. "Fighting all through the War," he said, "and I had to come back to the bolster. It's unnatural, isn't it?" '

Sarah lowered her eyes. She felt embarrassed, as if somebody had told her a filthy story. She had never liked filthy stories.

'She's a cruel woman is me mother; narrow, and cruel, and like all such women, bitchy. May is bitchy, but she's not narrow in that way. You know something, Sarah?' He was still bent towards her with his hands on his knees and she looked at him again. 'You've struck a blow for all of us the day. Every single one of us . . . Dan, Dad, Davie, and me. Oh yes . . . and me. For how many times have I wanted to say to her just what you said the day. You know, it's funny. We're known about the doors as a united family, yet each one of us hates her guts in some way . . . aw, don't let it trouble you, don't look so sad. Come on, cheer up. You've stood on your two feet today so you shouldn't look sad.' He took his hand from his knees and bent over her, and his tone dropped to a whisper as he said, 'I worry when you look sad. I do, I do . . . Sarah.' His hand came out to touch her cheek when she pressed herself away from him, saying under her breath, 'No, don't, don't. Don't, don't.'

'All right.' He straightened up and stood looking down at her for a moment before turning abruptly from her. 'I'll be seeing you,' he said.

247

She lay back in the chair. Her heart was pounding against her ribs. Why must he do it . . . touch her? Everything would be all right if he didn't touch her. When the beating subsided she thought of what he had said. She had struck a blow for all of them. Yes, she had struck a blow, and smashed the house. Very likely if she had kept her mouth shut this business would have died down and a veneer would have covered the real feelings of them all and they could have gone on with the daily business of living amicably – but never again. The blow she had struck had severed the lives of the two houses; and in her own house there stood David, Dan, and John, with her father-in-law astraddle the wreckage. But standing alone in the rooms of the other house was Mary Hetherington; bereft of her menfolk. This knowledge brought no feeling of triumph to Sarah, only awareness of the hard bitter woman's pain.

6

Sarah felt dreadful. She longed to go in to Dan to help as usual, to see to him, but she knew that even if she had the courage to walk up the next yard she would find the door bolted against her.

She had tidied upstairs. She had done her

kitchen and dusted the few bits of furniture that were in the front room. She had prepared the dinner far in advance of its time. And now, taking up some socks of David's she sat down near the fire. She didn't feel well – she supposed it was the upset of last night – she felt all to pot. She said to herself, Get up and make yourself a cup of strong coffee – coffee was David's innovation. He liked it. He liked it better than tea. She wasn't very struck on it herself, but David said it bucked you up.

As she snapped off the wool from the sock there was a flick of shadow against the left-hand pane of the kitchen window. This meant there was someone at the back door. She was in the scullery before they knocked, and when she opened the door her mouth did not drop open into a gape of surprise, it clamped closed, her lips losing their full shape in a tight line. 'What do you want?'

'You were always civil, weren't you?'

'I asked you what you want?'

'Just a word.'

Her tongue drew a quick line over her upper lip before she said, 'Get it out then.'

'Well.' He moved from one foot to the other; then rubbed his thumb under his nose and brought his eyebrows close together before saying, 'It's a bit private like, I don't think I'd do me talking out here.'

She stood staring at him. She wanted to bang the door in his face. She remembered that he had been trying to see her before this. Without a word she pulled the door wide to give him plenty of room to pass her, she had never liked getting close to him – there was a smell about him, a body smell. Even when he had washed himself down there had still been that smell, a smoky, sweet, funny smell.

In the kitchen she kept her distance from him. She did not ask him to sit down but stood looking at him, waiting. He was looking about him, a smile on his face. When he looked like this she could understand anyone thinking he was a quiet, inoffensive little chap.

'You've got it nice . . . grand. Did well for yourself, didn't you?' He was still smiling as if in approbation. 'I'll sit down a minute, off me legs. I've been to the doctor's with me back . . . I'm on the sick. They stopped me dole.'

So that was it. He had come cadging. He had a nerve. She repeated the words in her mind, slow, deep, and emphatic. By! Yes . . . he had a nerve all right. Then, as she had guessed, it came.

'I was wondering if you could spare me a few bob to tide me over.' He had not said, us over, which would have meant he wanted the money for the house.

Her face was hard, her voice equally so, as she rapped out, 'I haven't any money to give or lend.'

'No?' He shook his head slowly.

'No, not now or any other time.'

'But your man's doing all right, he's got a

permanent job. From three pounds five a week they get in the dock office, I understand.'

'It doesn't matter what they get, or what you understand, I've got no money to give you; it takes me all my time to manage. And now you'll have to go. I've got to go out.'

He sighed here, then leant his short body forward until his elbows were resting on his knees, his hands hanging idly downwards, his whole impression one of relaxation. 'It's a pity.' He sounded sorry.

She was puzzled by his reaction. She had expected him to bounce to his feet and tell her what he thought she was, a bloody upstart. Instead he started talking about David.

'Nice fellow, that man of yours. Did he tell you I had a word with him on the road the other day?'

David hadn't told her.

'He asked me how long I'd been out and he gave me a bob.'

Oh David, David, what a silly thing to do. But that was David.

'I should think he was a chap in a thousand, straight like; no side to him. I was talking to some of 'em at the dock gates and they said he was the civilist fellow in the office.' He lifted his eyes upwards looking at her under his lids. 'You've been lucky, you know. You fell on your feet. It'd be a pity if you were knocked on your back now, wouldn't it?'

Her brows came together. 'Knocked on me back? What are you getting at? Look.' She did not go near him, but she bent her body towards him. 'I don't know what you're yammering on about or what you're leading up to. I only know one thing: coming from you it won't be any good.'

'Well, it's all how you look at it, isn't it? A thing is good or bad how you look at it, that's what I say . . . The mother's a bit of a tartar.' He jerked his head towards the wall. 'Thinks herself somebody, I hear. Never out of the Baptist chapel they say. Narrow as they come. No understanding. Now our lot can booze and whore and think nowt of it . . .'

'I'll have none of that talk in my house.'

'Well, I was just explaining, no offence. But you know yourself we're all human, you should know that better than anybody.' He was smiling again, nodding at her now. 'But what a Catholic would laugh off a Baptist would hang you for.'

Sarah was standing straight now, stiff and tall, her hands gripped in front of her waist. There had come upon her a terrible feeling of apprehension. It might only be imagination, she told herself, but the smell from him seemed to be filling the room. She felt faint, sick with it. He was staring at her, not speaking. She told herself not to let him see that she was agitated. That's what he wants, she said. Stand up to him like you did to her yesterday

. . . go on. She took a deep breath, then said, 'Look, if you've had your say you'd better go because I'm going out, I've told you.'

When he still did not answer but continued to look at her with his unblinking red eyes she withdrew one hand from the other hand, and, putting them behind her, supported herself against the edge of the table. And as she did so he said quietly, 'It's a pity the big fellow hadn't been single an' all, you'd have had your pick then.'

'W . . . w . . . what?'

'I said . . .'

She was away from the table now, standing over him, shouting, 'I heard what you said.' She glanced at the wall. She would hear her next door if she went on like this. Her voice dropping, she hissed at him, 'Don't think you can frighten me with anything your sewer mind can make up. All David's family come in here, his uncle and his father.'

'Oh?' He turned his eyes up towards her and his voice sounded almost childish. 'I didn't know they all came in, that's nice. But it wasn't that I was meaning. You see . . .' He pushed his head back as if to get a better view of her. 'About New Year's morning. You know the Collins, me cousins down Bogey Hill way, well, they asked me over for first footin'. I was a bit surprised like but I went, but didn't stay long, and on me way back Aa was took short.' He stopped at this point and Sarah closed her eyes and waited, her breath suspended, her whole life suspended. She waited.

'I went in one of the huts, you know, the end one on the waste land, and then I heard this coughing. Well, you know, there's always couples around there. I bumped into two or three on me way up, making the best of New Year's morning. Well, this couple began . . . well, they began to talk. At least he did, an' Aa was a bit surprised like. Well, you see what I mean.'

Sarah, her eyes open now, was pressing herself against the table; then her body, arching itself upwards, shot forward and she was hanging over him and words, each borne on a spurt of rage, came frothing from her mouth. 'You devil! You dirty, evil devil! It was nothing . . . nothing. I tell you it was nothing. Nothing happened.'

'No?' He seemed to be untroubled by her rage, and his voice still held a childish innocent note and he shook his head as if in perplexity.

'You dirty-minded swine!'

'Now, look, Sarah.' He got slowly to his feet. 'I don't want to quarrel with you. There's no reason. An' it wasn't my doings, was it? I just happened to be there, and there I had to stay. You wouldn't have liked me to show me face, now would you? I had to stay put for over ten minutes, you know.'

Oh God! Oh God! Oh God! Sarah bowed her head deeply.

'I couldn't close me ears, that's why I said it was a pity, a pity the big fellow's married, for he seems clean gone on you . . . Mind . . .' He moved his head slowly. 'I don't blame him, but it's awkward, isn't it? It's an awkward situation all round, I mean with your man being such a nice bloke an' his mother being such a tartar an' all that. And then the big fellow's got a bairn, hasn't he, and a wife that's a bit of a spitfire too as far as I can gather . . .'

'Shut up! Shut your evil mouth. I tell you, nothing happened, noth . . . ing, do you hear? Noth . . . ing.' Spurts of frothy saliva came from her mouth with the last word. A voice was going mad inside her now, urging, directing, yelling. Stand up to him. Don't let him get you. Tell him to go to hell and do what he likes . . . But he wouldn't go to hell. She would, she would be plunged into a living hell. If she hurt David in any way that would be hell. But what she could do was to take the wind out of this slimy devil's sails by telling David what had happened . . . And turn him against John? No, no. She could never do that. Then she must tell John . . . What, and have him murder this little reptile! Whatever road she tried to take out of this mess was blocked, she could see that. If she made a move in any direction she'd bring disaster on them all, the disaster that Mary Hetherington had prophesied, that the priest had prophesied. She remembered Father O'Malley's words: God works in strange ways, sometimes through a series of disasters. Her whole being trembled. It was as if he had known what was going to happen, as if he had a hand in the plan.

'I wouldn't take on like that, there's no need to upset yourself. I just thought I'd tell you and put you on your guard like in case you got careless.'

Her eyes were closed again. She could not bear to look at him in case she sprang on him and beat her fists into his face. Her mouth opened twice before she said, with eerie quietness, 'There was nothing happened, he was drunk.'

'Aye, I can believe that. Yes, New Year's morning, lots of funny things happen in drink. Meself, I've always steered clear of it, but there it is . . . Well, I just thought I'd pop in and tell you an' see if you had a couple of shillings on you. That's all I want, a couple of shillings until you see your way clear . . . anyway, what's five bob a week to keep everybody happy, eh? I ask you now.'

She was going to be sick. She was going to faint. She had never fainted in her life, but she wanted to faint now, to pass right out, for if she didn't she would do something to him, she knew she would.

She found herself at the cupboard next to the fireplace where she kept her bag, and, groping blindly in it, she found her purse, and taking from it a two-shilling piece she threw it with a backward movement on to the table. She heard it bounce twice; then from the corner of her eye she saw him stooping to pick it up from the floor.

'Thanks. Thanks, lass. Now don't worry, there's nothing to worry about. I won't tell your mother so you needn't worry, 'cos it would upset her, you know. She lays great store by your being up this end. It sort of makes up for the other one and the Arab like. There's nobody need know anything about this only you and me . . . and them concerned . . . Well, so long. Aa'll be seeing you. Aa'll pop over now and again. So long. Aa'll see meself out. Don't you bother.'

When she heard the door close she stood with her back pressed against the cupboard shelves. She would go mad. This would drive her mad. What could she do? She staggered to the table and gripped its edge until her nails broke. Then she was leaning over it, her stomach heaving. It seemed to turn over and rush upwards. The next moment she was standing over the sink vomiting.

She was still sick when David came in at dinner-time. 'What is it?' he said. 'Have you eaten something?'

She hung on to his hands tightly with both of hers, and she made herself smile when she gave him the news: 'I'm going to have a baby I think,' she said.

At two o'clock the following morning Sarah awoke screaming from a nightmare, and when

David held her, trying to assure her that she was awake and safe, she grabbed at him. 'I was in the mud. Everybody was in the mud, but they dragged me to the middle. I had it in my mouth and I was choking . . . Oh, David, it was awful, awful. I'm frightened, David.'

'There's nothing to be frightened about, darling; it was only a dream.'

Yes, it was only a dream. Her body slowly unwound against him. 'But it was worse than usual.' She said, 'It was worse than usual, much worse.'

'You've had it before then?'

She nodded against his breast. 'It started with an overdose of cough mixture my mother gave me.' She felt a tremor of laughter go through his body. 'Well, that's put paid to cough mixture.'

They lay silently, their bodies close, breathing almost the same breath, until David whispered, 'Don't let anything frighten you, dreams or anything else. And as long as you've got me I'll see to it that nothing does, not even . . .' He pressed his finger into her backbone and the pressure spelt 'mother'. 'You understand, love?'

Yes, she understood. She also understood that his words meant the exact opposite from what he thought. They meant, for as long as she had him she would know fear, the fear of her little world, her new superior little world, exploding.

PART THREE

1

'I think there's going to be a march,' said John.

'Where to?' asked David.

'London, of course.'

'It'll likely be the same as the one in Seaham Harbour when you met Ramsay MacDonald. Tea and soft soap and the promise that Jarrow would be kept in mind. That's three years ago.'

'We'll get results this time or else . . .'

'Or else what?' said David. 'Riots?'

'Aye, if necessary. But they don't want it to be like that; everything's going to be orderly, at least from our end. Ellen's coming with us.'

'Oh, that woman!' May's thin voice broke in on the men. 'My godfathers! You would think she was a priestess; I'm sick of the sound of Ellen Wilkinson's name.'

'Shut up!' John turned on her, spitting the words at her. 'You haven't got the list to lift a hand to help anybody, and you haven't a good word in your belly for those who do.'

May raked John with her cold glance before rising to her feet and saying, almost listlessly, 'Lift a hand? You've been lifting hands for years now, the great John the Baptist, and where's it got you? What's it got us?'

'As much as it's got anybody else in this town – a place the dole queue. If we hadn't fought, you and the likes of you would now be in Harton, that's if you could get in. You'd more likely be lying on the salt grass, as they did not fifty years ago, dying on a bit of sacking.'

'Oh, for God's sake! Let up, will you! I've heard it so often it's got whiskers.' May moved round the table, past Sarah, who sat silently sewing, and made her way towards the staircase door, saying, 'I'll call Paul down.' But before she reached it David spoke to her quietly, 'But he's right, you know, May. If it wasn't for the likes of John here and people like Alfred Rennie and Drummond . . .'

'Oh, David, don't you start . . . please. And tell me something I don't know. I'm sick of listening to the virtues of Drummond and Riley and Rennie and Thompson and the rest. Oh yes, and the Virgin Mary herself, Miss Ellen Wilkinson. But tell me, David . . .' She stepped back into the room, 'What have they done? All this cafuffling and what have they done?'

Before David could answer John was on his feet crying, 'They just keep men sane, that's all. Keep reminding them that they're men, that they might be down but not bloody well out. They're trying to feed their minds. At least, put into them as much as their depleted systems will allow them to take, so that when we march into London it won't be a band of ignorant numbskulls they'll be talking to, and that's what they take us for down there, a lot of bloody brainless numbskulls. And they're not alone in thinking along those lines, are they, May dear?'

They glared at each other for a moment. But just as May was about to speak John put in quickly, 'You won't come up to the rooms, will you? No, because you'd have to swallow your words. And, what's more, you might learn something . . . Oh, but you don't need to learn, do you? No, you know it all, don't you? Like them up there. Well, as I said, they'll get an eye-opener when we march in.'

'Da-di-da, da-di-da; tra-le-la-la.' May gave an imitation of blowing a bugle, and as John took a step forward David, catching his arm, said quickly, 'Now then, now then. Stop it, you two.'

'I'll make some tea.' Sarah rose from her chair, and, pushing the little dress she was smocking on to the dresser, went out into the scullery, while John, looking towards May again, said bitterly, 'One of these days I'll land you one and you'll not get up again.'

'Try it on.' She smiled at him as she rolled her head tauntingly on the back of her shoulders.

Then, going into the passage, she called upstairs, 'Paul! Paul, do you hear me? Come on. We're going over.'

There was some laughter and chatter from the room above, then a bouncing step on the stairs and a boy of about eight years old followed May into the kitchen. He was tall for his age and thin, and he looked like neither May nor John, but there was a suggestion of his father in his mercurial manner. With a flicking movement of his eyes he looked from his father to David and said, 'You'll never be able to make her spell, Uncle, I bet you won't. She can read long words, but she can't even spell cat.'

'What should I do with her? Bray her?' David made great play of rolling up his shirt-sleeves, and the boy laughed a high tinkling laugh. 'I can see you doing that, Uncle David. But you being a good speller and knowing about words, you'd think she could spell, wouldn't you? She's over five.'

'Yes, you would at that age.' David shook his head sadly at the boy, causing him to laugh again.

May, pushing at her son, now cried, 'Get going. It's a shame to waste two houses between you and her.'

'Aw, let's have a minute, Mam.' The boy swung away from her and went quickly round the table to where John sat moving cardboard letters with his finger.

'You playing Lexicon, Dad?'

'Do as your mother bids you.' John did not raise his eyes.

'You playing Lexicon, Uncle David?'

'Do you want to get shot, Paul Hetherington?' David looked into the boy's grinning face.

'I want to watch you play. Why are you always messing about with letters, Uncle? You should have been a teacher. Have you always messed about with letters, like when you was a young lad?'

'Yes, Paul, always. They've always fascinated me.'

'Did you hear me?'

'Yes, Mam. Just one minute, only one minute. Go on, Uncle Davie.'

David looked at May and shook his head.

'Why do they fascinate you, Uncle Davie?'

'Well, I suppose it's because a few lines differently arranged can tell you so much.'

'But they're not lines, Uncle Davie, they're squibbles and things.'

'No, they all start with lines. Look.' David took from his pocket a piece of string and, cutting it into lengths with his pen-knife, he placed one piece before him, then he bent another in two, and, sticking it in the middle of the first piece, he said, 'There you are, one straight line, another straight line, bent in two, stick them together and you've got K.' The boy nodded and David went on, 'Then you take another straight piece, put it next to the

K and you've got I. Now I is the most important letter in the alphabet; it not only means I, it means ME.' David thumped his chest in a number of places, 'It means all of ME. I've always thought the letter I was an amazing letter. You think of that straight line and then you think of what it means . . . you see?'

Paul nodded again, his eyes bright and twinkling.

'Then you want an S, so you take your straight line and you bend it like that . . . there.' He pointed. 'You've got an S.' He did the same again, then said, 'Look, another S, and what have you? Kiss.'

Paul thumped his uncle in the arm and laughed his high laugh. 'Do some more.'

'Oh no you don't. Come on.' May grabbed her son by the collar, swung him round and marched him out of the room.

In the scullery, protesting but still laughing, Paul grabbed at Sarah's skirt as he was hustled past her and cried, 'Goodnight, Aunt Sarah. She's not asleep. I bet you a shillin' she starts howling in a minute.'

'Goodnight, Paul. She'll get her bottom smacked if she does.'

'What you havin' for supper?'

This question brought May to a halt, and, turning towards Sarah, she said, 'Do you know something? I think he's got a tapeworm – I'm serious.' She nodded at Sarah. 'The minute he got in he had a basin of stew left over from the dinner. That was half-past four. When I went next door' – she jerked her head towards the scullery window – 'he was sitting up having a full tea with his grandad. Chips . . . the lot. And then I come over here and finds him scoffing again. And look at him.' She shook his collar. 'There's not a peck of flesh on his bones, people think he's starved. I tell you, he's got a tapeworm.'

Sarah smiled. 'Well, he never ails anything, does he?'

'Ail anything?' He hasn't got time, he's always eating.' She gave her son another shake, then pushed him out into the yard, saying, 'Goodnight then.'

'Goodnight, May.'

The door had hardly closed behind her when it was opened immediately and May, her face in the aperture, said, 'Tell him to get over home before twelve, will you? I hate to be woken up in the middle of the night.'

She was gone before Sarah could make any retort, but if she had thought of one she would not have been able to voice it. She stood for a moment looking out into the dark yard. What did she mean by that? May knew that she herself went up to bed and left them downstairs talking until all hours. She had likely meant nothing. What could she mean, anyway? But May was deep. No-one ever knew what May was thinking, you couldn't get to the bottom of her.

'Mammy! Mammy!' The cry came from almost above her head and she turned and, picking up the tray of tea, went into the kitchen.

David had half risen from his chair. 'I'll see to her,' he said.

'No, it's all right. Leave her to me.'

'She'll keep you going. She'll have you up there until dawn.'

'It's all right.' She put the tray on the corner of the table and went out and up the stairs, and when she entered her daughter's bedroom the child was sitting up in bed waiting for her.

'Paul didn't read me a story, Mammy.'

'Well, he was helping you with your spelling, wasn't he?'

'He wasn't. I was reading to him and when it was his turn Auntie May called.'

'Come on, lie down. What do you want?'

'Oh.' The child snuggled down into the bedclothes. 'Henny-penny and Cocky-locky and the sky is going to fall.'

Sarah pulled a chair towards the bedside, and, reaching out, picked up a thick-backed nursery book from the table. She had no need of the book, she knew the story word for word, but she flipped the pages over until she came to the story of Henny-penny and Cocky-locky going to tell the King the sky was going to fall. But before starting on it she cast a smiling glance down on her daughter and the child smiled back at her. Every now and again during the reading they would do this. Sarah would lift her head and look at the child and they would smile at each other. Almost from the day she was born it had been like that. They would look at each other and smile and become one.

Every time Sarah looked at this child of hers she knew she was the luckiest woman alive, for she not only had the child, she had its father. In this tiny world of hers she had everything, everything to make a woman happy. Was not David one of the few men in work? They had four meals a day, they owed no one, they had everything, everything that made for joy . . . that was David's phrase. He had said to her, 'I just can't understand about you having nerves, honey, you're not built like that. And we have everything, haven't we? Everything that makes for joy. Is there anything you want? Tell me. Tell me, is there anything in the world that I can give?' And then he had added quickly, 'That's a silly question on three pounds fifteen a week.'

On that occasion she had thrown herself into his arms and assured him with all her heart that he had given her the world. Then why had she got nerves? Why had the doctor said she was suffering from nerves? The doctor had said he thought she was worrying about something . . . What was she worrying about?

Again she had reassured him that she hadn't a worry in the world. Perhaps, she had said, something had happened to her when she was carrying Kathleen, for it was from when she was first pregnant that she had felt this way.

Yes, David remembered it was from the night she had the nightmare, the night following the day she had told him about the baby coming.

She came to the end of the story.

'There now, go to sleep.' Sarah closed the book.

'I haven't said my prayers, Mammy.'

'Yes, you have. You said them before you got into bed. You know you did.' She patted the plump cheek, then, bending over, she laid her mouth to it and was imprisoned by two podgy arms.

'Mammy.'

'Yes, darling.'

'Paul says he loves you.'

'Does he? That's nice. I love Paul too.'

'Paul says that when he grows up he's going to have a house with fifteen rooms and a big car.'

'Oh, I'm glad to hear that; we'll have to go and stay with him . . . Leave go, darling.'

As Sarah disengaged herself Kathleen said, 'I want Nancy, Mammy, to keep me warm.'

'Oh, Nancy's too hard, you might roll on her and hurt yourself. Have Peter, he's soft.'

'He kicks me, Mammy.'

'I'll tell him not to.' Sarah went to the corner of

the small room and from a shelf attached to the wall she took from among numerous toys a dilapidated velvet rabbit, and, holding it at arm's length as she walked to the bed, she said, 'If you kick Kathleen, Peter, you'll get your bottom smacked in the morning.' She placed the rabbit in the child's arms, kissed her once again, then saying as she put the light out, 'I'll leave the door open,' she went from the room and down the stairs.

Dan was in the kitchen now, sitting at the table shuffling a set of dominoes. He turned his head at Sarah's entry. 'Hello, there, how's it going?'

'Oh, all right, Dan.'

'Is she asleep?'

'Yes, she'll be off in a minute . . . I hope.' She smiled at him.

'You go to the doctor's today?'

'Yes.'

'What did he say?'

'Oh, nothing fresh, but he gave me a different bottle, it's very bitter.'

'That'll be for your appetite.'

Sarah picked up her sewing from the dresser again and seated herself in David's leather chair to the side of the fire and continued with the smocking. The dominoes clicked, and the two brothers and their uncle, all looking of a similar age now, played their nightly game. It had become almost a ritual, this gathering together each night from seven o'clock onwards. If, as they sometimes did, David and she went to the pictures, they would find Dan and John sitting at the table on their return. The key was always kept in the wash-house in between the legs of the poss stick which stood in the middle of the poss tub.

And Dan played on a Thursday night too now.

Sometimes they played Lexicon, or cards, but for the most part it was dominoes, and it was seldom that the evening did not end in some form of discussion. That their discourse kept clear of heated argument was due entirely to David's even temper and Dan's humour.

The only reason why David played games, Sarah thought, was to keep his fingers moving, for he missed his piano-playing. She had tried in every way she knew to persuade him to continue his practice, but his answer was always the same. When she was welcome next door he would start practising again. She had learned in her six years of marriage to David he could be stubborn, and it was surprising to her to realise that he could carry this stubbornness to great lengths. She knew that neither Dan nor John would have been so tenacious with regard to his principles. Although David still visited his mother his visits were short and they had become shorter with the years. The reason for this, Sarah knew, was that Mary Hetherington had not taken to her grand-daughter. Although David had not put this in actual words, she knew that he was aware of it.

David's voice now brought her attention to the table, and Dan, as he said, 'What's up with you the night, Dan? That's the seventh game you've lost, and you've doubled twice. That means you owe me . . .' He consulted a piece of paper in his hand, then looked up and laughed. 'Four pounds seven-and-sixpence. I'll let you off with the sixpence.'

'Will you have it now or wait till you get it?'

'I'll wait till I get it.'

'Aw.' Dan scraped his chair back from the table, and, lifting his thick hair from his scalp with his spread fingers, he said, 'To tell you the truth, me mind's not on it, it's miles away . . . in the shop.'

'In the shop?' John looked up from shuffling the cards. 'Anything wrong?'

'Well, yes and no. It's like this.' Dan leaned forwards his forearms on the table again, and looked from John to David. 'The old man made a proposition to me today and I don't really know what to do. It's like this. He's up against the wall now, like all the others; four shops have closed in the last month down the street and our books are so full of tick there isn't any margin left. One of the main snags is that some of them when they've any money go elsewhere, down to Shields Market or some such place. I've said to them, "Look, you can have what tick you like as long as you bring your little bit of ready in." Some of them do, but you just can't keep going on the few. Well, he called me

273

upstairs this morning, and there was the wife sitting. I tell you it was awful, but he put it to me plainly. He said he would have to shut up unless he could find a bit of ready to meet the bills. He's a proud old devil you know, but straight as a die. He's got his faults, but he's honest, and there he was, near tears. And the old woman, she was in tears. And he said to me without any palaver, "Well, Dan, what about it? What have you got left of your winnings?" "Well," I said, "I've got just over four hundred." '

Sarah's hands became still, the needle poised, and involuntarily she repeated, 'Four hundred?' And Dan, turning and looking at her, said, 'Yes, from me winnings. You know, out of *John Bull*.' Then, jerking his head round to David and shaking it, he muttered, 'Don't tell me you never told Sarah about it?'

'No, I never told her. There was no need. It's years ago you got it. I've n⸱ er thought about it.'

'That's him.' Dan was lo⸱king at Sarah now, smiling. 'Yes. I won six hundred in *John Bull* . . . Fashions, you know.'

'Really?' Sarah smiled. 'Fashions?'

'Yes, I was a dab hand at fashions. I knew absolutely nothing about them, so I came up . . . Well, there it is.' He looked at the men again. 'The old boy's offered me a partnership if I'll put me money in the shop. But he warned me, mind, that it might be like throwing it down the sink. If things

274

don't turn in another year, well, we'll be like the others, we'll be shut up. But the other side of it is that if I don't go in with him we'll be shut up in any case and soon, and I'll be out of a job. And if I don't get another I'll have to live on the four hundred, won't I? They won't give me dole with that gold mine in the bank, not likely. So it's really as broad as it's long. What do you say?' He looked from one to the other.

'You could start up on your own on four hundred,' said John.

'Oh no you couldn't, except in a huxter's shop; not a place like Campbell's. It's a well-established shop and it's got a licence too, you see. He's had that place thirty-eight years; in nineteen twenty-one he could have retired, for he was sitting pretty then. And there's another thing that needs thinking about. He said that if we can keep the place going he'll leave it to me, that's if his wife goes before him. If she doesn't, then I'll have to make her an allowance, but in the end it would be mine . . . It's not to be sneezed at, is it? What do you say, Davie?'

'I think it's worth taking a chance on, Dan, for in the long run you've got nothing to lose. Anyway, you've already made up your mind, haven't you?'

Dan's hand came out and he pushed at Davie, saying, 'Aye, I suppose I have. But I wanted to know what you think.'

'Go ahead,' said David. 'And all the luck in the world. You won't sink. I couldn't imagine you ever sinking.'

Shuffling the cards, John put in quietly, 'If you want an errand boy remember charity begins at home, I'm ready any time.'

Sarah, rising from her chair, looked at Dan. 'I'll make a cup of tea, and we'll drink to it,' she said, smiling.

'That's the ticket, Sarah. And look . . .' He grabbed at her arm. 'When I have me . . . me chain of shops running from Shields Pier to the Swing Bridge in Newcastle, you know what? I'll buy you a car and a mink coat.'

'Thank you very much.' She was laughing now. 'But I'd rather have a wireless set.'

'Oh, but you're getting a wireless set; John's making you a . . .'

'Your big mouth!' John slapped out at Dan, and Dan said, 'Aw, I'm sorry.' He turned to Sarah. 'It was to be a surprise.'

Sarah looked at John. He was dealing out the cards now. She did not say 'Thank you' immediately, but, turning to David, she asked, 'Did you know about this?'

He nodded at her and she said, 'And you let me go on talking about wirelesses . . . Oh.' She ruffled his hair, then, glancing towards John's still bent head, she said, 'I didn't know you could do wirelesses. Thanks, John.'

'That fellow can do anything,' said Dan, laughing. 'Anything he puts his hand to. He is a blooming genius.'

Sarah's words had sounded grateful, but as she went into the scullery the thought in her mind was, Why had he to be the one to give her things? He had made nearly all their furniture, except for the bed, the couch, and the armchair. And what would May say about this? Very likely nothing, but she would think and look all the more.

As she put the kettle on she found herself feeling sorry for anyone who had to live with May, and she dared now to say to herself, I'm sorry for him. Every day for the past six years she had suffered because of John. There were times when she hated him and her feelings would come out in her attitude towards him. And most of the time she was on her guard in case she would say something to him that would bring comment from David. Yet besides all her submerged feelings concerning him, she was sorry for this big, bustling, bumptious, and frustrated individual. And he was frustrated in so many ways. Unemployment to him was a disease that was eating into the very core of his being, and it wasn't lightened by the fact that his father, his uncle, and his brother were all in jobs. He was the one that could least suffer unemployment. There were times when, seeing him in the depths of depression, she had wanted to put her hand out and touch him, to give him comfort, but the fear that accompanied this desire almost paralysed her body, and she was thankful that it did. There had been one particular occasion during the past few years when she had been grateful, yes grateful that she was being blackmailed because of him; for if anything could prevent her softening towards him it was this weekly trial on her nerves. The situation had arisen when one day John had returned hungry and tired from a fruitless workers' march, to be greeted by May and her barbed tongue. He had come over into the kitchen here – she had been alone in the house and he rarely came in when she was alone now – and with the sadness of an aged man, he had asked, 'Can I rest awhile here, Sarah? I'm dog-beat and May's playing hell.' She had made him a meal, and then he had fallen asleep in David's chair, and it was as he slept that there came on her an almost uncontrollable desire for her hands to touch him. And she had flown upstairs and stayed there until David came in . . .

As she made the tea she thought, Him always making things for me, David must be blind. Then she attacked the suggestion with, Well, you don't want his eyes opened, do you? Oh, my God! No, no, never that. Rather the nauseating sight of her father, the parting weekly with the precious five shillings, and her visits to the doctor for her nerve tonic. But how much longer could it go on? She could see her nerves as worn wires, and the strength of a wire at its weakest part. What was her weakest part? There was no answer to this, and she mashed the tea and took it into the kitchen to drink to Dan's success.

2

Over the years Sarah and Phyllis had met once or twice a month. If the weather was fine they took a ride on the ferry across the river. At other times they would walk down towards the sea. They had never reached the sands, for the time they spent together as the years went on grew shorter. Phyllis had now three children to see to, and Sarah always wanted to get back home to be in when David returned from work. Neither of them visited the other's home. Their homes were rarely mentioned. Sarah's decision, years earlier, had come to nothing. She had too much on her mind.

On this Saturday morning Sarah stood in the shelter of a doorway in the Market Place looking over the stalls in the direction of Waterloo Vale where Phyllis was now living. They, as a rule, never met at the week-ends – week-ends were for the family and were a busy time – but this morning was an exception and it was Sarah who had written to Phyllis making the appointment.

The market was almost deserted except for the stalls and their owners. The cutting wind was carrying on it a thick rain almost like sleet, and it was only early October.

When she saw Phyllis moving rapidly with her light step across the cobbles towards her, she went to meet her. After both exclaiming about the wretchedness of the weather, Phyllis said, 'Let's go in here and sit down.'

'Here' was a working-man's café, and when they had taken their thick cups of dark-looking tea from the counter they sat in the corner of the dismal and almost empty room. After sipping from the steaming cup, Phyllis, holding her hands over it, said, 'Do you know any more? Have you heard anything?'

'No, nothing, only what's in the papers . . . Phyllis.' She leant towards her sister. 'Do you know anything about it?'

'Me?' Phyllis pressed herself against the back of the chair, repeating, 'Me? No. No, I don't, but by God I wish I'd thought of it years ago. Is he going to live?'

'I don't know. I just saw me mother for a minute yesterday. We hadn't got the paper on Thursday night, I knew nothing about it until she came in; she had just come back from the hospital. She said he was in an awful state.'

'Hell's cure to him. He's got what he's been asking for for years. Some bloke likely caught him snooping and beat him up. I only wish the polis hadn't come across him so soon; if he'd lain out all night he might have died from exposure . . . that's what they said in the paper an' all.'

Sarah bowed her head. The feeling of guilt lifted from her for a moment; she hadn't been the only one to think along these lines. But she doubted if Phyllis had prayed for him to die. She herself had prayed every minute since yesterday morning that he wouldn't regain consciousness.

'The paper says his arm's broken and he's got injuries to his head. Oh' – Phyllis took another quick sip of her tea – 'if anybody's got their deserts he's got his. It said in the paper a pair of binoculars were found near him that he used for bird-watching. My God, that's something . . . bird-watching. Birds all right. You wouldn't think a reporter would be so daft as to put it in. Him! A man like him bird-watching. But me mother told them that. She said she had to say something because of him going round with a spy glass. I wonder where he got the money from to get it because he hadn't got the guts to pinch. But what made you think I'd 'ad a hand in it?'

Sarah's head was lowered. She knew where he had got the money from, only too true she knew. She looked up quickly, saying now, 'Since he was found near Redhead's Docks down East Holborn way I thought . . . well, to tell you the truth, Phyllis, I thought you might know something about it.'

'No, no, I tell you I don't; but mind, if I'd known he was in the habit of coming down that way, take it from me I'd have done something about it. There's one or two blokes down there who'd beat up their mother for a pint. But he chose the wrong place to use his spy glass when he chose Holborn. It's as Ali says, he was likely watching a couple. But somebody was watching him, and they lathered him. And good luck I say, good luck to whoever it was.'

Yes, good luck to whoever it was. She endorsed that, oh, she did. She only wished they had done the job properly. Eeh! If only she could stop thinking like that . . . She finished her tea, then asked, 'How's the children?'

'Oh, I've got Jimmy in bed again, he never seems well. I've had the doctor. He just says, well, nothing's wrong with him really; give him plenty of fresh air and feed him well, he says. I can do that all right. He gets his grub, he's luckier than some. I thank God for the café every day of me life. Getting things at cost, it means a lot.'

'How is it going now?'

'Oh, just scraping along. In fact hardly that, nobody's got anything.'

'It's worse up in Jarrow.'

'Yes, I know. I went up there the other day. It's dead. I was glad to get back. While I was waiting for a tram there was a fellow talking to a group of them; they all looked as if the smell of a pot of stew

282

would knock them over. But the way this fellow was talking! Like a lawyer. And something he said stuck with me. It isn't very often I listen to the blah-blah-blahing. But it was true what he said. He said Jarrow had been raped and it had given birth to twins, hated twins, hunger and idleness. That's what he said.'

'He's right too, in a way, at least. Only I don't know so much about the idleness. All the men up there are trying to do something. John is forever helping to organise things. It's funny.' She smiled. 'He said the other day that a lot of the fellows have received an education through being on the dole, and when your stomach isn't full he says you can always think better.'

'I saw him in the market last Saturday afternoon. He was with a woman; she was youngish, but she looked a snipe. Would it be his wife?'

'Yes, that sounds like May.' Sarah nodded. 'Small, thin. And she's a snipe all right, you never know how you have her.'

Sarah now gathered her bag and gloves towards her, saying, 'I'll have to be moving, I've left Paul looking after Kathleen and they'll have the place turned upside-down.'

It wasn't until they were on the pavement that Phyllis turned towards Sarah, saying, 'Are you still wanting a piano for David?'

'Yes. You know I do. But I can't manage the money now.'

'This one's only four pounds. Ali says it's a bargain. You know, he said he'd keep a look-out for you. He takes adverts for the café window, it always helps, and he got this one for the piano. He even went and had a look at it. It's just off Fowler Street and the people are in straits. Ali says it's being given away.'

'But four pounds! I haven't got it, Phyllis. I've got about thirty shillings put by and that's the lot.'

'I could lend it to you. Oh, I'm not on me beam ends, don't you worry. I keep slipping a shilling or two into the old tin. Look, Sarah, you can have it and welcome.'

Sarah looked through the slanting rain over the market place towards St Hilda's Church and she thought that the morning had lightened, her future had lightened. She saw through the rain a space ahead without the dread of the tap on the back door on a Monday morning. Perhaps weeks, months of respite, perhaps a lifetime of release . . . If he should die. Oh, dear God, let him die . . . There she was again. It was dreadful to keep going on like this, wishing somebody dead. But he deserved to die; he was wicked, horrible. She felt at times she could embrace a reptile easier than she could look at him . . . And then there was Phyllis offering to lend her money for the piano. Yes, the morning was lighter.

'Look, will I tell Ali to put five shillings on it,

then you could go and have a look at it yourself, eh?'

'Yes, yes, Phyllis.' Sarah was nodding enthusiastically down on Phyllis. 'Yes, I'll come down on Monday, eh? What's the address?'

'Oh, I can't remember it off-hand. It'll be in the shop.' They looked at each other in silence for a moment, then Phyllis asked softly, 'Won't you come round to the house, Sarah? You've never been.'

'You've never asked me.' They smiled shyly at each other.

'It's seven, Waller Place.'

'Seven, Waller Place. All right, I'll come, Phyllis; I'll come in the afternoon after I've dropped Kathleen into school. About two, eh?'

'About two. But mind, don't expect too much. Although' – Phyllis's chin went up – 'I'm not ashamed of our place, I've got no reason to be. It's a damned sight better furnished than some of them at the other side of the town. I can tell you that.'

'I'd love to see it, Phyllis.'

'Well, Monday. So long, Sarah.'

'So long, Phyllis.'

They touched hands quickly, shyly, then went their separate ways, hurrying as if to get rid of their embarrassment.

It was as the tram came to a stop at the top of

Stanhope Road that the thought sprang into Sarah's mind: 'I'll pay a visit.' And just as the bell rang for the tram to move on again she jumped off and crossed the road and went down the gentle slope towards the church.

The church was empty and quiet. She blessed herself with holy water from the font, then went down the side aisle, past the pictures of the Stations of the Cross to the front pew before the altar of the Virgin Mary; and as always when she came to this church she felt in a strange way as if she had come home. But she hadn't been in the church for years, and over the past four years she had rarely seen the priest. Father O'Malley had apparently given her up as a bad job, but since Kathleen had started at St Peter and St Paul's school Father Bailey had been to see her twice. He was nice was Father Bailey, and he thought the world of Kathleen.

She began to pray. The Our Father, the Hail Mary. Then she repeated parrot-wise, 'Come, Holy Ghost, fill the hearts of thy faithful and kindle in them the fire of thy love. Send forth thy spirit and they shall be created and they shall renew the face of the earth.' All the set prayers of her childhood. And then she was talking to God, talking rapidly, beseechingly, asking Him of His mercy to take her father, to make him die. She bent her back until her buttocks were resting against the seat, and her head bowed on the back of the

286

seat in front of her; her forearms at each side of her head brought her hands clasped above her hat, and she talked to God as if He was before her, as if she was clutching His garments. Take him, O Lord, take him, because I'm frightened. I nearly hit him last week. Take him, O Lord. I can't bear the sight of him, he's evil, I'm afraid of what I might do. I've thought of doing just what this man's done to him, O Lord. I've thought of following him on a dark night, O God forgive me. Take him, Lord; please take him. And for no reason she could think of she found herself now repeating the seven capital or deadly sins. Pride, covetousness, lust, envy, gluttony, anger, and sloth.

'Sarah.'

She sprang back on to the seat, crouching against the pillar to the side of her, staring up at the hand that had touched her shoulder and the face above it.

'Are you all right, Sarah?'

'Y-e-s, Father. Oh, Father, you gave me a fright.'

'I'm sorry, Sarah.' The priest slowly sat down on the edge of the pew a few feet from her and he asked quietly, 'Are you in trouble, Sarah?'

She swallowed and moved her head as if in denial; yet its very action was an affirmative answer, and Father Bailey said, 'What is it? Can I help you? Dry your eyes.'

She fumbled in her bag for her handkerchief and dried her eyes and blew her nose, and then dried the fresh tears that were flowing down her cheeks.

'Is it your husband?'

'Oh, no. No!' The denial was emphatic. 'He's wonderful to me, Father. Believe me, no one on earth could be better. No. No.'

'It isn't the child, is it? There can't be anything wrong with Kathleen. I saw her yesterday.'

'No, Father, Kathleen's all right.'

'Wouldn't you like to tell me, Sarah?'

'Oh, Father.' Her whole body slumped against the pillar. Could she tell him. Not a living soul had she uttered a word to of the cause of her mental anguish over the past years. Everybody thought she had nerves, and indeed she had nerves now. But oh, the relief to be able to tell someone, to know that someone would understand, and this priest, this good priest, would understand. She wondered why she hadn't thought about it before. But then she remembered she had thought about telling it in confession and dismissed it. She lifted her eyes wearily to his now and asked quietly, 'Could you hear me in confession, Father?'

'Certainly, Sarah.' He held out his hand and raised her to her feet as if she was a sick person, and to him she was a sick person. Then he turned from her and moved out of the pew and up the church towards the confessional box, and he went into one door, and she into the other.

When she was kneeling on the kneeler, her face

to the wire mesh, she whispered, 'Will I start as if in confession, Father?'

'Yes, Sarah.' And so she began formally, 'Please, Father, give me your blessing for I have sinned' – this opening had always struck her as comical, for it seemed you were asking the priest to bless you because you had sinned – but not today. She went on, 'It is nearly six years since my last confession. I have only missed Mass a few times, but I have never been to Communion or my Easter duties.' She paused here, thinking of all the venal sins she had committed. Bouts of temper. Thinking unkind thoughts. Missing her morning and night prayers. All her small sins she told him, and then she paused again before saying, 'My main sin, Father, is wishing someone dead. It's about this I want to tell you.'

'Go on, Sarah, I'm listening.'

And so she told him. She told him exactly what happened on that New Year's morning, and she told him of the morning her father had visited her and his weekly visits since. Of the five shillings a week she paid him, and of the terror rising in her of late in case she would do him an injury. And lastly she told him of feeling glad, in fact joyful, when she heard he had been beaten into unconsciousness.

When she had finished, the priest made no sound and she remained still, waiting. And then he said a surprising thing, he said, 'Do you love this man, Sarah, your husband's brother?'

'No, no, Father.' Her reply was like rapid fire.

'In no way, Sarah? You haven't encouraged him to take a liberty with you?'

'No, Father, no. I was a little afraid of him because I think I knew what he was feeling.'

'And there was no answering response in you to this feeling?'

She waited before answering, and then said falteringly, 'He's a very attractive man, very virile. He's . . . he's unhappy with his wife, I know. I've felt . . . well, sorry for him at times. At times I wanted . . . I wanted to be kind to him. But no, Father, I've never encouraged him and . . . and I don't love him.' She could not say to the priest that there was some part of her that called to her husband's brother and made her ashamed that this part would rear up like a wild animal at times, and these times usually occurred with the gentle loving of David. It was then that this part of her would long for a different loving, a wild, frenzied, mad loving, a kind of loving she sensed on the New Year's morning when locked in John's embrace. No, she could not say this to the priest because she was only barely conscious of it. The thoughts in your head while your man was loving you, and the thoughts that filled it for the rest of the day and night belonged to two separate beings. But when these two beings attempted to merge, as they sometimes did in the light of day, she was overcome by a feeling she had to flay, and flay it she did. She flayed it with her happiness, the happiness given to her by David. She flayed it with the gratitude she owed to David. She flayed it with the passionate love she had for her child.

The priest was talking now. He was saying, 'You have been very silly, Sarah. You should never have given your father money in the first place.'

'I couldn't help it, Father. I knew he would have told my husband, and although David wouldn't have believed him, not really, it would have caused a difference between him and his brother, and he's very fond of his brother, they are very fond of each other. And then there was his mother. His mother doesn't like me, and I knew that if she heard about this, life would be unbearable for us all. Then there was my sister-in-law, John's wife. She's an odd type of girl. Well, what I mean is, Father, she seems quiet, but she's quarrelsome, hard. You see, I just had to keep my father quiet.'

'When he comes out of hospital – you must stop praying that he won't come out, Sarah, do you hear me?'

'Yes, Father.'

'Well, when he comes out you must tell him that you're going to give him no more money, and if he becomes nasty you must tell him you are going to the police.'

'But, Father!'

'Listen, Sarah. You must tell him that. You must frighten him off. Whether you go to the police or not is up to you, but blackmailing is a serious offence and they'll soon put him in his place. What you've got to realise is that he is undermining your health. You've lost a lot of weight, haven't you?'

'Yes, Father, two stone.'

'Well, you can't go on like that. You know what you should do, but you won't do it. But I feel that your husband should know about this. What I have seen of him he is a very reasonable man. I like him, Sarah.'

'Thank you, Father, but . . . but I couldn't tell him.'

'Well, leave it for a time until your father comes out of hospital, but in the meantime think about it seriously, think about confiding in your husband. Bring him down to me if you like and we'll talk it over.'

'I couldn't, Father. There are too many complications.'

'Well, you must do what you think best. And remember, Sarah, I'm always here if you should need me.'

'Thank you. Father. I feel better now.'

'Make a good act of contrition, Sarah.'

She came out of the confessional box and waited a moment and then the priest joined her; he walked with her to the door of the church and there, taking her hand in his, he said, 'Nothing matters if your conscience is clear . . . Make that your aim in life, Sarah. Keep your conscience clear.'

'Yes, Father.' She inclined her head towards him. 'Goodbye, Father, and thank you, thank you very much.'

'Goodbye, Sarah.'

She walked quietly down the steps of the church, past the station, and down the Dock Bank. The Bank, as usual, was black with men, some talking in groups, some standing silently against the rails, just looking out of the hungry present into the hungry future. No longer were they on the lookout for the gangers with the hope of being set on a boat, because the gangers, too, were standing staring. Gone from the Bank was that notable measured stride of the burly, proud captains; the noticeable bearing of the arrogant chief engineers. No longer were there strings of coolies shopping on the Bank, their bass bags swelled with fish, their bare knees pointing upwards as their seemingly unbending feet left the ground. The colour, the excitement, had gone from the docks.

Sarah cast her eyes towards the Dock offices as she passed them. David was in there. She knew where he would be sitting, the exact spot, to the right of the main door where you went in, and her glance towards the grimed window next to the door was tender.

David was lucky; he was one of the envied ones, he was in work. As long as the docks were moving at all he was secure, and she was secure. But David didn't give the docks credit of his security, he gave it to Mr Batty. He had once said to her when talking about the office, 'He feels he's tamed me . . . training me he would call it, so if there is any security in the job at all it's that, just that. He hasn't made life unbearable for me like he has for some. I feel he holds me up to himself as part of his success.'

'And you don't mind?' she had said to him.

'No.' He had smiled at her. 'Why should I? It pleases him and it doesn't hurt me.'

That was David, the gentle way every time. Oh, she thanked God for David. She felt lighter, happier. Why hadn't she gone to Father Bailey before. Oh, she wished she had.

It had stopped raining, so she decided to walk home, it would save the bus fare. She crossed over the road to the path that led under the dock arches. The arches were dark and dismal, the brickwork was as black as a singed bloater, and the water dribbled down the walls in rivulets of slimy green. But the arches left no impression on Sarah; they were part of the dismal whole, unseen, except on rare occasions, because of their familiarity.

The pavement bordered by the actual dock wall curved round by the bottom of Simonside Bank, the Bank which led into . . . the country, to the nice houses and Hedworth Hall and the Robin Hood and places like that. She hadn't been up into the country for years. As she looked up the steep incline of the bank she said to herself, 'I must start and take Kathleen for walks up there, away from the streets.' They could do it on a Sunday afternoon; she would speak to David.

She was turning her gaze away when it was pulled back again. A man had just rounded the bend. He came striding down the road, his step quick and purposeful, and as she watched him raise his hand quickly then break into a run she turned her head away and groaned inside. Oh, no, no, not this morning. Then fear came upon her. She would have to walk all the way home with him. What if her father . . . She closed her eyes. She had forgotten, he was in hospital. The relief scuttled the fear from her being and she turned and looked towards John as he came running up to her.

'Fancy seeing you . . . Here, give me your bag.' He took the bag from her hand.

'There's nothing in it,' she said.

'No, there's not.' He shook it up and down. 'Well, where've you been then?'

'To see Phyllis.'

'Oh, oh!' He was walking by her side now, suiting his step to hers. 'How is she?'

'Oh, she's fine.'

'I've been up to see Ted Cobber. He lives up near

Jarrow cemetery, but I wanted a walk so I came back the country way . . . getting in training. Him and me, we were mates for years. He's a bit cut up, he wasn't picked for the march.'

'Is he oldish?'

'No, no, same age as me about. But he didn't pass the doctor. We all had to go through an examination, you know. It's a wonder that he found two hundred fit among us when you take everything into consideration.' His voice was quiet, and Sarah nodded. 'Yes, it is a wonder,' she said.

They walked in silence for some minutes, and each second of each minute Sarah was aware of the man by her side. It was always like this when she was alone with him. She wanted to break the silence but couldn't, and was relieved when he said, 'I went up to get a loan of his ground sheet; he used to do a lot of cycling at one time and sleep out.'

'But you won't have to sleep out?'

'No. No. It's all been arranged in different town centres and places, but we'll likely have to sleep rough on the boards. But you can use a ground sheet to cover you in the rain, you know.'

He was excited about the march on Monday, the march from Jarrow to London, the march of protest against starvation, and he had talked of nothing else for weeks. She had become almost as familiar with the names of those chiefly concerned as May was. David Reilly, Councillor

Paddy Scullion, and Councillor Symonds; Councillor Studdick, the Conservative agent, and Harry Stoddard, his Labour counterpart. She knew that these latter two, political men from opposing sides, had been sent ahead – and together – to prepare the reception for the marchers in places like Harrogate, Leeds, Barnsley, Bedford, Luton, and other towns.

But the name mostly on John's lips was that of Ellen Wilkinson. Sarah had never seen Ellen Wilkinson. She didn't think of her as a woman, not an ordinary, normal woman. A woman who could lead men on a march to London could not be an ordinary, normal woman. In fact any woman who was in Parliament could, of course, not be ordinary. As for being normal, well, women had their place, hadn't they, and it wasn't really their place to yell their heads off among a lot of men in Parliament. So thought Sarah.

But John was quiet now. He was not talking at high speed about the arrangements and the arrangers, those for and those against. He wasn't wanting to wipe the floor with Bishop Hemsley Henson, Bishop of Durham, or worship at the feet of Bishop Gordon of Jarrow – his homage of the latter having nothing to do with the man being a churchman.

As Sarah glanced at him she was surprised at the unusual expression of sadness on his face; she had never seen him looking sad before.

Aggressive, bitter, cynical, jolly, rollicking, but never sad. He was looking ahead as he said, 'There's going to be a short service in Christ Church for the marchers afore we leave.'

'Oh, that'll be nice.' Her answer sounded inane, but it was all she could find to say. And then he asked, 'Would you come, Sarah?'

She flashed her eyes towards him. 'To church, you mean?'

'Yes.' He was still looking ahead.

'Yes . . . yes, all right, John. Yes, I'll come. May could call for me . . .'

'May's not coming, nor is me mother. Neither of them, but for different reasons. My mother wouldn't put her foot inside a church if it meant saving her life, or anybody else's for that matter. As for May, she neither believes in God . . . or man.' He stressed the last word. 'She says it's a lot of damned hypocrisy, the men going to church before the march, for ten to one there hadn't been a man Jack of us inside a church or chapel for years . . . and I suppose she's right in a way. But you know, this isn't just an ordinary march, at least I don't see it that way. They're marching from Scotland and Cumberland, and Yorkshire and Wales, and Durham, but ours is different somehow. Runciman's said that the Government could do nothing for Jarrow, that Jarrow must work out its own salvation – well, that's what we're doing in this march. Some of us might never

298

make it; it's a long way on two feet and mended shoes.' He looked down at his boots, and Sarah looked down at them too. They were newly cobbled. On each boot were two bulging patches of leather, but the boots were shining. As always John was tidy.

There came over her body now a softening, an enervating wave. Again, and almost unconsciously, her body and mind were forgiving him for all the trouble he had caused her. She even forgot for the moment that a short while ago she had knelt in an agony of mental suffering in the church. At this point there came into her mind what she termed a silly thought. I wish I was his mother, she said to herself. She seemed to see inside the big aggressive bulk of him to the everlasting little boy who needed someone to turn to, someone who would always listen to his prattling and who would push the black hair back from his brow as he talked . . .

'Keep your conscience clear. Make that your aim in life, Sarah. Keep your conscience clear.' The priest's words were loud in her head and she exclaimed to herself, Oh God! But I've done nothing, said nothing. She was throwing denials back at her mind now. It was just that when she was alone with him she felt something, a sympathy; it was nothing else, just a feeling of sympathy. He made her feel like this, as if he wanted her protection . . . Protection. John needing protection . . . huh! Don't be so daft. She threw scorn at herself. What he wanted was to bear her to the ground and crush her into it with love. Oh, she knew, she knew what John wanted. Her body told her what John wanted, and there she was talking about being a mother to him. She hadn't been honest with the priest . . . Oh, she had, she said; she hadn't thought like this when she was with the priest, it was only when she was alone with John that she thought like this. Oh God, she wished she was home. And why had she said she would go to the church on the Monday morning and neither the one or the other going. She herself had more than one reason why she shouldn't go. It was forbidden that a Catholic should partake of a service in another church; it was a sin, she knew that, yet she had said she would go. And after Father Bailey being so kind to her. Oh, she wished she was home.

They were walking in step silently, both looking ahead. Then John, picking up where he had left off a few minutes earlier, said, 'It's as if every one of us was going on a private mission. Not a man of us but wants everything to be ordered and who wants to thrust the word rabble down the necks of those that say that's what it'll be. I don't think there's been anything so well organised as this march for years. Nothing has come out of the North so well organised, I'd like to swear on that. That petition will be handed over to Parliament by men, not a rabble. And for the few that's against us we've got the majority with us. All Tyneside is behind us, and the Lord Mayor of Newcastle, Alderman Lock, is with us all the way. He's not standing aside and saying every man for himself, Jack. He says, and these are his very words, "Jarrow's troubles are our troubles", and . . . and you know, Sarah' – he turned his face fully towards her now – 'what a lot forget is that it's us the day, but it'll be them the morrow if the canker isn't stopped.'

When she didn't answer he waited for a moment before saying, 'Are you all right?'

'Yes, yes. It's just the damp gets into you with all this rain.'

Again he was looking ahead, and again he was silent for a time until he said, 'Have you been to the doctor's this week?'

'Yes.'

'What did he say?'

'Oh, just that I must eat more.' She forced herself to smile at him. 'And I told him I didn't mind losing weight, it was fashionable to be thin.'

He kept his eyes on her now as he asked quietly, 'Sarah, has your worry anything to do with me?' He put out his hand quickly towards her, exclaiming with concern, 'Look . . . look, don't jib away from me like that, I'm not going to take anything up; and I can't do anything, can I?' He moved his head round to indicate the open space of the Slacks and the broad daylight. 'It's only that I get worried at times. Aye, yes, I do.' He nodded his head quickly at her. 'I get worried about you because you never seem to have been right since . . . well . . .' He flung his head round on his shoulders and muttered through his teeth. 'Since that New Year's Eve. If it's about me you are worried you can put your mind at rest, it won't happen again, I've told you . . . There now.' He swung his head sideways once more. 'Well, is it me that's worrying you . . . I'm asking you?'

She was sweating now; she could feel it running down between her breasts and from her armpits. Never before had she wanted to pour out the truth to him. Hadn't she done enough pouring out for one morning? The distress in her was like froth in a bottle, and she knew that once it was released it would be difficult to stop the flow. One thing was sure: if she told him she would have no more trouble with her father. He would scare the daylights out of him, perhaps finish the job that the other fellow had started. She shivered on the thought . . . But there was another thing she could be sure of too. If she were to answer his question truthfully they would be drawn together, held together by ties stronger than those they would have created through any physical means. She could not explain to herself this knowledge of John's reaction, except that in fighting her father for her he would unconsciously cloak himself with moral righteousness. Moreover, he would glory in holding some part of her that was not David's.

She made herself aggressive both in voice and manner and used it as a screen behind which to hide as she cried, 'Why must you bring that up? And what makes you imagine you have anything to do with the way I feel? You've got a nerve, you know, John.' Her eyes were blinking, her chin was thrust out at him, and her step became uneven as she quickened it with an effort to move away from him.

'All right, all right.' His voice was calming. 'I only wondered. But don't take on. When you act like that you sound like May.' His voice was still calm.

She paused in her stride. 'I'm not like May.'

'No . . . no, you're not.' He was looking at her, his eyes soft, his whole expression tender. 'I'm sorry, I shouldn't have said that. No, thank God, you're not like May.'

Again they walked in silence. They were approaching the streets now, and when she turned into Camelia Street he turned too. He did not say, 'So long, I'll be seeing you.' Nor did he say, 'You don't mind if I drop in for a moment?' He just accompanied her home.

As they approached the front door they heard high laughter, and after she had knocked on the rapper there came a scurrying through the front room and the door was pulled open. And there stood Paul and Kathleen, their faces bright with careless childhood.

Kathleen was about to cry, 'Oh, Mummy!' when she saw John. Then, literally leaving the ground, she jumped from the high step into his arms, shouting, 'Uncle John! Why, Uncle John!' It was as if she hadn't seen him for days.

John walked through the front room with her legs straddled round his waist, his arms supporting her shoulders as her head dangled beyond them.

Paul, walking by Sarah's side into the kitchen, said under his breath, 'We've broken a cup and saucer, Auntie.'

'You didn't.' Kathleen was looking from her upside-down position towards Paul and she waved her arms at him now as she cried, 'You didn't, I did. I threw it at him, Mammy.'

'You what! Let her down, John.'

John, with a lift, planted the child on her feet, and Sarah, looking down at her daughter, said, 'You threw a cup and saucer at Paul? Why did you do that?'

Putting her hands behind her back, Kathleen sauntered towards the fender; then sat down on it before she answered, 'Just 'cos.'

'Never mind just 'cos.' Sarah's voice was stern. She turned to Paul. 'Why did she throw it at you, Paul?'

'He likely deserved it.' John gave his son a

304

gentle push that landed him in David's chair, and the boy, looking at Sarah, said, 'We . . . we were just playin'. I . . . I was teasing her.'

'You weren't, you were telling lies. You were . . . you were.' The little chin was thrust out at Paul. 'He said, Mammy . . .' She looked at Sarah now. 'He said you loved him better than me. So there. That's why I threw the cup and saucer at him. It hit the fender.' She looked down and pointed with her finger towards the brass rail that rimmed the steel fender, and she continued to look at it as she ended, 'And you don't, do you?'

'I was only teasing, Auntie.' The boy spoke with his head down, and Sarah turned her eyes away from him, away from her daughter, and away from John. She could not please her daughter by saying, 'Of course I don't,' because that would hurt the boy, and the boy was John's. What she did say was, 'You'll get a skelped behind, me lady, one of these days.'

Then she fell back on the old stand-by that helped her through trying moments and over little obstacles, and big obstacles too. She said, 'I'll make a cup of tea . . . we're froze.'

On the Monday morning Sarah stood outside the Jarrow Town Hall and watched the mayor review the men. Two hundred shabbily dressed, freshly shaved, tidy, thin men. She followed them as they marched to Christ Church, and as they entered a man stopped a boy in front of her from going in by saying, 'It's only the wives and mothers, lad.' For a moment she hesitated, but the man accepted her and she passed into the church and sat in the back row. The Mayor and Corporation were seated at the front, and Bishop Gordon took the service.

Sarah had never been in any but a Catholic church in her life, but she did not find this service strange, as she did not follow it. Her mind was elsewhere, for she was overcome by a feeling of deep sadness. Yet at the same time she was experiencing a sense of exhilaration, and she was wishing that she too could march with them. Oh, she wished she could. Oh, she told herself, she did.

The service over, they filed outside, and John came to her side. He had a groundsheet in a roll slung across his shoulders. He looked big and gaunt, yet he too looked elated.

'Well, this is it.' It sounded like the goodbye of a man going to war. She looked at him, but she could not speak. Sadness had excluded all other feelings. A couple to the right of them were enfolded in each other's arms; all about them people were embracing, wives, mothers, children, all clinging to men as if they were about to march to their deaths.

She should say something, but she could not translate her thoughts into words; her mind was a jumble and full of pain, as was her body. It was a strange pain, unlike anything she had experienced

fore. As the tears welled into her eyes, John's
ce moved before her like a reflection beneath
pling water. She heard him saying, softly,
arah, Sarah. Oh, Sarah.' He had hold of her hand
w. 'Thanks for coming. You can't believe what
means. Goodbye, Sarah.'

She could not even say his name or bid him
odbye. But her mind, still in a turmoil, was
eating a force which was driving something
rough her body, something that was beyond the
ice of conscience, that could not be held in
unds by discretion, discretion that would have
forced propriety. There was only inches
tween them, yet the distance seemed immense;
was as if she had to leap to reach him, but reach
m she did. Her mouth rested against his hard
w line just to the side of his lips. After a second
  hesitation, when she thought he would not
uch her, his arms came about her, and he held
r in a vice-like grip. Then she was standing
aking and blind among the other women, and
 was on the road, somewhere in the ranks.

With the pad of her thumb she swiftly wiped the
ars from her cheeks, and over the head of the
rong she saw him clearly. He was looking
wards her. He did not raise his hand in a last
lute, he just looked at her and held her gaze. She
atched him turn his head away, and it looked
e that of a conqueror.

A small woman to the side of her was crying.

She sniffed and blew her nose loudly. 'There the go,' she said; 'the skeletons of Palmers. It'll fruitless, the march. The shipyard's dead an' can't never be brought to life again.'

A woman standing behind Sarah said harshl 'Well, they'll have a damned good try. It's a goo job everybody doesn't think alike. When that l gets to London they may look like skeletons, b what they lack in flesh they'll make up for in spir By the livin' Harry they will that.'

The little woman, now apparently aiming make up for her despondency, looked at Sara and said, 'But your man'll be all right; he's big an tough looking, he'll stand it. His name Hetherington, isn't it . . . John? I've heard me s on about him. Have you any bairns?'

Sarah's mind was working now. Like a juggle it was tossing words here and there. Before sl had time to stop herself she said, 'I've one, but . . . he isn't my husband.'

'No!' There was surprise in the exclamation.

'He's my . . . my brother . . .'

'Oh.' The woman smiled as she put in, 'Aye, should have gathered that, you're both the sam build like, big strappin'.' Her smile became wide

Sarah turned slowly about. The marchers h disappeared; some of the crowd had moved wi them; the people about her were breaking into groups. She nodded farewell to the litt woman, then she found herself confronted by th woman behind her, who was looking at her through narrowed eyes, her whole expression one of close scrutiny, and she stopped Sarah's passage with her voice, saying quietly, 'Aa did washin' for Mrs Hetherington for years, it's the first time Aa knew she'd a daughter.'

Sarah took a great intake of breath and stammered, 'I didn't mean b-brother, I meant brother-in-law . . . but the woman' – she motioned her head towards the roadway where the little woman was now standing – 'she . . . she cut me off.'

'Aw, Aa see. Yes.' The head moved with each word the woman spoke. 'How is Mrs Hetherington these days?'

'Oh, she's quite well.'

'Tell her Hannah was askin' after her.'

'I will . . . goodbye.'

'Goodbye.'

Sarah knew what the woman was thinking as plainly as if she had yelled the words at her. 'Where's his wife then? Why couldn't she come?'

She did not take a bus from the town but kept walking, walking quickly as if this would enable her to get away from the condemning voice in her head which kept reiterating, 'You're mad, you're mad, you're mad, you're mad.' She had walked almost halfway home before she rounded on it. 'But I love David, I do.'

'You proved it, didn't you, to do that in the

open in front of everyone, to kiss him in the open.'

'It was nothing, I tell you, it was nothing. He looked so lonely. He is lonely. He hasn't got anybody.'

'That woman thought different; that woman knew he has a wife . . . And she knows his mother, think of that. You're mad, I tell you, stark staring mad. Now you won't only have your father on your tracks, you'll have the gossips. You could see by the look of her she was a talker.'

Just beyond the Don Bridge she stood for a moment looking down at the slimy banks of the river, between which the narrow stream of dark water made its way to the Tyne. She felt beaten, tired, and her mind was weary, too weary to erect any façade, too weary to cover up for John, or for herself. He's like a magnet, she thought, drawing badness from me body, from some black depths of me.

Father Bailey had said: Keep your conscience clear.

Kind Father Bailey.

But Father O'Malley had said no good ever came out of a mixed marriage.

Clever Father O'Malley.

But what do you say? The question seemed to rise from the black mud lining the river bank, the mud with which she was familiar in her nightmares, the mud which sucked her closer towards its middle each time she dreamed of it. But it was a challenge she could face in the daylight. Yet the voice which answered it was still weary. 'I'll never hurt, David,' it said. 'Never.'

She turned away and walked home, and the journey seemed never ending, like the years ahead.

PART FOUR

'This is the best place for you.' David touched Sarah's hair with his fingers as he leaned over the bed. 'If anybody should knock let them knock, I've been in and told Dan that you would be upstairs, and he's going across the road' – he motioned his head in the direction of the window – 'to tell our John that you're all locked up for the night. I've got my key, so you stay put. Do you hear?'

She nodded up at him and raised her mouth to his as he bent to kiss her.

When he withdrew his lips from hers he did not straighten up immediately but said, 'Of course, if there's a warning you'll go into the shelter; that's different.'

'Yes, if there's one I'll go in.' She put her hand out now and gripped his arm. 'You'll be careful?'

'I'll be careful.' He smiled down on her. 'But whatever's on, as soon as I go on duty the night becomes as dead as a doornail. I've been fire-watching now for two years and never put out as much as a candle. They just don't come my way . . . scared of me that's it.' He straightened up now but did not move from the bed. Instead, he sat down slowly on its edge and, taking her hand in

315

both of his, he looked at her for a long moment before saying, 'I wish I knew what's worrying you.' It seemed almost as if the word scared had prompted this question.

She moved her legs quickly and looked away from him as she answered, 'That's simple. Isn't everybody worried about the War dragging on like this?'

'I don't suppose you would have worried so much if they'd taken me.'

'Oh yes I would.' She was gazing up into his face now. 'I should have gone mad without you.'

'Look, Sarah.' He tapped her hand gently. 'I'm going to ask you something and I don't want you to get annoyed. It isn't the day or yesterday that it's been in my mind, it's been there for a long time, and somehow I've got an idea I'm right, because when our John's on leave you're as edgy as a foal.'

She had actually stopped breathing. She was staring at him, her eyes stretched wide.

'Now tell me, Sarah. Has he ever said anything to you . . . tried anything on?'

'No, no . . . No.' She was shaking her head rapidly, emphasising the denial of her words.

'Now, now, don't get yourself agitated. It was just an idea I got because, you know, you've never really been nice to our John. You're not snappy by nature.' He touched her cheek lovingly. 'But you've snapped at him, time and again, I've noticed it. And then this week, when he's been on leave, he's never been out of the house. And him drinking like a fish . . . well, I thought . . . perhaps he might have . . .'

'No, David, no.'

'All right, all right. Mind you' – he pointed his finger at her – 'I'm very fond of our John, but if I thought he'd ever said a wrong word to you I'd have him on his back as big as he is, and that would be the finish. As brothers go we've been close, very close, but there's some things I wouldn't stand, not from him or anyone else. I was for going for him last night, acting the goat like he did following you round . . .'

'Don't . . . don't quarrel with him, David, please. It's just that when he's on leave he goes a bit mad. I suppose it's understandable, him being stuck away in the far point of Scotland for months at a time, it . . . it must get him down. He's lonely there, and he's lonely here I think, and May . . . well, she . . .'

'Oh, May! May's the cause of his trouble, if you ask me. She's only got one thought in her head and that's the lad. There'll be trouble in that quarter, you'll see, for, as quiet as Paul is, he's got a will of his own, that boy. And if she brings her ruling hand down too heavy on him . . . Well. Of course the trouble with Paul too is that he's too fond of you. That gets under May's skin; it's evident.' He stopped speaking for a moment and stared at her, his head slightly to the side, his face wearing its usual gentle expression. And then he said softly, 'You've never liked our John, have you, Sarah?'

Her lids flickered just the slightest before she closed her eyes and brought her chin into the deep white flesh of her neck.

'It's all right, it's all right.' His voice was urgent yet consoling. 'I understand. And I'm glad in a way because John's always been a devil with women. You know me, don't you? I've never talked about him, or Dan, or their affairs. Dan, as far as I know, had that one woman and that was all, at least to my knowledge, but our John . . . aw, one was never any use to him. But I must say he steadied up after he married May. Then came the hard times afore the war and he hadn't any money to toss around, but since he joined the Air Force, I understand from Dan he's gone the whole hog again and that's why I didn't like the idea of him acting the goat with you, especially as you objected to it, as I could see you did without uttering a word.'

Sarah kept her eyes closed. Up till a moment ago her whole body had been full of fear; now, to it, was added pain. For days she had feared that John, with his boisterous drink-created hilarity, might go too far, might say something that would open David's eyes to this thing that was between them, this undeveloped thing that had been stunted in its growth, but which was nevertheless still alive. Twice during this past week she had

318

thought, If he hurts David he'll cook his own goose, he'll kill whatever is in me for him. But David must not be hurt. She would do anything to save David from hurt, mental hurt. This gentle creature, whose love had lifted her from the mire of the bottom end – this man without fire. This docile man. Docile, even at times to the point of boredom, yet who had brought her love for him almost to the peak of adoration. Nothing or nobody must hurt David, because David was gentle, kind and incapable of hurting any living thing.

Yet there was room in her for pain of a dimension equal to that of the protective fear. It was the pain of degradation and humiliation, as if her body had been assailed. The pain would have been understandable had she been John's wife, or even his woman, and heard he was carrying on with someone else. But as she was neither, why should such news, news of which she was already aware, hurt her so deeply? She couldn't really understand herself.

'Aw, don't be upset.' David was bending over her again, enfolding her in his arms. 'I don't mind how you feel about our John, believe me. In fact, to tell the truth I think I'm glad you feel that way. As long as you love me that's all I care about.'

'Oh, David, David.'

'There now, there now. Look, I've got to go. I should be there now. Old Butler's a stickler for time; that's what comes of being a sergeant in the First War. You know' – he smiled at her – 'some of them enjoy it, I know they do . . . There now, give us a smile, come on.'

She smiled at him; she put her arms about him and held him fiercely to her; and then they stared at each other for a moment before he pulled himself up from the bed.

'Go to sleep.'

'Goodnight, darling.'

'Goodnight, my love.'

He was at the door when she whispered, 'Look in on Kathleen, will you, and see her blackout's all right? She's a devil with that blind.'

'I will. Goodnight, love.'

Sarah was not asleep when at a quarter-past ten the siren sounded. It lifted her out of bed and to the bedroom door, and, pulling it open, she called quickly, 'Kathleen! Kathleen!' She had begun dressing before its wailing died away. She called again, 'Are you up, Kathleen?'

'Yes, Mam, I'm nearly ready.'

As Sarah hurried to the landing Kathleen came out of her bedroom, dressed in a siren suit and with an eiderdown over her arm. She was tall for fourteen and big-boned. In this way she took after Sarah, but her face held little resemblance as yet to her mother's, or yet her father's. If she resembled anyone it was her grandfather Hetherington, yet the resemblance to Stan stopped here, for her manner, unlike his, was quick, vivacious, even boisterous. She ran down the narrow stairs with the fleetness of a hare, crying up to Sarah behind her, 'I'll get the flask 'cos Uncle Dan will likely come in. Will I bring some cake?'

'Leave that alone' – Sarah's voice sounded unusually sharp – 'and get yourself over. I'll see to the flask and things. Go on now.'

'We'll both do it and we'll get there quicker. I'll put the kettle on.' She was flying into the kitchen as if partaking in a game.

'You know what your father said, we haven't to play about. Come on, let's get settled in, I can come in later and get the tea.'

'It won't take a minute . . . O-oh! Mam.'

The sound that cut off Kathleen's voice was a force that lifted her off her feet and sent her staggering against the wall.

Sarah found herself on the floor by David's chair. She was gripping handfuls of the mat. The house seemed to have stood on its end for a moment and was now settling back. As the gas flickered twice, then went out, she cried, 'Kathleen! Kathleen! Where are you? Are you all right?'

'Yes, yes.' Kathleen's voice was very small. 'It's a bomb somewhere . . . somewhere near, isn't it?'

Sarah pulled herself to her feet. There was cold air coming into the room and she said, 'Be careful, the window's broken. Where are you?' She groped forward until she found Kathleen's hand, and, pulling her towards her, she whispered, 'Let's get into the street.'

The front door was stuck, and as she tried to pull it open it was pushed from the outside and a voice out of the darkness said anxiously, 'Are you all right, Sarah?'

'Yes, Dad. Yes, we're all right. I thought the house was down . . . Where did it drop?'

'It must have been at the bottom end. We . . . we only got the blast.'

'The . . . bottom . . . end?' She repeated the words slowly, separating them. David was at the bottom end, that's where the post was. Her mother was at the bottom end too, but that didn't matter so much. David . . . David was on duty there. She gasped out now, 'Dad! Dad! David . . . he's on duty.'

'I know. Now keep calm, it'll likely not be anywhere near the houses. You go into the shelter . . . or, better still, come into ours.' His hand found her arm. 'Mary'll be glad if you'll come in. I know she will. It's hard for her to give in, she's made like that.'

'Yes, all right, I'll come, but later, Dad. Yes, yes, I'll come in later, but I must see if I can find David . . . he . . .' She stopped talking. A moment ago she hadn't been able to see Stan, and now his face, grey, thin, and pinched, was outlined before her and it was covered with a rosy glow.

'Fire. There's a fire, a big one.' She made to run from him when he caught her by both arms, crying, 'Now be sensible, Sarah; he's got his job to do. Be sensible. Get inside and I'll go and see how things are. Dan's already gone down.'

'No! No! . . . And there's me mother, it might be our street.' She pulled away from him. 'Look, Dad, take Kathleen in, I'll just go and see, I'll be back in a minute.' She grabbed Kathleen and pushed her towards her grandfather.

'But, Mam . . .'

'Do as you're told and stay where you are.' On this she turned from them and ran round the corner. The red glow was brighter here, shot through with flashes crossing the sky. It showed up the main road and lorries and moving shapes. There was a constant rattle of anti-aircraft fire, and from the distance there came two more dull thuds, heaving pressing thuds. She was half-way to the bottom end when her running was jerked to a stop and a voice said, 'Where are you off to, missis?'

She gasped and her head wobbled back and forwards on her shoulders before she could bring out, 'Howard Street. Me Mother . . . and me husband's on duty.'

'Take it easy, missis. Take it easy; get your breath . . .' He paused a moment before saying, 'I'm afraid the bottom end's had it; they must have been trying for the factory beyond. Four of the streets are like matchwood, at least as far as I can gather. Best keep away, you'd never get through, anyway.'

'But me . . . me . . . hus . . . husband. Hetherington's the name.'

'Oh, Hetherington . . . David. Oh, aye, I know David, missis. Well, look, let me take you back home now, come on.' His voice was gentle and he turned her about, but she jerked away from his hold.

'I've got to see if he's all right; the post is up that way.'

'Look, lass, you couldn't do anything; the place is a shambles, fire and all that, you can see for yourself.' He pointed upwards.

'I've got to go. I must find out. Leave go, please.'

He was gripping her by the shoulders, his voice harsh now. 'They've got their work cut out as it is, getting people out, them that's left. You'll know sooner or later, I only know the post has gone. But that doesn't say your husband's not all right, he could have been any place.'

Perhaps it was because he didn't expect any further resistance that he found himself stumbling back against the wall. Sarah was running like the wind now, gabbling over and over again in her mind, 'David! David! Oh, don't be dead, David!'

She was stopped before she reached Dudley Street or where Dudley Street had once been. There were a group of men frantically pulling hoses from a fire engine, and she fell headlong over a length of hose and on to her face. They picked her up, and one said, 'Steady, missis, steady on. You're going the wrong way; you must get out of this.' Another asked, 'Are you from here?'

She was standing on her feet supported between them; she was shaken with the fall and it rocked her words into a drunken mutter and she stuttered, 'Da . . . vid. I want Da . . . vid . . . my husband. Fi . . . fire-watching. He . . . he was f . . . fire-watching at the post.'

One of the men said something gently to her, but it was lost in the noise of the guns pop-popping overhead.

The older man shouted to someone and a woman came running. 'What is it?' she asked.

'Take her to headquarters.' He lifted Sarah's hand like that of a child towards her and the woman, who scarcely came up to Sarah's shoulder, put her arm around her waist and led her away. And she allowed herself to be led away from the burning tortured jumble of bricks, wood, and bodies. But when they reached the main road she said quietly to the woman, 'I'm going home, I live in Camelia Street.'

The woman still had her arm around Sarah's waist when they reached the front door.

It was three o'clock the next afternoon when they brought David home. John and Dan carried him in and laid him on the bed, and he still looked alive. He was unmarked except for the brick dust that covered him. They had found him in a pocket of beams. He had not died by being crushed, or by a blow, or yet by fire, he had died from shock. The heart that had stopped him passing for the Army had given up.

Sarah, alone in the room with him, knelt by the bedside. Gently she lifted up his hand, his long thin hand. It felt cool, not cold or clammy. He's not dead, she thought. He could be in a coma; they should do something. If he was dead she would be crying, wouldn't she, and she couldn't cry. She could only keep moaning, 'Oh, David, David.'

Not until she laid her face against his did it get through to her that he was really dead, and with this knowledge was born a strange weird feeling. It worked itself up from the core of her being. She felt its approach even through the subconscious layers of her mind, and when it burst the surface she screwed her eyes tightly shut for a moment against the black light of the startling truth it presented to her . . . She was relieved, she was glad that David was dead.

Oh, NO! NO! NO!

But yes, she was. Her mind, rocking from the impact of this knowledge, steadied itself and spoke to her with frightening calm reasoning. He'll never be unhappy through you now, it said. It couldn't have gone on; look at last night. There was a rift opening between him and John and because of you. He knew how John felt about you; he never said anything, but he knew. What he didn't know was how you felt. He died thinking you perfect; be glad of that.

Yes, she was glad of that. He had gone on loving her wholeheartedly to his last breath, and that was what she had prayed for, wasn't it? But it couldn't have gone on much longer, not if John had remained in England, and had kept getting leaves. She thought at times lately that she must tell David, she just must tell him why her father came so often when he got no welcome, when she even showed her hate of him. David had known that she gave him money, but he took it for granted that it was to help her mother, and she had not disabused him of this idea.

But now it was all over, the fear and the worry . . . and the love. She would never be loved again as David had loved her, never. Nor would she ever love again as she had loved David . . . She would never love again, except Kathleen. But that was a different kind of love. In a way she was free. Her mother was dead, her husband was dead . . . and her father was dead.

There came a gentle tapping on the bedroom door. She made no movement or sound, but she knew it was May who had entered the room.

'It's Mam, she's coming up.'

When Mary Hetherington entered the bedroom her eyes went straight to the figure lying on the bed and she moved slowly towards it; she did not look at Sarah or say any word to her.

On the older woman's approach Sarah had moved back from the bed, and now she stood looking towards her mother-in-law. She hadn't looked at her for years, not in the face. Mary Hetherington did not seem much older than on the day they had faced each other across the table in the living-room; the only difference about her was that her face looked sharper and harder. But this woman was David's mother, she would be sorrowing too. She was his mother and had loved him the best – more, oh, much more, than she had loved John, or even her husband, for that matter. She must remember that; she must remember that she was suffering at this moment.

When Mary Hetherington turned from the bed without having touched the figure that lay there, Sarah, making a valiant effort through compassion towards reconciliation, whispered brokenly, 'Will you help me to see to him?'

Mary Hetherington paused and she brought her

eyes from space to look at her daughter-in-law, and she kept them on her for a full minute while Sarah waited for her to speak. Then she turned her gaze away and with it her body. She did it with a measured timing that was an insult in itself, and with this timing in her step she went out of the room.

Sarah's lower jaw was trembling. When she tried to control it by clenching her teeth their chattering became loud in her head. It wasn't possible that anyone could keep up hate like that, and particularly at a time like this, but she had, David's mother had. Her face had been full of it. She had looked the picture of fury, as a female god might have looked, a jealous god . . .

'I'll give you a hand, Sarah.' May's voice was gentle, and Sarah, her throat swelled to bursting, murmured, 'Thank you, but if you don't mind, I'd . . . I'd rather see to him myself.'

'Very well.' May inclined her head, then went out, closing the bedroom door quietly after her, and Sarah set about the task of doing the last service she would ever do for David.

Two hours later Sarah sat in the kitchen; she felt drained and empty, yet filled with grief and still that strange, unwelcome sense of relief. Kathleen was standing on one side of her and Paul on the other. Kathleen was crying and Paul was not far from it. Sarah had hold of Kathleen's hand, and when Paul muttered, 'Oh, Auntie Sarah', she took his also.

The boy bent his willowy length towards her. He looked older than sixteen, he could have been eighteen, even nineteen, and he spoke like a man now as he said under his breath, 'Don't worry, Aunt Sarah, don't worry about anything. I'll see to you, I'll always see to you and Kathleen.' He flicked his eyes to the tear-drenched face of the girl who had always been his playmate. 'You'll neither of you want for anything, I'll see to that, I will.'

Sarah looked at the boy. He was a nice lad, a fine lad. Yes, she could imagine him meaning what he said, at least about Kathleen, because he was more than fond of Kathleen. He had never attempted to hide his feelings in that direction. But youth changed, all that was in the future. She could think of the future at this moment, at least for them, but there was no future for herself; she could see only a wilderness, a vast wilderness, in which she would walk until one day she met up with David again. It was funny how the habit of religion caught up with you when you were amidst death. She realised that the latter thought in her head could have been David speaking. He had said wise things had David.

Oh, David, David. How was she going to bear being alone, for from now on she would be entirely alone. Oh yes, there were the others. John.

he shuddered on the name. If only it had been he who had died. And then there was Dan. There would always be Dan. Dan was good and thoughtful and kind. He was like David was Dan, only different, more carefree, more careless, at least about things in general, but so good, oh, so good. Yes, there would always be Dan. And in the background, her father-in-law. But close, close to her there was Kathleen and Paul. Yes, Paul was close to her, closer to her than he was to his own mother. But why was her mind thinking like this, for it didn't matter who she had when she hadn't David.

She heard May's voice now coming from the room. It was low and murmuring. She was talking to Dan and John about something, likely the preparation for the funeral.

There came a knock on the back door and Paul said, 'I'll see who it is.' He hurried away through the scullery and she heard the murmur of voices. Then filling the doorway and pushing into the room were three figures. Two of the men she had not seen before, but the man they were supporting between them was her father, and the sight of him changed her world yet again. As she looked at the dirty, bedraggled, undersized man her body became charged with a force that brought her to her feet and sent the chair spinning backwards across the room. She felt her body and her head swelling into gigantic proportions; she had the

331

idea that her expanding flesh would push th
walls apart.

One of the men, looking at her across th
kitchen, said, 'They thought he was in the rubbl
but he just got the blast. He's been wanderin
about. He says you're his daughter, so w
brought . . .'

'GET HIM OUT!'

'But, missis.'

'GET HIM OUT!'

'But he's got no place to go . . .'

'What is it?' She heard Dan's voice behind her
then she heard John's voice saying, 'My God!' Sh
saw him move forward to her father. 'Well, yo
were lucky,' he said quietly.

Sarah glared at them, the big figure of John, th
small wizened figure of her father. Because c
these two men she was thankful, unnaturall
thankful that her man was dead. Her body wa
swelling, swelling; her lungs were pushing he
ribs out, there was pain all over her. She screame
again, 'Get him out, I tell you!'

All the faces were turned towards her, an
when no one moved, her hand, darted with th
swiftness of a panther's paw, grabbed the teapo
from the table, and, lifting it high, went to hurl
at the man who had seemingly come back from th
dead.

In a flash, almost as swift as that which ha
enabled her to grab up the teapot, John reache

her. With his body pressed against hers, his arms stretched wide, muscle to muscle, they stood outlined like a crooked cross for a second; then, as the teapot crashed to the floor, she heaved the gigantic structure that her body seemed to have become, and, like a wrestler throwing off an opponent, she hurled him from her. This was the second time she had been prevented from hitting her father with a teapot.

She could see the room once more. The two strangers had gone, her father with them. Dan, too, had gone. She could hear his voice from the yard exclaiming angrily, 'You'll just have to find some place but not here. Can't you see?'

There were only May and John left in the kitchen, and Kathleen. Kathleen was crouched in the far corner of the room, fear written all over her. It was the sight of her daughter's fear that seemed to pierce the swelling in her body. She felt herself running down like a deflated balloon as it were, and when she was her normal size again she looked from one to the other, from Kathleen to May, and then to John, and for the first time in her life she hated him, hated him at this moment almost as much as his mother hated her. Groping her way to David's chair, she dropped on to it, and, turning her face into the corner, she began to cry, tearing, agonised crying that knew no end.

PART FIVE

1

They left the tennis hut, their shoes and rackets swinging from their hands. They walked down by the wall of the workhouse, down Talbot Road and into Stanhope Road, and they never stopped talking, first one and then the other.

Paul at nineteen was half a head taller than Kathleen. His hair was dark and his eyes brown and his overall expression intense, yet attractive. His body had remained thin; unlike his father, he had no bulk.

Kathleen, on the other hand, had bulk; her body was just a younger edition of her mother's. She was not quite as pretty perhaps as Sarah had been at her age, but happier looking, freer.

Kathleen turned her bright gaze up to Paul now as she said, 'Don't you feel furious about having to do your National Service first? Why don't you go and tell them that you'll do it after you finish at Oxford? Some people do. Renee Patten said her cousin did it.'

'Don't talk dizzy. Renee Patten!' Paul gave an exaggerated sigh, and, turning a solemn countenance towards her, raised his free hand, and in a voice of a bishop intoning a blessing, began, 'My dear child, I do not intend to try to penetrate your dim wits again. After attempting and having failed on several occasions, to get the facts through your thick skull that my future hangs on a small matter of a small amount of money, small being a comparative word, I am dismayed ... indeed I am dismayed, dear child ...'

As she hit out at him with her racket he skipped aside into the road; then they came together again and went on down the street laughing.

'I know you've got to have money,' Kathleen began once more, stressing each word with deliberation. 'But I meant that if you were to put it to them they would give you the money to go up first and then you could do your National Service after.'

Again Paul sighed, another deep exaggerated sigh, and staring ahead, he said, as if reading from a letter now, 'My dear His Majesty's Forces. You know that I intend to serve you with all my brain and brawn for two years, and in return – I hope – you are going to feed me and fend for me during my stay in a certain celestial city. But would it be too much to ask if you would reverse the process and put off my sojourn with you until I have my fling in the said celestial city, while probing, of course, during the said fling, deeper into English Literature, so that after three years, when I gladly join you, a cross between a neologist and a paleographer – trusting by that time to have achieved

338

this distinction – you will understand how much more valuable I will be to my brothers in the barracks should they ever be lost for words . . .'

Again Kathleen's racket swung out. 'You think you're clever, don't you? You're swanking all the time. Neologist! Paleographer! I hope when you get to the British Museum they'll stuff you.'

Paul threw his head back and laughed, and in this action he took on a semblance of John.

'Yes, you can laugh, but listen; it's funny, isn't it, about you going in for words all because of Dad.' Her face had a thoughtful look now.

'Yes, it is funny when you come to think about it. And funny isn't the correct word but we'll skip it on this occasion.' He glanced teasingly towards her. But his flippancy didn't bring her to attack him with her tongue or racket, and picking up her mood, he went on. 'No, I don't suppose I'd ever have thought about words if it hadn't been for Uncle. I remember the first time he told me all words were straight lines. I didn't believe him. Even when he showed me, I didn't believe him, I wanted to argue with him. I suppose it was this feeling that years later made me get that book on Chinese writing. I remember thrusting it under his nose with a triumphant feeling and saying, "Straighten those out, Uncle David." He did laugh.'

'It's three years ago,' said Kathleen softly, 'and I still miss him. He was lovely was me Dad.'

They were walking down the bank now towards the church, quiet for the first time since they had left the tennis court, and when they came to the foot of the steps Kathleen stopped and said, 'I'm going to pay a visit.'

'OK.' He turned with her and walked up the steps.

At the church door Kathleen stopped again and, looking at him, said, 'Do you think you'd better. Me Aunt May will go for you.'

'She's not to know.'

'Well, it's odd but she has ways of finding out. You remember what she said a while ago: she said she could smell the incense off you.'

'That was sheer imagination. Anyway, I've always come in with you and I'm not going to stop now. Come on.' He pushed her forward into the dim porch.

The church was cool after the reflected heat of the pavements. Kathleen led the way down the side aisle to the front pew opposite the Lady altar. This was the pew her mother had always sat in when she came to church as a young girl. She prayed daily that she would one day return to it. She genuflected deeply before she entered the pew, then knelt down and, bowing her head, covered her face unselfconsciously with both hands.

Paul had not genuflected; nor did he kneel down, he just sat back on the seat and looked quietly about him. He had told himself a number of times that he didn't quite know what the attraction was about this place. It certainly wasn't the beautiful structure of the church, nor yet its interior decoration, for the stencils, to his mind, were horrible. Kathleen said the lads from the club usually did most of the decoration and everybody thought it was lovely; well, it certainly was a matter of opinion. Nor was he attracted by the statues, for they appeared crude to him, glaringly crude except perhaps the face of the Virgin, whose expression, he had the idea, seemed to change from time to time. No, he couldn't quite lay his finger on what drew him to this church. Was it because Kathleen loved it? Perhaps. He glanced towards her, her face still buried in her hands, and a feeling of exquisite tenderness flowed through him. She was lovely was Kathleen; everything about her was lovely, her face, her figure, her simplicity. She tried to be clever – he smiled inwardly – oh, she tried hard, but he hoped she would never be clever because it was that inbred simplicity and her uncluttered way of looking at things that he loved. She was like her mother in that way. His Aunt Sarah had the same qualities, an uncluttered way of thinking. But his Aunt Sarah never tried to be clever. She was one of those women who didn't need to be. He remembered his father saying that. He loved his Aunt Sarah, that's why he loved Kathleen, he supposed, because they were one. He would soon have to speak to his mother about Kathleen, and it wasn't going to be easy. She didn't like Kathleen, nor his Aunt Sarah. Why, he didn't really know. But then she liked so few people, so he supposed it wasn't so strange. But his father would welcome the idea of Kathleen as a daughter, for he thought the world of her. His mother had taunted him once by saying that his father thought more of Kathleen than he did of him, but it didn't matter; he was glad his father loved Kathleen . . . Yet he was getting away from the question uppermost in his mind, his attraction towards this church. Mr Rogers, his Sixth Form master, had had a pet theory. 'If you cannot control your thinking before you are twenty, then you'll never control it or anything else.'

He looked towards the High Altar. He liked the High Altar. Perhaps this was the main attraction, the High Altar, where, Kathleen had told him a long, long time ago, the priest brought Christ alive every day. He had laughed his head off about that at the time and teased the life out of her, and yet now, when he knew so much more, when for years he had been delving back into the strange history of language, where myths and magic were realities, he laughed no longer. But still he couldn't understand why, with his extended knowledge, the idea of a daily resurrection had become more credible to him. 'As the hart pants

342

after the foundations of water so does my soul pant after thee.' He had read these words in Kathleen's Prayer Book, and as they came to his mind now he felt strangely disturbed, as if he was being hurt by beauty.

Kathleen raised her head, blessed herself, then turned her face towards him and smiled. He rose to his feet and went out of the pew, and she followed him. He paused for a moment as she dipped her fingers into the holy water in the little font, then, watching her bless herself and genuflect again towards the main altar, he pushed open the door and let her pass out.

'Oh, wasn't it cool in there!' She drew in a deep breath, took a flying leap down the first flight of stairs, laughing over her shoulder at him as she cried, 'Oh, I always feel wonderful after I've been into church.'

He took the steps two at a time and caught up with her as she stepped on to the pavement, and they both bumped into Father Bailey.

'There you go, dunching into everybody.' The priest was steadying her, laughing down into her face.

'Oh, I'm sorry . . . I'm sorry, Father.'

'And so you should be, knocking poor old men over, going round wrecking joints.' He now stooped and stroked his knee.

'Wrecking joints?' They repeated the priest's slanging quip on high laughter.

'It's nothing to laugh about.' He wagged his finger at them. 'It's another joint I'm referring to . . . the tennis hut. Who broke the seat, eh? Who broke the back off the garden seat?'

'Oh, Father,' Kathleen put her hand across her mouth, and glanced at Paul. 'We were having a bit fun, a bit carry on.'

'A bit carry on!' He nodded at her with mock sternness. 'As far as I can gather there were ten of you having a bit carry on, and I want two shillings from each of you, understood?' He looked from one to the other, and Paul, nodding his head once, replied, 'Understood.' He did not say Father.

As he looked at the young boy the priest's expression changed, the smile which lifted his cheeks up into pouches under his eyes had a seriousness to it. 'I'm to congratulate you, Paul, I understand. Oxford? Now isn't that wonderful . . . a scholarship to Oxford! When do you go up?'

'Oh, not for some time, sir.' The sir came out naturally. 'I've got to do my National Service first.'

'When did you have your interview . . . I mean for Oxford?'

'Oh, before last Christmas.'

The priest nodded. 'You must have done well, you must have impressed them, indeed you must, to have got a scholarship.'

'Oh no, sir.' Paul's eyes narrowed and his mouth took on a humorous twist, and with a facetiousness of youth he went on, 'I was just dead lucky. The English tutor who took the interview happened to be a dialectologist, and, hearing my Geordie twang, he said, "By, lad, y'just watt Aa'm lukin' for. Aa can de aall the dialects but Aa get stumped wi' the Geordie. By, yo're a God-send, lad!"'

They were all laughing again, the priest heartily, and when Father Bailey laughed heartily the tears ran out of his eyes. 'Go on with you. Go on.' He pushed at Paul, then as he dried his eyes he exclaimed, 'Oh, I wonder if you're any good at languages . . . translating? Do you know any Spanish?'

'Spanish? No.' Paul shook his head. 'I'm sorry.' Father Bailey drew a piece of paper from his inside pocket and, after looking at it, he handed it to Paul, saying, 'Well, take a look at that and see if you can make anything of it.'

Paul took the paper on which was written the following:

Si Senor, Derdago, Forte Lorez Inaro.
Demainte Lorez Demis Trux,
Foolacoos Andens Andux.

Slowly he read aloud, 'Si Senor, Derdago.' Then looking at the priest he said, 'No, sir, I can't make head or tail of it . . . sorry.'

The priest shook his head solemnly. 'Well, if you can't read that it's a poor lookout for you up at Oxford,' and taking the paper from Paul he pointed his finger to each word translating, as he went, by splitting up the words. And what he read was:

Si Senor, der dey go, forty lorries in a row.
Dem ain't lorries, dem is trucks, full of coos and hens and ducks.

Paul and Kathleen looked at each other, then at the priest, then together they let out a howl of laughter, and again the tears ran from the priest's eyes. 'I had you that time . . . the last one's on me.'

'Oh, Father, you old twister!' Kathleen was pointing at the priest, and Paul through his laughter was crying, 'You wait, sir, I'll have my own back on you.'

'Any time, any time.' The priest was moving away from them now, waving his hand at them. 'Goodbye, goodbye.'

'Goodbye, Father.'

'Goodbye.' They called together.

Then, half running, half walking, in their laughter and excitement they went past the station calling to each other as if yards apart, 'Dem ain't lorries, dem is trucks, full of coos and hens and ducks.'

'Isn't Father Bailey lovely?'

'He's all right.' Paul was non-committal, mainly to tease her.

'He's not all right, he's lovely.' She swung her racket at him again in an upward movement, and he caught her arm and they struggled together until of a sudden Kathleen became still, and her face, losing its merriment, she whispered hastily under her breath, 'Give over, there's me grandda behind.'

Letting go of her, Paul glanced casually back up the road, and there, walking as always with his hands in his pockets, was the little man who Kathleen called grandda. Whenever Paul saw this man he would remind himself that there was no blood relation between his Aunt Sarah and Pat Bradley, and he was glad, even relieved. He would have hated to think there was anything of this man in his Aunt Sarah, or Kathleen.

They walked on quickly now, sedately, a space and silence between them. Kathleen said quietly, 'He gives me the creeps.'

'Don't let him worry you.'

'He worries me mother. He's started coming round again. He hasn't been for months. He's been living with his cousins, but they've had a row and now he's in digs and he doesn't like them. He wants to come and live with us.' She glanced towards Paul. 'I think I would die if he lived with us. I couldn't bear him in the house. But, anyway, I needn't worry about that, for me mother can't stand the sight of him. She's warned him time and time again, but he still comes. There's some people think we should have him because we've got room. Betty Lawson said last term when we had a quarrel that everybody knew that my mother was hard because she wouldn't give her own father house room after the blitz that time. The quarrel was nothing to do with Mam or anything else, it was about netball, but she brought that up. So people think that Mam is hard. She isn't, is she?'

'Aunt Sarah, hard? Good Lord, no. She's too soft, if anything. Don't you take any notice. People only get half of the story, then they make up the other half. Aunt Sarah's got reason to hate his guts because he led her and your Aunt Phyllis a life of it when they were young. Dad told me all about it.'

Kathleen said now, 'Let's get the bus. I want to get home. He might catch up on us. Look! There's one coming in, we'll just make it.'

Simultaneously they began to run, and they caught the bus.

Fifteen minutes later, laughing again, they came up the backyard and burst into the kitchen on Sarah and Phyllis.

'Oh, hello, Aunt Phyllis.'

'Hello, Kathleen pet; been playing tennis?'

'Yes, Aunt Phyllis.' She threw her racket and shoes on to the armchair, and Sarah, turning from the table where she was rolling out pastry, said, 'Now get those off there, Kathleen. I've told you before.'

348

'OK, Mam. OK, Mam.' And picking up the racket and holding it at arm's length and dangling it from her fingers, she asked innocently, 'Where'll I put it, Mam?'

Sarah and Phyllis exchanged glances, and Sarah, trying to suppress a smile, said, 'Wherever you're going to put it you'd better get it there and quick!' She turned round sharply, her hand extended to give her daughter a wallop across the buttocks, but Kathleen, leaping past Paul and towards the scullery, cried, 'Save me! Save me!'

'Save yourself, you're big enough.' With manly indifference Paul sauntered to the hearth and, jerking his head at Phyllis, exclaimed in throaty tones, 'That's telling 'em.' Whereupon Phyllis let out a bellow of a laugh. Sarah too laughed, but as she trimmed the pastry from the edge of a large plate she said without looking at Paul, 'Your mother's been across, Paul. She wondered if you were back.'

'Oh.' The laughter slid from Paul's face and again he said, 'Oh,' then added, 'I'd better be getting over.'

'Where you going?' Kathleen was entering the kitchen again.

'Over home, of course . . . I have one, you know . . . a home.' He thrust his head down to her.

'I didn't say you hadn't, there's nobody arguing with you. I'll come over with you.'

Before Paul could make any reply Sarah put in

349

quietly, 'No, Kathleen, I want you for a moment. Let Paul go over home.'

'But . . .'

'Never mind any buts. Go on, Paul.' She smiled at the boy, and Paul, returning her smile, said, 'Be seeing you.' He made a small swipe with his racket in Kathleen's direction then went out.

'What do you want me for, Mam?'

'Never you mind, that can wait. You haven't been in the house five minutes.'

'Do you want me to do something?'

'No, I just want you to stay put for five minutes.' She turned, and, looking down at her daughter, smiled at her. And Kathleen, as always, returned her smile, but pursing her mouth and grinning now, her expression saying, 'Anything to humour you.'

'Well, I must be off, Sarah.' Phyllis rose to her feet.

'Oh, wait a minute, I'll make a cup of tea before you go.'

'You'll not. I've had two lots of tea since I've been in. You'll drown me in tea. It's a wonder your stomach's not poisoned. How many times do you have it at work?'

'Oh, only twice. In the morning and afternoon break.'

'When are you going back?'

'Monday, I suppose, if he'll sign me off. It seems daft to catch a cold, weather like this, doesn't it?

It's sweltering. But they're worse in the summer.'

'Will you be able to come down at the weekend?'

'Yes, I'll likely be at the market; I'll look in.'

'Bring Kathleen with you.' Phyllis looked towards her niece, and added quietly, 'You don't often look in on us. The lads love you to come. Young Dick said to me the other day, why weren't there any girls in our family, and I said to him the doctor thought I could look after boys better; he said me hands are too hard for braying girls with.'

Kathleen just smiled at this quip, she did not laugh, and Phyllis, turning abruptly away, said, 'Here's me for the road. Bye-bye, Kathleen.'

'Bye-bye, Aunt Phyllis.'

Clapping her hands over the board, then drying the remainder of the flour from them on her apron, Sarah followed Phyllis into the passage.

When they reached the door they stood for a moment looking down into the street, and Phyllis said, 'She's bats about Paul, isn't she? How's it going to work out?'

'Oh, it'll take its course.'

'What if they want to get married?'

'I hope they will.'

'You do?'

'Yes, why not?'

The sisters looked at each other, and Phyllis, her head drooping, said, 'Nothing, I suppose. There's not so much pressure against cousins marrying

351

the day.' Then, glancing quickly up, she asked, 'You really want them to?'

'Yes.' Sarah was now staring out into the street. 'It's about the only thing I do want.'

'Why don't you marry again?' Phyllis's voice was gentle. 'You could, you know. You're bonnier now than you were at twenty, being thinner, except for your bust . . . you're stuck with that.' Sarah pushed her and they both laughed. Then Phyllis ended, 'Well, you wouldn't have to go to the factory day in and day out if you did.'

'I prefer the factory.'

'Well, I suppose you know your own road best, like us all.' She paused here before asking, 'How long are you going to keep Kathleen at school?'

'As long as she can stay. She'll never reach Paul's standard. But that doesn't matter; the main thing for her is an education so there won't be so much difference between them.'

'You've got it all cut and dried, haven't you?' Phyllis was smiling her understanding smile. 'Well, that's how it should be. I wish I could do the same for even one of my four, but they haven't a pennorth of brains atween them, except for making money, that is, and Ronnie isn't bad on the piano.' She laughed. 'Oh, they'll make out all right, the money way. You'd think our Jimmy was seventy instead of seventeen. And do you know that it was him who discovered ice-cream?' She pushed her fist into Sarah's arm. 'Yes, ice-cream hadn't been heard of until our Jimmy struck it. Anyway' – her laughter was high now – 'he's making money out of it, so good luck to him.'

As Phyllis's loud laugh floated into the street Sarah glanced towards the door that was only a few yards from her own, and she made a warning sign to Phyllis, and Phyllis, clapping her hand over her mouth, drew her head into her shoulders. 'Sorry,' she whispered. Then, looking towards the other door, she asked, 'No sign of a thaw?'

Sarah shook her head. 'I don't want any thaw now.'

'It would drive me round the bend. Do you mean to say she still doesn't open her mouth to you?'

'Not a word, and when we pass in the street she could be blind, she doesn't even see me. But there it is.' Sarah gave a small smile. 'It doesn't matter, it doesn't matter any more. You know, I forget she's there. For days on end I forget she's there.'

'Does the old man still pop in?'

'Oh yes, once or twice a week, mostly at the weekend. And Kathleen goes in and out.'

'If she was mine I wouldn't let her darken the door. If they wouldn't have me they damn well wouldn't have her.'

'No, I would never stop her. After all, she's her grandmother.'

'Well, as I said, better you than me. I couldn't

put up with it. I must be off . . . Well, see you at the Assizes.'

To this macabre but colloquial parting Sarah laughed and replied, 'Yes. See you at the Assizes.' Which saying they were to recall within a matter of hours. 'My love to the boys,' she added softly.

'I'll tell them. So long.'

Going back through the front room, Sarah thought, It's odd what Phyllis thinks she couldn't stand, and her standing the stigma of the Arabs for years and still keeping her flag flying . . . Phyllis was a good lass. Yes, she was indeed. And she had spunk. By, she had that!

'I'm not going down to Aunt Phyllis's on Saturday, Mam.' Kathleen was waiting for her when she entered the kitchen.

'All right, all right, there's nobody forcing you.' Sarah's tone was tart.

'Well, I can't help it, Mam; I've tried.'

Sarah was at the table again, her back to her daughter and, her voice quiet now, she said, 'I know you can't. We'll not go into it, it's all right.'

Kathleen sat down in what had been David's chair, and she bowed her head as she said, 'I like Aunt Phyllis, I do. She's nice, and she's a good sort . . . but the boys, and Ali . . . Well, somehow . . .'

Sarah turned from the board. 'It's all right, dear.' Her manner was soothing. 'I know how you feel, so don't worry. But all you've got to do is to remember that the boys can't help looking like Arabs and that they're nice boys, they are.'

'I know.' Kathleen was mumbling now. 'But it's since Iris Bannister got to know about it and she told the others. And just before the holidays, just as recently as that, Peggy Crofton, the sneaky little cat, came up to me and said, "It isn't true, is it, that your auntie lives among the Arabs?" I could have smacked her face. I nearly did.'

'Coloured folk are marrying white folk all the time now and it's only ignorant people who make something out of it. You've got to look at it like that. And those girls ought to be ashamed of themselves. And them with their education an' all.'

'Education!' Kathleen sniffed. 'Iris Bannister lives in Westhoe village. Their house – I've seen it – it's not much bigger than this, but because she lives in Westhoe she thinks she's the last word, and she's always telling you about the private school she went to before she came to the High School. Betty Chalmers says it was a potty little place, just a house run by two people, old maids, who hadn't even been teachers, but of course they were very . . . very refeened, and they talked like this.' Kathleen screwed up her nose and lifted her upper lip into a point showing two large white front teeth, and as her mother burst out laughing her face fell into its natural lines again, and she too laughed as she said, 'Betty Chalmers can do it wonderfully, she'd make you scream.'

'Oh, dear, dear.' Sarah, still laughing, shook her

head at the tragedies of youth, but when Kathleen, rising from the chair, said, 'I think I'll go across to my Aunt May's for a bit,' Sarah stopped laughing and answered quickly, 'No, I wouldn't. Your Aunt May doesn't see much of Paul and you know he'll be gone soon.'

'Well, that's why . . .'

'But you must think of your Aunt May, Kathleen . . . Oh' – Sarah tapped her brow with the knuckle of her thumb – 'I forgot to tell you. Lorna MacKay called in this morning. She wanted you to go and hear her new record.'

'Oh, bust.'

'But I thought you liked Lorna?'

'I do, I do, but then Michael will likely be in.'

Sarah smiled. 'You used to like Michael, too, at one time.'

'Yes . . . well, I suppose I did. He's all right but he's always asking me to go out now, to the pictures and places.'

'Well, you go to the pictures with Paul, don't you?'

'Yes, I know, but that's different. But that's what he said too: I went to the pictures with Paul.'

'And what did you say to that?' Sarah was smiling quietly as she worked away at the table.

'Oh, I said . . . well . . .' Kathleen paused and gave a hick of a laugh. 'Well, I said, you let me go with Paul because he was my cousin, but you thought I wasn't old enough to go out with him.' Her voice became smothered with suppressed laughter.

'You little monkey!' Sarah was looking at her daughter, her eyes bright. 'Anyway, I would go up and see Lorna.' It was an order put gently over.

'Oh, all right. It'll be an educational afternoon,' she sighed, 'interposed with a running commentary on . . . our Michael.' Here she mimicked Lorna's voice and attitude. 'Our Michael's earning sixteen pounds a week and him only nineteen, and when he gets to the coal face he can make over twenty pounds a week, he can.' She waggled her plump, adolescent body, and Sarah said, 'Now don't be catty.'

'Well, she's always on about the money their Michael's making. Always getting a dig in that Paul won't be making any for years. She even said that her mother said that Paul would be twenty-three before he earned a penny.'

'Did she now?'

'Yes, she did.'

'Well, Paul has got something money can't buy, you tell her that.'

'I have; and I really don't believe that Michael makes sixteen pounds a week, do you?'

'Oh yes, they can make that at the pits now doing overtime. And I shouldn't be surprised that he reaches twenty when he gets to the face. Coal is like gold now. And long may it last for them, they've had it rough long enough.'

'I'd hate to marry a pitman.' Kathleen was sauntering to the door as Sarah said, 'Well, don't.'

'I won't.' And once again they looked at each other and once again they laughed.

'I won't stay long,' said Kathleen.

'There's no need to hurry. If Paul comes over I'll come up and knock for you.'

'You will?' Kathleen's face brightened. 'OK. Bye-bye.'

'Bye-bye, my dear.'

Paul, Paul, Paul; Paul all the time, waking and sleeping. Would she change? She was only sixteen, she might. But no, Sarah shook her head at the thought. She was held fast. Although Paul did not look like his father, there emanated from him the same virile attraction. No, Kathleen wouldn't change. She prayed to God she wouldn't, anyway, because if she did, well then . . . Sarah's hands became quiet on the board and she looked at the wall opposite. All her efforts, all her self-denial, all her trying to do the right thing would have been in vain, wouldn't it? Still staring at the wall, she saw there the day of her choice. It happened six months ago in this very kitchen. John had been out of the Air Force for eighteen months then and was doing well in his wireless business. That's how he had started, talking about the shop. 'I'm on to something here, Sarah,' he had said. 'You'd never believe the money that's in it. Joe's opening another shop in Wallsend and I'm going to keep

358

on with the Newcastle one and see to the workshops. And if we can get a likely enough fellow we'll open one down here in Shields. Everybody is wireless mad. And you know another thing that's going to boom . . . television. I bet you a shilling before ten years is out everybody'll have a television in their own house.'

'Television? Just what is television?'

'The pictures, that's what it is, the pictures.'

'And in your own house?' She had laughed as one would at a tall story.

He had shaken his head solemnly at her. 'It's a fact, Sarah. Fellows have been working on this long before the War and now they're getting pictures from London. I'm telling you, it's no fairy-tale. And we're in on the ground floor, Joe and me.' He had looked away from her at this point and said, 'That's one good thing that came out of the Air Force anyway, Joe and me stuck in that godforsaken hole planning what we'd do together after the War. Joe was to do the talking and the buying, and I was to do the making, wirelesses and that, and see to the production end. And that's how it has worked out. When I think of those years on the dole . . . years . . . my God, it was an eternity! I can't believe this is really happening to us . . . I've bought a car, Sarah.'

'A car?' Her eyes screwed up at him.

'Yes, a dandy. I got it as a snip. It's secondhand, but it was lying up all through the War. A nineteen thirty-eight Rover, a beautiful job, like a Rolls-Royce, it is, honest.'

'Oh, John.' She had looked at him softly and smiled. She was pleased for him. Success would ease the turbulence in him, part of it at any rate.

He had said, then 'I made plans at the end of the War, Sarah, not only with Joe, with meself. I said, I'll make money, real money, and then I'll buy me out, so to speak, and I'll do what I've longed to do for years.'

Her body had become stiff, rigid, but she had remained silent as he went on, 'I've had enough, a bellyful if anyone has. I'm not God's gift to woman, I know. Oh, I know, nobody better, but that's over. I've got money now and I'll have a hell of a lot more before I've finished. But I'm determined on one thing . . . May's not going to wallow in it. No, by God, I'll see to that. I'd rather give it to all the whores in the town.'

She had exclaimed aloud at this and he had cut in abruptly saying, 'You don't know what it's been like, Sarah. She's me mother all over, only in a different way. A damned sight worse if you ask me. No, I've made up me mind.'

She had said at this point, in a voice she could scarcely hear herself, 'Aren't you forgetting about Paul?'

'No, I'm not!' he had barked back at her. 'Paul will know where he's going in a few months' time. He'll have to do his National Service, anyway, and once he leaves the house he'll be on his own and my life sentence'll be finished.'

She had looked at him then and stated flatly, 'Paul is in love with Kathleen and she with him.'

His mouth had dropped open and he had gaped at her; for a full minute he had gaped at her before he said, 'But they're just kids; they've been brought up together.'

'It's more than that, at least I think so. Anyway, I'll have to wait and see.'

He had taken a step towards her, crying, 'Look, Sarah!' but with her outstretched hand she had stopped him. She had not touched him, she had just put her arm out towards him, her hand raised vertically.

'I'm waiting,' she said. 'Kathleen is the only thing that matters to me, you've got to know that.'

'I do know it, but I'm willing to take a chance, I'm willing to take what's left.'

She had her head bowed on her chest when she murmured, 'There's time enough for that.'

Again he looked at her for a long, long moment, and then characteristically he spoke the truth. 'There might be for you, but not for me. I'm at the end of my tether, Sarah. I'm made that way . . . There's got to be somebody . . . For years and years I've wanted it to be you.'

'I cannot help you,' she said. Her head was still lowered.

At this he had turned and walked out. It had all

been comparatively quiet and orderly, the arranging of their future lives.

Sarah brought her attention back to the table. She gathered the scraps of pastry up, pressed them together, then rolled them out. As she lined an oven plate she saw Dan come in from the back lane and her face brightened.

When he entered the kitchen he sniffed, saying, 'Coo! That smells good. What is it?'

'Oh, just odds and ends; they're always hungry.'

'They are? You mean Paul. If you were to be paid for all the food he's eaten here you'd have a tidy sum.'

'Oh, that.' She gave an impatient toss of her head. 'I've got to bake, anyway. She can tuck it away like a young horse an' all.'

'By! It's hot.'

'I'll make you a cup of tea.'

'No, no, I won't be staying a minute.' Yet as he spoke he sat down by the side of the table.

Sarah looked at him. 'But it's Wednesday; you're off, aren't you?'

'The shop's closed.' He nodded at her. 'I'm off that far, but I'm going up again; the old lady wants some rooms turned round.' He bounced his head. 'She's got an idea, and she's working on it. She thinks I can't see it . . . She wants me to go and live up there.'

'Really!'

'Aye. She's lonely since the old man went. I've known this has been coming for some time, and' – he wagged his finger at Sarah – 'it wouldn't be a bad thing, it wouldn't at that, for she's a dear old soul. I'm more than a bit fond of her, and, as she says, the place'll be mine some time ... You know.' He rested his elbow on the table and pushed against a glass bottle lying on its side, and Sarah exclaimed quickly, 'Look, you'll get flour all over you.' As she lifted the bottle out of his way, he said, 'That's a cute idea, using a bottle for a rolling-pin. Where'd you find that?'

'Oh, in a magazine. It works an' all. You fill it with cold water and it helps to keep the pastry firm.'

'Well, well, I wonder what next. But as I was saying. You know, Sarah, there's kind people in the world, and those two have been pure gold to me, and not a drop of blood between us. Strangers can be kinder than your own, don't you think?' He did not wait for her to comment on this but went on, 'I did meself a good turn the day I put that four hundred into the business; they've paid me back a thousandfold ... Well, not quite,' he laughed. 'But you know what I mean. And now this changing round of rooms. There's six of them, you know, fine big ones at that, and well furnished. Oh, aye, they've got some nice pieces, and she's been on about making two flats of it for some time now. She keeps saying two people could live here

363

amicably and not get in each other's hair . . . Poor old soul! I've known what she's been driving at, but I've never let on. You see, it's going to be difficult, I mean leaving next door.'

'Yes.' Sarah nodded down at him. 'That is going to be difficult. I don't think you should do it, Dan; she would be lonely without you.'

Dan stared at her for a moment before saying, 'You know, you're a remarkable woman, Sarah. I've always thought that.'

'Oh, don't make game, Dan. Remarkable, huh! I know just how remarkable I am.' She was nodding her head slowly at him.

'I'm not making game, not on this matter, I'm not. I know what I think. Here you are trying to persuade me not to leave her because you think she would be lonely. She's got Stan, she's got John and May across the way, she's got two grandchildren, and you say she'll be lonely. After the way she's treated you, you can still feel sorry for her.'

'She's not a happy woman . . . inside. That's what I mean. And unhappy people are lonely. We are all lonely in a way, but unhappy people are more lonely.'

'Yes, I suppose you're right there. But there's another thing against it, but I suppose you wouldn't notice. I wouldn't be able to pop in here every day.'

'Oh, I'd notice that all right, Dan.' She stood

with her hands resting on the table, her body leaning towards him. 'I just don't know what I would have done without you, Dan. I've . . . I've never said this before, but I think that at the beginning I would have gone clean off my head, really off my head, if it hadn't been for you. Oh, I know what it would be like if you stopped popping in.'

Dan stared at her, his eyes holding no vestige of humour now. Then, pushing his fingers through his thick greying hair, he rose abruptly and went towards the fireplace and stood looking down into the empty grate. And Sarah stood by the table, her hands moving nervously and without purpose until he said, 'Have you talked to John lately?'

'John?' The name said like that jerked her into stiffness and she twisted her head over her shoulder and looked towards his back. And again she said, 'John?'

'There's going to be a bust-up there and it's a pity. He should let the lad get settled first. Although in a way I don't blame him, he's had it rough since he came back. It was bad enough before the War.'

She watched him turn slowly towards her now and he held her gaze when he spoke, 'He's going to leave May.'

There was a pressure in her throat as if from the point of a bone; the feeling would not allow her to swallow. Yet this was not news to her, she had known it was going to happen.

She heard him say, 'What are you going to do, Sarah?'

'Me? . . . Me?' She moved her head from side to side in one wide startled sweep. 'Nothing, nothing. Why . . . why should I?' She sounded indignant. But she could not keep her eyes on his and her lids dropped over them; then her head moved downwards. She felt him coming towards her, and when he was near he said, 'I'm glad of that, Sarah, I'm glad. I'll tell the old lady that I won't be moving up there, at least not for the present. I'll be going now. So long, Sarah.'

'So long, Dan.'

She waited for him to move, and when he didn't she looked up. She looked into the kindly face of this man – this man who had about him the gentleness of David and the virility of John. It was a strange attractive combination, seeing that he was also the brother of her mother-in-law. When he put out his hand and touched her cheek gently it was as if David had come alive. He turned from her and went out.

As Sarah watched him go down the backyard, pausing to turn off the dripping tap before going into the back lane, she did not think of him, nor yet of John, nor yet of David, but she thought of the woman next door who was mother and sister to these three men, and the words she had once spoken resounded loudly through the kitchen: 'You have taken my menfolk.'

Her head drooped again and she supported her brow with the palm of her hand. Then, blinking rapidly, she said to herself, 'I'll make a cup of tea before I clear.'

As she sat drinking her tea she thought of what the years had done to her, of what loving a number of people had done to her. She had loved David . . . Oh, yes, she had. But she had passioned for John. Without loving him she had wanted him. She realised that. During the first month of her marriage her body had in a way become a university for her natural desire, but she had learned so quickly in this direction that her tutor was left far behind on a plane from which he had not the power to propel himself. David was not ruthless enough, not brutal enough, not selfish enough. John in this particular field would have been all three.

She pulled at the neck of her blouse to give herself air. She felt as if she was going to suffocate, the room was stifling. She rose and went to the window and pushed it further upwards, and as she did so there walked in through the back door the thin wizened figure of her father. He saw her almost at the same moment as she caught sight of him, and to prevent the door being locked in his face he sprinted up the yard.

Breathing heavily, Sarah turned to the table. It was no good rushing into the scullery, he'd be in by now. The next moment his voice came from behind her, not placating as it was once, but surly. 'You would have shut me out, wouldn't you?'

She did not answer him for a moment, and then she said in a voice so unlike her own that it was impossible to imagine herself speaking, 'I've told you not to come here. Can't you take a telling?' But she knew that she became an entirely different being when confronted with this man.

'Aa've got no place else to go, Aa've been turned out.'

'It isn't the first time, you can find other lodgings.'

'Aa can't, not on my money; only place is a hovel.'

'It's of no interest to me where you stay, I've told you before. Now get out.' She still had her back towards him.

'Folks is talkin'. You with a room goin' beggin' and me on the street. You'd see me in the work-house.'

'Yes, I would.'

'Well, you won't then, I'm comin' here.'

She turned towards him now, her eyes wide. 'You're what? You'll come here over my dead body. You've blackmailed me for years, but now, as I told you before, the only one I was afraid of you hurting has gone. And you can say what you damn well like now, it makes no difference. Go on, get on with it; shout about all you think you know.'

368

'You're speaking out of turn, you should think a bit afore you open your mouth so wide.' He was speaking slowly, quietly.

She narrowed her eyes at him. She couldn't follow him. What did he mean? What was he alluding to? He had got something else into that warped, twisted mind of his. 'What are you up to now?' she said from between her teeth.

He peered at her through his bleary eyes. There was a trickle of saliva running from one corner of his mouth. He asked again, 'Aa y' goin' to give me that room? You'll be sorry if y' don't, mind. Aa'm tellin' you, you'll be sorry.'

'Get out!' she took a step from the table, a threatening step, but he did not move.

' Y' could handle me if y' liked. It would be worth your while, Aa'm tellin' you.'

'Get out!'

'Aye, aall right then. If y' want it that way, Aa will. An' Aa'll find those two an' tell 'em.'

Her face screwed up. 'Those two? What two? Who you talking about?'

'The bairns.'

'The bairns?' she repeated.

'Aye, that's what Aa said, the bairns. Do Aa need t' name 'em. Aa'll tell 'em they'd better go careful.'

Her face was slowly stretching. She mouthed the word 'careful', but without a sound.

'They were carrying on together down the

369

station bank, rolling about; they're ready to jump into bed any minute, and they can't, can they?' He stared into her wild, startled face. 'Y' mustn't let that happen, must you? It'd be unnatural, wouldn't it? After you given 'em the same faather an' all . . . Well, didn't you? She was born practically nine months to the minute from one o'clock on that New Year's morning on the waste land, where you and the big fellow were neckin'. An' that's putting it mildly, isn't it? If there'd been nowt in it, do you think you'd have paid up all these years . . . You had somethin' to hide all right, an' y' still have.'

Once before she had experienced the feeling of her body swelling to explosive point; the feeling was with her again only more intense, more terrible. She felt her rage lift her off her feet. She swung round to the table and grabbed up the first thing that came to hand, which was the rolling-pin bottle filled with water, and she hurled it at him. As he turned his face from the onslaught it caught him full on the temple and he dropped like a stone.

She was standing, her back to the table, hanging on to its edge. She was aware that someone was in the yard, but she didn't know who; her body was still swelling, her head seemed to fill the room. She could feel her eyes stretching to snapping point as she watched the blood flow over the lino. The bigger her body grew, the quieter she became inside, it was as if she was being carried away into a great silence. Even when she saw May burst into the room with Paul by her side she made no sound. She watched May kneeling on the floor, she saw her raise his head up, then put her hand inside his waistcoat. May looked more human in this moment than she had ever seen her before. 'He's dead,' she said.

Sarah knew he was dead. She knew as soon as the bottle had hit him that he had died. She was glad he was dead. Oh, she was glad he was dead. He could never hurt or terrify her again. He could never hurt anyone again. He could never hurt Kathleen now . . . that was the important thing, he could never hurt Kathleen. Kathleen was safe, safe, safe. And Paul too; yes, Paul was safe too. They were both safe.

2

Time was only in the mind. David had said that. He had read it some place. He had said how true it was . . . Time was only in the mind. She herself knew how true it was now, for time had almost ceased to exist for her. Soon she knew that time, as the mind knew it, would end altogether, but it wasn't worrying her. Her mind had rejected time as it had all other things. If it thought about anything clearly it was that it wished . . . it . . . was all over. She wasn't afraid of the end; she had even said so to the priest. At times her mind came back into the present sufficiently to answer questions if it considered they needed answering. When the priest spoke to her of God she almost laughed; the thought of God was ludicrous to her now, really funny. When her mind was on this other plane she was amazed at the credulity of all the people who believed in this thing called God, this thing that had become an . . . it, to her. Her mind admitted to this 'it' being alive, yet at the same time she saw it as inanimate because it was without feeling for the human being. She felt a malicious desire now to bring her thoughts from this far-away plane and hurl them at the priest, hurl 'it' at the priest. But the priest was Father Bailey, and he was kind was Father Bailey. But he kept repeating one thing to her, trying to drag an answer from her, a response. 'You've got to tell them, Sarah,' he kept saying. 'And today. It'll be your last chance. Tell them that he blackmailed you for years. Tell them. Do you hear me, Sarah? Sarah.'

She bowed her head before his pitying gaze. He could no nothing. Being a priest, his tongue was tied. And she would do nothing, because if she opened her mouth she could only tell them half the truth. She could say: My father blackmailed me because he thought I had been with John and I hadn't. But would they believe her? No. No. They would say, those clever ones in the court, they would say, Then why did you pay him to keep silent? And then it would become complicated. She couldn't begin to tell them why at first she paid him to keep silent, it was all too far in the past. Even if she could explain it would bear no weight. She alone knew the thing that would bear weight. Her father had known it and now he was dead. He was dead because he had created it . . . this thing, this thing that she alone knew now and must hide. And it was a lie this thing, the biggest lie of the lot, but nevertheless she must hide it because if she once showed it the light everyone would believe it. There was never smoke without fire, they would say. Yes, yes, that's why she had paid up all the years, they would say. Then they would look at Kathleen and Paul and remember they had been inseparable since they were babies. They would remember that John loved Kathleen like a father . . . But, she needn't worry, they wouldn't remember, for they wouldn't hear the lie spoken, the lie that would help her to live. It would die with her. Kathleen would be safe.

The priest went away and the warders came, two of them. One of them had a nice face, she had a kind voice too. She was about Sarah's own age and she took Sarah's hand and patted it before they mounted the steps. But when she sat down beside Sarah her face looked cold and remote . . .

Sarah looked around the court-room, her head moving slowly as if with an effort. There was Phyllis, her face filled with two great compassion-filled eyes. Dear Phyllis. And next to her was Ali and Jimmy . . . They were nice, Ali and Jimmy.

There was Dan, his eyes waiting for her. Something in her stretched out towards him and said, Don't cry any more; don't cry any more, Dan. And next to him was Kathleen, her face like paste, and her eyes like great dark pools, pools full of pity. The thing inside her stretched out to Kathleen, it leaped to Kathleen and said, 'Oh, my dear, my dear! Don't worry, you'll be all right.' And then there was Paul. Paul's head was down and he was not looking at her, he never looked at her. A voice from the far-away plane cried out to Paul, 'Look at me, Paul, I'm not bad. Please look at me.' But Paul refused to look at her. Next to Paul sat May, and May was looking at her. But what was May thinking? No-one ever knew what May was thinking. There was a man sitting next to May but Sarah did not look at him, or say his name to herself, for it was because of him, because he had been born, because the desire of his body was the ruling power in his life, that she was sitting here now . . . I'll see you at the Assizes . . . I'll see you at the Assizes.

Her mind slipped away on to the distant plane again, and from it she heard faintly the voice of the prosecuting counsel, the man who seemed to hate her. He talked as if he had known her from birth and as if she had never done a decent thing in her life. Why was he talking about her like that? He also seemed to hate the nice man who was defending her. He said nasty things to him, spiteful, sarcastic things, and they always referred to her. Her counsel was now speaking to the judge, asking to bring forward another witness. Time passed and then she was looking at a man in the box. She couldn't remember ever having seen him in her life. Of course that was natural because he had just said he lived in Wallsend and she didn't know anybody in Wallsend. He said his name was James Ballast and that his brother had once beaten up the deceased man.

'Why did your brother beat up the deceased man?' asked the nice man.

Because the deceased was always spying on courting couples, the man said. He had been spying on his brother, and his brother laid a trap for him, then beat him up.

'Where is your brother now?' asked the nice man.

'He's dead,' said the man in the box. 'He died in the War.'

The cool voice from the high bench cut through the examination, saying, 'What is all this? This has no bearing on the case at all.'

'I'm just trying to show, my lord,' said the nice man, 'what kind of man the deceased was.'

'We are not here to deal with the dead man's character,' said the cool voice. 'We are here to prove or disprove murder. Why have you raked up such a witness?'

'The man offered himself as a witness, me Lord. He thought he could help the accused.'

'And apparently you did too?'

'Yes, me Lord.'

People were kind. It was as Dan always kept saying, people were kind . . . all except the prosecuting counsel. He was standing in front of the jury now, telling them how bad she was. He even remembered to tell them about the day after the big raid when she wouldn't give her father shelter and had screamed at him and had gone to throw something at him.

People had long memories, May had a long memory. It was she who had told them that bit when she was asked if she had ever seen her raise her hand to her father before. May had a lot in common with the prosecuting counsel.

Then the nice man was talking to the jury. He was telling them what she had gone through in her childhood, how she had feared the deceased, how he had beaten her and her sister . . . Phyllis had told them all about that, and Phyllis had been fearless. Phyllis wasn't frightened of anybody. She had said to them, 'I always wanted to kill him and many a time I said I would, and I would if I'd got the chance.' The judge had told her to stop talking, and when she wouldn't he had warned her she would be put out of the court. He had warned her twice because she was always jumping up and down in her seat.

Now the jury filed out of the benches and went into a room and the warders took her downstairs and the kind one squeezed her shoulder, but she said nothing. They wanted her to eat and drink, but all she wanted was a cup of tea. And then it didn't taste like tea, not her kind of tea.

She sat staring ahead, waiting, her hands joined in her lap. Time passed. She supposed it was hours, she didn't know. Everybody seemed restless. The policeman came and spoke to her; even the stiff-looking ones spoke nicely. Then they went and talked in the passage outside. She heard a voice say, 'Well, he didn't find her insane, did he? And he examined her long enough. She's just withdrawn herself. They do, you know. She'll likely be like that until near the end . . . if there's an end.' 'Ssh!' said somebody else. 'Ssh!' and the voice answered, 'It's all right, she doesn't take it in.'

And then of a sudden they took her upstairs, and there they all were in their places as if there had been no long interval. And one man from the benches stood up and the judge asked him a question, and he said, 'We have found the prisoner guilty of manslaughter, my lord. Because we are agreed that there was no premeditation to kill.'

Her mind began to race now, flying away to reach the plane, the safe plane, where the voice of the judge couldn't follow, but even when she reached it she couldn't shut the voice out. Two sentences came floating to her. One was, 'The jury have agreed your act was unpremeditated.' But for some reason she got the impression that he didn't agree with the jury's verdict. The second sentence was: 'Nevertheless you have killed a man and been found guilty of manslaughter; therefore I sentence you to prison for fifteen years.'

Her mind was shot from the plane and into her head again. She wasn't to die, she wasn't going to die. She was surprised, amazed. Then her mind whimpered, but fifteen years! Fifteen years! Then she heard Phyllis screaming: 'It's monstrous! Cruel! He should've been dead years ago, the swine! I wish I had done it myself, I tell you. Oh, my God! Sarah, Sarah! Fifteen years! God Almighty!' Phyllis's voice trailed away as they pulled her from the court.

Just before she was led downstairs she glanced towards her family. They were all standing as if petrified, looking at her, all with the exception of John. Perhaps it was because he was not looking at her that her eyes went involuntarily to him. His head was bowed deep and his face was covered with his hands.

3

The day was dull, the world was dull. Everything was crazy; he was crazy. At times he thought he was going stark staring mad. Everybody had changed since the trial; everybody and everything had changed . . . But some of them had changed before the trial. Paul had. What was up with the lad? Just look how he was treating Kathleen.

In three rapid strides John was at the window looking down into the yard seeing Kathleen going through the back door and across the lane into her own backyard. Because it was still her own backyard, she had refused to budge. But she was no longer a young girl skipping and gay; she had grown up overnight, as it were, and the transition had left her dazed. She wanted help, comfort, and the one who could give her the most comfort was turning his back on her. Why? Why? Well, he would find out; he would have something to say to that young squirt, he would that.

As he turned from the window about to stalk from the room, Paul entered, and John stood aside and let him reach the fireplace before he started: 'Look, what's the matter with you these days? We've all had a shock, but the one that's troubled most is Kathleen and she needs your help. And what have you done? You've kept clear of her for

weeks as if she's got the mange. I don't like it.'
John's face screwed up, his lips leaving his teeth.
'I don't like the trait in your character that makes
you shy off when you're most needed. Even if
your Aunt Sarah has done something wrong, and
that's a matter of opinion, you cannot hold
Kathleen accountable for it. But that's what you're
doing. Every time she walks in the door you go
out. Now look here, let's get this straight.'

'I want to talk to you.' Paul's voice was quiet,
cold and quiet.

'Then talk. Fire ahead.'

John looked at his son and waited, and when he
did not begin he said brusquely, 'What's holding
you up? I thought you wanted to . . . ?'

'I'm going to become a priest.'

The silence in the room was like sound ampli-
fied; it penetrated through the cries of the children
outside in the back lane, through a man calling a
boy's name, through the high cry of a baby.

'Say that again.' John's tone sounded ordinary.

'You heard what I said.'

'Aye . . . aye, I thought I did. I thought you said,
"I'm going to become a priest." That's what I
thought you said.'

'And that is what I said.'

John pulled his chin into his neck, pushing out
the flesh that looked tough and thick like a reddy-
brown hide. 'You're going to become . . . ? Look,
lad, have you gone barmy?'

'No.'

'But you said a priest . . . not a minister, or a curate, but a priest?'

'That's what I said.'

'A Catholic priest?'

'A Catholic priest.'

'You trying to make me do something – hit you, knock you out or something?'

'It won't make any difference what you do.'

'It won't, eh? Get out.' John swung his arm in a half-circle motion indicating the door, but as Paul turned towards it he sprang across the room barring his way, crying, 'No begod! What am I saying? You'll not get out of here until I hear you talk sense . . . Priest! You're going to become a priest . . . Over my bloody dead body you will. Now sit down.' He pointed to a chair. 'Sit down and let's hear what all this is about.'

The boy moved with seeming quietness towards the chair and sat on its edge and waited; and John, towering over him, demanded, 'Well now, get going. Since when have you had the idea you're going to be a priest?' His voice was sneering.

Paul turned his white face up to his father's. 'Since the day my Aunt Sarah killed her father.'

The answer nonplussed John and it brought his shoulders back and his head up. It brought the lids of his eyes together, and he asked, puzzled, 'But what has that to do with this business? There's no connection that I can see.'

'You can't?'

'No, I can't.'

'I happened to hear what her father said before she hit him.'

'But you said . . . you said you didn't hear anything. You told them in court . . . only a babble of voices, you said.'

'I know what I told them.' Paul now thrust out his arm as if pushing his father aside, and, getting to his feet, he moved a few steps backwards, putting distance between them before he spoke again. 'The old man said Kathleen and I were acting like a courting couple and we shouldn't because . . . because you had fathered us both.'

The telling silence took over again until John whispered, 'I had what?' He brought his hand up to his chin, the forefinger pressing below his lower lip, and as if coming out of a daze he repeated, 'I had what? God Almighty!' With a movement of his leg he flicked the chair across the room, and as it crashed against the fender he cried, 'He said that? Well, let me tell you, son, and I'm swearing it on God's oath, it's a bloody lie . . . a bloody lie. Do you hear?' His voice was high now.

'Yes, I hear, but I also heard the old man remind my Aunt Sarah of the night Kathleen had been conceived. It was on New Year's morning nineteen and thirty on the waste ground . . . Kathleen's birthday is on the fourth of October.'

John stood as if someone had hit him a

382

resounding blow, a blow that should have felled him to the ground. He swayed slightly, his hand moving now round his face, his eyes blinking; he had difficulty in speaking and when he did his voice had a note of pleading in it. 'Paul . . . listen, Paul boy. It's not true. Your Aunt Sarah and I did stand round there that night, and we talked. We talked because . . . Oh, my God! What does it matter now? I loved your Aunt Sarah, but nothing . . . ever . . . happened between us. You've got to believe me. Your Aunt Sarah's a good woman.'

'If nothing happened, then why did she let her father blackmail her all these years?'

'Blackmail her?' The word sprung John's brows upwards. 'What are you saying? Have you gone barmy?'

'No, I've not gone barmy, and you know I haven't. She'd been paying him money for years to keep quiet about that night.'

'Christ alive!' Slowly John turned his gaze from his son and going towards the fallen chair he picked it up, and when it was righted he sat down, gripping the seat with his hands as if to support himself. His mind in a blinding turmoil, he was seeing a picture which covered the years; Sarah's nerves, her tenseness, her terror of being left alone with him. Aye, she had been terrified, and with what reason! God Almighty! . . . God Almighty! 'Paul.' He put out a shaking hand towards his son, and his lips moved, trying to form the words that would establish his innocence in the boy's mind, but they were ineffective when they came. His tone held no conviction, he was too dazed to be convincing. 'There was nothing, Paul, nothing, nothing, between your Aunt Sarah and me. That swine of a man must have heard us talking that night and held it over her. She loved your Uncle Davie. There was only one person for her, she could see nobody but your Uncle Davie. It was likely because she didn't want trouble, and didn't want to hurt him, that she paid up. But, my God . . . !' His hands dropped to his side. 'My God! What she must have gone through.' Now his voice roughened and strengthened. 'You should have spoken up and told them, it would have helped her.'

'Would it? Would it have helped if they had thought she was carrying on with you and that you were Kathleen's father? Would it have helped her?' Paul's voice was accusing.

John shook his head. 'No. I suppose you're right. But, Paul . . .' He leant well forward from the chair. 'You've got to believe me, and you've got to make things right between you and Kathleen.'

Paul moved to the side of the table and he looked down at it before he said, 'That's over. We were like brother and sister, anyway. We were brought up too close.'

'But you're not brother and sister, or half-brother and sister. You could get married.'

'No.' The boy's voice was so harsh it could have been John himself speaking. The tables seemed to be turned; it was the boy who had the strength and John who was the weaker in this moment. 'I'm going through with this. I know now it was what I wanted to do all along. I was always attracted to the Catholic Church.'

'Oh, my God! Don't talk, boy, don't talk.' John's head was bowed forward, his hands supporting his brow.

'I've got to talk, and now. In six days' time I'll be in the Army . . . I've been taking a form of instruction from Father Bailey, a very preliminary form. He has told me of all the obstacles that are in my way, so you won't be the only one who will try to put a spoke into the wheel. I've got to convince them that I'm serious. I've got to see the Bishop, Bishop McCormack, and Father Bailey wouldn't make the appointment until I'd told you everything.'

'That's bloody kind of him.' John was rearing now. 'I'll have something to say to this Father Bailey, and one thing will be that you can't do a damn thing about it. I've got the idea that you're under my jurisdiction until you're twenty-one.'

'I know all about that, we've gone into that. You can get a Court Order to prevent me from becoming a priest. You can also prevent me turning a Catholic while I'm a minor, but I'll be twenty-one before I come out of the Army, and

385

until then you or no one else can stop me reading and learning. I'll be getting myself ready . . .'

'For Christ's sake! Shut up, will you! Be quiet, before I do something to you . . . And' – he paused – 'where does the university come in in all this?'

'I won't be going to Oxford. I can take my degrees while I'm studying. I'll likely go to Ushaw College near Durham.'

John bounced to his feet. He still looked dazed, but he sounded more like himself when he cried, 'Ushaw College, be buggered! I'll see you in hell first before I'll let you go through with this. You're mad. This business has turned your brain. As for those bloody cunning priests, wait till I get my tongue round them . . . and my hands.' He doubled his fist and shook it towards Paul. 'You know something? I'd rather see you dead than let you go through with this. Now get out.' He turned his back on his son and looked into the fire, and Paul moved slowly from the table and went to the door and opened it, and his intake of breath brought John's head round quickly to see May standing in the doorway. There was no need to wonder if she had heard anything; her face told him that there was nothing she hadn't heard; she must have been there all the time.

As Paul hesitated and looked at her she said evenly, in the ice-rimmed tone that was natural to her, 'Go on out, I'll see you later.' Then she went into the room and closed the door.

May stood with her back to the door, not leaning against it; she did not look in need of support, her small compact body was rigid with the white heat of hate. 'So!' she said.

'Aye. So. Well, you heard what he said.'

'Yes, I heard what he said, but I lay no stock on that. I understand my son where you never did. A priest indeed! He means that as a girl would mean it – if she said she was going to be a nun after being let down. I'll see to him presently. It isn't him I want to talk about now, it's you . . . and her!'

John's lips met in a straight line, the corners pulled in as if he was sucking.

'That's it, get ready to do battle. Get ready to lie your way out.'

'I've got no need to lie about anything and I'm not going to, so don't worry your head on that score.'

'Yes, I loved your Aunt Sarah.' She was mimicking his tone now, her face spread into a mirthless leer. Then as if a switch had changed her expression, her face was straight. The muscles tight and her eyes flint-hard as she spat at him, 'There was a pair of you. The big fellow and the big, fat floppy-breasted bitch.'

As she watched him silently writhing, she taunted him, 'Why don't you say something? At least defend her and say she wasn't a floppy-breasted bitch, she was beautiful. Aye, like a sow on her side she was beautiful all right.' She paused again. Then her voice dropping deep into her throat, she muttered, 'There could be another killing this very minute.'

'Aye, there could. So look out, I'm telling you.' His words sounded thick and fuddled as if he were drunk.

'I'm not frightened of you and your bulk, and you know it . . . To think that all these years, you and her . . . I could spit on you.'

'You're barking up the wrong tree as usual.' John moved his head slowly. 'It's true what I said and I'm not going to deny it. I was in love with her, and still am if you want to know, so coat that with your venom and burn it through . . . But there's been nothing between us, not a damn thing. That first New Year's Eve I tried to kiss her coming back from her mother's, but that's all that happened – she soon put me in me place. And I'm going to tell you something, right now I'm going to tell you something. If it hadn't been for our Davie the tale would have been different, for I would have taken her – and I could have – and I'd have left you high and dry. Twenty years I've sat like a mute under your tongue, but now it's finished. So you know.'

May was standing within an arm's length of him. She looked up at him, her thin face wearing a twisted smile, and her voice sounded deceptively normal when she said, 'That's where you're wrong, John. Things are only beginning; you forget about Kathleen.'

'You can do nothing there; Kathleen isn't mine.'

'Can you prove it?' The smile slid from her face. 'If you went on your bended knees at this moment I wouldn't believe you, nor would anybody else. You've always been very fond . . . fond, that's a light term for your feeling for Kathleen, isn't it? You liked her better than you did your own son. You've never had much use for Paul, have you? Oh no. But Kathleen looks like her mother, doesn't she, and she takes after you, doesn't she? There's nothing of Davie in her, but you stick out a mile. Helter-skelter, never stay still. That's Kathleen . . . just like her father, eh?'

'I tell you you're barking up the wrong tree.' John's voice, although loud, sounded weary.

'I don't think so. In fact, I'm sure I'm not.' May was talking in a conversational tone now. 'If your dear Sarah had nothing to hide, why didn't she bring this all out at the trial; it would have helped her, she would have gained sympathy, a woman who had been blackmailed for years. But no, she was frightened because she knew that if she opened her mouth the cat would be out of the bag. As Paul said, Kathleen's birthday is on the fourth of October. You haven't to do much counting up from the first of January have you?'

'Look!' He was bawling now. 'You can talk until you're sick and you'd still be wrong. I tell you . . .'

'You can tell me nothing. Now you listen to me.' May's tone changed yet again; her face was tight, bitter. 'As I see it, your dear Sarah took a longer stretch than she need have done just to save Kathleen knowing the truth. Well . . . now listen hard, big fellow, because if you make a mistake it'll be a pity. If you think you're going to wait for her coming out you're mistaken, because if you as much as go and visit her, just once, I'll go across that back lane and I'll tell our dear Kathleen who her daddy is. You know, there are more ways of killing a cat than drowning it. And just think how Dan would take this bit of news . . . and your Dad. Oh, you wouldn't care what your mother thought, in fact you'd like to hit your mother with this, but not the other two. Oh no, you'd like to keep their good opinion, wouldn't you? All men together.' She stepped back quickly as John advanced towards her. 'Don't try it,' she said. 'Don't try it, I warn you.'

They stood staring at each other, the hate like molten lead between them. It was May who moved first. She turned from him, showing her disdain by giving him her back, and as she reached the door she looked over her shoulder towards him and said evenly, 'The way business is going we want a better address, don't you think? I'll look for a place down Westhoe in Shields, it's nice down there. And by the way, if you should get the idea into your head to let the business go flat to spite me, remember it would be a pity to think that your dear Sarah had sacrificed herself in vain, wouldn't it?'

When the door had closed on her, John turned slowly and went to the window, and, looking out across the back lane, he gazed down into Sarah's yard, into Sarah's kitchen window, and he said aloud: 'All this because of those few minutes that night. God Almighty! First her going through it, and now me. But I'm not Sarah. How long can I hold out? God Almighty!'

PART SIX

1

It was nineteen-fifty seven and Dan's birthday, and he was fifty-seven years old. He stood appraising himself in the wardrobe mirror. He was still upright and his figure hadn't fattened. He patted his flat tummy – he was too much on his feet to get any flesh on there. His hair, although quite thick, was a grisly grey, and there was no bright twinkle in his eyes now. They had a serious look, as had the whole of his face. He remarked to himself on the seriousness of his expression and thought, You've got to feel light inside. What you feel like inside always tells. But the mirror presented him with a smart, well-set-up man, a prosperous man. But what, he asked himself, was prosperity if there was nobody to share it? Well, things would be different within a week. Yes, the week ahead would be a very telling time. Now he must get going; he did not want to keep Kathleen and the Sunday dinner waiting.

He went out of the bedroom and stepped into a large carpeted hallway. He walked across it and into a sitting-room. It looked an extremely comfortable, and well-furnished room. He put a wire guard round the fire, went to the window, and looked down into the main street for a moment. It looked utterly deserted, as a shopping thoroughfare always does on a Sunday. Unconsciously he arranged the velvet curtains; then with one last look round the room he went out into the hall again, took his overcoat out of an oak wardrobe standing near the door, adjusted his trilby hat, and picked up a pair of fur-lined leather gloves from a small table. Going out, he locked the door and descended the carpeted stairs to the street, and there, getting into his car, he drove the two miles to the Fifteen Streets.

There was another car parked outside of the house he now thought of as Kathleen's. He drew up behind it, but when he alighted he did not go into Kathleen's, but went around the corner and into the back door of number one.

Mary Hetherington was setting the table for the dinner. She turned from a sideboard drawer with some cutlery in her hand and, looking casually at Dan, said, 'You're early.'

'Yes, I am a bit. Stan out?'

'He's next door.'

Dan stood with his back to the fire. He held his hat and his gloves in his hand and watched his sister laying three places at the table – May always came over to dinner on a Sunday now.

She went into the scullery next and filled a glass jug with water, and when she returned and set the jug on the corner of the table, and straightened the knives again, she said, 'Well?'

'Well, what?'

'Well, what have you arranged? You know what I mean.'

Dan remained silent, looking at this woman as he had looked at her over the years wondering how he ever came from the same source. She was seventy now and still upright – her tightly-laced stays helped here. But there was no help for her face; her skin looked like old Chinese silk that had cracked here and there where it had been folded. Her eyes still held the alert quality; that had never diminished, for it had been fed continuously on bitterness.

'You're not bringing her back here?'

'Where else can she go?'

'I don't care where she goes, you know that, but I'm warning you not to bring her back here.'

'Her home's next door, her daughter is next door, you seem to forget that.'

'I forget nothing, nothing.'

'No, you don't, Mary, you forget nothing. Forgiveness isn't in you, and the odd thing about it is that she had never done a damn thing to you.'

'What! What do you say? And, by the way, I'll thank you not to swear in my house. And as to her not doing a thing to me, how can you stand there and say that? You know she ruined this family. She broke it up.'

'She did no such thing.'

Mary Hetherington drew herself up. 'I'm not going to argue with you, you've always been soft. But I warn you, if you bring that woman next door it will mean trouble. You wouldn't want Kathleen's life to be broken, too, would you?'

'There's no fear of that.'

'Just you wait and see.' She nodded warningly at him. 'They should never have let her out of a sudden like this, she should have been made to do the full fifteen years.'

Dan pulled the rim of his hat through his hands, then, moving from the fireplace, he walked past her. He did not exchange any form of farewell, and he went out, closing the door none too gently.

No sooner had he gone than Mary Hetherington was out of the room and up the stairs and into the back bedroom, and there she stood to the side of the curtain watching him crossing the lane to May's back door. She saw him go up the yard and into the house, and as she stood waiting she glanced at the little clock on the mantelshelf. When he came out she looked at the clock again. He had been in there nearly fifteen minutes. She smiled to herself, a tight, satisfied smile, then went out of the room and down the stairs.

Meals at Kathleen's were never talkative or boisterous affairs. Kathleen had lost the art of laughter ten years ago, but today's meal was even quieter than usual. Dan sat opposite to Kathleen, and to her right sat her husband, Michael, and to her left, in a high chair and close to her, was a two-year-old baby girl.

Kathleen was nearly twenty-seven but she looked older, she looked a woman well into her thirties. Her face over the years had taken on a resemblance to Sarah's, but she had not Sarah's expression. There was a solemness about Kathleen's face now, an innate sadness printed on it. The look had been there for years. At first it had not been permanent; the day it became permanent was the day that Paul had been ordained a priest. That was over three years ago. Three months from that particular day she married Michael MacKay.

Michael, Dan thought, was a good fellow, and in a way Kathleen was lucky. Feeling as she did, and acting at times as if she wasn't aware of anybody, it said a great deal for him that he never lost patience with her. It was well for her that he had loved her for a long time – ever since he was a lad, in fact. At the same time Dan thought it was a bit hard on him.

From the day they had taken Sarah from the house to the magistrates' court at Clervaux Terrace in Jarrow Dan had made it his home and for over six years he had looked after Kathleen, right until the time Michael took over. On that day he had moved to the shop. Braving Mary Hetherington's tongue, he had taken his belongings and gone up to his new home. And now he held pleasant memories of two peaceful years with Mrs Campbell. But since the old lady had died over a year ago he had lived on his own. He didn't like living on his own and he had for some time now been hoping to change this state of affairs. But, like everything else, the outcome of this hope remained to be seen.

The meal over, he sat with Jessica on his knee making her laugh while Kathleen and Michael washed-up the dinner things. Then Michael took the child upstairs to bed, and Kathleen and he were alone together. Having so much to say, they said nothing, each waiting for the other to make an opening. Kathleen busied herself in putting the room to rights, placing the modern dining chairs, with the different-coloured leather seats, under the table, pushing the G-Plan armchairs into different positions. There was not a piece of the old furniture to be seen throughout the house. The whole place had been re-decorated and re-furnished.

At last Kathleen came and sat down by Dan, and, putting her hands between her knees, she looked at him as she said, 'How do you think it will work out, Uncle Dan?'

'We'll just have to wait and see, Kathleen, that's all.'

'I'm terrified.'

'What is there to be terrified about? She's your

mother, remember that, and a good woman. A good woman, Kathleen. I've told you again and again, Sarah is a good woman.'

'If I only didn't believe . . .' Kathleen's head dropped down to her chest.

'But you've got to believe it, Kathleen, because it's the truth, I believe it. I know your Uncle John, I know him inside out. I tell you he almost went on his bended knees to prove it to me. You know he was fond – oh, more than fond of your father; there was a strong tie between them, a strong, strong tie, and your Uncle John admitted that if David hadn't been your father he would have gone off with your mother, but . . . well, he, in his own way . . . well, he loved your father, he couldn't bring himself to hurt him . . . David was your father, Kathleen.'

She looked at him, saying quietly, 'You know, Uncle Dan, I think I could be happy now if I could just believe it. I've tried, but I keep remembering . . . I keep remembering my Uncle John and . . . and him always being over here, and how he used to look at her . . . and Aunt May's jealousy, and her not liking me.'

'Look, Kathleen, we've been over all this before, it's old ground; but I say again, what your Uncle John felt for your mother we all felt in one way or another. She was a very fetching woman and she didn't go out of her way to attract anybody. She wasn't smart-tongued like your Aunt May, or clever in any way; she was just nice and kind . . . loving, sort of. And then the way she looked . . . you look like her, you know, Kathleen.'

Kathleen was on her feet. 'Don't say that, Uncle Dan.'

'I'm going to say it. And don't take that tone, Kathleen, it's a compliment.'

Kathleen turned from him and walked to the kitchen window, and from there she said, 'About Wednesday – will you pick me up? I'm leaving Jessica with Michael's mother. I'm not telling Grannie I'm going, she'd go mad.'

'I've got it all arranged. I'm picking up your Aunt Phyllis at half-past nine, that should get us there in time.'

Dan was standing behind Kathleen now, with his hand on her shoulder. 'Don't worry, my dear; things are going to turn out all right. Believe me.' His tone was emphatic. 'Just believe me. And try and remember that she'll be in a state too. She's been away for ten years, she'll be changed. She's likely as fearful of coming back as you are of her coming.'

Kathleen did not reply to this, but said, 'That tea. I suppose it's kind of them to want to welcome her back like that, but having a tea in the street and putting flags out, because that's what they'll do down there. You would still think they lived in the ramshackle houses the way they go on. And when me grannie knows she'll be wild . . . wild.'

402

'Well, there's nothing we can do about that, it's their way of expressing their feelings.'

'But she didn't know hardly any of them from the bottom end, not for years.'

He patted her shoulder, saying, 'It'll all be over this time next week. Everything will have settled down by then. You'll see, you'll see.'

'This time next week.' Kathleen muttered the words to herself as she looked up over the chimneypots and into the sky. She had tried to readjust her life, she had tried to close the wound, but on Wednesday, between her grannie, her Aunt May, and her mother, the wound would not only be torn open again – she would be rent apart.

2

Before she had done a month of her sentence Sarah's mind came down from the plane to which it had escaped: time had a different meaning now. She got up with it early in the morning, in the mornings that always seemed like night, and the daytime was broken up into pieces of time; pieces when she ate colourless food, when she walked round a square; when she worked in a laundry; when she ate again, and worked again, and ate again, and then went to bed while it was still day.

Nevertheless she longed for this time when she could go to bed, not to sleep or rest but to be by herself.

That was the most difficult thing: getting herself used to time, time being used in a different way from that in which she had used it before. Everything inside was connected with time; everybody was doing time. But she found you can get used to anything; so she got used to using time. She had to, as she had to get used to not being nauseated with the smell, the smell of urine. In the block it permeated the air; even in the laundry, where there was soap and water, the smell still hung around some of the women. She liked few of the women; there was one, but she went out after six years. Her name was Gladys and she had liked reading. She had looked after the library. It was because of her that Sarah had got the job helping in the library for an hour after tea. So for over six years she had accepted time. It would be thought she hadn't much choice, yet some didn't accept it, and for them life was a living hell.

But her acceptance ended one visiting day when Dan had said to her from across the table, 'Kathleen is going to get married.' Her heart had come alive at that moment. But she didn't know for how short a time. Kathleen hadn't been to visit her for four months, and she had written her only short, terse letters. She was at work and she couldn't get off, she had a cold. Then Dan, his head bowed, had said, 'I've got to tell you this, Sarah. She's marrying Michael MacKay.'

She had mouthed the name without a sound, then asked gropingly, 'Why, Dan, why?' and he had to say to her:

'Paul has become a priest.'

'A priest!' It was the first time she had heard anything about Paul and the priesthood. She had been hurt sore that he had never been near her, nor yet had written her a scribe of the pen, she couldn't understand it. But then there were lots of things she couldn't understand, such as Kathleen's aloof attitude. Her daughter seemed to have turned against her . . . This was torture.

Her mind dizzying as it had been wont to do, she asked again, 'But why, Dan, why?'

He had been forced to tell her the truth, the truth as Paul thought he had heard it, and, thinking she might as well know the rest, he went on to tell her of John, how he had left May and gone to live in Newcastle. But he did not tell her that he was living with a girl young enough to be his daughter, he couldn't tell her that. Nor that on the day he had broke away from May she had gone over to Kathleen's and told her why Paul was becoming a priest. There are things you cannot get the tongue to speak.

But Sarah had not been concerned at what was happening to John or May, she could only think of Kathleen and Paul. Paul a priest! It was unbelievable. Just because he had heard what was said that day, that terrible but fading day. Why was God doing this to her? Perhaps he was answering Father O'Malley's prayer and wreaking more vengeance on her. Perhaps, she thought, it was meant that she should go through all this just so Paul could become a priest. But no. No. She wouldn't think like that. She had given up thinking like a Catholic, she was no longer a Catholic. She was no longer anything that was connected with a God. She was just no longer anything. She didn't want to go on. She was finished. Paul a priest! A Protestant, with his mother and father bigots. Paul a priest! And then it had penetrated through her mind, the real reason – half-brother and sister, Oh, Kathleen! Oh, poor, poor Kathleen! It was all crazy . . . mad, mad. Who was causing this to happen, anyway? God? . . . God was mad.

It was from this time that she spent three months in the prison hospital, but she could not die. Her body, although thin and a shadow of its former self, would not give her up. Her mind was ready any moment, and it did its best to force her release, but it failed. And when she left the hospital they did not put her back into the laundry; her time was spent between the sewing-room and the library. And through this change she got to know, and in fact become friendly with a warden called Peters. Her life was now lived on a level plane, orderly, monotonous. Until one day, without any warning, she was told she was going to be released.

It was seven o'clock on a Monday morning when Sarah stood with one foot outside the prison gates. The officer said to her, 'Will you be all right? I think you should have told them it was today.'

Sarah shook her head. 'I would rather it was this way.' She spoke in an undertone as if afraid of disturbing someone.

'Goodbye, Mrs Hetherington, and good luck.' The officer was smiling and holding out her hand, and Sarah took it. 'Thank you,' she said. 'You've been kind.' Then she turned away.

She did not feel the strangeness of being in the open for the first moment because she was thinking . . . Mrs Hetherington, she was . . . Mrs for the first time in years. She was Mrs. Then she looked across the road. The other side looked far away. When her legs began to tremble she said to herself, It's no different to walking inside, and she kept on. The clothes that she was wearing felt strange, loose, as if she had no body to support them. She looked down at herself. She was so thin now. All except her bust. Her bust hadn't altered so much. The officer had joked with her and said she had a figure like Marilyn Monroe. Were people looking at her? No, no, they weren't. She passed a woman and glanced at her, but the woman was looking ahead. She felt surprised at this. Wasn't there some kind of a stamp on her to tell people where she had come from? When she reached the corner of the road she had the desire to run back and bang on the prison gates. She felt frightened; she was by herself and she hadn't been by herself for a long, long time. She wanted someone near, not to touch, oh no, but just to know that they were near . . . But yes . . . yes, she did . . . she did want someone to touch, a hand to hold. She had been silly, telling them it was Wednesday she was coming out. She should have told them it was today. But she couldn't face a street tea, anything but face a street tea and a sea of curious faces. She had told the warden that and the warden had understood. Dan said people were kind and this was their way of showing their kindness. Perhaps . . . but she didn't want this kind of kindness. Doubtless they had deluded themselves into thinking that in getting up a street tea and a jollification for her coming home they were doing her a kindness, but what they were really doing was giving themselves a bit of cheap sensation. She was not surprised at her own insight into human nature, for, as the idleness of the dole years ago had turned many a man towards self-education, so had her years of confinement and daily dealing with books tutored her mind a little, at least, to a certain stage of analytical reasoning. It had happened unobtrusively, so unobtrusively that she was unaware of the change. And yet she knew she was different, her way of thinking was different. She felt that she would never know fear as she had known it before; in a way it had overstepped itself. But being afraid, and facing a table full of laughing faces and questing eyes set out in the open street, was a different thing. If it were to rain they would hold it in the factory hall; they were prepared for all contingencies. But wherever it was held they would have provided the opportunity to gape and question . . .'What's it like in there, Sarah? What did they do to you? Did you ever get solitary? Come on, woman, open up, you're among friends.' And she was not exaggerating in imagining the trend the reception would take. She knew what some of them at the bottom end were like, and it would doubtless have been these very people who had proposed the welcome home tea, and their every probe would be in good part. Oh yes, everything would be in good part; it was a favourite cover-up for curiosity, the term, good part. And if she didn't take everything in good part, she would be damned . . . She couldn't have stood it . . .

The officer had told her the way to the station. She turned right down the street, then left, and left again, across a square, up another street, and there it was, the station. She didn't remember seeing it before, but she must have seen it, at least once, when they brought her here from the magistrates' court in Jarrow. 'You are committed in custody to await trial at Durham Assizes.'

The man at the ticket office said, 'What do you say, missis? Speak up.'

'A single to Newcastle.'

'A single to Newcastle . . . there you are.'

She put the change in her bag. It was funny having a bag hanging from your arm, it felt awkward. She thought people must think how stiffly she held her arm with the bag on it.

She had the carriage to herself all the way to Newcastle, and she did not stand up and walk from one window to the other taking her fill of both views, but sat quietly in the corner, her back straight, her head turned towards the changing scenery. The trees looked bonny, oh so bonny. The sun turned their browning leaves to glittering gold and bronze. She realised she was looking at colour. She had missed colour; oh yes, she had missed colour. She had always kept her home colourful. Cushion covers made from cheap remnants, curtains with patterns on, never Nottingham lace curtains . . . How would the kitchen look? She turned her mind deliberately from the kitchen, saying to herself, One thing at a time. You'll get the bus outside Newcastle station, it isn't likely that the stop will be changed; and then you'll get off at the corner . . . One thing at a time.

The bus stop was changed. 'Which part of

Jarrow do you want to go?' said a man in a peaked cap.

'The Fifteen Streets,' she said.

'Oh, down that far? Oh well then, you can get either the one that will take you the Robin Hood way, or there's the other that goes straight through the town. The town one, I think, that's the one you want. And it's in, look, over there.'

Sarah thanked him; then boarded the bus, taking a seat right up at the front.

'Which part of the Fifteen Streets do you want?' the conductor asked her. 'It's a long walk if you get off at the wrong end.'

'The ... top end?' She put this as a question and he replied, 'Oh yes. Well, I'll tell you when to get off.' Evidently he thought of her as someone who didn't know where she was going.

And from Hebburn onwards Sarah saw that she didn't know where she was going. The immediate landscape had changed; the places which she had last seen as open stretches of flat land were now covered with houses, dozens of houses, hundreds of houses. Here and there, she would think to herself, Yes, I remember that; that is the way to the ferry; that is the way to the church near Dee Street. We should be nearing the church bank now, and the park, and the quay corner.

At the quay corner she saw the church of St Paul. It looked so much smaller than she remembered; it looked lost, forgotten. She felt akin to it.

Then the bus conductor came up to her and said, 'This is your stop, missis.' She followed him down the bus without looking to see where she was and the next minute she was on the main road. From the pavement she looked up at him puzzled, and he said, 'This is the top end, the top end of the Fifteen Streets . . . All right?'

She nodded her head slowly at him, and he rang the bell and the bus sped away. But he paused a while to look at her.

She stood looking across the road. He had put her off at the wrong end, he had put her off at the bottom end. But it was a different bottom end from when she had last seen it. Then there had been an open space where the four streets had stood before the night of the raid. Now before her were stretched not only four streets but street after street of new houses all with little gardens in front and bigger gardens behind. She walked slowly across the road, and she was at the end of the first street. There was a fancy board supported by two stout wooden pillars at the corner, and on it was written: Churchill Street. She began to walk past the corner of the streets going in the direction the bus had taken. The second street was called Eisenhower Avenue. This was about where they had lived, she thought. The following street was Montgomery Terrace, on and on; Wavell Avenue, Laurence Street, all new streets, all named after men of war. Here and there, there were children playing in back gardens, but except in the distance she saw no adults. Being nearly two o'clock, the men had returned to work and the women were taking it easy for an hour, things seemingly hadn't altered that much. On and on, slowly, towards the top end she went. And then abruptly the new houses ceased and she could see ahead four of the original streets, and the contrast gave her a shock. Like beggars lying at the rich man's gate the four streets lay at the foot of the new estate, and they looked dirty, old, and shrunken. Her step became slower. She knew now why the bus conductor had put her off at the other end of the streets. The situation of the place had turned a complete somersault; the top end had now become the bottom end. Yet among the people in the new houses were those who still thought along the lines of street teas. Places, she realised, could be altered or renewed in a week, a month, a year, but not people. It took the accumulated years of a generation and perhaps another to alter people, turn them from their inbred ways. The Fifteen Streets would be the Fifteen Streets until this generation died, that was certain. It was only the status of the Streets themselves that had turned the somersault. The sight of Camelia Street staggered her. This was the place she had once invested with royal status. Here she had lived in the glory of exclusiveness. For years she had thanked God at night in her prayers for depositing her at this end.

In the middle of the street two motor-cycles leaned against the kerb, their new brightness forcing its way through the shadow cast by the dismal houses. There were also three cars standing in the roadway, one of them outside her own door – she still thought of it as her own door. The car would be Michael's. Fancy him having a car; fancy anybody who lived here having a car.

She was standing at the door now, her hand half-raised to the knocker. But before she touched it she gripped the front of her coat and shook herself. Now then, steady, steady . . . take it easy, one thing at a time.

When the door opened, there stood Kathleen. Sarah watched her mouth drop into a loose gape, then close on a gasp: 'Wh . . . why,' she stammered. 'I thought . . . What brought you? Who's brought you?' She shook her head wildly, and then, pulling the door further open, she added, 'Come in.'

It was as if she were bidding a stranger enter, and, like a stranger, Sarah walked into what had been her home, for immediately she crossed the threshold the change sprang at her. She would have had to be blind not to take it in in one glance.

Kathleen walked sideways along the little passage through the front room and into the kitchen; she had her hand extended as if for guidance, but she didn't touch her mother.

In the kitchen they stood looking at each other,

Kathleen with her hands joined at her throat. The action was painful to Sarah, for it gave away Kathleen's distress.

'You said Wednesday.'

'Yes, yes, I know, Kathleen, but I . . . I couldn't bear them making a tea and all that.'

'Oh.' Kathleen jerked her chin up as if in understanding, and then she said, 'Sit down. Why, sit down.' She pulled a chair hastily forward. It was one of the coloured-seated dining chairs and Sarah looked at it before she sat on it.

'I'll tell Michael. He's on night shift, but he would be getting up shortly.'

'Don't wake him, there's plenty of time.' Sarah was still speaking in that peculiar undertone she had come to use over the years.

'Oh, I'll tell him, I'll tell him.'

Kathleen almost ran from the room and she went up the stairs calling loudly, 'Michael! Michael!'

Sarah listened now to Kathleen's quick steps overhead. She heard the murmur of her speaking rapidly, warningly, and she bowed her head. How was she going to bear it? . . . One thing at a time, one thing at a time. Once today was over it wouldn't be so bad. She reminded herself that she was sitting in her own kitchen, she was home. But was she? She raised her head and looked about her. There wasn't a stick of furniture that she could recognise as hers. She experienced a new kind of pain.

When Kathleen came down the stairs there were footsteps behind her, and Sarah turned her head to look at the man entering the room. He was dressed in trousers and shirt; his sandy hair was ruffled, and his eyes still full of sleep, but she recognised Michael MacKay. He hadn't changed much. He was older of course.

'Well, hello, there,' he said.

'Hello, Michael,' she answered.

'We weren't expecting you the day. You should have told us, coming all that way by yourself.'

He was trying to be kind, not to show his surprise, not to let her see that he was put out in any way. 'Have you had a cup of tea?' he said.

'No, not yet.' She smiled towards Kathleen.

'We'll make one in a jiffy,' he said and went into the scullery.

Yes, Michael was nice. As Dan said, Kathleen could have done a lot worse. But Michael wasn't Paul . . . Oh, Paul . . . Paul. But she mustn't think of Paul . . . One thing at a time.

'How's the baby?' she said looking up at Kathleen.

'Oh, she's fine, she's asleep.' She made for the door again. 'I'll bring her down.'

'Kathleen.' Sarah's voice halted her. 'Don't . . . don't disturb her, there'll be plenty of time.'

'Yes, yes, of course.' After a pause Kathleen came back towards the table, and, standing before her mother, she said, 'Take your hat off . . . take your things off.'

Sarah reached up and slowly she removed her hat. Then, standing up, she took off her coat. As she put her hand up to smooth back her hair in which there was still not a thread of grey Michael entered the kitchen. He had a tray in his hand and he stopped dead for a moment and looked at Sarah. He saw a woman so like his wife that the resemblance startled him. When she'd had her coat and hat on he hadn't seen it so clearly, but now he was seeing them together. It was a strange experience. The only difference was that the older woman had a better figure and a softer face. Yes . . . yes, he had to admit that to himself. Even after all she had gone through, and she must have had a packet, she didn't look hard or bitter. Not that Kathleen looked hard or bitter; but there was a set look about her face that didn't show in her mother's. He sighed and smiled. Things wouldn't be too bad. Better than he'd thought. Now that her mother was out Kathleen might forget about the past. He hoped to God she would, anyway. 'There you are.' He placed the tray on the table. 'Nothing like a cup of char.' As he poured out the tea he looked at Sarah and said, 'We'll have to get your room ready, but that won't take long, it only needs the bed putting up. We can take the cot out any time.'

'But' – Sarah shook her head – 'the little boxroom will do me. Don't move anything.'

'There isn't a boxroom any more.' Kathleen was looking at the fire. 'Michael made it into a bathroom.'

'Oh!' Sarah glanced at Michael. 'That's nice. Oh, it's nice to have a bathroom.'

They were sitting, the three of them, drinking their tea when silence attacked them, the awkward horrible silence that yells aloud, and Sarah was just about to break it, she was just about to say, 'Don't worry. I won't be in your way. I'll get a job and then perhaps I'll find a little place of my own.' That is what she was going to say when the back door opened and Kathleen jerked out of her chair as if she had been shot.

There was the sound of steps in the scullery. The kitchen door opened and Mary Hetherington entered the room, and perhaps for the first time in years she was caught off her guard, and it registered on her face which showed utter and blank surprise.

Sarah's heart was beating wildly. This was the moment she had dreaded, more so than entering her old home again and the meeting with Kathleen. Yet she had never imagined herself being actually confronted by her mother-in-law. Being passed by her in the street, yes; ignored, yes. At the same time being made vitally aware of her hate and loathing, but she had never imagined her walking into the kitchen like this. She had come in as if she were used to coming in . . . Yes, undoubtedly she was used to coming in.

Michael, trying to smooth over the tense moment, said, 'Come and sit down, Gran. I've just made some tea. Have a . . .'

Mary Hetherington, indicating with a swift movement of her arm towards him that she wished him to be quiet, he became quiet. His voice trailed away and he looked sharply at his wife, but Kathleen was looking at no one. She had her head down. It looked as if she were rejecting something, something shameful.

'So you've come!' Mary Hetherington's voice was thick, like someone who was gone in drink. 'How soon are you going?'

Sarah did not rise to her feet nor did she make any retort, but she sat, her stomach sick, looking up at this old woman, and she saw that she was old, and her hate was old, but strong still, stronger if anything. Sarah could see it all clearly. This hate-filled woman had taken Kathleen under her wing, not with the desire of protecting her, but of separating her from herself, from contamination with herself. That's how she would think of it.

'Look, Gran.' Michael was tentatively appealing again, and again he was silenced by a more violent wave of the hand now as Mary Hetherington repeated, 'When are you going? I asked you a question.'

Sarah had got out of the habit of talking. You didn't talk in there, you listened, and you only spoke when you were asked a question. She had been asked a question and now she forced herself to answer it. She said softly, 'I've come home . . .'

Before Sarah's lips settled on the last word Mary Hetherington charged in, crying, 'Home! This is no longer your home. You gave up this home ten years ago.'

Sarah, her voice still level, her words still spoken in that peculiar undertone, said, 'The rent book's still in my name. Dan said . . .'

'Dan said! Dan said!' There was scorn in Mary Hetherington's voice. 'I know what Dan said. What he doesn't know is that Michael had it transferred to his name two years ago. And look round you. Is there a stick of yours here? No, not so much as would fill a matchbox. Your home! Now again I say to you . . . When are you going?'

'Gran . . . Gran, stop it. I tell you, stop it! Leave her alone; it's my affair, our affair.' Kathleen was confronting her grandmother now, swallowing between each word, daring to oppose this woman who had imposed her rule on her.

'You leave this to me, Kathleen. Unless you want your life ruined and Michael in trouble . . . because let me tell you—' The old woman leant towards Kathleen and wagged her finger at her. 'As sure as God's in heaven she'll have Michael.

She'll have your husband; no man is safe within a mile of her. They're never too old, they're never too young. I'm speaking from experience.'

Sarah rose to her feet, not hastily; she just rose from the chair, as if she were being pulled up by a mechanical device. She was trembling all over. She had a desire to cry, but she could neither cry nor speak; she could just stand, her hands on the table looking towards this hate-corroded being.

'You don't believe me?' Mary Hetherington lifted her eyes from Kathleen and brought them to Michael. 'I'll bet all I own this moment that within a few weeks, yes, within a few weeks she'll have set her cap at you and you won't know where you are.'

'Now look, Gran, stop talking like that. Let up. There's a limit.' Michael was obviously embarrassed and he wagged his head, his gaze directed towards the floor.

'You want proof . . . I'll give it to you.' The old woman swung round and, snatching at the curtain, lifted it into a loop, and as she did so Kathleen cried, 'No, no, Gran . . . don't bring Aunt May over . . . please!' She went to pull the curtain from her grandmother, but the old woman pushed her aside.

'Far better bring May across than have your home broken up. Leave it alone, I want May here. This woman took your Aunt May's man . . . my son, when she was only married a few weeks to my other son. She takes everything . . . everything with trousers on.'

Years ago Sarah would have thought, She's talking like one of the women at the bottom end; now she could only think, I'll have to go . . . I'll have to go . . . I can't bear it. Something will happen if I don't get out. Oh, my God!

She turned her head wildly now in the direction of the couch where lay her hat, coat and bag, and then her head was jerked back with startling suddenness to her mother-in-law again. Mary Hetherington was glaring at Kathleen and saying, 'She deprived my son, my David, of fatherhood. I've told you what she did, but you only half believed me. But let May confront her with it; yes, let May con . . .'

'Be quiet! You evil creature . . . be quiet!'

They were all looking at Sarah now. A different Sarah. Not the Sarah that Mary Hetherington remembered, nor the Sarah that Kathleen remembered as her mother, nor yet was there any connection with the Sarah who had sat so timidly before them only a few minutes earlier. The tall, pale, wide-eyed woman before them had a majestic bearing, a towering majestic bearing; there was no aggressiveness in her attitude, yet it held them all still. She stared at her mother-in-law for a full minute in silence before she began to speak again.

Her voice too was different now, the tone

strong, the words crisp, yet quiet. 'I'm not going to let you get away with this. Oh, no, not with this. From the day we met you've hated me; you've sent your venom and your spleen through that wall there at me' – she pointed – 'until the very bricks were tense with the atmosphere you created. You hated me because David loved me; you hated the idea that I could make him happy. Me!' She pressed her finger gently into her breast. 'The scum from the bottom end. That's how you thought of me, wasn't it? And you couldn't bear the thought that I'd brought your favourite son alive; you couldn't bear the thought that in my kitchen your menfolk found peace from your nagging. That's all they came in here for, just to get away from your nagging. They were sick of listening to the gaffer of God.' She did not fire a barbed shaft here by adding, 'That was David's name for you' – but went on, 'From the moment I came into your life, you have tried to ruin me; every bit as much as my father did, you tried . . . '

'How . . . how can you stand there and speak the name of your . . .'

Sarah cut Mary Hetherington's words off with an uplifting movement of her head: 'I dare speak his name. I have paid for what I did . . . I'm free . . . and I dare speak his name. He doesn't trouble my conscience, he never has. Let that horrify you.' She paused for a second before going on. 'But that's beside the point . . . As I said, there's one thing you're not going to do. You're not going to burn that last lie into my daughter's mind.' Sarah now switched her eyes to Kathleen, and her voice had a ring of command in it. 'Kathleen,' she said, 'listen to me . . . listen closely to me. I never once went with your Uncle John . . . you understand? NEVER ONCE. Not once . . . Your Uncle John loved me. Once he kissed me, once on New Year's morning, nineteen-thirty, near the bottom end. I'd been to first-foot my mother. He came over with me because everybody else was joining in the jollification, and he kissed me and we talked. That was all. And my father heard what we talked about. Well, you know all about that part of it. The next time was the morning he marched to London with the hunger marchers. Neither his wife nor his mother would go to see him off; he asked me if I would, and that morning I kissed him . . . on the cheek. That, Kathleen, is the story of the vileness between your Uncle John and me. And that, when you sum it all up, is what I've done time for.'

Kathleen was looking at Sarah, staring up into her face. As they once used to look at each other and laugh, now they were looking at each other, but there was no laughter between them. As Sarah stared into the sad pleading countenance of her daughter she knew that she had to do something to give the seal of truth to her words. Her eyes flicked from Kathleen's face to the wall. There, hanging on it was a modern version of the picture of the Sacred Heart of Jesus. Like everything else, it was new.

It was the only holy picture in the room; likely it was Michael's choice, for he was a strong Catholic. She had never hung holy pictures in the house during her married life, but she remembered a similar one to this hanging in the kitchen when she was a child. The picture, although in a plain modern frame, held the same face of Christ, the same head and shoulders with the hand across the chest, palm up holding on it his bleeding heart, the blood dripping down through his fingers. She no longer believed in God or Jesus, or in any other symbol of the Catholic Church, but Kathleen did, and always would. With a swift movement she stepped to the wall and, lifting the picture by its string, brought it to Kathleen, and, laying it flat on one hand, she put the fingers of her other hand at the centre of the heart. But before she spoke she turned her eyes from Kathleen and fixed them on Mary Hetherington, and it was to her she said, 'I swear by the Sacred Heart of Jesus that what I have said is true.' Then, looking at Kathleen again, she said, 'David was your father, Kathleen.'

Sarah imagined she saw a cloud lift from Kathleen's face, leaving it a shade lighter. She turned from her now and hung the picture back on the wall. Then once again she looked at her mother-in-law. It was evident that Mary

Hetherington had received a setback, but it was also evident that she wasn't beaten, and she showed this by renewing her attack almost immediately. With a deriding mirthless laugh, and addressing no one in particular, she cried, 'Well! You can take that bit of acting for what it's worth, and from where it comes. The Sacred Heart of Jesus . . . Huh! But the Lord isn't mocked . . . Let me tell you, the mills of God grind slow, but they grind exceeding small.'

'The mills of God!' Sarah repeated, shaking her head slowly as she looked now almost pityingly at the old woman. 'Though the mills of God grind slowly, yet they grind exceeding small; though with patience he stands waiting, with exactness grinds he all.' Sarah sensed immediately that her mother-in-law had never heard the second line of the quotation, and in this moment she felt a strange feeling of superiority over her . . . Prison life had done something for her after all. It had introduced her to the library, from where she had gathered a small amount of knowledge, small because her need in this direction was small, for she had never aspired to education – not for herself; all she had aspired to was to talk properly, as she put it to her herself, to be able to pass herself. She had always had this desire. Hadn't she longed for a dictionary when she was a girl just so that she could pass herself in conversation?

Her voice held an authoritative note as she

repeated now, 'With exactness grinds he all. But not all . . . oh no, because you know what? He's blind, your miller, blind and vindictive. Indiscriminately doling out pain and agony, that's your God. Well, all I hope is that His groping hands don't find you, for even now I don't wish you your just deserts. I just pity you. I always have, you know . . . So there, you have it.'

With her bearing upright and dignified, she turned from the bitter face to the couch, and, picking up her coat, she put it on. And as she did so, Kathleen cried, 'Where you going? Oh, Mam, where you going?'

'Don't worry.' She smiled a sad faint smile at her daughter. 'Don't worry,' she said again. She put on her hat and picked up her bag. Then once again she turned, and, looking her mother-in-law straight in her eyes, she held her gaze for a moment before leaving the room. But she had just reached the in-between door when Mary Hetherington's voice sent its last bolt at her: 'And leave our Dan alone,' she cried, 'Him and May's going to be married. He spent enough years looking after you and yours, so let him do what he likes with the remainder of his life. Do that one decent thing at least.'

Her words halted Sarah, but only for a second. She went on through the front room into the passage. But when she reached the door Kathleen was behind her, and her hands on her Mother's shoulders, she turned her round and looked into her face for a moment before enfolding her in her arms, crying through her tears, 'Oh, Mam . . . Mam.'

'There, there. Don't upset yourself.'

'I believe you. I want you to know I believe you.'

Sarah remained quiet, and they clung together for a moment longer.

'Where you going?'

'Down to Phyllis's.'

'Look.' Kathleen was whispering now, her face close to Sarah's. 'We want to get a house away from here. We'll get fixed up, and you can come with us then. I would like it. Oh, I would, I would.'

'We'll see, we'll see. Don't worry.' Sarah opened the door, and Kathleen stood on the top step clinging on to her hand, saying, 'Oh, Mam. Oh, Mam.'

When there came to them from the kitchen the sound of raised voices, Sarah knew that May had arrived. She couldn't face May, she had stood all she could from them all. She knew she was going to break down, but she didn't want to upset Kathleen any more. She said hastily, 'Pop down to your Aunt Phyllis's when you can. Goodbye, my dear. Goodbye, my dear.'

Once again Kathleen had her arms around her; once again they clung together. Then Sarah was walking quickly away.

She could restrain the outlet no longer. When

she reached the main road the tears were raining down her face, and she walked with her head down. The road between the Fifteen Streets and the New Buildings at East Jarrow was practically empty, but a woman who had passed her came running back after her, saying, 'What's the matter, lass? Are you in trouble?' Sarah did not look at the woman but shook her head. And the woman, walking by her side now, said, 'Can I help you, hinny?'

She raised her eyes to the woman and managed to say, 'No, thank you.'

As the woman looked at her her face crinkled slowly with recognition, but Sarah stopped her making any exclamation by waving her off with her hand; then she said, 'I'm sorry, just let me be,' and hurried on, leaving the woman standing on the pavement looking after her.

It was as she neared the New Buildings that the car drew up alongside the kerb. Michael had only a coat over his shirt and his hair was still ruffled. He said softly, 'Get in.' And she got in, still with her head bowed, the tears washing down her face.

Michael sat in deep embarrassed silence looking at her before starting the car, then he muttered, 'I'm sorry.' After a short while he asked quietly, 'Do you know the house?'

'It's in Laygate.'

He went through Tyne Dock, cut through the Deans, and they were in Laygate before she spoke again. 'She's an old devil.' He kept his eyes on the road as he spoke. 'I've had a job to keep me tongue meself. She's always trying to dominate Kathleen. I was goin' to try and get a job away last year in one of the Durham pits so we could move, but then things got a bit shaky. They're closing some pits down, so you've got to stay put. But I'll get a place out of it now. I told her afore I left just what I thought about her.'

There was an audible groan inside Sarah now. If Mary Hetherington wanted anything to confirm all she had said, Michael turning on her would have proved how right she had been about her daughter-in-law. She said now under her breath, 'It's the ice-cream café on the right.'

He helped her out of the car, then followed her into the shop.

Behind the counter stood a tall youth with Arab features and a fairish skin. And talking to him was a woman, a shortish, fat woman. She turned at the approach of customers, then her mouth springing open, she cried, 'Sarah! Why, Sarah! The day? You've come the day?' She was round the counter and they were holding each other. With tears running down her cheeks Phyllis kept repeating, 'Sarah! Oh, Sarah!' She held her at arm's length. 'Oh, lass, lass, am I glad to see you!' Becoming aware of the interest of the only two customers in the shop, she cried, 'Come on, away up out of this.' She went to pull Sarah forward; but pausing, she looked at her son, shouting to him as if he was streets away, 'You remember your Aunt Sarah, don't you?'

The young man smiled shyly. 'Yes . . . yes. Hello Aunt Sarah.'

'Hello . . .' Sarah didn't remember this one's name, and Phyllis cried, 'He's Joss, the youngest. Look at him, he's twice my size. But come on, come on . . . Come on, Michael.' Her arm extended, she drew Michael after them towards a door at the end of the long café. And leading the way up the stairs and into a large living-room, expensively if not artistically furnished, she turned again to Sarah. And now like a child she stood in front of her and laid her head on her breast. 'Oh, Sarah, lass! Oh, Sarah!' she said softly.

Sarah was overcome with emotion. Here indeed was a welcome. In the home of her sister who had married an Arab, a man who had always slightly repulsed her. Though Ali had always treated her with kindness, she had never met him but she had thought, How could our Phyllis do it? But she knew that Ali too would welcome her, warmly, sincerely. Life was strange. Oh, indeed, life was strange.

'Here, let me get your things off.' Phyllis was now pulling at Sarah's coat. 'We'll have a slap-up meal the night. I had it all prepared, in me mind that is, for Wednesday. What happened?'

Briefly, Sarah told her.

431

'Aw well, I see your point.' As Phyllis nodded it was evident to Sarah that she didn't quite see eye to eye with her in the matter of a street party. If Phyllis had spoken the truth she would have said, 'Well, I think it was jolly decent of them to think of such a thing.'

'Sit down, Michael. Sit down. And we'll have a cup of tea . . . Oh no we won't.' She raised her arm in a Hitler-like salute. 'We'll have something stronger to begin with, we will that.'

'Not for me, thanks all the same.' Michael smiled widely at her. 'I'm driving. And I've got to get back. In fact, I'd better be going. But I'll look in again.' He nodded his head quickly.

'Oh . . . Oh, all right then.' Phyllis didn't detain him, she wanted Sarah to herself.

'I'll be seeing you.' He was speaking to Sarah now in an undertone. 'I'll bring Kathleen down.'

'Will you, Michael? Oh, that's kind of you.'

'The night, if you like.'

'Please. Oh, thanks, Michael, thanks.'

'Don't you worry.' He nodded his head down to her. 'Things'll pan out, you'll see. Now don't you worry.' He stood looking at her sympathetically for a moment before going to the door where Phyllis was waiting. And as he passed her he motioned to her with his head, and Phyllis, picking up the signal, turned to Sarah and said, 'I'll just see him down the stairs in case he breaks his neck. They're a bit dark. Go in the kitchen and get that tea under way. Make yourself busy, for if I know you, you'd rather tea than anything else.'

The sisters smiled at each other. The years seemed to have slipped away. Phyllis went out and closed the door, and Sarah went into the kitchen.

Here again everything was expensive and over-crowded. An outsize fridge, an electric washing machine, an electric food mixer . . . the lot. And Sarah was glad, glad that Phyllis had the things that stood for success.

She had made the tea and had it in the living-room before Phyllis returned. Phyllis's face was straight as she entered the room, and, looking across at Sarah, she said quietly, 'Michael's told me . . . You just got in about two? God, what a reception!' She came and stood close to Sarah, looking up into her face. 'But, anyway, you'd have likely got it on Wednesday, so it's over you. She's a sod. She's a sod of a woman if ever there's one. Sit down, lass, sit down and let's have a drink.' She pressed Sarah gently into an armchair. 'Will you have a drop of something in yours?' She pointed to the tea.

'No, Phyllis, no. Just a good cup of tea, that's all I want.' She smiled. 'I've longed for a real good cup of tea.'

Phyllis turned from her, and going to a cocktail-cabinet that stood in the corner of the room, she brought out a bottle, saying as she did so, 'I could go up there and pulverise that old bitch. I could that, this very minute.' She came back to the table and poured a generous measure of whisky into her own tea. Then, sitting down, she raised her cup to Sarah, saying, 'Here's to us, lass. Here's to us. We'll never be parted again. At least not if I can help it. You can stay here until you die. You can have a job if you want it, or you can leave it alone, it's all up to you. You've got nothing to worry about, not any more.'

'Oh, Phyllis.' Her sister's kindness was almost as painful as her mother-in-law's attack. She said again, 'Oh, Phyllis.'

Phyllis took a long drink from her cup; then, putting it down on the table, she wiped her mouth with the pad of her thumb, and, looking across the room towards the window, she said, thoughtfully, 'What I cannot understand is this business about Dan and May. Michael's just told me. I would have thought he had more sense.' She looked towards Sarah. But Sarah's head was bowed; she was staring down into her teacup. Then, lifting the cup to her lips, she took a long drink, as if something warm might soothe the new pain that had entered into her . . . Dan and May. Well, why not? Dan deserved happiness; Dan had been so good to her; pure gold Dan had been all through. He had been so kind and attentive that she had come to think of Dan as her main support; she had imagined him supporting her, at least morally, through the first strange months of her release. She remembered the time when he had told her that Paul had become a priest and that Kathleen was going to marry Michael. She had given up then, yet all the time a hand had been holding hers . . . Dan's hand, and it was this hand that had pulled her back into existence. Whatever happened there would always be Dan. He had even said those words to her, time and again, time and again. When he had come to visit her he had said in some way, 'You've got me; you'll always have me; I'll always be there, Sarah.'

Phyllis was saying, 'I'm beginning to see the light. She wouldn't give John a divorce, not for years. That lass had three bairns to him; she was likely in a stew in case he'd walk out on her. You could never tell with a bloke like that. But he did try, I'll say that much for him. He tried again and again to get May to agree to a divorce, but she wouldn't bite. But then, just about eighteen months ago, she tells him to go ahead, and early on this year it went through. And now he's married at last. Aw, Sarah!' Phyllis put her fingers over her mouth and shook her head slowly. 'This doesn't hurt you, does it, to know this?'

'No . . . no, Phyllis. Don't worry. Ten years is a long time; you have time to think in ten years. If you haven't got to worry about eating, or the rent, or firing, or light, you've got to put your mind to work in some way. I set mine the task of straightening up my thinking, and learning not to be afraid of being afraid.'

Phyllis lay back in the corner of the couch and her eyes narrowed as she looked at Sarah. And she said quietly, 'You've changed, you know; you've changed, Sarah.'

'I hope so,' said Sarah.

'Oh, I don't.' Phyllis was bending forward, her hand touching Sarah's knee. And Sarah covered it with her own as she said, 'Come on, it's your turn. Tell me about the family.'

'Oh, you know all about them; I've kept you informed over the years. Things are just the same. They're all set in the cafés. We did think about taking another, but Ali's biding his time; things are not as bright as they were a few years ago, you know. Oh, by the way, Ronnie's in Newcastle with the band this weekend.'

'Oh, is he? I'd love to hear him play.'

'It's funny that, isn't it?' said Phyllis. 'I mean how he became a pianist . . . all through that old four-pound piano. You remember?'

Sarah remembered . . . the day that she had kissed John, before he had marched off to London. And that dinner-time, to take her mind off things, she had told David that she was going down to see a second-hand piano, and to her amazement he had put his foot down and said he was having no piano in the house. 'Don't you see, it will only make matters worse,' he had said as he inclined his head towards the wall. She had written and told Phyllis. And Phyllis had written back to say it was all right, and that, anyway, Ali had bought the piano himself, he thought it would do for the bairn. And it had done for the bairn. Her second eldest son had become a first-class pianist.

'I would never have thought about a piano for meself, or any of us,' went on Phyllis. 'But there, it's fate; we had to have that piano because playing the piano is the only thing Ronnie lives for . . .'

For the next hour they talked, as they always had done when they were together; they talked until the light went. Phyllis was pulling herself to her feet, saying, 'What about a little light on the subject,' when a voice called from the foot of the stairs, 'Mum! Mum!'

'What is it now?' Phyllis went to the door and, opening it, cried, 'What is it? Can't you manage without me for five minutes?'

'There's someone to see you. It's Mr Blythe.'

'Dan?' Sarah rose to her feet. Of a sudden she felt nervous, uncomfortable. For the first time in her life she didn't want to come face to face with Dan.

Dan paused in the doorway a moment, then came swiftly forward, and, taking her hands in his, said, 'Why, Sarah! You silly lass, you silly lass. You should have told me.'

'It's all right, Dan. It's better this way.'

'Better?' He withdrew his hands from hers, and

his face became solemn, almost stern. 'Not from what Michael told me on the phone. That woman will go off her head one of these days . . . But perhaps it's all for the good . . . I mean you coming today, Sarah.'

'Yes, perhaps, Dan.'

He was standing away from her, looking at her now, his attitude slightly uneasy, and Phyllis, quick to sense this, jumped into the awkward breach by exclaiming loudly, 'Well, you'll stay to tea, Dan. Now, I'm not taking no.' She flapped her hand at him, although he had made no sign of refusal to her offer. Then going to the sideboard and taking out a cloth, she spread it over the dining-table, talking all the time.

'Well, this is a get-together, the first of many, I hope . . . and how's business, Dan?'

'Oh, pretty fair, you know, Phyllis, pretty fair.'

He was sitting to the side of Sarah now but not looking at her. He kept his eyes on Phyllis as he talked, and it would seem that the state of business at the moment was all that concerned him. 'We've all been making hay in the last few years, but it looks like the harvest's over. The dole circle's enclosing the Tyne again, I can feel it. I bet you can an' all in your weekly returns.'

'Well yes, you're right there, Dan. I won't say they're as shining as they were a couple of years ago.'

'No. And they won't be for a long time again. A

438

grocer's shop is a money thermometer; I've seen it again and again. And what have we now? Unemployment, getting worse every week. It's bad when it hits the young 'uns, the lads just out of their time. Just the twenties over again: they do their apprenticeships and then they're stood off.'

'Still, you're not in the workhouse yet, Dan.' Phyllis was smiling at him.

And he returned her smile with a laugh. 'No, not yet, Phyllis. On the doorstep, like, looking through the gates as it were, but not quite in.'

They both laughed together, and Phyllis asked now, 'Well, what about a mixed grill? I've got some nice chops and sausages. What about it?'

'Not for me, Phyllis. A cup of tea and a toasted tea-cake. Now I wouldn't turn my nose up at that.'

'How about you, Sarah?'

'I'll just have the same. No grill, Phyllis. Not yet, anyway.'

'Well, you're customers that's easily served. And I bet you don't leave a tip . . . Mean lot!' In mock indignation she stalked into the kitchen. And they were left alone.

Dan, turning fully round in his chair, now looked at this woman who had never, in his eyes, changed one iota from the first time he had seen her across the tea-table on her first visit to the house.

And Sarah was looking at him, at his kindly face, still handsome, but perhaps not so jolly

439

looking as when he was younger. And the more she looked at him the more she ached inside. She was feeling more lost at this moment than she had done since the prison gates had closed behind her.

'How you feeling?'

'Oh, all right, Dan.'

'You're not. You can't fool me. Look.' He leaned forward and gripped her hands. 'I've got something I want to say to you.'

She closed her eyes for a second; then forced herself to open them and look at him and wait. Dan deserved to be happy.

She watched his lips move two or three times before they formed words, and then he was speaking hesitantly.

'I wanted to give you this gradually, not spring it on you. I wanted to do things gently, take perhaps a week over it. Not because I wanted to wait a week. No, but because I wanted to give you time to settle in. Time to think. Not feel you were forced to do anything you didn't want. But now, what Michael told me on the phone has altered everything. I could go up there and slap her mouth for her, I could really . . . Saying that me and May . . .'

'It's all right, Dan.' She was holding his hands now, and she was looking down at them. 'It's all right, I understand.'

'Oh no you don't. You don't. That's what I'm

440

getting at; that's what I'm trying to say. Look, Sarah, I'd have to be damned hard up for a woman and gone in the head before I'd go within a mile of May. All the way down in the car coming here, you know I really felt frightened. I can see it all now: Mary's plans. And May's an' all. The divorce and everything, after she had sat tight for years. And then her coming up to the shop and wanting to do things upstairs. I cooled her off there, but I still didn't guess, and I kept on going across on a Sunday to have a word with her – I always have since John left. But my God in Heaven! Men are infants! That's all we are, infants . . . Sarah . . . oh, lass, don't cry.' He put his hand up to her face and wiped away the tears.

'It's all right, Dan, it's all right.'

'Can I go on?'

'Yes, Dan, yes.'

He looked down at their joined hands now, and with his voice scarcely above a whisper, he said, 'I've waited a long time. Every day of ten years I've waited, knowingly waited, knowing what I was going to say to you the minute you came out. I've waited with hope these last ten years. And you might as well know it. I've waited from the first minute I saw you, but without hope . . . Mary was right about one thing, you know, Sarah: you did take us all. But not from her, because she never had us . . . Now don't get upset. Aw don't, you could no more help the lot of us coming to you than a flower can help itself opening to the sun. Anyway, I've thought and planned what I would say to you. Sometimes, especially at nights, I got worried. I'm not young any more; I'm ten years older than you; and whereas, as you hardly look – and I mean this, Sarah – with all you've gone through you hardly look a day older than when I first saw you. I could even say you were better looking, if that is possible. Well, what I was going to say to you after you'd got your breath was . . . Will you have me, Sarah?' He waited. Then in a small voice: 'Will you?'

'Dan. Oh, Dan.'

He slipped from his chair on to his knees by her side, and his arms going about her, he waited. 'Will you?'

She nodded slowly.

His head was on her breast now, as Phyllis's had been, and she laid her cheek on his hair. She did not ask herself if she loved Dan; she didn't, not as she had loved David, and again not as she had loved John. But this was a new kind of feeling, a feeling of warmth, of tenderness, a feeling without fear, without worry, a feeling that expressed laughter because she couldn't see herself living with Dan and not laughing.

It was as if Dan had read her thoughts, for he said, 'I'll give you everything I have, Sarah. There'll be no fifty-fifty, you can have all I've got.

I've enough money put by to see us out comfortably. I've got enough to enable us to laugh.' He raised his head and looked at her. 'You were made for laughter, Sarah, laughter and jollity. But you've never had it; it's always been damped down one way or another.'

'Oh, Dan . . . Dan.' She was gazing at him, but she could see him only through a thick mist.

'I love you, Sarah.'

The tears still running, she smiled at him.

'And now I'm going to do something I've waited a long time to do.' And on this he bent forward and kissed her. His lips hard and firm; he kissed her full on the mouth. Then, getting to his feet and holding out his hands, he pulled her upwards and into his arms.

Holding close, they looked at each other. Then through her tears Sarah laughed. She laughed haltingly but freely for the first time in years. And she said to him, her voice cracking, 'How's Mrs Flaherty? Is she still alive?' She was giving him a lead to make her laugh, more and more, more and more.

Dan's head was back now, his laughter filling the room. And so he stayed for a moment before bringing it forward again to look at her and say, 'Alive and kicking. Oh, the things I'll tell you about Mrs Flaherty! You'll split your sides.'

But what he said to her now about Mrs Flaherty was: 'You know, over all the years when she was reduced to twopennorth of bacon scraps she would always say, "God's good. Aw, God's good." She hadn't a thing in the world to be thankful for, but always she would say that . . . God's good. Well, here's me. I have everything at this minute to be thankful for, and I say with Mrs Flaherty, God's good.'

No recess in her mind questioned Dan's conception of God, nor yet the God of Mrs Flaherty who had inspired faith even through hunger. Perhaps there were millions of gods. Perhaps every man had his own god, and as he saw him in life so he found him in death . . . Gods like Mrs Flaherty's, gods like Dan's . . . and David's, who weren't acknowledged, only lived. Gods like Father Bailey's. Then there were the gods of the Father O'Malleys, and the gods of men like her father and the gods of the Mary Hetheringtons, and these gods were all blind millers. These were terrible gods, and their followers could be terrible people.

Phyllis came from the kitchen now, crying, 'I couldn't leave the toast. What are you two la . . . ?' She brought herself to a halt and looked at them for a full minute before flinging her arms wide and rushing at them. And as they entwined her in their embrace she lent her head once again on Sarah's breast, and between laughter and tears she too said, 'Aw, lass, God's good. When all's said and done, God's good.'

Though the mills of God grind slowly,
Yet they grind exceeding small;
Though with patience He stands waiting,
With exactness grinds He all.

THE END

BOOKS BY CATHERINE COOKSON

NOVELS

Kate Hannigan
The Fifteen Streets
Colour Blind
Maggie Rowan
Rooney
The Menagerie
Slinky Jane
Fanny McBride
Fenwick Houses
Heritage of Folly
The Garment
The Fen Tiger
The Blind Miller
House of Men
Hannah Massey
The Long Corridor
The Unbaited Trap
Katie Mulholland
The Round Tower
The Nice Bloke
The Glass Virgin
The Invitation
The Dwelling Place
Feathers in the Fire
Pure as the Lily
The Mallen Streak
The Mallen Girl
The Mallen Litter
The Invisible Cord
The Gambling Man
The Tide of Life
The Slow Awakening
The Iron Facade
The Girl
The Cinder Path
Miss Martha Mary Crawford
The Man Who Cried
Tilly Trotter
Tilly Trotter Wed
Tilly Trotter Widowed

The Whip
Hamilton
The Black Velvet Gown
Goodbye Hamilton
A Dinner of Herbs
Harold
The Moth
Bill Bailey
Bill Bailey's Lot
Bill Bailey's Daughter
The Parson's Daughter
The Cultured Handmaiden
The Harrogate Secret
The Black Candle
The Wingless Bird
The Gillyvors
My Beloved Son
The Rag Nymph
The House of Women
The Maltese Angel
The Year of the Virgins
The Golden Straw
Justice is a Woman
The Tinker's Girl
A Ruthless Need
The Obsession
The Upstart
The Branded Man
The Bonny Dawn
The Bondage of Love
The Desert Crop
The Lady on My Left
The Solace of Sin
Riley
The Blind Years
The Thursday Friend
A House Divided
Kate Hannigan's Girl
Rosie of the River
The Silent Lady

THE MARY ANN STORIES

A Grand Man
The Lord and Mary Ann
The Devil and Mary Ann
Love and Mary Ann

Life and Mary Ann
Marriage and Mary Ann
Mary Ann's Angels
Mary Ann and Bill

FOR CHILDREN

Matty Doolin
Joe and the Gladiator
The Nipper
Rory's Fortune
Our John Willie

Mrs Flannagan's Trumpet
Go Tell It To Mrs Golightly
Lanky Jones
Nancy Nutall and the Mongrel
Bill and the Mary Ann Shaughnessy

AUTOBIOGRAPHY

Our Kate
Catherine Cookson Country
Just a Saying

Let Me Make Myself Plain
Plainer Still

SHORT STORIES

The Simple Soul and other Stories

THE TINKER'S GIRL
by Catherine Cookson

Just before her fifteenth birthday Jinnie Howlett is offered a position as maid-of-all-work at a farm near the Cumbrian border. She hopes this will be a welcome relief from the workhouse she knows all too well.

But when she meets her brutish employers Jinnie realizes one life of drudgery has been exchanged for another. She is grateful when one of the sons befriends her, but it isn't long before Jinnie sees how tempting life is beyond her place of work . . .

Set in the early 1870s, *The Tinker's Girl* is a delightful read, brilliantly capturing the life and fortunes of a spirited servant girl.

9780552156691

CORGI BOOKS

KATIE MULHOLLAND
by Catherine Cookson

As the daughter of a mining family, Katie
Mulholland is forced to find work as a scullery
maid for the Rosiers. But the beautiful young girl
soon captures the eye of her employer's evil son, a
seducer who uses force when charm fails and
leaves her pregnant.

Quick to dismiss Katie, the family forces her into
a loveless marriage with the cruel manager of the
Rosier mines. But Katie's fate changes course
when one man offers her the opportunity to make
her own fortune, and to discover real love . . .

Spanning Katie's life from 1860 to the height of
the Second World War, this is a triumphant,
timeless drama from the pen of a skilled
storyteller.

9780552156660

CORGI BOOKS